IN HER NAME:
CONFEDERATION

By
Michael R. Hicks

For Mom and Dad.
The best parents a kid could wish for.

WHAT READERS ARE SAYING

"This is one of those books that I could not put down. Well written, interesting characters. The hero was a hero because he adapted to the environments that he had been thrust into. the characters so intrigued me that I also purchased the two sequels. They did not disappoint."

"If you're reading this, you've already read Empire and are wondering if the story holds up for the reast of the series. It does. The main characters stay true to who they are while adapting to their new situations. I expected my enjoyment to diminish with Reza outside the Empire but it did not. Hicks manages to keep your interest, keep the pace, and still build a convincing and captivating plot. Well done."

"This is a great continuation of the first book and starts off at a good clip. It relates the story of the main character after his return to human space and also builds up some relationships both positive and negative that the author really plays well with in this and the last book of this story. While I was not 'on the edge' during most of this book it is good simply for the character building it provides. You really get to know the main character and feel with him in his exile from the empire."

"An excellent read and highly recommended."

"I highly recommend this whole series, truly a remarkable story. The alien culture is rich and nuanced, as are the characters. Warning, this will suck you in!"

"I appreciated this novel more than I appreciated the original if just because this showed he could keep up a good, consistent storyline. It makes me more than a little anxious to read the final novel in this trilogy!"

"The plot and descriptive language was just as thrilling in this book as it was in the first. There were parts of the book where I could not stop reading, and stayed up late to find out what was going on. Just like in the first book,

Mr. Hicks pulls at each of your emotions. There is a bad guy in this book that would easily fall into my "Top 10 bad guys" list."

"This is my first review ever for a book and I have only one word for this series - Gripping! Michael's ability to draw you into the story and root for both sides of a conflict is truly a gift. I am so glad I still have 2 more books to read! Keep them coming Mike!"

Discover Other Books By Michael R. Hicks

The *In Her Name* Series
First Contact
Legend Of The Sword
Dead Soul
Empire
Confederation
Final Battle
From Chaos Born

"Boxed Set" Collections
In Her Name (Omnibus)
In Her Name: The Last War

Thrillers
Season Of The Harvest

Visit *AuthorMichaelHicks.com* for the latest updates!

ONE

"It's going to be light soon."

The statement was more than simple fact. Coming from the young Marine corporal, whose left leg ended halfway down his thigh, the bloody stump capped with crude bandages that now reeked of gangrene, the words were a prophecy of doom. Like many of the others clustered around him, broken and beaten, he was beyond fear. He had spent most of the previous night taken with fever, whispering or crying for the wife he would never see again, the daughter he had never seen beyond the image of the hologram he held clutched to his lacerated chest. There were dozens more just like him crammed into the stone church, waiting for morning. Waiting to die. "They'll be coming."

"Rest easy, my son," Father Hernandez soothed, kneeling down to give the man a drink of water from the clay pitcher he carried. "Conserve your strength. The Lord shall protect and provide for us. You are safe here."

"Bullshit."

Hernandez turned to find Lieutenant Jodi Ellen Mackenzie, Confederation Navy, glaring at him from where she knelt next to a fallen Marine officer. Her foul mouth concealed a heart of gold and a mountain of determination, both to survive and to keep the people who depended on her – now including these Marines – alive. Momentarily turning her attention from Hernandez, Mackenzie closed Colonel Moreau's eyes with a gentle brush of her hand.

Another life taken in vain, Hernandez thought sadly. How many horrors had he witnessed these past, what, weeks? Months? And how many were yet to come? But he refused to relent in his undying passion that his way, the way of the Church into which he had been born and raised, and finally had come to lead, was the way of righteousness.

"Please, lieutenant," he asked as one of the parish's monks made his way to the side of the dead Marine colonel to mutter the last rites over her cooling body, "do not blaspheme in my church." He had said the very same thing to her countless times, but each time he convinced himself that it was the first and only transgression, and that she would eventually give in to his gentle reason. He was not, nor had he ever become, angry with her, for he was a man of great if not quite infinite patience and gentleness. He looked upon those two traits and his belief in God as the trinity that defined and guided his life. They had served him and his small rural parish well for many years, through much adversity and hardship. He had no intention of abandoning those tenets now, in the face of this unusual woman or the great Enemy, the demons, that had come from the skies. "Please," he said again.

Mackenzie rolled her eyes tiredly and shrugged. "Sure, Father," she said in a less than respectful tone. "Let's see, what is it you guys say? Forgive me, Father, for I have sinned?" She came to stand next to him, the light from the candle in his hand flickering against her face like a trapped butterfly. "The only sin that I've seen is you and all your people sitting around on your butts while these poor bastards," she jabbed a finger at one of the rows of wounded that now populated the church, "throw their gonads in the grinder for you." She saw him glance at Colonel Moreau's body, now covered with a shroud of rough burlap. "She can't help you anymore, priest," Mackenzie muttered, more to herself than for his benefit. Moreau had been as sympathetic to Hernandez's beliefs as much as Jodi was not. "I guess I'm in charge of this butcher shop now." She closed her eyes and shook her head. "Jesus."

Hernandez regarded her for a moment, taken not so much by the callousness of her words but by her appearance. Even exhausted, coated with grime and smelling of weeks-old sweat (water conservation and Kreelan attacks having rendered bathing an obsolete luxury), she was more than beautiful. Although Father Hernandez and the other dozen monks who tended to the parishioners of Saint Mary's of Rutan had taken the vows of celibacy, he could not deny the effect she had on him and, he suspected, on more than one of the monks under his charge. Even for a man of sixty-five, aged to seventy or eighty by a rough life on a world not known for its kindness, she was a temptation for the imagination, if not for the flesh. Hernandez did not consider himself a scholar, but he had read many of the great literary works of ancient times, some even in the original Latin and Greek, and he knew that Helen of Troy could have been no more radiant in her appearance. He could hardly intuit the heritage that gave her the black silken hair and coffee skin from which her ice blue eyes blazed. In his mind he saw the bloodlines of a Nubian queen merged with that of a fierce Norseman. Perhaps such was the case, the result of some unlikely but divine rendezvous somewhere on the ancient seas of Terra.

"You're staring, father," she said with a tired sigh. It was always the same, she thought. Ever since she was ten and about to bloom into the woman she someday would become, she had been the object of unwanted interest from men. The boys in her classes, sometimes the teachers; countless smiling faces had flooded by over the years, remaining as leering gargoyles in her memory. The only man she had ever truly loved had been her father, who had been immune to her unintentional power: he was blind from birth, beyond even the hope of reconstructive surgery. Jodi was sure that the fate that had placed this curse on him had been a blessing in disguise for her and for their relationship. He had never seen her beauty beyond what the loving touch of his fingers upon her face could reveal, and so he had never felt the craving or lust that her appearance seemed to inspire in so many others. He had always been wonderful to her, and there were no words to describe her love for him.

Jodi and her mother had been equally close, and with her Jodi had shared her feelings, her apprehensions, as she grew. But while her mother could well understand Jodi's feelings, she had never been able to truly grasp the depth of her daughter's concerns, and in the honesty they had always shared, she had never claimed to. Arlene Mackenzie was a beautiful woman in her own right, but she knew quite well that Jodi was several orders of magnitude higher on whatever primal scale was used to judge subjective beauty. Jodi was only thankful that her mother had never been jealous of the power her daughter could wield over others if she had ever chosen to, which she never had. Jodi had always been very close to her parents, and she reluctantly admitted to herself that right now she, Jodi Mackenzie, veteran fighter pilot of the Black Widow Squadron, missed them terribly. The priest's appraising stare only made her miss them more.

"What's the matter, father?" she said finally, her skin prickling with anger. "Did you get tired of popping your altar boys?"

Red-faced, Hernandez averted his gaze. A nearby monk glanced in their direction, a comic look of shock on his face. The Marines lying on the floor beside them were in no condition to notice their exchange.

"Please," Hernandez said quietly, his voice choked with shame, "forgive my trespass. I cannot deny a certain weakness for your beauty, foolish old man that I am. That is an often unavoidable pitfall of the flesh of which we are all made, and even a hearty pursuit of God's Truth cannot always prevent the serpent from striking. But I assure you," he went on, finally returning her angry gaze, "that the vows I took when a very young man have been faithfully kept, and will remain unbroken for as long as I live." Hernandez offered a tentative smile. "As beautiful as you are, I don't feel in need of a cold shower."

Jodi's anger dissipated at the old joke that sometimes was not so funny for those in Hernandez's position. More important, she appreciated the priest's guts for admitting his weakness with such sincerity. That, she thought, was something rare on the outback colony worlds, where men were still men and women were still cattle.

"Maybe you don't," she told him, her mouth calling forth a tired but sincere smile of forgiveness, simultaneously wrinkling her nose in a mockery of the body odor they all shared, "but I could sure as hell use one."

Visibly relieved and letting her latest blasphemy pass unnoticed, Hernandez took the opportunity to change the subject. "Now that you are in command," he asked seriously, "what do you intend to do?"

"That's a good question," she said quietly, turning the issue over in her mind like a stringy chunk of beef on a spit, a tough morsel to chew on, but all that was available. She looked around, surveying the dark stone cathedral that had been her unexpected garrison and home for nearly three weeks. Shot down by Kreelan ground fire while supporting the Marine combat regiment that had been dispatched to Rutan, she had bailed out of her stricken fighter a few kilometers from the village of the same name, and that was where she had been stranded ever since. She had never worried about being shot at while floating down on the parachute, watching as her fighter obliterated itself against a cliff face five kilometers away, because in all the years of the war, the Kreelans had never attacked anyone who had bailed out. At least, that is, until the unlucky individual reached the ground.

In Jodi's case, friendly troops happened to reach her first, but that was the beginning and the end of her good fortune. As she was drifting toward the black-green forest in which Rutan was nestled, the Hood, her squadron's home carrier, and her escorts were taking a beating at the hands of two Kreelan heavy cruisers that a few days earlier had landed an enemy force to clean out the human settlement. After destroying her tormentors in a running fight that had lasted nearly three days, Hood had informed the regimental commander, Colonel Moreau, that the ship would be unable to resume station over Rutan: her battle damage required immediate withdrawal to the nearest port and a drydock. The captain expressed his sincere regrets to Moreau, but he could not face another engagement with any hope of his ship and her escorts surviving. There were no other Kreelan ships in the area, and Kreelan forces on the planet were judged to be roughly even to what the regiment could field, plus whatever help the Territorial Army could provide. On paper, at least, it looked to be a fair fight.

But neither Hood's captain, nor the Marines who had come to defend the planet had counted on a colony made up entirely of pacifists. Normally, the two thousand-strong Marine regiment would have been able to count on support from the local Territorial Army command that was supposed to be established on every human-settled world in the Confederation. In the case of Rutan, that should have been an additional five to eight thousand able-bodied adults with at least rudimentary weapons, if not proper light infantry combat gear.

Unfortunately, the intelligence files had contained nothing about the colony's disdain of violence. But that was hardly surprising, considering that the information contained in the files was for an entirely different settlement. Only the data on the planet's physical characteristics – weather, gravity, and the like – happened to be correct. Someone had called it an administrative error, but most of the Marines had more colorful names for the mistake that was to cost them their lives. They were bitter indeed when they discovered that what should have been a comparatively swift human victory through sheer weight of numbers rapidly became a struggle for survival against the most tenacious and implacable enemy that humans had ever encountered.

Now, a month after the Marines had leaped from the assault boats under protective fighter cover from Jodi's Black Widows, the proud 373d Marine Assault Regiment (Guards) had been reduced to twenty-two effectives, eighty-six walking wounded, and nearly five-hundred stretcher cases, most of them crammed into St. Mary's. The rest of the original one thousand, nine hundred and thirty-seven members of the original Marine force lay scattered in the forests around the village, dead. Among the casualties were the regiment's surgeon and all thirty-one medics. The survivors now had to rely on the primitive skills of the two local physicians (Jodi preferred to think of them as witch doctors), plus whatever nursing Hernandez and his monks could provide.

The remainder of the population, on order of the Council of Elders and with Hernandez's recommendation, had holed themselves up in their homes to await the outcome of the battle. Jodi had often pondered the blind luck that had led Rutan's founders to build their village in the hollow of a great cliff that towered over the forest, much like an ancient native American civilization had done over a millennia before on Terra: it had been the key to their survival thus far. An ordinary rural settlement, situated in the open, would have forced the defenders to spread themselves impossibly thin to protect their uncooperative civilian hosts.

On the other hand, Jodi thought, depressing herself still further, the human contingent was now completely trapped. While the village's natural defenses helped to keep the enemy out, and the sturdy stone construction made its dwellings almost impervious to the small arms fire the Kreelans occasionally deigned to use, they also left no escape route open to the defenders. There was only one way in, and one way out.

She thought of how close victory could have been, had the villagers cooperated. But Colonel Moreau and her Marines had dished out punishment as well as they had taken it, inflicting at least as many casualties as they had themselves taken. Jodi was convinced that even now a completely untrained and moderately motivated militia, led by the few remaining able-bodied Marines, could take the field. They were the defenders, and in this battle of attrition the humans had at least one advantage: they knew where the Kreelans would attack, and when. The enemy did not apply the principles of Clausewitz or Sun Tzu to their tactics and strategy. In fact, it was not entirely clear at times if they really had either, or cared. This confused the bulk of their human opponents, who were conditioned to deal with "logical" objectives like capturing terrain or severing enemy lines of communication, all of which – hopefully – would help accomplish some particular strategic objective.

More often than not, however, the Kreelans simply preferred a stand-up brawl that was more typical of the knights of Medieval Europe than the technologically advanced race they otherwise were. Rarely did they seek a decisive advantage, mostly preferring to duke it out one-on-one, or even conferring a numerical or qualitative edge to the humans. They used their more advanced weapons to strip the humans of theirs, lowering the level of technology employed on the battlefield to not much more than rifles, knives, fists and claws.

The humiliating – and frightening – thing, Jodi thought, was that they usually won, even when fighting at a disadvantage.

Here, on Rutan, Jodi knew that even now the remaining Kreelans were massing for an attack on the village. The first shots would be fired at dawn, as they had for the last three weeks. She also knew that this would probably be their last fight. There simply were not enough able bodies left to cover all the holes in their flagging defenses. Once the Marine line finally broke, the civilians who cowered in their shuttered homes would be massacred.

"Father," she said, trying to drive away the oppressive desperation of their situation, "I'm going to ask you this one last time: will you please at least let people, anyone who wants to, pick up a weapon and help us. You don't have to ask for volunteers, just let them do whatever–"

"And I have told you, Lieutenant Mackenzie," he replied, gently but firmly cutting her off, "that I shall permit no such thing." Jodi, her cheeks flushed with frustration and rising anger, opened her mouth to say something, but Hernandez waved her into silence. "I grieve terribly for the deaths and suffering of these courageous people," he went on quietly, "but we long ago set aside violence as a part of our lives. Rutan has not had a violent crime committed in nearly a century, and neither I nor the council will condone our people taking up arms for any reason, even our own self-preservation. We did not ask you to intercede on our behalf; you came of your own accord, uninvited. I am truly sorry, but this is how it must be."

Jodi just stared at him for a minute, trying to calm herself down. It made her so mad to know that her demise – as well as that of the Marines around her – could have been so easily prevented. She wanted to scream at the old man, but she was too tired, too worn out. "This is probably going to be it, you know," she told him quietly so the others nearby could not hear. Most of them knew that their number was going to come up this morning, but she did not see any sense in advertising the fact. "They're going to get through us today, and then you're going to have a real bloodbath on your hands, father. All your little sheep, hiding in their comfy houses, are going to get more than fleeced. They'll be slaughtered to the last child."

"I am an old man," he told her solemnly, "but I am still young enough at heart to believe, to have faith in God. I don't believe that divine miracles disappeared with the passage of Jesus our Lord from the earth. God has already granted us one miracle in our time of need: your coming to protect us as the enemy was knocking at our gates. I believe that He has not yet abandoned us."

Jodi regarded him coldly. She liked him, respected him. Deep down, she wanted to believe him. She wanted to throw herself on her knees and beg forgiveness if only things would just be all right, if the enemy would just disappear, if someone would wake her up from this nightmare. But she knew it was an illusion. The enemy was not about to simply be sucked into some miraculous celestial vacuum cleaner. The wounded and dying around her and the bloody carnage outside the village gates was clear evidence that, if there was a God, His benign interests were obviously elsewhere, not worth expending on the inhabitants of this insignificant grain of dust in the cosmos. No, she thought grimly. The Kreelans would not just go away, whisked to some never-never-land by a momentarily preoccupied God. They had to be fought and killed to the last warrior, hacked to pieces, exterminated. Only then would Jodi feel justified in thinking about tomorrow.

"The only miracle," she told him, "would be if you and your people suddenly got some balls." Turning on her heel, Jodi stalked away toward the rear of the church to get her equipment ready for what she already thought of as Mackenzie's Last Stand.

Father Hernandez stared after her, not knowing if he should be angry or ashamed at the woman's words. His leathery face shrouded in a frown, he bent to his work, doing what he could to comfort the wounded.

God has not abandoned us, he told himself fiercely. He has not.

Amid the cries of the wounded and the dying, Father Hernandez prayed.

* * *

Jodi picked up the ancient-looking pitcher and poured some cold water into the hand-made clay basin. After soaking a worn strip of cotton cloth, she wiped her face and neck, scraping off some of the grime and dirt that had accumulated since the last time she had allowed herself such a luxury. She considered undoing her uniform and wiping down the rest of her body, but decided against it; not out of modesty, but because she did not have the time.

Here, alone in Father Hernandez's private quarters submerged beneath and far behind the altar, she could have danced nude had she wished. Hernandez had donated his tiny rectory to the female officers, insisting that they take any necessary moments of privacy there. Jodi had originally resented it as a sexually oriented distinction that she initially found offensive, but Colonel Moreau had accepted, if only to mollify the headstrong priest. But now, Jodi was glad to have this little room to herself, just to be alone for a little while. There were no other occupants. She and Jeannette Moreau had been the last two, and now Moreau was gone. That left Jodi as not just the last surviving female officer, but the last surviving officer, period.

She looked for a moment into the palm-sized oval of polished metal that Father Hernandez used for a mirror, studying the face she saw there. She was not afraid of having to lead the Marines in what was probably going to be their last battle, for she had been doing that since shortly after she had been shot down and Moreau had needed her to fill in for Marine officers she had lost. Jodi had not had the Marines' specialized training, but she was tough and quick, both mentally and physically. It had not taken her long to prove that she was more than just another pretty fighter jock, and the Marines had quickly adopted her as one of their own. The Marine NCOs had given her a crash course in how to fight that made a mockery of the self-defense training she had received as a part of her pilot training. And, fitted with a Marine camouflage uniform and armor, she was indistinguishable on the battlefield from her rival service colleagues, such was her courage and tenacity. She had put their teaching to good use and had somehow survived, keeping as many of her people alive as she could in the process.

She set the mirror down. She could handle the upcoming fight, win or lose. She was ready, except for the one thought that nipped at her heels like a small but vicious dog: she was afraid to die. Unlike many of those in her profession, she was terrified not just of how she died, but of death itself. The courage to face the end of life – or at least to ignore the possibility that death would someday come – was the one thing neither her parents nor the years she had spent fighting the Kreelans had given her. Her only religion was flying, but it was little consolation when faced with the prospect of the end of one's existence. Jodi was and always had been an atheist, despite her parents' best efforts, and it had made her life somewhat more straightforward, if not necessarily easier. It was only when one contemplated the end of the line that things became complicated. Not surprisingly, Father Hernandez had taken up the challenge with his customary gusto, but Jodi had argued him to a standstill, as she had with other would-be converters. A belief in any afterlife required a kind of faith that Jodi just did not have, and their intellectual sparring had left them consistently deadlocked, if for no other reason than Hernandez could not prove to her that there was a God or Devil, Heaven or Hell. Her beliefs, of course, did not require proof of anything except the given facts of human existence and the inevitability of death.

Therefore, she had little trouble defending her own views while easily finding logical faults in his. Faith, virtually by definition, transcended logic and empirical knowledge, which always made it vulnerable to attack. Still, Jodi respected the man's vehemence in his beliefs, and was even a little afraid on a few occasions that maybe – just maybe – he might have something. But then he would go on about his "miracles" or some other patent silliness, blowing away any thoughts Jodi might have had of more closely examining her own beliefs.

Despite his apparent latent lecherous tendencies, for which Jodi easily forgave him, she liked the old man, and knew she was going to miss talking to him about things most of her regular companions took for granted.

But the person she would miss the most was her squadron commander, with whom Jodi had fallen hopelessly in love when they met four years before. Jodi tried desperately to push from her mind any thoughts of the woman she loved for fear that she would break down and cry now, just before her last battle. But the image of the woman's face and the imagined sound of her voice were more powerful than the fear of failure, even the fear of death. Jodi knew that the lover of her dreams would never look upon her as anything more than a close friend, because she had chosen a different way of living, finding whatever solace she required with men. Outside of one very tentative advance that was gently rejected, Jodi had never done anything to change her love's beliefs, and had done everything she could to remain her closest and best friend, no matter the pain it had sometimes caused her.

Jodi knew she would never see her again.

"Come on, Mackenzie," she chided herself as she wiped a threatening tear from her eye. "Get a fucking grip."

Grimacing at the opaque water left in the basin after rinsing out the rag, Jodi forced herself back to the present and bent to the task of putting on her armor, donated by a Marine who no longer needed it.

The candle on the washbasin table suddenly flickered, a tiny wisp of black smoke trailing toward the ceiling as the flame threatened to die. Then it steadied again, continuing to throw its melancholy light into the rectory.

Jodi, concentrating on closing a bent latch on her chest plate, did not need to look up. She had not heard the door open, but had no doubt that the regiment's acting sergeant major had come to fetch her.

"I'll be there in a minute, Braddock," she said, smiling. She liked the crusty NCO, lech or not. "If you want a peek or a piece of ass, you'd better try the monks' quarters." She finished dealing with the recalcitrant latch on her breastplate, then grabbed her helmet and turned toward the door. Braddock had been almost like a big brother to her since she had fallen from the sky, and she was going to give him one last bit of hell before they plunged into the real thing. "This is off limits to enlisted scum–"

There was someone – some thing – in the rectory with her, all right, but it was not Braddock. Looming in the shadows just beyond the candle's reach, she saw that it was neither a Marine nor one of the church's robed inhabitants. In fact, it did not appear to be human at all.

Her hand instinctively went to the pistol at her waist, but she never had a chance. With lightening speed, so quick that it was only a dark blur in the dim candlelight, the thing covered the two or so meters between them. Before Jodi's hand was halfway to the gun she sought, her arms were pinned to her sides in a grip of steel as the Kreelan warrior embraced her. As she opened her mouth to shout a warning to the others, a gauntleted hand clamped down over her lips, sealing her scream in a tomb of silence and rapier-sharp claws that rested precariously against her cheek. She struggled, throwing her weight from side to side and flinging her knees upward in hopes of catching the warrior in the crotch and at least throwing her off balance, but it was to no avail. It was like she was being held by a massive slab of granite. The pressure around her ribs suddenly increased, crushing the air out of her lungs and threatening to break her upper arms. Gasping through her nose, she closed her eyes and relented, helplessly surrendering herself to the inevitable.

But Death did not come. Instead, the pressure eased to a bearable, if not exactly gentle, level. Then she felt the hand over her mouth slowly move away. She wanted to scream, but knew it was probably futile. The warrior now holding her was stronger than anything or anyone she had ever encountered, and she had no doubt that with a single determined twitch the arm still around her chest could crush the life out of her. She bit her lip, stifling a moan that threatened to bubble from her throat. Her eyes were still closed; she had seen enough Kreelans close up to know that there was nothing there that she wanted to see. It was sometimes better not to look Death in the face.

She heard a tiny metallic click in the darkness. So quiet that normally she would never have noticed it, the sound echoed in her skull like a thunderclap. It was a knife, she thought. Or worse. Involuntarily, cursing her body for its weakness in the face – literally – of the enemy, she began to tremble. She didn't want to be afraid, now that her time had really come, but she was, anyway.

Something touched her face. She tried to jerk her head away, but realized that she had nowhere to go. Her breath was coming in shallow pants, like an overweight dog forced to run at his master's side under a hot sun. The dark world behind her closed eyes was beginning to spin, and suddenly the most important thing in that tiny world seemed to be that she was on the verge of losing control of her bladder.

She felt something against her face again, but this time she did not try to draw away. She knew that it must be a knife, drawing a pencil-thin bead of blood down her cheek, painless because it was so sharp. Strange, she thought, that the Kreelans so often used knives and swords when they had such weapons built into their bodies. Of course, she absently reflected, as she imagined the skin of her face being carved away, they used their claws often enough, too.

The knife – What else could it be? she wondered – slowly traced the bones of her cheeks, then moved along her proud and intelligent brow, pausing as if to investigate the anomaly of her eyebrows, of which the Kreelans had nothing but a ridge of horn. Then she felt it spiral around her right ear, then move to her lips.

God, she thought, there won't be anything left of me. She wanted to cry at what must be happening to her once-beautiful face, but she stifled the urge. It would avail her nothing. Surprisingly, she neither felt nor smelled any blood, which should by now be pouring from her wounds and streaming in rivers down her face and neck.

Whatever it was continued to probe at her lips, gently insinuating itself into her mouth to brush against her teeth. Like some absurd dental probe, it dallied at her canines. Then the thing – a finger, she suddenly realized – extracted itself, leaving Jodi to ponder the tracks and swirls upon her skin that were now burned into her memory.

Again, she waited. She wondered how much time had passed, hoping that someone would come looking for her and burn this alien thing into carbon. But a hasty reflection revealed that only a minute or two, if that, could have passed since the thing mysteriously appeared. And how–

Her thought was suddenly interrupted by a sensation she instinctively recognized, and it jolted her with the force of electricity. She had no idea what had run its course over her face only a moment before, but what touched her now was immediately recognizable. A palm, a hand, gently brushing against her face. She could tell even without seeing it that it was rough, callused, but warm and almost timid in its touch.

Unable to control her curiosity at what was happening, and against her better judgment, she forced her eyes open.

What she saw in the dim candlelight stole her breath away: a face that was unmistakably human. The skin, while not exactly any easily catalogued shade, was obviously not the cobalt blue of the enemy. She could see eyebrows where there should be none, and hair that was somehow of the wrong texture – a bit too fine, perhaps – and undeniably not the ubiquitous black found among the Kreelan species. It was instead a dark shade of brown. Even the general shape of the face was different, slightly narrower in a jaw that did not have to accommodate large canines. He even smelled human somehow, if for no other reason than the almost-sweet musky smell of Kreelan skin was absent from the air.

But even with all the other differences immediately noticeable, the most obvious giveaway was the eyes. They were not the silver-flecked luminescent feline eyes of the Kreelans, but displayed dark, round pupils surrounded by irises that were an unusual color and brilliance of green, easily seen even in this murky light and with the pupils dilated fully open. The eyes were not exactly cold, but were nonetheless inscrutable, impenetrable, and she could see that the intelligence that lay behind those eyes was not human, not by any measure.

There was another difference, too. It was more difficult to pin down until she noticed the shape of the chest plate against which she was pinned. The creature – human or otherwise – that now held her captive was male. It was not just the chest plate's lack of the two protrusions that customarily accommodated the females' breasts that grabbed her attention. It was also her instinctive understanding of the signals that defined sexual orientation on a primal level, the way one could tell if an unseen speaker was a man or woman. And the individual now holding her was unmistakably male.

She blinked once, twice, to make sure she was not just seeing things, but the human apparition in Kreelan garb remained. It – he – stared at her, unblinking, as he gently ran his hand over her face, acting as if he had never seen another of his own kind.

It was then that she saw the wet streaks on his face. He was crying. That sight shocked her more than anything else.

"Who..." Jodi whispered, trying not to speak too loudly for fear of frightening her captor into using his powerful grip to silence her, "... who are you?"

His hand stopped its inquisitive caressing, and he cocked his head slightly, his face silently voicing the obvious fact that he did not understand her words.

Jodi slowly repeated the question, for lack of any better ideas at the moment. "Who are you?" she asked him again, slowly.

His lips pursed as if he was about to speak, but then he frowned. He did not understand.

Awkwardly, her movements hampered by his arm around her chest, she began to raise a hand toward him. His grip tightened at her movement, eliciting a grunt of air being pushed out of her lungs, and his eyes flashed an unmistakable warning. But Jodi was unperturbed, and after a moment of indecision, he allowed her to continue.

"I'm not going to hurt you," she said, hoping that she sounded convincing. She did not really know what she should – or could – do in her present situation. On the one hand, she desperately wished that one of the Marines outside would suddenly burst in and free her from this surreal rendezvous. On the other, she found herself oddly captivated by this... man. If he was what he appeared to be, a human somehow converted by the Kreelans, and not one of the Marines playing out a cruel joke at the eleventh hour, his discovery might be terribly important. Assuming, of course, that any of the humans here survived long enough to tell someone about him.

And that he would allow her to live.

Tentatively, she touched the hand that had been exploring her face, feeling a tiny jolt of excitement, almost like an electric shock, as her fingertips touched his skin.

"Please," she said, her trembling fingers exploring his opened palm, "let me go. I'm not going to hurt you. I promise." She almost laughed at the words. Here she was, pinned by a man who had extraordinary strength and whose intentions were entirely unknown, saying that she was not going to hurt him. It was ludicrous.

But, much to her surprise, it worked. Slowly, his other arm fell away from her, and she breathed in a deep sigh of relief. He was holding her hand now, gently, as if he was afraid of damaging it, and his blazing green eyes were locked on her face, waiting. It was her move.

"Thank you," she said, taking a small step backward, giving herself a little breathing room, but not moving so far as to arouse any suspicion that she might be trying to flee. Besides, with him between her and the door, and only a tiny dirty window looking to the outside behind her, there was nowhere for her to escape to.

Taking his hand, she held it to her chest, just above her breasts. "Jodi," she said, hoping to convey the idea of a name to her uninvited guest. She felt slightly foolish, because she had no idea if Kreelans even had names. No one knew the answers to even the most mundane questions about their culture. "Jodi," she repeated. Then she moved his hand to his armored chest, gingerly, shocked at how warm the ebony metal was, and asked, hoping her tone might convey her message better than the words themselves, "Do you have a name?"

He looked at her for a moment, his brow furrowed in concentration. Then his eyes cleared. In a quiet tenor that made Jodi's flesh prickle with excitement, he said, "Reza."

"Reza," Jodi repeated, smiling as she felt a shudder of nervous relief through her body. Perhaps he was not going to kill her after all. At least she had some hope, now. She might yet leave this room alive. Surely he would not bother with this little game if he had come only to kill her. But then again...

"Say my name, Reza," she said, moving his hand back to her chest. "Jodi," she said.

"Jo-dee," he managed. Even that simple utterance was nearly lost to the guttural accent that filtered his speech.

"Good," she said, elated by this tiny success. She edged slightly to one side, trying to move closer to the door without him becoming suspicious of her intentions. "Come on, now. Say it again."

He did, and she nodded, breathing a little easier. As she looked at him, forcing herself to ignore the door that was only a few feet away, but still so far out of reach, she was taken by the moist tracks that ran down his face.

With her free hand, she touched them, feeling the wetness against her fingertips. "Why are you crying?" she whispered wonderingly. She did not expect an answer.

Reza worked his mouth, as if he wanted – or was at least trying – to say something more than just repeat her name, but a change flashed across his face, a look of such cunning and knowing in his expression that it frightened Jodi. His eyes narrowed suddenly, and he took hold of her and spun her around in his arms like they were on a dance floor, whirling to some insane waltz. In the blink of an eye, she found herself facing the door to the rectory, staring into Gunnery Sergeant Braddock's surprised and confused face as he opened the door.

"You, ah, all right there, ma'am?" the regiment's acting sergeant major asked quietly, a frown of concern turning down the corners of his mouth as his hand gripped his rifle a little tighter.

Jodi spun back around to where Reza was and found... nothing. She was alone in the rectory.

"There was..." she began, then shook her head. "I... I mean... oh, shit." She looked back at Braddock, her face pale, then reddening from embarrassment. She was shaking. "I think I'm flipping out, gunny," she said with a nervous smile. "I could've sworn I was just talking to a Kreelan that looked like a human, a man."

"That'd be a bit odd for you, wouldn't it?" he joked, poking fun at her sexual preference, but he got only an uneasy grimace in return. Jeez, he thought, she's really spooked. He came up to her and put a hand on her shoulder, offering her a sympathetic smile. "Look," he said quietly, "I know what you mean, lieutenant. I've had some pretty freaky spells myself lately. We're just strung out a bit thin, getting tired and a little jumpy, is all. You'll be okay." He handed her the helmet that had been sitting on the priest's tiny bed. "We've still got a job to do, ma'am. Morning's on the way, and our blue-skinned lady friends will be along any time, now, I imagine. I'll get the troops started along while you get your stuff together. Maybe we can have one last formation before the carny starts."

"Yeah, sure," she said, trying to control the trembling that was shaking her so hard that her teeth threatened to chatter as if she were freezing. "Thanks, Braddock," she told him.

Favoring her with a compassionate smile, he left her in peace. A moment later she could hear him barking orders in the main part of the church, rousing the remainder of the able-bodied Marines to yet another fight, their last. Shaking her head in wonder, Jodi rubbed her eyes, then stopped.

Her fingertips were noticeably moist. With her heart tripping in her chest, she looked at them, saw them glistening wetly in the candlelight. Cautiously, she put a finger to her lips, tasted it with the tip of her tongue. It was not water, nor was it the bitter taste of sweat. She tasted the soft saltiness of human tears.

"Jesus," she whispered to herself. "What the hell is going on?"

* * *

She met Father Hernandez as she was moving toward the front of the church and the roughly aligned ranks of her gathered command.

"I see that, yet again, you refuse to have faith, lieutenant," he said somberly, his eyes dark with concern. He had said the same thing to all of them every morning that they had gone out to fight, hoping that someone would accept his wisdom as the truth and lay down their weapons to let God do the work of feeding them to the Kreelans' claws. "If only you would believe, God would–"

"Please, father," she said, cutting him off more harshly than she meant to. But the incident, hallucination, or whatever the hell it had been back in the rectory had really rattled her, and she did not need his well-intentioned mumbo-jumbo right now. "I don't have time."

She tried to push her way past him, but he held her up, a restraining hand on her arm. "Wait," he said, studying her face closely. "You saw something, didn't you?"

There was no disguising the look of surprise on her face at his question. "What the hell are you talking about?" she blustered, trying to pull away.

"In there, in the rectory," Hernandez persisted, his eyes boring into hers with an intensity she had never seen in him before. He gripped her arm fiercely, and she suddenly did not have the strength to struggle against him. It reminded her too much of what had happened only a few minutes ago. "I know when people have seen something that has touched them deeply, Jodi, and you have that look. Tell me what you saw."

"I didn't see anything," she lied, looking away toward the crucifix hanging above the altar. The wooden statue of Christ, forever pinned to the cross by its ankles and wrists, wept bloody tears. A shiver went down her spine as she imagined the statue's eyes opening, revealing a pair of unfathomable green eyes. "Please, father, let me go." She looked at him with pleading eyes that were on the verge of tears. "Please."

Sighing in resignation, the old priest released her arm. "You can close your eyes and ears to all that you might see and hear, you can pretend that it never happened, whatever it was, but He is persistent, Jodi," he said. "Even you cannot ignore God's Truth forever." He leaned forward and kissed her lightly on the forehead, surprising her. "Go then, child. I do not believe in what you do, but that will never stop me from praying for your safety and your soul."

Jodi managed a smile that might have been more appropriate on the face of a ten-year old girl who had yet to experience the pain and sufferings of adult life. "Thanks, father. For whatever it's worth–"

"Lieutenant!" Braddock's voice boomed through the church over a sudden hubbub that had broken out near the great wooden doors that led to the outside. "Lieutenant Mackenzie! You better take a look at this!"

"Now what..." Jodi muttered under her breath as she made her way through the rows of invalid Marines, running toward the doorway.

"What is it?" she demanded as she pulled up short next to Braddock.

Her voice was all business now, the acting sergeant major saw. She had it back together. Good, he thought. "Look," he said, pointing through the partially opened doors toward the village gates. "Just who – or what – the hell is that?"

Jodi looked toward where Braddock was pointing. The village gates were at the apex of the semicircular stone wall that formed Rutan's external periphery beyond the cliff into which the settlement was recessed. The church, located under the protective shelter of the cliff itself, was in line with the gates and elevated by nearly fifteen meters, giving anyone at the church's entrance an unobstructed view of the approaches to the village. The only approach of concern to the Marines had been the stone bridge that spanned the swift-flowing Trinity River. It was there, along the deforested stretch from the river to the village gates, that most of the battles for Rutan had been fought. The Kreelans had taken refuge in the thick forest on the far side, unable to find any suitable ground closer or to either side of the village, and it was from across the bridge that they attacked each morning. It had not been so in the first week or two, when they had engaged in fluid battles away from the village. But after the humans' heavy weapons and vehicles had finally been knocked out, the Kreelans had set aside their more powerful war machines and contented themselves with a small war of attrition, virtually forcing the humans into daily fights at close quarters, often hand-to-hand.

"I don't see..."

Then suddenly her voice died. There, facing the bridge and the Kreelans already advancing across it, was the man who had come to her in the rectory, standing like an alien-inspired Horatius.

"Reza," she whispered. She suddenly felt very, very cold.

Braddock was staring at her. "Is... is that him?" he whispered incredulously. "He was real?"

"Looks that way," Jodi replied hoarsely. She did not have enough energy for anything more. "I, ah, think we better get out there and get ready. Don't you?"

"Yeah," Braddock replied absently as he pulled out his field glasses and held them up to his eyes, focusing quickly for a better look.

But neither of them moved. Behind them, the Marines murmured among themselves, unsure and afraid at their leaders' strange behavior. A few of them were standing up on pews to see what was happening, peering out the narrow windows and reporting the action to their fellows. The church grew uncharacteristically silent, even for a holy place filled with the injured and dying.

Nearby, Father Hernandez watched the two figures peering out the door. A curious smile crept onto his face.

Fascinated into inaction by what they saw, Jodi and Braddock watched the Kreelan phalanx converge on the mysterious figure that awaited them.

* * *

La'ana-Ti'er stepped forward from the group of warriors who had come in search of combat. Kneeling, she saluted her superior. Behind her, the other warriors kneeled as one.

"Greetings, Reza of the Desh-Ka," she said humbly. "Honored are we that you are among us, and saddened are we that your song no longer sings in our veins." She bowed her head. "To cross swords with you is an honor of which I am unworthy."

Reza regarded her quietly for a moment. He was chilled by the emptiness he felt at no longer being able to hear in his heart what she and the others could, at being unable to feel the Empress's will as a palpable sensation. Although he had possessed that ability for only a brief period, its absence now was nearly unbearable. The severed braid that had been his spiritual lifeline to the Empress throbbed like a violated nerve.

"Rise, La'ana-Ti'er," he told her. They clasped arms in greeting, as if they had known each other their entire lives, had been comrades, friends, as if they were not about to join in a battle to kill one another. "It is Her will." He was left to interpret Her desires from his own memories of what once was. With his banishment to this place, wherever it was, all he had left were his memories and the single, lonely melody that sang to him in the voice of his own spirit.

La'ana-Ti'er looked upon him with respectful and sympathetic eyes. She did not pity him, for pity was beyond her emotional abilities; she mourned him. "Should you perish on the field of battle this day," she told him, "it will bring me no joy, no glory. I will fight you as I have fought all others, but I pray to Her that mine shall not be the sword to strike you down and cast you into darkness." She dropped her eyes.

"My thanks, warrior," he told her quietly, "and may thy Way be long and glorious." He drew in a breath. "Let it begin."

* * *

Jodi blinked at the sudden violence that erupted on the bridge. One moment, the Kreelans who had come to finish them off were all bowing in front of the strange man who had come to her. In the next there was nothing to see but a whirlwind of clashing swords and armor. A memory came to her from her days as a child on Terra, when a neighbor boy released a single black ant into the midst of a nest of red ones. The savagery and intensity she had seen in that tiny microcosm of violence was an echo of the bloody chaos she was witnessing now. The church reverberated with the crash of steel upon steel, the cries of blood lust and pain raising gooseflesh on her arms.

"What the hell's going on?" Braddock whispered, his eyes glued to the binoculars. "Lord of All, they're fighting each other!"

"Can you see him?" Jodi asked. Her eyesight was phenomenal, but the distance was just too great to make out any details in the raging rabble that had consumed the old stone bridge. All she could see was a swirling humanoid mass, with a body plummeting – hurled might be a better word, she thought – now and again from the bridge like a carelessly tossed stone. She had lost sight of the man after the first second or two as he waded into the Kreelans' midst, his sword cutting a swath of destruction before him.

"Yeah... No... What the hell?" Braddock wiped his eyes with his hands before looking again through the binoculars. "I see him in one place, then he just seems to pop up in another. Damn, but this is weird, lieutenant." He turned to her. "Should we go take a closer look?"

"How much ammo have we got?" she asked.

Braddock gave her a grim smile. "After we redistributed last night, three rounds per rifle and a handful of sidearm ammunition that isn't worth shit. Everybody's got their bayonets fixed for the rest of it."

Jodi sighed, still concentrating on the scene being played out on the bridge. It was no worse than she expected. "Let's do it."

Braddock turned to the Marines now clustered behind them. "ALL RIGHT!" he boomed. "MOVE OUT!"

Twenty-two Marines and one marooned naval flight officer burst from the safety of the church's stone walls and began to move in a snaking skirmish line toward where the unexpected battle still raged at fever pitch.

* * *

Reza paid no attention to his eyes and ears, for he had no real need of them at the moment. His spirit could sense his surroundings, sense his opponents far better. He was living in a state of semi-suspended time as the battle went on, his opponents appearing to move in slow motion, giving him time to analyze and attack with totally inhuman efficiency, his body and mind acting far outside the normal laws that governed physical existence. His fellow warriors knew that they would die at his hand, but none of them would ever have dreamed of turning their backs upon an opportunity to face a Desh-Ka in a battle to the death. It was unspeakably rare to engage in such a contest since the Empire had been born; the Empress had sought external enemies to fight, allowing Her children only to fight for honor among themselves in the Challenge, without intentionally killing one another except in the most extreme of circumstances. To face one so skilled, regardless of whether they lived or died, would bring much honor to the Empress and their Way.

Now their blood keened with the thrill of combat, and as they died, slain upon Reza's sword, their spirits joined the host that awaited them and welcomed them into the Afterlife. By ranks they charged the warrior priest who for the briefest of times had been a part of their people, throwing themselves into his scything blade like berserkers bent upon self-destruction. Time and again they converged upon him in a ring, swords and axes and pikes raised to attack, and time and again he destroyed them. There was no sorrow in his soul for their passing, save that they would no longer know the primal power of battle, and never again could bring glory to Her name through the defeat of an able foe.

At last, it was over. His great sword still held at the ready, Reza surveyed the now-quiet scene of carnage around him. There were no more opponents to fight, no one else to kill. The bridge was slick with the blood that still poured from the dead Kreelans' veins, blood that turned the churning white water of the river below to a ghastly crimson swirl. La'ana-Ti'er's lifeless body lay nearby, her hand pressed to the hole in her breast, just above her heart, where Reza's sword had found its mark.

Replacing his bloodied weapon in the scabbard on his back, he knelt next to her. He saw Esah-Zhurah's face on the woman sprawled beside him, and a terrible realization struck him. He knew that he would see his mate's face upon every warrior he fought, and would feel the pain of loneliness that now tore at his heart, that burned like fire in his blood, for every moment of his life. Worse, he knew that she would be enduring the same pain, and would never again sense his love, or feel his touch.

He had touched her for the last time but a short while ago, and already it seemed like an eternity.

He bowed his head and wept.

* * *

"My God," someone whispered.

Only a few minutes after Jodi, Braddock, and the others had reached the village wall, only a hundred meters or so from the church, the battle was over. The Marines who now overlooked the scene on the bridge were not new to battle and its attendant horrors, but none of them had ever witnessed anything like this. Even Braddock, a veteran of eight years of hard campaigning ashore and on the ships of the fleet, had to look away from what he saw. Fifty warriors, perhaps more, lay dead upon the gore-soaked bridge, or were now floating downstream toward the distant Providence Sea. They had ceased to be a threat to the inhabitants of Rutan, and Braddock seriously doubted that there were any more to contend with, except maybe injured warriors who would only kill themselves to prevent capture.

Braddock turned to Mackenzie. "Looks like Father Hernandez got his bloody miracle, doesn't it?"

"Yeah," she whispered, still not believing the incredible ferocity and power of the man who now knelt quietly among the dead. "I guess so." Somewhere down the line of Marines, huddled against the stone of the chest-high wall, someone vomited, and Jodi fiercely restrained the urge to do the same.

"What do we do now?" Braddock asked, clutching his pulse rifle like a security blanket.

Jodi licked her lips, but there was no moisture in her mouth, her tongue dry as a dead, sun-bleached lizard carcass.

"Oh, shit," she murmured to herself. There was only one thing they could do. She began to undo her helmet and the web gear that held her remaining weapons and ammunition. "I want you to keep everyone down, out of sight, unless I call for help," she told him.

"What are you going to do?" he asked, suddenly afraid that she really had flipped. "You're not going out there by yourself, are you?" he asked, incredulous. "After what we just saw?"

Shrugging out of her armor, glad to be free again from its clinging embrace, Jodi smiled with courage she didn't feel inside and said, "That's the point, Braddock. After what I just saw, I have no intention of giving him the idea that I'm a Bad Guy. I don't know how he's choosing his enemies, since he just waxed a wagon-load of what I suppose are – were – his own people. But walking up to him with a bunch of weapons in hand doesn't seem too bright." Finally free of all the encumbrances demanded by modern warfare, she fixed Braddock with a look of concern that failed to mask her fear. "If he polished off that crowd by himself," she said quietly, "we wouldn't stand a chance against him should he decide to turn on us. I don't know who – or what – he is, but he scares the piss out of me, and I want to do everything I can to try and get us on his good side before he starts looking for some more trouble to get into."

Standing up, she put her hands on top of the wall. She did not have the patience to walk the fifteen yards to the bolted gates. "Give me a boost, will you?"

"You're nuts, el-tee," Braddock grumbled as he made a stirrup with his hands to help lift her over the wall.

"Look at it this way," she told him as she clambered to the top. "At least he's human. Besides," she went on with faked cheerfulness as she dropped to the ground on the far side, "I know his name. Maybe he'll take me out for a beer."

Worried like an older brother whose sister has a date with a known psychopath, Braddock kept an uneasy watch through the sight of his pulse rifle. He kept the cross hairs centered on the strange warrior's head, as Jodi slowly made her way toward the bridge and the silent, alien figure that knelt there.

The closer she got to the bridge, the faster Jodi's forced upbeat attitude evaporated. She was excited, which was good in a way, but she was also terrified after what she had just witnessed. The memory of this man holding her captive only a little while ago, holding her closer than she had ever allowed a man to hold her, overshadowed all her other thoughts. It was also a sliver of hope: he had not harmed her then, and she prayed to whatever deity might listen that he would not harm her now.

As she stepped onto the old stone blocks and saw more closely the destruction that lay just a few meters away, she stopped. The thought that one individual, wielding what she had always considered to be a very primitive weapon, a sword, had shed so much blood in so brief a time, was beyond her understanding.

But looking at Reza now, she saw no trace of the monstrous killing machine that had slain her enemies only minutes before. He appeared bowed under, crushed by some incredible pressure, as if his spirit was that of an old, broken man.

Stepping gingerly around the ravaged Kreelan bodies, Jodi slowly made her way toward him.

"Reza," she said quietly from a meter or so away, trying not to startle him.

After a moment, he slowly lifted his head to look at her, and she cringed at the blood that had spattered onto his armor and his face, coating him like a layer of crimson skin. He stared at her with his unblinking green eyes, and she began to tremble at what she saw there, not out of fear, but with compassion for another human being's pain. Kneeling beside him, she took the sweat-stained bandanna from around her neck and began to gently wipe some of the dark Kreelan blood from his face. "It's okay now," she soothed. "Everything will be all right now."

Reza did not understand her words, but her feelings were as plain to him as if they had been written in stone. He had found a friend.

TWO

Fleet Admiral Hercule L'Houillier was not by nature an excitable man. Small in stature, but with the courage – or so some said, and he would sometimes allow himself to believe – of a lion, he had survived many long years of combat by maintaining his composure and his wits in the most desperate situations. His war record and an instinctive political savvy eventually had placed him in the position of Supreme Commander of the Confederation High Command, the highest military posting in the human sphere.

But today, during the emotional discussions and heated arguments that had swept over his staff and the other assembled notables sitting around the table, his normally placid demeanor had been shaken with the possibilities and responsibilities that now lay before him. Around him, the other members of the hastily assembled commission continued to argue while L'Houillier remained content to listen. He would take the floor when he judged the time was right.

"I tell you, this is the first and only opportunity of its kind! We must take full advantage of it, regardless of the consequences for a single individual." Major General Tensch, a notable conservative on the crisis council that had been convened to review the situation, had echoed his sentiments with the dedication of a modern-day Cato. "The destruction of–"

"Yes, general, we know," interrupted a woman with close-cropped blond hair who wore an extremely expensive – and attractive – suit of red silk. "'The destruction of the enemy is the first and only priority,'" Melissa Savitch, a delegate from the General Counsel's office, finished for him, rolling her eyes in disgust. "Your single-minded approach to the issue has been well noted on numerous occasions, general. However, there is more at stake here than the information you can pull from this man like juice squeezed from a grapefruit. Until we have all the facts at our disposal, we just don't know what we're dealing with, and this office will not support the kind of action you are advocating." Looking around the table, careful to make eye contact with every one of the people gathered around her, she went on, "I would like to remind you, all of you, that we are discussing the future and well-being of a Confederation citizen here, not one of the enemy."

"I think that has yet to be determined, Ms. Savitch," interjected T'nisha Matabele, a young aide to Senator Sirikwa. She was standing in for the senator who was at the moment dozens of parsecs away on Achilles and unable to return in time for the meeting. "There is no evidence to prove beyond a shadow of a doubt, as your office loves to quote, that this – what's his name – Reza Gard was forcibly abducted by the enemy." She paused, confident now that she had everyone's attention. She did not bother to feel foolish for momentarily forgetting the subject's name. That wasn't important. "At this point, there is no way at all to prove his identity, even if we had a DNA sample right here. All we have is a report that he presented local Marine Corps authorities with a letter allegedly written by a war hero who died over fifteen years ago in an enemy attack that has never been explained in terms of motive or method. Any records on this Reza Gard were destroyed there, and the chances of stumbling across any validating birth or orphanage records on another planet are slim, to say the least. In my estimation, the entire affair is simply too convenient. I think the enemy is trying to lead us on somehow." She looked around the table, daring anyone to contradict her assessment of the situation. "While I sympathize with Counselor Savitch's position," she went on smoothly, wearing her conceit like an overpriced perfume, "I firmly believe, and am going to recommend to the senator as our course of action, that a deep-core brain scan is the best approach to deal with this... problem."

"I agree," said General Tensch, obviously satisfied with her reasoning, and certainly with her conclusion.

Melissa Savitch noted with dismay that more than half the heads in the room and on the far end of the holo links bobbed their assent. Some of the fence sitters just took a side, she thought. She was about to make a rebuttal when another voice intervened.

"Poppycock."

As one, the three dozen heads, real and holo projections, turned toward a huge bear of a man in a dress black Navy uniform who sat in the shadows at the periphery of the gathered luminaries. The gravelly voice, barely understandable through a carefully cultivated Russian accent, belonged to Vice Admiral Evgeni Zhukovski, one of the Confederation's most brilliant officers and an unabashed Russophile. His left breast boasting more ribbons and decorations than most of the others in the room had ever seen in their lives, Zhukovski had more than paid his dues to humanity. Glaring at

Matabele with his one good eye, the High Command's Chief of Intelligence did not try to conceal his contempt for her and some of the others in the room. After facing the Kreelan enemy so many times in his life, the potential opponents arrayed around him now seemed entirely laughable, save that they had a great deal to say about their race's survival. It was what continually terrified him away from retirement.

Squinting theatrically at the table console, Zhukovski said, "Obviously, I have been remiss in my understanding of what was said in good Lieutenant Mackenzie's report, as well as progress of war in general," he paused, glancing at Counselor Savitch, "and articles of Confederation Constitution in particular. Perhaps review of facts may help eliminate ignorance of old sailor.

"Fact," he said, thrusting his right index finger into the air as if he was poking out someone's eye. "Since war began long ago, certain humans have tried to betray their own kind – for whatever insane reason – and Kreelans have never accepted them." He paused, glaring at Matabele, then at Tensch. "Never. In fact, from what little is known from exposed cases, would-be betrayers fare even worse than normal victims, getting nothing for their trouble but slow and painful death. This is no war of nation against nation, fighting over land or competing ideologies, where at least some participants of both sides may find something in common, even if only greed, and therefore find reason to betray side they are supposed to be on. We have nothing in common with Kreelans. Or, if we do, we do not know what. Nearly century later, we know nothing of their language, culture, customs; nothing of their motivations, their weaknesses: only their name – and even that we assume from what dying Kreelans have said before death. We know much about their biology, but we cannot explain what we see. And their technology, which covers such wide scope, we do not understand on anything other than strictly application level, and sometimes not even that. They build incredibly advanced starships to come and find us, and then use swords and spears to kill us."

He had to pause for a minute, taking a dramatically noisy gulp from his water glass. "Please excuse," he said, cutting off one of Tensch's supporters before he could open his mouth, "I am not finished yet." After another gulp, he went on. "Now, where was I? Ah, yes. So, we know nothing of importance, really, about our enemy, which makes basic tenet of most human martial philosophies, 'know your enemy,' rather useless, da?

"Another fact: over fifteen years ago, planet Hallmark blows up. Poof. No distress signals, no evidence that orbital defenses worked, nothing. No people left, all blown to little pieces. We know it was Kreelan handiwork, because navigational traces were found in system and orbital defenses destroyed, but we do not know how or why. Bigger question is why did they only use this weapon that one time? Why not use it on all human planets? And why use it on defenseless Hallmark, world of orphan children, in first place? Could they not find better target? What were they doing there, and why did they not want us to find out about it, why cover their tracks with such vigor?

"Now, fact that brought us together today." He pointed at the console and the display of Jodi Mackenzie's report. "Less than twenty-four hours ago, strange young man masquerading in Kreelan armor shows up on tiny settlement where Marines are, shall we say, not doing well. According to young Lieutenant Mackenzie's report, he somehow appeared inside and somehow got out of small room that had only one door, and that was watched by remnants of Marine regiment on far side – all without being seen." He jabbed his finger in the air again. "Then he appears on field of battle and proceeds to kill over fifty Kreelan warriors by himself in close combat in only minutes."

"So what, admiral?" Anthony Childers, another senatorial aid filling in for his master, asked. "First of all, how do we know this Mackenzie is reliable and not just coming up with some nutty concoction to get back to her ship or something? Frankly, I find it hard to accept this magical mumbo-jumbo about popping in and out of rooms like a cheap magician." Heads nodded around the room, with several hands covering not-so-innocent smiles. "Secondly, this guy killing a bunch of his own doesn't prove anything. He could have done that just to get into the confidence of those grunts down there on the colony, and from the way this drippy report reads, he did a damn fine job."

Zhukovski could do nothing but glare at the man. The admiral lost his arm and an eye nearly ten years before after ramming his dying ship into a Kreelan destroyer, and he now regretted not having taken up the surgeons' suggestion that he get a prosthetic. He would have liked to strangle Childers, but would have needed two hands to grasp the man's fleshy neck. "I will ignore insulting comments to men and women of military services," he growled, his accent deepening. "Not having served any time in military sometimes makes people say and do unkind things to those who have, instead of truly appreciating their sacrifice."

Childers reddened at the insult. It was not a widely known fact that he had obtained an under-the-table exemption from mandated military service through the intercession of his powerful shipping magnate father, and he would have preferred to keep it that way, especially in this crowd.

Zhukovski knew that he had just made yet another enemy by humiliating the man, but he did not care. What could they do, retire him? He shrugged. Childers had more than deserved it.

"But, comrade," Zhukovski went on, "to answer question, I have reviewed Mackenzie's records in detail. I have no reason at all to believe that what she said is not so. As for this Reza Gard pulling off so-called 'snow job,' I do not believe it. As Chief of Intelligence, I cannot and will not rule it out as possibility, but it goes against what few hard facts we have obtained, and – more importantly – nearly century of deadly experience."

"Then what exactly do you believe, admiral?" Melissa Savitch asked. Based on previous encounters with the man, she had long regarded Zhukovski as another conservative military hard case whose brain functioned on one level only, if at all. But she got the feeling that she was in for a surprise.

Zhukovski regarded her quietly before he answered. What a strange world I live in, he thought to himself, considering that this woman, who usually was in vehement opposition to his position, now appeared to be his only potential ally. He had noticed the shift in the room, seeing that the likes of Tensch and Matabele now had clear control of those who would allow others to make their decisions for them, and those who simply wished to be politically correct.

"Yes admiral," Tensch prodded acidly, "please enlighten us."

"Very well," Zhukovski replied, biting his tongue to keep from telling Tensch how much he needed to be enlightened. "I believe that we must take this Reza Gard at face value until or unless he shows us otherwise. He perhaps is only one who can answer our questions, even if only about his own personal history, about what happened to Hallmark and why."

"So why the big argument, admiral?" Matabele interrupted, even more impatient and self-important than Tensch. She flashed a quick glance at Childers, just to let him know that she had usurped his influence, and was immune to attack, at least from that angle: she had done her time in the Territorial Army. "Why worry about whether he's for real or not, when a core scan can tell us all we need to know right away?"

"Two reasons, young lady," Zhukovski sighed as if he was speaking to a complete idiot. "First, while I confess I am not overly moved by Counselor Savitch's emotive arguments, I nonetheless support her position. This is not because I am great humanitarian that you know me to be," he noticed Savitch suppressing a smile, "but because of something she herself commented upon very early in our meeting today. It is something all of you have so far overlooked or ignored: I believe Reza Gard is not a spy, something for which our enemy has no use, but some kind of emissary from the Empire."

The room suddenly became a maelstrom of gesturing hands and animated faces that matched the flurry of conversation that erupted at the admiral's statement. Melissa Savitch was impressed not only by what the man had said, but by the contrast in effects between when she had brought up the idea this morning and now. Her attempt had been solidly brushed off by everyone who cared to comment on it. But after Zhukovski's delivery into the vacuum left by all the arguing and fighting that had gone on all day, the delegates at least were willing to shout about it.

The man has timing, she had to admit to herself.

Admiral L'Houillier let the pandemonium continue for a few moments before he brought the meeting back to order with several raps of the gavel upon the table. "Order!" he called. "Order!" The conversations rapidly tapered to silence.

The admiral directed his attention to Zhukovski. "Evgeni, you said there were two reasons to take this individual at his word. You elaborated on the first. What was the second?"

"The second is that he presented to good Lieutenant Mackenzie what I believe to be authentic letter written by retired Marine Colonel Hickock, may he rest in peace." Again he studied the transmitted image of the yellowing letter, his old friend's distinctive scrawl immediately recognizable. Wiley, he thought sadly, whatever became of you? "Kreelans," he went on, not wanting to think of how few old friends he had left, "have never shown interest in our literature and correspondence, even military signals as far as we can tell, approaching fray each time as if they were rediscovering us. There is no reason to suspect that he was given letter with intent to use it as bona fides for espionage. Besides, if that was truth, why would he appear in guise that was so obviously Kreelan? Because they do not know how to spy on us properly? Bah." He shook his great head. "I believe letter is real, and that Reza Gard knew Colonel Hickock at some time before he came under control of Empire. And, if estimate of Reza's age is good to within few years, only place they could have met would have been on Hallmark when he was young boy."

"Which we can't prove," said Melissa. It was not an attack against Zhukovski's reasoning, but a statement of unfortunate fact.

"Da. Which we cannot prove. For now, anyway."

Tensch was shaking his head. "I'm sorry admiral," he said, "but all that's fantasy, as far as I'm concerned. I understand your respect for Colonel Hickock, but that has nothing to do with the subject of this meeting. We're talking about a human being who was indoctrinated into the Kreelan Empire, and then returned to the human sphere for reasons unknown. I believe he poses a serious security threat and I think he should be dealt with accordingly. Assuming he cooperated, it might take years to reintroduce him to humanity, and that's time that we just don't have." Tensch's expression hardened. "If he has to be sacrificed, so be it."

Zhukovski leaned forward like a cat about to pounce. The balance of power in the room had shifted again, with most of the delegates on the fence again, and he was determined that Tensch and his band of reactionaries would not have their way. Zhukovski had a gut feeling that the young man now waiting in a monastery on a faraway colony could be the deciding factor in humanity's continued survival, and he was not about to let a mistake here seal the fate of Zhukovski's great-grandchildren. His gut instincts had seldom steered him wrong, and he was not about to dismiss them now.

"Then perhaps you will be one to carry out deep-core on him?" he hissed. Tensch looked shocked. "Surely you, much-decorated general of the Marine Corps, will have no difficulty in getting man who slaughtered fifty Kreelan warriors single-handed to willingly submit to excruciating procedure that will leave him as permanent vegetable?" He swept his hand around the room, then banged it against the console in front of him so hard that the entire table shook. "You do not seem to understand, my friends. If half of what Mackenzie's report says is true, you may not have any choice but to accept him for what he claims to be, because we may not be able to control him – may not even be able to kill him – otherwise."

The room was dead silent. Very few of them had considered the problem from that angle. They had been so concerned with the end result that they had ignored the difficulties of how to achieve it. Clearly, assuming the report from Rutan was credible, if Reza did not want to submit to the deep-core scan, it was extremely unlikely that he could be convinced or coerced into doing so. Jodi Mackenzie had not reported any trouble with him, but she had been treating him well. So far, it seemed that her approach of kindness and respect was paying off.

"What is it that you suggest we do, Admiral Zhukovski?" L'Houillier's question told the others in the room that Zhukovski's recommendation would be undersigned by the Supreme Commander. L'Houillier had listened patiently to all the arguments during the day, not because he did not have his own views, but because a committee had to be allowed the latitude to discuss what it might in order to reach a workable consensus. It was the chairman's job to keep it on track without crushing it with his or her own bias. But there came a time when discussion had to end and a decision had to be made. Zhukovski's arguments, judging by the expressions on the faces of those around him, had carried the field. They had also convinced the Supreme Commander. There might still be opportunities for some of the others to dissent L'Houillier's decision to go with Zhukovski's recommendations, but not in this room, and not today.

No, L'Houillier thought. If anyone wants to take it up later, they will have to do so with the president himself.

Inwardly relieved, but not showing it except for a surreptitious wink in Melissa Savitch's direction, Zhukovski said, "I propose that we do exactly what Colonel Hickock originally intended, admiral. I believe that Reza Gard should be inducted into Marine training and put into military service, at which he appears to excel already, at earliest possible convenience."

Tensch was about to interrupt when L'Houillier angrily hammered the gavel against the table. Tensch visibly jumped, startled by the sound. His face reddening with anger, the general bit his tongue as he gave L'Houillier a glare the admiral returned until Tensch, thinking better of it, looked away.

"As I was saying," Zhukovski went on, allowing himself only a moment to relish Tensch's humiliation, "this will serve several purposes. It will let Gard do what he apparently wishes, which will make him easier, perhaps, to deal with in near term.

"Second, military training centers are good place to indoctrinate people into Confederation. Long ago, concept was called 'school of nation,' and it is no less applicable in this case. He will learn language and customs, how to be more human and less alien.

"Third," Zhukovski continued, "military service will make it easier for us to watch him without him feeling like he is being watched. There will always be someone – superior, subordinate, whoever – nearby. If he is not who he says, or does something untoward, it is more likely to be noticed than if he is given job selling flowers on street corner or reading poetry on mall.

"Finally, we will learn much more from him if he willingly cooperates, which I feel is based in large degree on what we decide today, how we treat him in future. That way, we get much more information over time. I know that time is factor, because it translates directly into lives lost. I have children, grandchildren, and great-grandchildren, and many members of my family have already given their lives to our cause, and I understand this well. But war has gone on for century already, and I doubt there is knowledge in his head that will let us win in week, if at all." He nodded to Tensch. "Also, those who would like to do core scan on brain forget one very important thing: we have no Kreelan linguists and thought interpreters to go through what might come out of your chekist machine. We have never successfully interpreted their language, and know nothing of their cultural images. I do not think Gard's brain will provide convenient translation for data thus extracted."

L'Houillier nodded, satisfied with the intelligence officer's reasoning. "Very well, admiral," he said. "Please meet with the operations officer and work out the details as soon as possible, beginning with the retrieval of Reza Gard and the Marines now on Rutan. That operation has uncompromising priority over all other tasks for the fleet, and the operations orders will carry my signature. Once that has been arranged, I want you to work out a long-term development plan for this young man and have a draft copy to me by twelve-hundred hours the day after tomorrow. After I have reviewed it, we will brief your plan to the president and Special Council as soon as possible." He made a few quick scribbles on the table's scratchpad, putting notes in his daily log file for later retrieval in the privacy of his office. Then he looked up and surveyed the committee members. "Ladies and gentlemen, does anyone have anything else to add?" Aside from a few disappointed looks, no one did. They were all anxious to get back to their parent organizations and agencies to hatch their own operations. "Very well then. This meeting is hereby adjourned."

The gavel pounded the table a final time.

History, Evgeni Zhukovski thought somberly to himself, has just been made. He prayed to God that they had made the right decision.

THREE

"This just came in, ma'am." A young Marine handed Jodi a message.

Jodi took it and gave the man a quick nod. "Thank you, corporal."

Braddock saw her face light up. "What is it?"

"Task Force-85 is on its way," she told him, "ETA thirty-six hours." It was not their home task force, TF-1051, but it would do.

"Hot damn!" Braddock cried. "Man, that's the quickest reaction I've ever seen from fleet."

Smiling with excitement, she read him part of the message: "As of 2385.146.1958T, prior regimental mission and priorities rescinded, repeat, rescinded. New priority as follows: imperative that safety and well-being of subject Reza Gard be maintained until arrival TF-85. Regiment is to stand down except for security details until relief arrival."

She turned to Reza, who knelt quietly on the ground nearby, watching her and Braddock's conversation as if he were a dog listening to its masters talking to one another, intensely interested, but unable to understand.

"Well, my friend," she said happily, "it seems as though somebody thinks you're awfully important."

"Yeah, enough to send a whole frigging task force!" Braddock announced.

Reza cocked his head at her words, his expression intense but unreadable, and she found herself pierced by his gaze. The hearts you could break with those green eyes of yours, she thought to herself, then smiled. She knew that hers would not be among them.

* * *

"Nothing's ever easy, is it?" Braddock sighed.

Jodi looked through the trees to the village walls and the several thousand heads peering over it. They had thought that the news of the task force's approach would make everyone happy. While the Marines had been elated, the Rutanians had taken a somewhat different approach to the news. A hastily called council meeting that had excluded Jodi and the Marines had ended with demands that Reza be brought into the village for what Hernandez had called an "inquisition."

Had her orders not been so out of the ordinary and Hernandez's request not so blunt – it was very obviously a demand – Jodi might have considered taking Reza into the village herself so Hernandez and the others might meet the instrument of their salvation that morning.

But, in light of the strange circumstances and fearing for Reza's safety – and that of the villagers – Jodi had managed to follow orders for once and refused. Much to her surprise, Hernandez had stalked away, silent with what could only be rage.

Not long afterward she heard Father Hernandez on the steps of the church. He was shouting something about "the Antichrist," and she ordered Braddock to have his Marines keep the townspeople back behind the wall while she took Reza to a secluded stand of trees where they could be fairly comfortable, yet inconspicuous. They were out of sight of the townspeople, but Jodi could still see out to keep an eye on things.

After seeing to the positioning of his Marines, Braddock had joined her, careful to let Reza see that he had no weapons. Reza accepted his presence without any comment other than his unblinking stare.

"I hope these people don't decide to do anything rash," Braddock murmured, looking back toward the city gates. Through his field glasses, he could see that the number of gesticulating hands and angry, frightened faces had multiplied considerably since his last observation. "Tomlinson," he said into his comm link, "what's the situation over there?"

Lance Corporal Raleigh Tomlinson's voice crackled back through the receiver in his ear. "I don't like it, gunny. These people are starting to look a little ugly, if you know what I mean. I'm not a Christian, but I know that some of the stuff they're saying isn't real nice. They're starting to get pretty hot under the collar, and I heard some saying stuff about crossing over the wall, mention of heretics, and so on. Looks like the old priest is making it into a religious hocus-pocus thing, talking about 'signs' and the Antichrist and such. He and some of the others on their council have been shouting garbage like that at me for the last couple hours." He paused. "I don't know, gunny, looks like refusing to let them talk to whoever you've got there might have been a bad idea. It kind of reminds me of when we were on Dehra Dun a couple years ago."

Braddock frowned. "Okay. Keep me posted, and for God's sake don't feel bashful about singing out."

"Roger. Tomlinson out."

"What about Dehra Dun?" Jodi asked, having heard the conversation through her own comm link. "What happened there?"

The gunnery sergeant looked at Reza, then at the gates, before he turned to face her. "Two years ago, when the regiment was due for some R-and-R, the task force dropped us off on Dehra Dun before moving off to a rendezvous to take on the regiment scheduled to replace us in the line. Dehra Dun wasn't described in the info bulletins as a garden spot, but it didn't look too bad." He shook his head slowly. "Man, were we in for a surprise.

"About a week after we arrived, me, Tomlinson, and a few others from my old squad were wandering around the capital when we saw an inter-city bus cream some poor kid that just ran out in the road. We were gonna try and see if we could help, but we couldn't get near the accident. It seemed like people all of a sudden just appeared out of nowhere and surrounded that bus like a human wall. They didn't do or say much of anything at first, like they were only rubbernecks or something. Then somebody shouted something and it set them off. First it was only murmurs and grumbling, but in a few minutes they were all shouting and angry as hell, buzzing around that bus like a bunch of hornets. It wasn't long after that when they started in, attacking those poor bastards in the bus. Even then, the driver might have been able to get away, but he waited too long. He never should have stopped." The memory gave him the shivers. "The crowd ripped open that bus like an army of red ants tearing into a caterpillar. They dragged all those people off, maybe a couple dozen, and beat every last one of them to death. They took the driver, who was probably already dead, and trussed him between a couple of skimmers. They took off in different directions, and that was the last of him." He smiled grimly. "Then they turned on us."

Jodi silently wondered if he had ever told this story to anyone before. She had only known the man for several weeks, but she felt she knew him well. In the daily battles they had fought, she had never seen him show fear; he had been an idyllic leader to his Marines, fierce and courageous, and a welcome support for her. It was difficult to imagine him being any other way. But, listening to his tale, she caught a glimpse of something else, of a time when Gunnery Sergeant Tony Braddock had indeed been afraid.

He looked back at the crowd that was beginning to gather at the city gates. "I had already gotten my people moving back down the street, away from the trouble, but it wasn't soon enough." He made a nervous laugh that caught in his throat. "You can't imagine what it feels like to be running like hell, with the ground shaking under your feet and your ears filled with the screaming of a few thousand pissed-off indigs chasing after you. Lord of All," he said quietly, "I've never been so scared by anything, before or since."

"Why were they after you guys?" Jodi asked. "You didn't do anything."

Braddock shrugged. "Who knows? I guess it was because we were there, and we were different. Just like the people on that bus. They happened to be Muslims on their way through a Hindu town to somewhere else. But, from what we read later about the place, it just as easily could have been a bunch of Hindus in a Muslim town. Wouldn't have mattered a bit.

"Anyway, we managed to get away with a few cuts and bruises from bottles and rocks, running fast enough to leave most of the rioters behind to look for someone else to beat up on. A few minutes later, a bunch of Territorial Army guys were heading back down the street to bust some heads and get those people under control, but it was too late for the people on that bus, and almost too late for us." He shook his head. "The news reported that eighty people died and over three hundred were injured in the rioting that day. That's what you get when religious fervor mixes with fear and hate. A bloody frigging mess."

There were over four thousand adults in the village of Rutan, Jodi thought. What if Father Hernandez's zealous pacifism was fired into righteous anger and fear? Jodi, while not an ardent student of history, had read enough to know that some of humanity's bloodiest wars had been fought in the name of one god or another. And the Rutanians outnumbered her Marines by about two hundred to one.

"Jesus," she whispered.

* * *

For one of the few times in his life, Father Hernandez was truly enraged. He was angry that he and his people were being held like prisoners within their own walls by the people who allegedly had been sent to protect them from the Enemy, from the powers unleashed by Satan upon the Universe. How ironic, he thought: the miracle for which he had prayed, and which he at first thought had been answered this very morning, appeared to be only an agent of the Evil One, a demon under whose enchantment the Marines beyond the gates had fallen. When he had seen Jodi's face that morning, he knew that she had seen a sign, but he had been so sure that it had been from God that he had never even considered the possibility of Satan's deceitful treachery. That morning he was certain that his call to God for help had been answered, and that an angel had been sent to save and protect them from the demonic hordes that had descended unbidden from the skies.

But it had not been so. As the last of the Marines followed the young Navy lieutenant down Waybridge Street toward the city gates, Father Hernandez had finally allowed himself the privilege of gazing firsthand upon the miracle God had delivered. At first, he was sure that his eyes were deceiving him, but then it became clear: an angel had arrived, no doubt, but it was not from above. As the thing made some unholy communion with its fellow demons, Hernandez understood that the angel before his eyes was the Angel of Death. He became sure of it as the beast suddenly turned upon its own kind in a ritual of slaughter designed to seduce the Marines in a demonstration of power, of a kind they could easily understand and accept.

Now, as he stood at the gates, he knew that Satan had won the hearts of these strangers with his clever tricks. The unbelievers stood now facing the thousands of Hernandez's flock, uniformed victims of a plague that needed no rats to spread. He felt pity for them, especially Mackenzie and Braddock, whom he had come to like and admire a great deal. But they apparently had never had the strength of faith possessed by Hernandez and his people, and so they were unprepared for Satan's insidious assault. God's miracle would indeed come, but it would be wrought by the hands of His faithful servants. It was a thought that repelled Hernandez and his fellows because they so abhorred violence. But it also thrilled them that God was giving them this opportunity to strike back at Satan, using their own hands as the divine instruments of the Evil One's undoing.

Still, Hernandez was a stubborn man, even in carrying out God's just vengeance. He had spent most of the years of his life saving souls, and he would not be content with himself until every avenue into the hearts of the weak had been tested. Not every man and woman on Rutan had died in the last half century with the Savior in their hearts, but none of them had died without hearing Hernandez's voice at least once in their lives, begging them to open their hearts to Him and be saved. He had encountered Satan's mark many times over the years, and only on a few occasions had he been forced to concede defeat or resort to the staff and rod. He knew his enemy was tenacious, and he was determined to be no less so.

"Corporal!" he called to the nearest Marine on the other side of the wall. "You must allow us to see the thing, that we may know if it is Satan's messenger!" Hernandez was as conscious as Corporal Tomlinson of the townspeople's increasingly agitated state, but he viewed it from a different perspective. What Tomlinson saw as religious fervor about to explode into undirected violence, Hernandez viewed as the gradual massing of God's power within his people. It was the means to slay the embodiment of Evil that had arisen, as champion of its own kind in a contest to be fought not for blood, but for the souls of Hernandez's people. "Please, corporal, you must let me speak with Lieutenant Mackenzie!"

He saw the Marine speak into his communications device, but knew that this meant nothing. He was merely sending information to be used by the Evil One cowering among the trees. Around Hernandez, men with crude weapons – hoes, scythes, axes – quietly began to move from the rear of the crowd toward the wall, to act as the vanguard of God's army.

Dread and excitement competing for dominance in his heart, Hernandez waited.

* * *

"I think we've got what's called 'a situation,' el-tee," Braddock said. "Farm tools and axes may not be much, but it's more than a match for whatever force we can muster against them."

"I don't want that to happen, dammit," she hissed. Tomlinson's last report had been the first page in the last chapter of tranquility; the next move would be a very short-lived battle between the Marines and a few thousand frenzied villagers, and she and Braddock both knew that the Marines would not be among the victors. "Tomlinson," she called over the comm link.

"Yes, ma'am," answered the young corporal's voice, a bit uneasily.

"Tomlinson, tell Father Hernandez that he and one other person – only one – of his choice, can come out here. Tell him, again, that we don't want trouble, but that we're dealing with something – someone – that's very dangerous and his people need to stay where they are for their own good. You got that?"

"Roger, ma'am. Right away. Out." He sounded relieved.

Jodi watched through her binoculars as Tomlinson called out to the priest who waited by the gates.

"Here they come," Braddock said as Father Hernandez and a somewhat younger man whom Braddock knew to be on the council quickly passed out of the gate and came toward them at a brisk walk. Hernandez, in fact, was walking so fast that the other man occasionally had to trot to keep up. The gunnery sergeant went out to meet them.

"Listen, Father–"

"No, my son, there is no time for talk!" Hernandez brushed by Braddock as if he were a pocket of cold air. "I know that Satan has already worked his powers upon you, and that you are now his unwitting servant. My only hope is that you can yet be saved from his clutches!"

"Wait!" Braddock cried, torn between tackling the old man and risking the consequences or letting him charge into the tines of Reza's claws. He decided that he had no choice but to opt for the latter.

Storming into the little clearing, Hernandez found only Jodi. "Where is he?" Hernandez demanded, his eyes darting into the shadows of the trees that lay around him like the bars of a cage. "Where is the servant of the Antichrist?"

"Father Hernandez," Jodi said evenly, straining to control the anger and fear that sought to creep into her voice, "if you turn around, very slowly, you'll see."

"Enough games, child!" he said angrily. "There is no–" He felt a tap on his arm, and turned to find his companion staring at something behind them, his eyes wide with disbelief.

Following his companion's gaze, Hernandez found what he had come for. "Mary, mother of God," he whispered as he crossed himself.

Backlit by the sun, Reza was an animate shadow that soundlessly stepped a pace closer to the elderly priest and the councilman. Jodi had not seen or heard him get up and move to where he stood now, even though he had been right beside her a moment before. More fascinating, however, was that when she did not look directly at him, if she looked at Braddock or the priest and Reza was only in her peripheral vision, he completely disappeared, as if he were an illusion, not really there.

"Please, father," she said quietly, keeping her eyes riveted on Reza, "don't make any sudden moves or threaten him. He has been very cooperative, but he's a complete unknown. Anything might set him off."

"What has he said to you, child," Hernandez said through his astonishment at the apparition before him, "to convince you that the ways of Darkness are best?"

Jodi shook her head. "Father, he hasn't said a word other than what I believe to be his name, which is Reza. I don't think he knows our language, or if he does, he's either forgotten it or has just chosen not to communicate with us."

"Foolish child," Hernandez chided softly. "So easily have you been led astray." He held up the wooden crucifix that hung from around his neck on a length of ivory cord. "As darkness flees from the light, so too does Evil retreat from the sign of the cross." Like a mythical vampire hunter, pushing the stunned councilman aside, Hernandez stalked toward Reza, the crucifix thrust before him just like the weapon he believed his faith to be.

"Father, no!" Both Jodi and Braddock reacted instantly, trying to stop the priest from carrying out this lunatic act of self-destruction, but they may as well have been miles away. In a movement so swift that it barely registered in Jodi's brain, Reza's sword sang from the sheath on his back, the ornate blade reflecting the glory of the sun as it sought its target. The air was filled with the ring of metal striking bone, and Father Hernandez crumpled to the ground at Reza's feet. As he fell, the tip of Reza's sword caught the cord of the crucifix, deftly lifting it from around the priest's neck and prying the cross from Hernandez's powerless hands. With a tiny flick, the cross flew into the air to land in Reza's outstretched fingers.

The councilman dropped to his knees and began to pray for deliverance with eyes tightly closed as Jodi and Braddock knelt beside the fallen priest.

"Oh, shit," Jodi cried. "You stupid old fool, I tried to warn you."

"I don't see any blood," Braddock remarked quietly. His eyes and hands worked over Hernandez's body, but there did not appear to be any sign of injury. "Reza's sword was so bloody fast I didn't even see where it hit him," he muttered. But then he saw the swelling near Hernandez's hairline, where the flat of Reza's sword must have hit the old priest's head.

Hernandez moaned, and his eyes flickered open. "Has the beast fled?" he whispered.

"Father," Jodi said, relieved that he seemed to be all right, "just be thankful you're still alive, although I can't figure out how. Where are you hurt?"

"My head," he groaned, his face wrinkling in pain, "but that is not important. Where is the child of Satan?"

"At the moment," she told him, taking a quick glance at Reza, "your demon is giving your crucifix a good looking over."

That was something Hernandez did not expect to hear. "That cannot be!" he exclaimed. Struggling mightily against the hands that sought to gently restrain him, he propped himself up on his elbows to see for himself.

There, as Jodi had told him, stood Reza, raptly staring at the crucifix in one hand, his sword held easily at his side in his other, the shimmering tip held just above the ground. He turned the old wooden cross over in his taloned hand with great care, as if it were a priceless family heirloom that had survived generations of hardship to arrive safely in his hands. Then, as if noticing the others for the first time, he leaned over Hernandez and dangled the cross by the cord from his fingers. Speechless, the old man reached for it with one trembling hand, and the cross came away in his fist.

"This cannot be so," he whispered. "All my life, I have believed that evil must flee from God's sign, but Satan has somehow transcended even this."

"Have you ever considered," Jodi told him, "that maybe you're not being confronted with something evil? Just because he's different, he's not necessarily the work of the devil, you know. Braddock and I are different from you, but you didn't seem to have too much trouble accepting us."

Hernandez shook his head, stubborn to the last. "It is not the same."

"No," Jodi said, "it's not. It looks like he's more like you than we are."

"What does that..." His voice died as he watched Reza pull something from a black leather pouch at his waist. Looking at it carefully, as if not sure of what he was seeing, an almost-human expression – longing, perhaps – crossed his face before the inscrutable alien mask descended once more. Squatting down, Reza held out his hand to Hernandez, palm up. Something small glittered on his palm.

Slowly reaching forward, careful to avoid the rapier claws at the ends of Reza's fingers, Hernandez came away with a chain that was attached to a small crucifix that might be worn around one's neck. The metal of the crucifix and the chain had long since oxidized to an inky blackness, but the few spots where the original material showed through left no doubt that it was made of silver. Rubbing his fingers over the surface of the cross, he was rewarded with a dull glimmer of beauty. Holding the cross from the chain, he looked at Reza. "This is yours?"

Reza seemed to concentrate for a moment, then slowly and deliberately nodded his head.

Hernandez could not say what lay in the green eyes that were fixed upon him, but he could not honestly tell himself that he believed this stranger was lying to him, or was in any apparent way an instrument of evil.

Perhaps Jodi is right, he thought. Although Satan could choose any form he wished, why would he choose such an easily penetrated disguise? Were there not better forms in which to deceive the simple folk of Rutan? The chameleon seeks to blend in with its surroundings, he thought now, not to stand apart from them. Hernandez's people had been segregated from the human sphere for many years, making Rutan a place where different ways of any sort were viewed with skepticism, especially since the harshness of life ruled heavily in favor of community over individuality. Just as Jesus had shown his disciples the need to seek out and touch those who were wretched in the eyes of their fellow men, so too had Hernandez striven to reach out to others. Not with his staff or a scathing tongue, but with his love and compassion. He was not yet ready to dismiss his fears that this Reza was an instrument of the Devil. But he was prepared to consider the alternative, that this was a man like any other in the eyes of God, flawed and imperfect, molded of the same clay by His hands. For Hernandez, that was still a great leap of faith, but it was a chasm he was sure – in time, at least – he could cross.

But for now, holding the tiny crucifix in his hand, he could not restrain himself from asking one more question of the stranger looming over him. "Do you believe in God?"

Reza cocked his head to one side in what Jodi now thought of as some kind of Kreelan gesture or body language, and then he looked to her and Braddock, in turn, as if for help.

"I don't think he understands the question Father," she said. "Sometimes, it's almost as if he can sense your thoughts or feelings and react to them, and not the words you say. But that's only been with very simple or obvious things. What you're asking now, especially after what he must have lived through in the Empire, goes well beyond the simple and obvious, even if you just want a yes-or-no answer."

Hernandez nodded, favoring Reza with a smile that was sincere, if not entirely trusting. "So true," he said. The priest was more inclined to believe in Reza now, because he was sure that a demon under Satan's power would have tried to deceive the priest with an answer, be it yes or no, because Hernandez wanted so badly to hear it.

Somewhat relieved, he would be content to wait for the Truth to be revealed.

* * *

As evening turned to night, the trio began to tire under Reza's unflinching gaze. It was not long after four bedrolls were brought from the village and a fire started that all of them were ready for sleep.

All, that is, except Reza. Eschewing the bedroll and the fire's warmth for the lonely chill of the nearby darkness, he knelt on the ground at the edge of the grove and stared into the star-filled sky.

"Do you suppose he is praying?" Father Hernandez asked. The possibility that this strange man knew of the existence of God was quickly becoming an obsession with him. Hernandez was aware that he was falling into that spider's web, but he was powerless against the force that propelled him into it.

"He might," Braddock said. "But it looks more to me like he's homesick as hell... ah, sorry padre."

Hernandez waved it off "I am used to it by now," he sighed, gesturing at Jodi, who rolled her eyes. "But what makes you think he is homesick and not simply praying, perhaps confessing for killing those on the bridge this morning?"

Jodi frowned, not so much at Hernandez's curiosity at Reza's beliefs, but that he automatically seemed to equate the killing of anyone or anything – regardless of the circumstances – to some form of murder. She was not happy to have to kill anyone, either, but there were circumstances that justified, even necessitated, the taking of another being's life. In the war against the Empire, the Kreelans had laid the ground rules: fight and have a chance or die. Even among humankind, the score was often the same. Jodi had been forced to kill a man once as he brutally assaulted and then tried to rape a woman in a suburban park on Old Terra. Jodi had not known either of them, she had only been a casual stroller-by, but her duty then had been every bit as clear as the duties she had sworn in her commissioning oath to undertake on the part of her race. She had felt terrible after the fact, was sickened by the knowledge that one human being could do something like that to another when the survival of their entire race was in jeopardy in a much larger war. But she had never, not once in all the years that had passed, regretted shooting the man when he turned with a knife to fight her off. He had been an enemy to everything Jodi believed in, perhaps even more so than the Kreelans were. To Jodi, not having tried to help the woman would have left nothing inside her but intolerable guilt. Perhaps if Father Hernandez underwent a similar experience, he might gain an appreciation for what lay beyond the idealistic cloak of his pacifism.

"Before I joined the Corps," Braddock told them quietly, not noticing the momentary glare Jodi leveled at the priest, "I spent my whole life in a little town on Timor. I worked as a mechanic after I got out of secondary school. I did all right, but I never would have gotten rich at it." He smiled wistfully, suddenly remembering how awful it had been, how wonderful it had been. The long hours, the hard work, the ribbing he had taken from his friends because he studied in his free time instead of playing pool at the local bar. The loves he had had, had lost. It had been his home, and he knew it always would be. "I never saw anywhere else on that whole planet, just that little town. Doing or seeing other things was something I didn't think about much, because I didn't really have time for it, not when you have to do all you can just to get food on the family's table.

"But then my draft notice was posted, and I decided to join the Marines. I figured it was a better shot than the Navy. No offense, ma'am." Jodi shook her head. The two of them had shared times that had long since dissolved any seriousness in jibes about their rival services. "After the papers were signed, I felt good about it. My folks and little sister would have money to make ends meet, and I'd get to see something of the outside, which really began to appeal to me after a while. And fighting, that was something I'd always been good at, since I was a little kid. And if I was going to be fighting the Blues, so much the better."

He looked at Reza. "It wasn't like I thought it would be, though. Boot camp went by in a flash, all of us so busy we didn't have time to think about anything but making it through the next day.

"But when I reached the regiment and saw what the war really meant to a grunt like me, to all of us, I suddenly realized that I'd probably never see home again, except maybe in a box. It hit me just like that. That night, while we were waiting to ship out to the fleet, I went off by myself a little ways and knelt on the ground, just like Reza there. I looked up at the sky, but damned if I could figure out which star was home, where Mom and Dad and Lucille were. All I wanted then, more than anything in the world, was to be at home, sitting in the kitchen and having dinner with my folks, or maybe having a beer with Dad out on the porch, a thousand other little things. I wanted to be home so bad that I just started bawling like a baby." Braddock was silent for a moment, taking the time to look at the stars himself. "Since then, Father, I've seen a thousand other guys and gals do the exact same thing. He might be praying all right, but if he is, my money says that it's not inspired by guilt from his work this morning. If he's praying, it's a wish to wake up from all this and be at home, wherever his home might be, tucked into a nice warm bed."

The three of them were silent with their own thoughts for a while.

"Well, folks," Braddock said, finally breaking the spell and stretching out with obvious pleasure on the heavily padded bedroll, the first real chance to sleep that he could claim to have had for the better part of a month or more, "I think I'm going to shut down for the night. I don't know about you, but this Marine needs his beauty sleep real, real bad. 'Night, all."

"Goodnight, my son," Hernandez replied. He, too, was tired from the ordeals of the last weeks, and today especially. His mind was wound tight as a clock spring, but his body needed rest. "I think I will avail myself of sleep, as well. Goodnight, Jodi."

"Goodnight, Father, gunny." Jodi sat at the fire by herself for a while, still thinking about what Braddock had said. That Reza might be homesick had not occurred to her. She had naïvely assumed that Reza would be happy to be back in the Confederation, among his own people. She saw how precious the old letter from Colonel Hickock was to him and the respect he had shown Braddock after Reza understood that Braddock was a Marine.

But believing that Reza should be happy to be "home" again had been silly, she understood now. Whatever Reza was thinking, it could hardly be from a perspective akin to hers. After all, how long had he been under the Empire's influence? Since early childhood? Since birth? And what – if anything – was left inside him that someone could point to and say, "That is human"? What did he really have in common with anyone in the human sphere, other than his genetic origins?

It was these questions that brought on a sudden wave of compassion for the dark, silent figure kneeling a few meters away. In the short time since he had been among them, he had demonstrated powers that made Jodi wonder if her disbelief in the supernatural, benign or otherwise, might be unjustified, and she wondered with uneasy curiosity at what other secrets might yet lay cloaked behind his green eyes. But for all that, he still boasted at least some of the frailties of his kind. He could shed tears of sadness, although she did not know exactly why he might be sad. Looking at him now, she knew that he could feel loneliness, too, just as Braddock had thought. Severed from the culture he had grown up in and whomever he might have been close to, how could it be any other way?

Quietly, so as not to disturb Braddock or the snoring priest, Jodi got up from her bedroll and went to sit beside Reza.

"Listen," she said softly as he turned to her, the pendants on the collar around his neck glittering brightly in the glow of the fire, "I know you can't understand what I'm saying, but I want you to know that you don't have to be alone." She reached out and found one of his hands. With the armored gauntlet and its rapier claws, it seemed huge and menacing against her tender flesh, but she held it anyway. "I don't know why you're here, or what or who you left behind. I hope that maybe you'll tell me those things someday, when we can speak in a language we both understand, because I really would like to know. Because I care. And there will be others who will care about you, too, and will be your friends." She touched his face with her other hand. There were no tears there now, just his glowing eyes. "I'm sure life won't be easy for you," she went on. "It never is for people who are different from the others around them, and you're different from every other human being who has ever lived. But you're still human, and that's what counts most. It'll be enough. I know it will."

She heard a tiny click, the same strange noise as when he had been holding her in the rectory, as he took off one of his gauntlets and clipped it to his waist. He took her hand in his, flesh against flesh, and did what Jodi thought was the most extraordinary thing.

Shyly, like a bewildered teenage boy on his first date, he smiled.

* * *

Jodi dreamed. Her nose was filled with the heady aroma of meat cooking over an open fire, and saliva flowed in her mouth like the warm waters of a deep subterranean river. Her stomach growled in her dream, and she moaned with almost sexual pleasure at the prospect of feasting on a thick, juicy steak, even one out of the shipboard food processors.

The dream, strange though some might have considered it, was rooted in one of Jodi's deepest desires since she had been marooned on Rutan. Penned up within the village walls for most of their stay, unable to hunt because of the threat from the Kreelans, the Marines had been eating little more than the stored bread, beans, and some vegetables of dubious origin. The Rutanians, being vegetarians, found this no great hardship, but Jodi and many of Colonel Moreau's people had become almost desperate for the taste of meat, especially when edible game was so plentiful in the nearby forest. Father Hernandez had chided her that it was an addictive vice akin to overindulgence in alcohol, and Jodi had not argued the point. If he and his people were content to live eating nothing but what came directly from plants grown and harvested by their own hands, Jodi would be the last to condemn them. But she and many of the others wanted something more.

She turned over on her side as the object in her dream floated into crystal-clear focus: a thick tender sirloin, this time not lean and healthy, but edged with a centimeter of delicious fat. Its plate-sized sides were streaked with the charring marks from the grill and carried the scent of the rare mesquite charcoal used to cook it.

Her stomach growled so loudly that it woke her up. Up to that point, the dream had been more satisfying and pleasurable than any sexual fantasy she could recall, if not because of its vividness, then perhaps because she had not eaten since the afternoon two days before.

"Oh, shit," she moaned, putting one hand over her empty belly, wishing she were back in the village rather than out here. But even though the villagers had all peacefully returned to their homes and the village was quiet, there was still a great deal of uncertainty regarding Reza. In light of that and Jodi's unusual orders regarding Reza's safety, she, Braddock and the priest had decided to remain in the tree grove – surrounded by the remaining Marines – to await the arrival of TF-85 and keep Reza company.

The culinary dream fading, Jodi came fully awake, her stomach grumbling even louder. The bedroll next to hers, where she had finally convinced Reza to lay down and sleep, was empty. "Where's–"

As she turned toward the fire and where Braddock and Father Hernandez had made their beds, her breath caught in her throat. Not five feet away, suspended on a spit over red-hot coals, was a forest gazelle. The aroma of cooking meat was nearly overwhelming, and she realized that this is what had prompted the dream about the steak. Her mouth suddenly was awash in saliva in anticipation of biting into the golden brown meat.

"Maybe there is a God," she murmured.

"To hear such words from your lips," came Father Hernandez's cheery voice from somewhere on the other side of the roasting animal, "makes me think that you are not quite as stubborn as me after all." His head popped up, his cherubic smile clearly visible through the smoke of the mystery barbecue. "Would you care to be baptized in the river this morning, good daughter?"

"Very funny, pious priest," she said. She was not sure which was worse, being baptized into something she had never understood, or having someone dunk her in the freezing glacier water of the nearby river. She had always thought that was a truly moronic idea. "Where's Reza? And where did this come from, besides heaven?"

"Reza and your gunny," he said, as always emphasizing the term as if he had never heard it before, "headed off toward the river a short while ago, presumably to take a refreshing dip while leaving me temporarily in charge of this most awful effort." He made a show of rotating the carcass a quarter turn on the spit, his face a tight grimace of disgust. "I awoke to this horrid vision when dawn broke. Reza must have killed the poor thing some time during the night and prepared it for your culinary pleasure."

"You just don't know what's good for you, Father," she said, taking one last look at the savory meat and wondering how Reza could have done all that without any of them waking up. Then again, they were all exhausted, and Jodi knew she probably could have slept through a hailstorm. "Since you're doing such a good job, I'll let you be and check out what the boys are doing down at the river."

"Wait! Don't leave me with this... this thing," Hernandez called, but Jodi paid him no attention as she trotted toward the sound of the rushing water. "Lord, forgive me for saying this," he muttered, glaring at the roasting beast, "but great should be my reward in Heaven for enduring such trials."

Jodi found Braddock sitting on the bank, a slender blade of grass protruding from his lips. Beside him Reza's armor and clothing lay in a meticulously ordered stack, but its owner was nowhere to be found. "Where is he?" she asked.

Braddock pointed to a group of rocks in the middle of a swirling mass of white water a few meters from shore. "In there somewhere."

"What do you mean?" she asked, panicked. "Can he even swim?"

Braddock chuckled. "He's already been to the far side and back. Underwater the whole way on a single breath. I don't think we have to worry about him drowning any time soon."

Jodi eyed the river, gauging its width. She figured she might make it a quarter of the way to the far side in one breath on a good day with a tailwind, but certainly not in the current that flowed here. "Shit," she said.

"Yeah," Braddock agreed.

Sitting down beside him, she asked, "Why didn't you wake me up?"

"Officers get cranky when they don't get enough sleep," he said lightly. "And you haven't had much sleep since you bailed out over this rock."

"So, are you saying that I'm cranky?"

Braddock laughed. The atmosphere around them had changed; the battle was over, the pressure was off. Reza's appearance was an enigma, but no immediate threat had materialized from him. Braddock felt like a human being again, instead of a cornered animal fighting for its existence. "No comment."

"Braddock," she said, serious now.

"Yeah."

"For whatever it's worth, thanks for keeping me in one piece."

He nodded, then gave her a mischievous smile. "It's only because I kept hoping you'd go straight and surrender to my masculine charms."

Jodi laughed so hard that her stomach began to hurt. "I'm sorry," she said finally, trying to control the spasms when she saw his face redden slightly. He had said it as a joke, but she could tell that there had been more than a grain of truth to his words. "Tony, really, I'm sorry. I didn't mean to... well, you know. Make you feel bad. I mean, off-duty, I'd like to be friends," she shrugged, "as much as officers and NCOs are supposed to be, anyway. But that's all I can ever be with you."

"Oh, hell, Mackenzie," he sighed wistfully, "I know that. It's just wishful thinking, is all. I won't hold it against you. Too much."

"Thanks," she said, patting his arm. He was a good man, a rare commodity on any world, and a good friend, which sometimes was even more difficult to find.

He suddenly nodded toward the water. "There's our boy."

Jodi looked up to find Reza standing chest-deep in the water, his gaze fixed on her.

"Hey, I think he's got the hots for you, too."

"Oh, stop it," Jodi chastened him, but she wondered if what Braddock said wasn't at least partially true. While Reza seemed to have bonded to Braddock and at least tolerated Father Hernandez, he related to her almost like a newborn chick that had imprinted itself on a surrogate mother. The bond did not seem to be sexually motivated; then again, there was no way for Jodi to really know, either way. Until Reza could be taught Standard – or he could teach someone Kreelan – only the most rudimentary communications could be exchanged. "He's only interested in me for my mind."

"Oh, Christ," Braddock moaned, "he can't be that desperate."

Reza watched them curiously, then energetically gestured at them with an outstretched hand, beckoning them to join him.

"Looks like he wants some company," Braddock said, shaking his head and holding up his hands in deferment. "He tried to get me in there earlier, but this is one I'll pass on."

"What's the matter? Is tough old gunny afraid to show off his wares?"

Braddock snorted. "Come on. You know how cold that water is. One step in there and I'd be groping around for a week trying to get a grip on myself again. If Reza can swim around like a beluga whale, power to him. I'll just sit nice and dry and stinky for right now, thanks very much."

"You better turn around, then," she told him as she began to undo the catches on her combat smock. "No free peeks unless you do the same."

"Jodi," he cried, "are you crazy? You'll freeze in there!"

"I know," she sighed as she made him turn around to face the sloping wall of the river bank, "but they don't heat the water in the village, either, and I'd rather not be the star of another peepshow for Hernandez's monks. I found the little hole they drilled in the wall of the bath." After this little discovery, the priest had been livid with his charges, and a severe tongue-lashing left them suitably terror- and guilt-stricken. But that was all ancient history now, having taken place soon after Jodi had bailed out, when such luxuries as personal hygiene had still been possible for the human combatants. "I figure I can jump in, scream, rub off some of the scum and get some of the shit out of my hair, and then jump back out and dry off with my smock and get dressed again before I turn into a popsicle."

"You're nuts," Braddock said, exasperated, as he faced the opposite direction. He heard the whisper and rasp of the heavy combat uniform against Jodi's skin as she undressed behind him. With a subtle movement, he extracted a small mirror, much like those used by dentists before more sophisticated scanners became available, from a cargo pocket on his uniform. He had used it on many occasions to see around corners without exposing his head to attack, and the seemingly primitive device had saved him from becoming a headless wonder on more than one occasion. He had to smile to himself. The young Navy lieutenant was going to have to work harder to outwit this Marine.

Holding it up in such a way as to not be too obvious, he took a surreptitious look at the scene behind him. He let his breath out slowly at what he saw when Jodi's undershirt and panties slid to the ground. Braddock had intimately known more women than he sometimes cared to admit, but none of them compared to this one. A non-practicing Christian, he marveled at how Jodi could look at herself in a mirror and still not believe that the Universe was a divine creation.

Feeling a rush of heat, he decided that he better put the mirror away.

"You can look after I get in the water," she told him firmly.

"Whatever you say, ma'am," he replied innocently.

Jodi gingerly stepped toward the water, suddenly wondering if this was not a serious error in judgment on her part. "What the hell," she sighed as the icy water touched her feet, bubbling around her ankles. Reza watched her patiently. "Here goes," she cried, diving headfirst into the water.

There was cold, and then there was cold. Jodi's reaction left no doubt as to what her body thought.

"Shit!" she cried as her head broke the surface. Her heart was pounding and she could barely breathe, but she was still alive. As she stood precariously on the bottom, resisting the swirling currents around her, the water came to just above her breasts. "God, Reza," she exclaimed, "how can you stand this?"

Reza, of course, did not reply, but watched with great interest as Jodi began to rub her skin with her hands and then rinse out her hair to clean off some of the accumulated grit and grime.

As she was dunking her head under, coaxing water into her hair, a sudden surge of the current knocked her off balance. Her arms flailing desperately, she lost her footing and was pulled under. She opened her mouth to cry out, but there was nothing but water, and it eagerly rushed into the void between her parted lips.

But just as suddenly as the crisis arose, it was put to an end. She felt a pair of strong arms gently grasp her around the chest and pull her away from the current. Her head broke the water, and the first thing she saw was Braddock, quickly wading into the water toward her, his face torn with concern.

"Are you all right?" he yelled.

"Yes," she managed, spitting water from her mouth. Luckily, she had not inhaled any water. "I'm okay."

"Goddamn stupid officers," he grumbled as he watched, unsure if it was necessary to go any further into the water. "Never have a lick of sense." After another moment of hesitation, he decided that Reza could handle her safety better than he could, and he beat a hasty retreat to the shore, already wet up to his waist and feeling every inch of it.

As Braddock was trudging back to dry land and comparative warmth, Jodi turned to Reza, who had one arm around her torso and the other under her legs, holding her like a groom carrying his bride across some watery threshold. She thought she could feel the heat of his body where his skin touched hers, although she knew that was impossible in water so cold. The muscles of his arms and chest, difficult to see in the water, felt as hard and resilient as his armor.

"Thank you," she told him. She kissed him on the cheek, just below an old scar that ran down his face over his left eye. Wrapping her arms around his neck, she let him carry her from the water, overseen by the ever-watchful gunnery sergeant.

"Hell," Braddock muttered, "I should have just gone skinny dipping." He was soaked past his waist and already shaking with cold, and now had no dry clothes to change into.

"We can dry off near the fire," Jodi told him as they reached the bank, "while we're having something to eat."

"Amen to that."

"Is everything all right?" Father Hernandez appeared from the direction of the camp. "I came to tell you that this barbarian ritual of barbecue appears to be nearing..." His voice trailed off and his eyes grew suddenly wide. "Sweet Mary, mother of God," he whispered.

"What's wrong, Father?" Jodi asked as Reza set her down. She thought for a moment that he was looking at her, but he was not. As alluring as any man might normally have found her, particularly naked, the old priest's eyes were firmly fixed on Reza. She turned to see what he was looking at. "Is Reza well-hung, or some...thing..."

Following Hernandez's gaze, she saw that Reza's skin boasted some differences that she at once found fascinating and repellant, things that she could not have seen with his armor on. For one thing, he had no hair except on his head. His groin and underarms were bereft of even a single pubic hair, and she could not see a single strand on his chest or arms, either, even a patch of downy fuzz. And on his face, there was not even a trace of a beard's shadow.

But that was not what really caught her attention. It was the scars. She had seen the half-dozen or so on his face, of course, and had thought it unfortunate that such a handsome man had to carry such terrible marks, especially the long one that ran over his left eye. But the highways of pinkish tendrils that coiled and meandered over the taut muscles of his body was like nothing she had ever seen. It was like a catalogue of pain and suffering, from the tiny puckers that seemed little more than oversized pinpricks to the scar in his side that looked like someone had skewered him like the gazelle now roasting on the fire. Leaning to one side, she caught a glimpse of a matching scar in his back. She had seen enough entry-exit wound combinations to know what one looked like. He had been stabbed clean through with what must have been a sword, just below the heart, and had lived to tell about it.

Urged on by morbid fascination, forgetting both her nakedness and the cold water that clung to her skin, she slowly circled this stranger, marveling at the unspeakable cruelty he must have endured.

"My God, Reza," she whispered, "what did they do to you?" She gently touched his back where seven jagged scars remained where the Kreelan barbed whip must have once struck him. Running a finger over the scar where another sword had pierced him, she traced the gnarled tissue that was as long as her palm and almost as thick as her hand.

"Yeah," Braddock said quietly, "he carries quite a history, doesn't he?" He had already seen the scars, when Reza undressed to go swimming. Braddock had seen enough scars to not be shocked by Reza's appearance, but he was still impressed that a man, any man, could endure such punishment and still function. "Look," he went on, "I don't know about you all, but I'm heading back to the fire. I'm freezing my ass and I'm starving." He looked at Jodi until they made eye contact. "And I'd recommend you get dressed and do the same."

"I will... ah, prepare some dry things for you," Father Hernandez said quickly. He had gotten an eyeful of Reza, and was not about to stay long enough that his attention wandered to the other exposed body standing on the river bank. He hurried back toward the camp, trailed only slightly by Braddock, who was now so cold his teeth were chattering.

Entranced as Jodi was by the tale seared into Reza's skin, her own body finally made known its own needs. "We'd better get dressed before we freeze," she said. Despite the warmth of the morning air, the cold water had penetrated to her core, and the last thing she wanted was to catch pneumonia just as the task force arrived and she had to start answering a lot of questions. She hurriedly wiped herself off with the battered smock. "Here," she said, turning to hand it to him. "I know it's grungy and a little wet, but you can still dry yourself off..." She felt her knees turn to rubber as she turned back around to him and saw what was happening. The camouflage smock dropped from her hand to the ground at her feet.

Reza still stood beside her, except that now wisps of steam were streaming from his skin and hair like cold water evaporating from hot pavement. She could feel the heat radiating from him like she was standing near an open fire.

"This is impossible," she whispered, reaching out to touch him. His flesh was hot, much hotter than any fever a human being could survive, and painful to her touch. "Reza, what are you?" she whispered.

Never letting her eyes wander from the spectacle, she managed to dress herself, her only oversight being that her undershirt was on backwards. When the steam stopped streaming from Reza's body, he, too, began to dress. His body completely dry, he put on his clothing in a precise ritual that Jodi found utterly fascinating. Watching his hands and the rest of his body move through their motions was like watching a precision drill team performing a ballet.

As she led him back to where Braddock was carving the meat from the cooked gazelle, Jodi wondered about the man who walked beside her, thinking that maybe Hernandez's first thoughts, that he was some kind of messenger from God, might not have been too far from the truth.

FOUR

Commodore Mauritius Sinclaire was known and loved by his sailors as a jovial man who was not above the occasional bout of wildness that had been part of naval tradition since men had first set sail upon the seas of Earth. The red-haired commander of one of the Confederation's finest task forces was claimed to have shared a pint or two, and sometimes a glass of something more sturdy, with the lowly sailors of his command, and was even reputed to have lost a game of poker now and then. Or so the senior chiefs would boast in front of the wide-eyed young sailors who had just set foot on the steel-plated decks of the task force's men-of-war.

Unlike so many of his peers, Sinclaire spent as much time as he could prowling the lower decks of the ships of his command. He sought out contact with the men and women who only bore a few red or white stripes on their sleeves, listening to what they had to say, telling them the things he thought they deserved to hear and reassuring them that what they did really mattered. Having started his naval career nearly thirty years before as a lowly machinist's mate on a long-dead destroyer, Sinclaire was a firm believer in the extraordinary strength and wisdom of the common man and woman.

He liked to laugh and tell jokes, and was as colorful and alive as his family's clan heritage had destined him to be. More than that, since the day he pledged himself to the Navy at the tender age of sixteen he had seen enough of death to know how precious life was, how dear and worthwhile, and he was loathe to squander it wastefully, or to see it so disposed. Honest to a fault and just as outspoken, his thoughts and tongue had cost him more than one promotion, but it was a price he was more than willing to pay to maintain his personal and professional integrity. He was certainly no angel, but no god could deny that Sinclaire had always tried his best to do what was decent and right.

And doing that was just what perplexed him now. "Blast it, doctor," he growled, "I understand your point, but my orders – our orders – say that we are to treat him as an ambassador until the powers-that-be decide just where this lad's supposed to fit into our way of doing things."

"That's all fine and good, commodore," said Deliha Rabat, the chief of the army of scientists, philosophers, clerics, diplomats, and seemingly countless other last-minute arrivals that had swarmed aboard the battlecruiser Aboukir for this mission. "But the Council expects a lot in the way of results out of this group before we reach Earth, and the only way that's going to happen is if we approach this from the scientific standpoint that it clearly warrants." She frowned theatrically. "I'm not talking about putting him in a straight jacket, for the love of All. But you have to remember: we're dealing with a complete unknown here, and – in my professional opinion – you would be well advised to follow my recommendations on this and keep him in a suitably appointed cell in the brig where he can be observed properly and kept under control." She paused a moment, waiting just until Sinclaire was about to speak. "Remember, commodore," she interjected as he was opening his mouth to reply, "you have the crew of the Aboukir to consider, as well. This man could prove quite dangerous."

Sinclaire clamped his jaws shut. If there was one thing he could not stand, it was when someone tried to use his vested concern for those under his command as leverage to influence him into making a particular decision. "I thank you for your concern for Captain Jhansi's crew, doctor," he said coldly, noting with satisfaction the rise of color in Rabat's olive cheeks, "but I've my orders, and nothing you've said has convinced me that there's any reason to deviate from them. Any results you want to present to the Council will have to be the fruits of your own hard labor and Reza Gard's willing cooperation. You'll get no support for coercion of any kind from me. Thank you, doctor, and I'll see you in the landing bay at fourteen-hundred sharp." With that, Sinclaire returned to studying his data terminal.

Deliha Rabat, Ph.D., M.T.S., etc., etc., had been dismissed.

The commodore did not have to look up to feel the hateful glare he received before she whirled around and stalked out of his day cabin.

* * *

"That's where we're going," Jodi told Reza, pointing out the shuttle's small viewport at the rapidly growing bulk of the Aboukir, orbiting majestically against the backdrop of the blue-green sphere of sunlit Rutan. She watched as he peered intently through the clear plastisteel, leaning further and further out of his seat until his nose bumped against the glass and he recoiled slightly, like a dog discovering a see-through door for the first time.

How much like a child he seems, she thought. There was so much she would have liked to know about him, but she knew that the knowledge would be someone else's to learn first. Jodi was a fighter pilot, not a trained interrogator, diplomat, or liberal arts teacher, and her home was with her squadron on the Hood. She had been informed that a shuttle had been prepared to take her to Ekaterina III where Hood was being repaired and refitted after her last mauling; Jodi should arrive there just before the battlecruiser was ready to sortie once again. She looked forward to returning to her squadron-mates and flying duty, but she could not shake the feeling of envy toward whoever would come after her and tap into the treasure trove of information now sitting beside her.

In the seats opposite sat Braddock and Father Hernandez. Braddock, sound asleep, snored open-mouthed in a ritual of fighting men and women that went back centuries: the delight of sleep after a battle fought and won.

Father Hernandez also had his eyes closed, but for an entirely different reason. Born on a planet without indigenous spacecraft – or even the most primitive of atmospheric craft, for that matter – he had developed a sudden and dramatic case of motion sickness when the shuttle lifted from Rutan, and had kept his eyes closed and his mouth moving in quiet prayer ever since. Jodi was sure his handprints would be left ever afterward in the shuttle, permanently embedded in the plastic armrests of his seat.

Those who had sent the task force had not planned on his coming with them, nor had it been planned by anyone on Rutan other than Father Hernandez himself. In what Jodi took to be a shocking course of action for one of their people, he had insisted on coming with them.

"But Father," Jodi had tried to explain as Hernandez strode up the shuttle's ramp amidst the survivors of Braddock's regiment, clutching the leather satchel that contained his Bible and few worldly belongings, "this isn't a taxi service. If you come with us, there's no telling when you'll be coming back. This task force is bound for Terra, and not many ships happen out this way—"

Hernandez waved her off. "So much the better, child, that I may see St. Peter's and the other great cathedrals of Terra with my own eyes." He tried to smile, but she was not returning it. For once, her irreverence had disappeared, replaced with a businesslike attitude that would have been well placed on a pit-bull terrier. "My child," he went on softly as the Marines trudged by behind them, "my time in this life wanes, and my service to my parish is nearly complete. Only next year was young Father Castillo to take my place at the altar. While there was a time when I looked forward to quiet contemplation and study of the scriptures to pass my days before Judgment, it holds promise for me no longer." He gestured toward the hatchway where Braddock had already led Reza to get him settled in for the flight up to

Aboukir. "God has offered me something more, a final challenge for my mind and my faith before I come before Him. There are things I must know about this young man's spirit, things that will forever consume my curiosity if I do not make this journey of discovery, a journey perhaps not much different than his own. I realize I am not a distinguished scientist or scholar as are those of the group you have told me await him, but I am in no less need of the knowledge that they also seek, and I am determined to find out what I must know. If I cannot go as a priest and friend, then I will go as a representative of the planet Rutan, of Reza's chosen place of redemption."

Slowly, Jodi nodded. "All right, you nutty priest," she said. "I just wanted to make sure you knew what you were getting into."

Hernandez smiled. "The Lord does make some allowance for fools, young lady."

"That He does," Jodi said under her breath as she helped Hernandez with his bundle of belongings and led him into the beckoning interior of the shuttle.

Returning her thoughts to the present, she asked, "How are you doing, Father?"

Hernandez hazarded a peek out of one eye, immediately snapping it shut again. "I am fine," he announced flatly.

"Liar." Grinning, she turned to the viewport again, trying hard not to laugh at all the nose prints Reza had left on the clearsteel.

"It won't be long now," she told him, reaching out to hold his hand, careful to avoid the razor-sharp talons.

Outside, a great cavern appeared in Aboukir's starboard flank as the shuttle's course brought them in sight of one of the battlecruiser's enormous flight bays.

* * *

"Attention on deck!" As the hundreds of officers and assembled crew of Aboukir snapped to attention, fifty Marines and the same number of seamen, all in dress uniform, filed down each side of the red carpet that had been rolled up to where the shuttle's main gangway was just now lowering. Unseen by most of the assemblage was the reserve gangway on the vessel's opposite side through which the regiment's wounded were already being taken off to sickbay. Sinclaire had orders to treat Reza as if he had diplomatic status, but he would never put protocol before the care of the injured.

The commodore, accompanied by Aboukir's captain and Dr. Rabat, waited at the end of the honor guard as a kind of abbreviated receiving line. Rabat's presence there rather irked Sinclaire, but there was nothing he could do about it. She was the Council's designated diplomatic liaison in this matter, in addition to being the research team chief. Besides, it was all he could do to limit the number of official greeters to the three of them: Rabat had wanted her entire team there, plus a boatload of people from the Department of State. On that score, however, Sinclaire had been firm, and Rabat had reluctantly conceded the point. The other members of her team were stuck in the ship's compartments set aside for their research, jealously watching the closed circuit feeds scattered around the flight bay.

The gangway hissed to the floor, and Sinclaire felt his fists begin to clench. So much could go wrong, from the inconsequential to the horribly disastrous. He had wanted to greet Reza with a very small party of people in a neutral atmosphere. Rabat had conjured up a circus, and this time he had been almost powerless to resist her demands.

"Present... ARMS!" The honor guard snapped their rifles in a salute and the ten-person band began to play La Marseillaise, the Confederation's official anthem, just as Braddock stepped down the ramp, a wobbly Father Hernandez on his arm. The gunnery sergeant was obviously mortified, returning the salute with as much dignity as he could muster. Father Hernandez smiled beneficently and waved at the receiving party with his free hand.

"What a bloody cock-up," Captain Jhansi muttered.

Braddock quickly dragged Hernandez down the carpet, his borrowed and badly fitting uniform and Father Hernandez's simple cassock contrasting poorly with the bright scarlet of the carpet and the immaculate uniforms of the honor guard. He came before Sinclaire and brought himself to attention, snapping a smart salute to the task force commander. "Commodore," he said formally, trying to see past the absurdity of it all, "may I present Father Hernandez of Rutan."

"Father," Sinclaire extended a hand in sincere greeting. From what he had heard, Hernandez could be something of a character, and he genuinely looked forward to talking with him. But that would have to be later.

"Thank you, commodore," Hernandez said sheepishly. "I apologize for what I gather was a breach of protocol, but I could stay on that machine no longer."

"Quite all right, Father," Sinclaire said, turning to Braddock. "And you, gunny, welcome back to the fleet. You and your people did a damn fine job."

"Thank you, sir—"

"Excuse me," Deliha Rabat interrupted impatiently. "With all due respect, we aren't here for you gentlemen. Where's Reza Gard?"

"Take a look," Braddock said coldly, pointing toward the shuttle, wondering who this egotistical woman might be. He would have liked to tell her to take a hike instead, but he doubted the commodore would have approved.

On that count, however, Braddock would have been quite incorrect.

"Where?" She snapped. "I don't see – oh..."

A sudden hush had fallen over the flight bay. The band stopped playing, the instruments falling into silence as if on a prearranged cue. Every individual present had been told what to expect, most had even seen holo movies as children depicting such fiction as men or women under Kreelan influence, but no one ever expected to see it as part of undeniable reality.

With Jodi holding one hand, reassuring him that those he was about to encounter meant him no harm, Reza stepped down the ramp. The blue rune of the Desh-Ka burned like a star on his breastplate and in the eyestone of his collar, the medallions that made up his name glinting like diamonds in the bay's harsh lighting. He paused a moment to take in his surroundings, his eyes roaming around the huge bay, the brilliant lights and strange mechanical shapes, and the colorfully dressed humans who apparently were there to greet him. He gathered that this spectacle of warriors and the humans with instruments that made strange noises – a band, he suddenly remembered – were for his benefit, and he felt honored by the display.

Sinclaire watched as the young man released Jodi's hand and stepped from the gangway onto the red carpet, and was suddenly struck by how fitting it seemed for him to be cast against such a background, a prince from some exotic and faraway kingdom here on a state visit. The silence magnified the dignity and grace of Reza's approach, and he was thankful that the band had ceased its playing of the Confederation anthem.

After an initial assessment of his new environment, Reza turned his attention to the three figures standing at the head of the warrior line, evidently serving as his immediate destination for the rendering of greetings. Two men and a woman, Reza instantly knew that these three were in their own different ways the most powerful beings on this vessel. The swarthy red-haired man was empowered to take or give life to those who served him; he was the one whose words guided the others, whose power extended beyond the walls of this ship to realms somewhere beyond. The man next to him, with skin the color of night and with little flesh on his bones, was of lesser stature than the red-haired one, but held similar powers over those within the confines of this ship. He was the vessel's master. Lastly, there was the woman, who seemed at once to be the least powerful of the three among all the souls Reza could sense around him now, but who perhaps carried more influence than the other two with authorities even higher. He could also sense that while the men were extremely curious about him and somewhat fearful, the woman had some keener interest that instantly set Reza on his guard.

With this one, he told himself, you must be careful.

"Commodore Sinclaire," Jodi announced officially as she led Reza to the end of the carpet and a new way of life, "let me present Reza Gard." For a moment, she considered adding "formerly of the Kreelan Empire," but thought better of it. For one thing, she did not wish to put words in Reza's mouth, especially when they could not speak the same language yet. For another, she did not know if it was true. "Reza," she said, "this is Commodore Sinclaire, the Commander of Task Force 85."

Sinclaire extended a paw toward Reza. While the shaking of hands was hardly the standard greeting among all humans, it was Sinclaire's. "In the name of the Confederation people and government, I bid you welcome Reza, welcome home."

There was an uncomfortable moment as Reza simply stared at Sinclaire. An air of tension began to build from the earlier excitement, and several of the Marines in the honor guard clenched their fists in worry as they threw sidelong glances toward where Sinclaire and Reza faced one another. Marine sharpshooters in the distant shadows of the flight bay tightened their fingers slightly on the triggers of their weapons, all pointed at Reza's head.

Much to everyone's surprise – and relief – Reza did not accept the commodore's offered hand. Instead, he knelt down on one knee and made what could only be a salute, bringing his left fist over his right breast.

"Well, I will be damned," Sinclaire breathed. "Come on, now, lad, get on your feet." With sinewy grace, Reza rose to his full height, turning toward Captain Jhansi. "This is Captain Michel Jhansi," Sinclaire said, exhilarated by this living enigma and what he might represent, "commander of the C.S.S. Aboukir, the vessel you're now on."

Reza nodded respectfully, but did not salute. He did not render the traditional Kreelan greeting of gripping arms to any of them, for they were not of the Way, and to do so was forbidden.

"And this," Sinclaire said, managing a neutral tone in his voice, "is Dr. Deliha Rabat, the diplomatic representative of the Confederation Council and head of your debriefing team."

Sinclaire felt a sense of grim satisfaction in the way Reza stared at her, and he thought that there was just an instant when something recognizably human passed over his face. Suspicion.

The commodore smiled to himself. The boy hasn't but set eyes on her, he thought, and already he's made her game. If he understood things right, Dr. Rabat was in for a real tussle.

With the initial pleasantries out of the way, Sinclaire led the Aboukir's little diplomatic group out of the landing bay to the ship's conference complex where Reza's reintroduction to humanity was to begin without delay.

Behind them, the dead and wounded Marines from Rutan continued to pour from the shuttle.

* * *

"Are you sure you won't change your mind?" Braddock's question was as much personal as professional. He might never get a chance to be her lover, but he still liked her more than just about anyone he had ever met. Even if she was an officer. "I mean, I'm sure the commodore could find some way to keep you on for a while. The Aboukir could use another hot jock, or so I hear."

"No," Jodi said quietly. "I need to get back to the Hood. They'll be deploying again in not too long, and I want to be on her when she does. Besides, I can't stand to be on the same ship as that Rabat bitch." It had taken as long as the time needed for Jodi and Braddock to shower, clean up, and change into clean uniforms for the New Order to emerge: Rabat had literally ordered Sinclaire to get Jodi, Braddock, and Hernandez out of her way. Regretfully, he had been forced to oblige. And that meant no more contact with Reza until Rabat deemed it necessary and acceptable. Jodi wanted to spit. "There's nothing more I can do here now, I'm afraid." She smiled then. "Look, playing Marine was fun, but I'd prefer to leave it to the pros. I miss flying too much." *And my commander,* she added silently to herself

"Lieutenant," a flight-suited petty officer called from the interior of the fast cutter that would take her to the Hood's drydock on Ekaterina III, "any time you're ready ma'am."

Jodi was grateful for the interruption. She hated protracted good-byes. No, she corrected herself. She hated good-byes, period. Too often they were permanently sealed with the mark of Death. "Time to go," she said, extending her hand. "Take care, gunny."

"You, too, el-tee. Drop me a line sometime." He shook her hand, his big and callused paw swallowing her trim and efficient palm. After only a second of consideration, he drew her close and hugged her. Jodi returned the affection with a tight squeeze of her arms around his neck.

"That's a promise," she said, fighting back tears. She picked up her gear bag that held a souvenir Marine uniform and some other tokens the men and women of the regiment had given her, and walked up the gangway into the cutter.

Braddock waved to her, but she did not turn around to see. The bay's outer door closed, and a moment later there was a subtle thump as the little ship left its berth for open space.

Frowning, he began the long trip back to the barracks bays where the remnants of his regiment were bedding down.

On board the cutter, Jodi sat in the cramped passenger cabin adjoining the two-person cockpit. There were no other passengers for this particular flight. In her hands was the wooden crucifix, his own, that Father Hernandez had given her as a parting gift. She had always disdained the existence of any Supreme Being, no matter what the name or religion. But something – she was not sure if it was hope or fear of what Reza might bring to the human universe – drove her to do something she had never honestly done in her entire life.

She prayed.

* * *

Father Hernandez sat alone in the ship's chapel. As on all ships of the Confederation Navy, it was an All-Faith chapel that welcomed the worshippers of all humanity's religions. It was so universal, in fact, that not even the most common objects of Earth-descended faiths were displayed. Instead, a single word adorned the pulpit that stood before the plastisteel pews: Welcome. Services were delivered every day of the week for each of the major denominations on the ship. While this meant that some religions were not always attended to directly, the ship's chaplain was skillful enough that all who wished to worship in public and with their fellows found a place in his words. Depending on the service being given, the walls that were now a soft white could be altered to show the inside of a great cathedral, a mosque or synagogue, or any of a thousand other places of faith, even an open mountaintop with white clouds and blue sky. Hernandez had been struck dumb the first time he had seen the wizardry that made such miracles possible. No such technology existed on his world.

Since Rabat had exiled him and the others from Reza's company, he had had one thing he had not wanted: too much time to ponder his own fate. While he was confident that there would come a time when he would have his chance to ask Reza the questions upon which he had become fixated, his obsessive interest held no patience to wait. And yet, he must, for there was no alternative. He was virtually a captive aboard this ship now. While he was free to roam throughout all but the most restricted areas, he could not venture beyond the confines of the metal hull; he could not return home.

But Hernandez was not sure, thinking about it for the thousandth time, if he even wanted to return home. To gaze from the steps of his church to where Reza had fought the invading demons to a standstill, to see the grove of trees where the young man had taken an old man's foolishness in good humor when he could just as easily have taken his life. Each day would only bring the same unanswered questions, the same nagging thoughts about things of the spirit that only Reza could answer. For if he, raised somehow by these horrid alien beings, perchance believed in the one God, was there not the chance for peace in the name of fellowship?

Besides, to return to Rutan prematurely would only be to disturb the simple but fulfilling way of life that his people had worked so hard for so many years to preserve. He was an outsider now, possessed of alien, perhaps even heretical thoughts that would pollute the pure stream from which he had been spawned. They would welcome him back with open arms, of course, but he would be forever lost to their way of understanding.

In his hands he held the tiny silver crucifix, which he had asked to borrow from Reza and had not been able to return. It had been a measure of spite on his part that he had not mentioned it to his present keepers, and guilt nagged at him for still having it. He consoled himself that it would be well taken care of until it could be returned. His own he had given to young Jodi, in what he knew were vain hopes that she would come to her senses and realize that there were greater things in the Universe even than the alien hordes that sought to destroy God's work. He was fond of the young woman, and hated terribly to see her go. But he knew that her work was important to defend Creation against the monsters that had raised Reza.

And now, the more he thought of it, the more he became convinced that Reza was genuine, that some spark of goodness, of godliness, had led him home, to stay raising his hand against those of his own kind. Perhaps, he thought wonderingly, Jodi was right when she said that different was not always evil, not always bad. To judge by outward appearances had led them to the brink of disaster before Reza had literally beaten sense into Hernandez, and the old priest vowed to change his ways, to never repeat that most human of mistakes.

* * *

Deliha Rabat watched silently as the young petty officer struggled to get back into his uniform, nearly laughing as he fell over backwards onto the bed while pulling his pants back on. He was fifteen minutes late for his duty station on the bridge.

"You'd better slow down, dear," she chided, thinking that he had been even more comical in bed. And just as hurried. Deliha was still well within her prime and attractive to both sexes, and when the fancy took her, she allowed her body the occasional pleasurable tryst. Unfortunately, it always seemed that her taste in bed partners was even worse than her choice in professional associates. None of them ever seemed to measure up. It was a paradox whose solution consistently eluded her.

"I'll, uh, I'll see you later?" the man stuttered as he finished dressing and hurried for the door.

"Don't be ridiculous," Deliha said absently, already having dismissed him from her mind. He had rated very low on her bedroom scale; masturbation would have provided a lot more enjoyment than his frenzied thrusts, and without the resultant mess. That he was now conveniently leaving behind.

With an unsure wave, he disappeared into the corridor, and the door swished closed behind him.

"Imbecile," she muttered.

As she rose to go to the bathroom and clean herself up, she contemplated her situation with a sense of frustration. Their voyage was almost over, with Earth only a few days away, and she felt she had very little to show for it. Oh, yes, the dietary team was ecstatic: they now knew what Reza liked to eat (nearly raw meat and a particular lager originally brewed in Earth's Australia), had studied his body's fantastic metabolism (but did not know how he achieved it), etc., etc. The linguistic team, led by Dr. Chuen, had made what even Rabat had to admit was phenomenal progress in teaching Reza Standard, although it was clearly due to Reza's learning skills, not Chuen's teaching.

But there had been no reciprocation on Reza's part. No matter how hard any of them tried, he refused to utter a single Kreelan word or discuss anything dealing with the Empire. Of greater annoyance, even granting his limited vocabulary in Standard, was that he refused to divulge the reason for his returning to humanity. It was as if he had simply been born again right out of his mother's womb and had no idea what they were talking about.

But that, Deliha was sure, was rubbish. Reza understood precisely what they were after, but was simply refusing to part with any information any more than he would part with his clothes: no one could convince him to stop wearing his Kreelan garb and dress in something a little more... fashionable. That and his habit of staring at people with the strange alien expression he always seemed to wear became unsettling after a while.

No, she thought, the bastard is hiding something. No, she corrected herself, he's hiding everything. And that was where most of her anxiety was focused, because that was her field, and thus her responsibility: psychoanalysis. It was her job to find out what made Reza tick, how he thought, what he thought, and why. She was fascinated at the prospect of his having psychological aberrations – and possibly superior abilities – that mirrored his physical ones, but he refused to cooperate with her at all. He would not let anyone get near him with any kind of physical probe (they still had been unable to draw a basic blood sample), and he became silent as a stone when she entered the room. It was as if he hated her personally, or at least despised her, and she could not understand why. It was small consolation that there were others on the team with whom he acted the same.

At least Dr. Chuen was able to deal with him, she thought sourly. Fool that the man was, his talent with languages was as unequaled as it was genuine, and she had to admit that it was good fortune that he was in the pool of lucky people Reza had chosen to open up to. But even Chuen was not immune to Reza's stubbornness, she thought, smiling to herself. His "human Rosetta stone" remained silent about the Kreelan language that Chuen had been so hoping to understand.

"What am I doing wrong?" she asked herself aloud. While she was at the top of her field in several esoteric areas of psychological research, her bedside manner left much to be desired, not that she particularly cared. She was more at home dealing with drugged criminal patients strapped into deep-core machines than she was with a highly intelligent and alert individual. Mentally, she went over every step and action she had taken with him, looking for some clue as to why he was holding out against her, but she could come up with nothing. Except spite, perhaps.

She finished her business in the bathroom and returned to the bedroom, this time sitting behind the desk monitor. It showed Dr. Juanita Feron, one of her team, sitting with Reza and giving him what Deliha recognized as one of the simplified versions of the Baumgartner-Rollmann intelligence tests that didn't depend on language.

"Good luck, you idiot," Deliha sneered as she called up a cup of hot tea from the food processor, recalling her own miserable luck while attempting to administer a similar test, several times. When she had laid out all the test pieces, of which there were nearly two hundred, each of which had to be arranged precisely within a defined work area, he had simply turned his attention to the room's viewport and ignored her. She had done everything short of physically touching him (she had wanted to throttle him, she thought angrily) to get him to pay attention, all to no avail. Now, she decided she was going to sit back and watch Feron's humiliation at the hands of this beast. "Go ahead, Juanita, lay it all out for him so he can spit in your eye." It occurred to her that this was Feron's first chance at him. She was not one of Deliha's protégés, and had been near the bottom of the access list. So much the better, Deliha thought savagely. This should be a good introduction for her to Kreelan manners.

Deliha leaned forward, watching Feron's lips move as she explained what she wanted Reza to do in a way she hoped he could grasp with his limited – albeit rapidly expanding – understanding of Standard. Rabat had turned down the sound during her little interlude with the awkward petty officer, and she had no interest to hear the test explained again. She had already heard it a thousand times. And so had Reza.

She took another sip of her tea, closing her eyes and pondering why Fate had cast her such a difficult nut to crack. Things would have been a lot smoother and more effective if the Council had just authorized a deep-core scan. Such a pity.

When she looked at the screen again, she was so surprised at what she saw that she spilled the tea in her lap.

"Dammit!" she snarled as the hot liquid burned her upper thighs. "You bastard!" The puzzle, which normally took someone with a genius-level IQ almost five minutes to complete, was half done in little over sixty seconds. Deliha wanted to vomit at the sight of Feron's overjoyed expression, completely overlooking the enormous significance of what Reza was doing.

Cursing every god and person that came to mind – Reza most of all – Rabat threw on some clothes and headed for the conference center, leaving the mute screen and Reza's contemplative face behind.

FIVE

Jodi was never so glad to get off of a ship as she was to leave the Aboukir's cutter. While the crew was a good one and the ship was fast, the voyage to Ekaterina III had taken what had seemed like forever. The fact that Jodi had not been allowed by the cutter's captain to get any cockpit time had not helped.

But thoughts of the cutter – indeed of the last few months – faded with every step she took toward Berth 12A, where Hood was tied up for repairs in Ekaterina's huge orbital shipyards. While Jodi had been sorely tempted to take one of the shuttles, she decided to stretch her legs after being so cramped in the cutter. It was worth the hour-long walk to get back to the ship.

At long last, there she was: C.S.S. Hood. The shipwrights of Trivandrum had built more than legendary striking power into their metal leviathan. The Hood, among humanity's most powerful warships, was also a beauty to the eye. Unlike many of her sister ships-of-the-line, she was not a collection of angular plates and protrusions that gave so many vessels an insectile appearance. Hood was a collection of finely modeled curves, streamlined and sleek, as if her destiny was to navigate through some terrestrial ocean as had her namesake centuries before. But in that beauty also lay strength, both in the armor that made up her thick protective hide and the weapons that bristled from her hull like the thorns of a rose.

But her last battle had severely tried her strength, as the carbonized craters and streaks, the breached hangar deck and ruptured gangway hatch attested. Most of her damage had already been patched, but there would be some ugly scars that would endure with the ship until her retirement by age or by fire.

You're still a tough old bitch, Jodi thought admiringly.

Pausing on the ramp just before reaching the new gangway hatch, Jodi snapped a salute to the Confederation flag suspended nearly a kilometer away on Hood's stern, before stepping up to the ensign who was the officer of the watch and rendering the same courtesy. "Lieutenant Mackenzie, reporting aboard."

The young woman's eyes lit up as she returned the salute. "Yes, ma'am," she said cordially. "Welcome back. The captain pays his respects, and will see you when he returns from shore leave."

"Thanks, ensign." As Jodi made her way over the decks she had come to know so well, greeting the few members of the crew who were not on rotation down to the planet surface, her excitement began to build. The sounds and smells of the great ship, the thrum that she knew was there but could not quite hear: all the many things that made the ship a living thing. It was her home.

There was a moment, just a tiny fraction of a second, as she was approaching her destination that she was afraid, terrified, that one tiny thing might have changed. Holding her breath, she approached the door and read the names on the assignment placard. There were two. One was hers. The other was...

Jodi burst through the door, knowing that her roommate and commander would be there. She always was.

"I'm back!" she shouted like a giddy teenage girl who had just been asked to the prom by the most sought-after male – or female, as the case might be – in school.

The woman inside, dressed in her duty fatigues, practically fell out of the chair where she had been writing performance evaluations of her pilots.

"Jodi!" her commander cried as she fell into Jodi's embrace. "Mon Dieu, I was so worried about you! Are you all right?"

"Yes, Nikki," Jodi said, "I'm okay. Oh, God, am I glad to be back."

Later, there would be many stories exchanged for the time they had been away from one another. But for now, Nicole Carré was content to hold her only real friend tightly, both of them crying tears of relief that the other was still alive and, for the moment, out of harm's way.

* * *

Ekaterina III boasted one of the strongest military forces in the human sphere, both in terms of its ground forces and the naval squadrons patrolling her system, guarding the enormous orbital shipyards. If there was a safe place in the known human galaxy, with the possible exception of Earth itself, it was here.

And that was how Jodi felt now. Safe, content. She was still riding an emotional roller coaster that alternated between the exhausted depression of the furious fighting she had seen on Rutan and the hyperventilated feeling of knowing she was back with the woman she loved. The fact that her love was unrequited, that Nicole Carré had long ago made it clear that she could never be more than a close friend, did not – and never had – been an obstacle for Jodi's tacit affection. It was enough to know that Nicole cared, loving Jodi as a friend. That they had never shared a passionate moment together was something Jodi had decided she could live with. The physical expressions of her love for Nicole were discretely diverted toward others who were more than happy to receive them, and who willingly did their best to satisfy Jodi's needs in return.

As for Nicole, Jodi knew that she had been with men on a few rare occasions, but nothing had ever come of any of these relationships. Nicole's life was her job, and Jodi doubted that there was anyone in the Fleet who did it better: Nicole Carré lived and breathed fighters. Living so long in such a lethal profession was beyond the ability of all but a very few. Nicole Carré was among them. Her mastery of technique and relentless aggression in the cockpit had quickly earned her commander's stripes and a squadron command, and she was now on the verge of putting on another stripe and taking over Hood's entire wing. Her cold demeanor had earned her the call sign Ice Queen since early on in flight training. But Jodi knew there was more, much more, beneath the flawless porcelain skin of her commander.

Nicole's professional and personal aloofness gave Jodi a certain sense of security, the feeling that she would always be the one to whom Nicole would turn in times of need. And so it had been for the years they had known each other. Jodi, her own flying skills having proven quite lethal to the enemy, had sacrificed promotions and choice assignments to stay with Nicole. Jodi obstinately refused her friend's pleas – and several direct orders – to take her own command and develop her career, and at last Nicole had given up after Jodi had laid her heart bare. It was then that Nicole fully realized how dependent she was on Jodi for support, lover or not; Nicole could not deny the fact that she herself was only human, and needed someone by her side. That someone just happened to be Jodi Mackenzie.

Still, Jodi could not help but be sad for her friend. She needed love just as a flower needs the light of the sun, but would never find it. As much as she wanted Nicole for herself, she would have been happy to see someone sweep her off her feet, to love her like Jodi would have loved to. That was the measure of Jodi's love.

"Jodi, what is wrong?"

Nicole's question caught her off guard. "Nothing," Jodi said, pushing away the thoughts of what could never be. "I... I was just thinking how good dinner was." She smiled. "It's been a long time since I've had food like this." She laughed nervously. "It'll probably make me barf."

"Do not be silly," Nicole said, letting Jodi's white lie pass for the time being. She knew that if something was bothering her, she would speak up about it sooner or later. Fishing for a little humor to brighten up her friend, Nicole made a theater out of looking over their plates, at the devastated remains of an authentic lobster dinner that had cost Nicole half a month's pay in the best restaurant in the port. It had been worth every credit, both for the food itself and to help welcome Jodi home. "The day you become sick from good food is the day the goat becomes the gourmet, oui?" Leaning forward, she took one of Jodi's hands in hers. "I am glad you are back, my friend."

"Me, too," Jodi rasped. She was afraid that she would break down and start bawling with joy. She squeezed Nicole's hand tightly.

Nicole smiled. She so much wished that Jodi would find someone she could be truly happy with, for she had so much to give. But Nicole knew that this was not going to happen any time soon; Jodi had made that quite clear. Sitting across from her, Nicole was painfully aware just how attractive Jodi was to the people around her. From surreptitious glances to unabashed stares, easily a dozen people close by were more than casually interested in her friend. If only...

But it was not to be. Not yet, anyway. Jodi was content with the way things were and, as fate would have it, so was Nicole. They were a good team.

"Jodi," Nicole asked, "what is that?" She had seen a strange bit of jewelry hanging from Jodi's neck that she had not noticed before. It looked like nothing more than a loop of twine or very fine rope cascading down into her ample cleavage.

"Oh," Jodi said. "It's a gift from someone I met on Rutan." She looked sheepish as she held up the small wooden crucifix that Hernandez had given her.

"May I see it?" Nicole asked, curious as to the origins of this token and who had gotten Jodi Mackenzie, of all people, to take up religion.

"Sure," Jodi slipped it from around her neck and handed it across the table.

"Does this mean you are a believer?" Nicole asked, curious as she examined the cross in her hands.

"No," Jodi answered immediately. "Yes. Maybe." She threw her head back in exasperation. "Hell, I don't know. I prayed on the way here from Rutan, on the shuttle. Can you believe that? I meant it, too. But now, I don't know. How can anyone believe in any God when the universe is as fucked up as ours is?"

"That is what faith is supposed to be about, or so they say," Nicole answered distantly. "To believe in something you have accepted to be true, but that sometimes seems to go against all that you see." She was quiet for a moment as she turned the old cross in her hands. "I used to have one of these, given me by my mother. That, and the clothes on my back, was all that was left to me when my parents died. There was a time when I believed in such things as God, but that was a long time ago, when I was very young, before the realities of life showed my beliefs to be painfully foolish."

"What happened to it?" Jodi asked softly, more to draw the pain out of her friend than to satisfy any sense of curiosity. Nicole had never spoken much about her childhood. But Jodi figured that this was a harmless question now. "The cross, I mean. Do you just not wear it anymore?"

Nicole shook her head and smiled, but Jodi could see that her eyes were misting over. She had never seen Nicole like this. "Nikki," she said quickly, "I'm sorry, I didn't mean to upset you. You don't have to–"

"It is all right," Nicole told her as her mind paged back to those distant years of her youth. "It has just been a very long time since I have thought of it, that is all. When I was a young girl, after my parents died and I was put into an orphanage, I had a friend. A boy who was very special to me. Since I was older, I was able to leave the orphanage before him, to go to the academy. I gave my crucifix to him to keep for me, the only special thing I had for the person I held most dear."

"What happened?" Jodi asked, watching Nicole turn the wooden cross over in her hands. "He blew you off, didn't he?"

"No," Nicole said with a force that startled Jodi. "No," she went on more softly now, "he would never have done that. Never. We wrote each other often, and I counted each passing day toward the time when he could join me. I would have been a senior by the time he could have come, but we would have had some time together. I knew even then that we were terribly young, mere children, but still, I had hopes and dreams for the two of us, and I knew he did, too.

"Then, in my first year at the academy, I was going back to visit him when I found out that the orphanage had been attacked, that the entire planet had been wiped out." She smiled bitterly. How many times had she relived that day in her nightmares? "The silver of my mother's cross burned away with the rest of Hallmark's atmosphere. Along with him."

Looking up at Jodi and seeing her shocked expression, Nicole apologized. "Jodi, I am sorry for bringing up such unpleasant a subject." Pretending she had something in her eye, a convenient excuse to wipe away a tear that threatened to fall, she asked, "Did you wish to go see the show tonight at Wilmington's, or... Jodi, what is wrong?"

"Did... did you say Hallmark?" Jodi rasped.

"Yes," Nicole said, confused and growing concerned at her friend's alarming change in expression. She looked like she was going into shock. "Jodi, tell me what's—"

"What was his name?" Jodi demanded suddenly.

"Jodi, why—"

"Dammit, Nicole, what was his name?" Jodi practically shouted from across the table. Around them, conversations ceased as people turned to stare.

"Reza," Nicole said, looking at Jodi as if she had gone mad. "Reza Gard. Why? What does it matter? What is wrong with you?"

Jodi felt her heart hammering in her chest, and she was becoming lightheaded to the point of dizziness. "What did he look like?" she asked, licking her lips and leaning forward as if she were physically starving for the words that were to come from Nicole's lips.

"He... he was just a boy then—"

"Did he have green eyes that you couldn't turn away from?"

That shocked Nicole. "Yes," she said, her face knotting with concern. "How—"

"Did he have a scar over his left eye, like this?" Jodi ran a fingernail over her left eye, just touching the skin of her forehead and cheek. "And dark brown hair?"

"Yes. Yes," Nicole croaked. A strange sense of déjà vu was creeping over her, leaving her skin tingling and a distinctly unpleasant feeling in the pit of her stomach. "Jodi—"

"Did your mother's cross have '3089' engraved on the back of it?"

"Yes. That was the year my parents were married." She suddenly reached for Jodi's hands. "Jodi, what is going on?"

"Oh, God, Nicole," Jodi said, fighting hard to contain her excitement, oblivious to the crowd of onlookers who had forsaken their dinner to watch the spectacle these two were providing. "He didn't die on Hallmark," she blurted, her words rushing forth in a stream. "He showed up on Rutan, carrying an endorsement letter from some Colonel Hickock and your mother's crucifix. He was brought up by the Kreelans, as one of them. He taught me his name. He's on his way to Earth right now aboard—"

"That is not possible!" Nicole shouted. But how else could Jodi possibly know these things? she demanded of herself. And who else could it be? Jodi began to fade behind a curtain of swirling black spots that suddenly began to pool in Nicole's vision.

"Nicole, it's true! I swear!"

"Reza... alive?" Nicole, wide-eyed, shook her head as the blood drained from her face.

"Nicole, I'm sorry, but – Nicole? Nicole!"

But Nicole could no longer hear what Jodi or anyone else was saying. Her eyes rolled back to expose the whites, and she fell from her chair to land at the feet of the shocked restaurant manager who had just emerged from the kitchen to see what all the fuss was about.

* * *

Jodi sat in a chair next to Nicole's bed, keeping watch over her friend as the sleep drugs did their work. In what had seemed like a trek born of a novel of the surreal, Jodi had somehow gotten Nicole back to the Hood. The chief surgeon examined her and put her on bed rest for twenty-four hours with a diagnosis of emotional trauma. Jodi felt awful.

But as she sat there, holding Nicole's hand, she realized why Nicole had reacted so strongly to the news that Reza had not died, but had been raised by their enemies: even though she had been so young, she had never let go of him, never stopped loving him. She had taken on the occasional lover, but never had she allowed the relationship to blossom into something more substantial than the satisfaction of the most basic primal needs. Somehow, inside, she had gone on believing that he could not really be dead, that somehow he would return like a fairytale hero to claim her heart, a modern Prince Charming, snatched from the jaws of Death. While Jodi knew that Reza was not – or at least did not seem to be – bent on the destruction of humanity, and perhaps just the opposite, his Kreelan upbringing and all the negative implications that lay therein could not be ignored. And to Nicole, who had not yet given Jodi time to explain all the things that had happened on Rutan, it must have seemed like her long-lost knight in shining armor had returned as some infamous Black Knight, corrupted and evil. The Reza Jodi had seen would be nothing like what Nicole remembered. She was bound to be taken aback, Jodi thought, perhaps even horrified.

"It's not that way, Nikki," Jodi said quietly, although she knew Nicole could not hear her through the narcotic fog that had been required to sedate her shocked brain. "I just wish you could have been there to see him. Maybe, maybe when that stupid bitch Rabat finally gets done with him, you'll get your chance. But..." Jodi sighed.

Despite the guilty feelings that the thought evoked, Jodi could not help but wonder if such a meeting would be a good thing for her. Reza represented a change in the equation of her relationship with Nicole, and that was something she was distinctly uncomfortable with.

On the other hand, if the two of them did share something, it would be so much more than Nicole had now.

An idea suddenly congealed in her mind, and she acted on impulse, calling the captain's yeoman.

"Yes, ma'am?" the young man answered.

"I'd like to speak to the captain as soon as possible," she said. "Please tell him it's extremely urgent."

"Just a moment." The boyish face was replaced by the Hood's coat of arms for a moment.

"Yes, Mackenzie, what is it?" The captain's face suddenly appeared, his short-cropped gray hair forming a silvery helmet on his head. From the rough leather jacket she saw on him, she knew he had just gotten back from shore leave, and his face made it clear that whatever she had to say, it had better be good.

"Sir, I'd like your permission to go to Earth with Commander Carré. She has knowledge that is vital to an ongoing Confederation intelligence project..."

SIX

Deliha Rabat was her usual flawless self. Despite too little sleep and horrendous stress, most of it produced by her own imagination, she was outwardly calm and collected. But under the plastic veneer she wore in front of her masters, there lurked a seething core of disappointment with herself and resentment toward the successful members of her team, her jealousy at their success a mountain that towered beyond the shadow of her own failure.

Now, standing before the Council and the president, she had to submit herself to what many lesser souls would have considered the final humiliation, the results of the debriefing that they had conducted on the Aboukir on the way to Earth. But to her, it was a challenge, and one that she eagerly accepted. She knew the human mind well, in all its various malignant forms, and was thus well prepared for her time before the Council.

The other researchers had told the Council their golden tales of success: of how phenomenally Reza had scored in language, spatial concepts, and certain types of mathematics; of his superhuman physical strength and mental acuity; of how his physiology was still basically human, yet fundamentally different in ways that were not entirely understood, as if Reza were the product of an extremely successful genetic engineering project that was well beyond human means to fully understand, let alone duplicate. Even the things at which Reza did not excel, but was merely human and thus flawed, were laid at the Council's feet where they were examined with the enthusiastic but often myopic vision of those disposed to power but often ignorant of the value of the individual.

Needless to say, they were entranced by the work that had been accomplished in the short trip to Earth, and none of the notables present commented on the lack of personal success on Rabat's part. This, of course, only fueled the fire of her malice.

Following the completion of Dr. Chuen's impassioned presentation, the last of her team chiefs to speak, she stood up and took her place at the podium that stood like the hub of the half-wheel of padded chairs from which the eyes of the Council looked down upon her.

"Mr. President," she said in her best subordinate voice, "ladies and gentlemen of the Council, let me conclude the research team's statements with some observations that may serve as food for thought as the Council considers the subject's place and future within the Confederation."

Rabat did not notice the Navy yeoman who entered through the room's rear doors like a stealthy field mouse and hurriedly sought out Admiral Zhukovski, who sat beside Melissa Savitch in the small audience arrayed well behind the podium. Zhukovski listened to the man for a moment, then dismissed him. Melissa noted the fleeting impression of a smile across his face, but he refused to answer her signaled question: What was that about?

"As you have already heard," Deliha went on, "while the subject has adapted extremely well to Standard, he has not uttered a single word of his adopted language, nor has he given any insight whatsoever into Kreelan customs or capabilities outside of those with which he, personally, is endowed.

"In short, he has consciously withheld information that is vital to the security of the Confederation, despite the clear understanding on his part of our need to learn of his experiences. Further, the physiological alterations to the subject apparently have been accompanied by no less significant psychological changes, which undoubtedly are responsible for the subject's genius level scoring in several areas of the psychological test battery and a phenomenal score in the extra-sensory perception portion of the tests."

Several of the council members raised their eyebrows at that. It was common knowledge that some individuals possessed a certain "sixth sense," in some cases active at a level that could be measured with the appropriate scientific techniques. However, Reza's test results weren't simply phenomenal; they were literally off the charts.

"Finally," Rabat continued, "it is my professional opinion and conclusion, as leader of the debriefing mission, that this physiological and psychological transformation was indeed deliberate on the part of unknown powers within the Kreelan Empire, and was done with malignant intent toward the Human Confederation. This leads me to recommend to the Council that the subject be treated as a significant threat to Confederation security, and should be peaceably confined while a much more thorough interrogation is undertaken using all measures appropriate to the potential threat."

The room fell into a quiet, uneasy murmur. While at home or at meetings dealing with the social welfare of their frequently embattled worlds, the members of the Council generally were predisposed to show dignified compassion. But in matters of security, brought up in the dark times of a seemingly endless war that had cost billions of lives and dozens of worlds destroyed, a more callused eye was focused on matters such as those at hand; conflict did little to instill trust in those besieged.

It's happening again, Melissa Savitch thought to herself as she saw the mood of the room swing from nearly awestruck interest to fearful muttered musings. Rabat had even managed to play Reza's strengths against him, Melissa saw now, using his superior abilities to highlight the fears Rabat was trying to draw out. Melissa's spine became a rod of iron as she made to stand up and take a stand against this insanity. This was not about any threat to Confederation security, it was not about Reza's right to be human if he so chose. It was about power. "I object to—"

"Ladies and gentlemen," Zhukovski rumbled, his good hand unobtrusively drawing Melissa back down into her seat, its strength communicating her need to cooperate quickly, "Gospodin Prezident and Council, I would like to speak, if I may."

Without another word, Melissa sat down.

"By all means, Admiral Zhukovski," the president said pleasantly, but with a poker face to conceal any thoughts of his own. While Zhukovski was one of the only people in the room whose judgment he truly trusted, the president also had to be a politician, which sometimes forced him to ignore good advice for far less noble purposes. They were on far more delicate ground than even Zhukovski probably realized. Mistakes here could trigger political repercussions that could topple the present government, and the president chose not to think about what would happen to the Confederation as a democracy if that happened.

Zhukovski bowed his head to honor his commander-in-chief before he began to speak. "It seems we find ourselves balancing future of entire race on outcome of one man's knowledge, and yet again are tempted into quick solution based on scant knowledge we ourselves possess. And all of this based on premise that Reza is not necessarily Confederation citizen, that he is different, not one of our kollektiv, and thus may be treated in any fashion found desirable and convenient, even unto death.

"But this... rationale, it would seem, now has – how do we call it? – litmus test." He held aloft the message the yeoman had left with him. "It has come to my attention that certain young Navy officer has personal knowledge of Reza Gard as youth on Hallmark."

This caused a stir of surprise in the audience and across the semicircle of the Council.

"Do you mean to say, admiral," boomed Senator Borge, the president's chief rival from the Opposition Party, "that this person knew Reza from before the Kreelan attack?"

"Exactly so, honorable senator," Zhukovski told him. "And to answer any question of how viable is her knowledge, I submit that it would be in best interests of all concerned if this officer was allowed re-introduction to Reza in hopes of verifying his identity, and to perhaps help build personal and cultural bridge he may cross to join our culture." He glared at Rabat and Major General Tensch, who still openly advocated a deep-core procedure on Reza, whether he was found to still hold citizenship or not. "I would also suggest that reintroduction be made here, for all members to witness. Only a few who now sit in this room have ever laid eyes on young man whose fate we charge ourselves with deciding. It would be only fair to him." And to ourselves, he added silently. "I am sure Dr. Rabat's host of experts can provide Council verification of Admiral L'Houillier's officer, that she is telling truth both about what she knows and about whatever may take place should Council agree to such meeting between her and Reza."

"Do you feel confident that this is so, Dr. Rabat?" the president asked.

Rabat seethed at the way Zhukovski had boxed her into a corner, but there was no alternative, for the moment, at least. She had to cooperate or she would look like that fool Tensch.

"Of course, sir," she admitted evenly. "I think even Reza has been baselined enough to know if he is telling the truth." This was the best compromise statement she could make without leaving herself open to charges of outright lying; in all the time the team had worked with Reza, not one single time had he lied or even bent the truth, to the best of their knowledge. If he did not wish to address something, he would simply remain silent. Apparently, silence or the complete truth were the only options available to his tongue. "And the officer Admiral Zhukovski has mentioned should be easy enough to deal with."

Neither Zhukovski nor Admiral L'Houillier liked the open conceit in her voice, but there was nothing to be done about it at present.

"Very well," the president said briskly. "Admiral L'Houillier, Dr. Rabat, set this up as soon as possible. Ladies and gentlemen, this meeting is adjourned until then."

Two raps of the gavel, and it was over.

* * *

The president. Reza mulled over the word and its significance. The humans did not have an Empress as did his own people. This they had told him, the words sparking dim memories of things he might at some time have known long ago. But seeking the knowledge of the human child who lay somewhere deep within him was by and large fruitless, for he was no longer a boy, nor was he truly human any longer. He had to learn everything anew.

Although it was very difficult in the beginning, he understood most of what they spoke to him now, and he could answer intelligibly. He felt their frustration when they asked him about things that dealt with the Way and his people, of the Empress and Her designs, and he became mute. Those things were not privy to any not of the Way, and although he no longer was bound to Her and his sisters in spirit, he did not feel compelled to cast aside his vows and beliefs. His honor was Kreelan, as was his soul, and these things he pledged to forever uphold as inviolate. He had tried to communicate this to the "scientists," but they had not taken his words as final. There were things he could tell them, perhaps, that would not endanger his honor or bring shame before Her eyes. But he sensed that the time was not yet right, that those who had swarmed around him in the bowels of the great ship like starving carrion eaters were but lackeys to a greater power.

The president. Undoubtedly not endowed with Her powers or divine grace, Reza understood that this person was the most high among humanity, the giver of laws, the maker of war, the one with final responsibility for all that happened or did not happen in the human realm. It was initially difficult for Reza to accept that the leader of humanity was a male. He had thought the scientists had been telling him a joke, as they periodically were wont to do to test his understanding of the concepts he was relearning, human-style humor not least among them. Doubting their words, Reza had demanded that they produce a likeness of this person, and they did so, presenting him with a small life-like image of a stately, if not quite regal, man wrapped in brightly colored scarlet cloth, with vibrant insignias and other ornaments around his neck and arms. His hair was a silvery gray, a handsome contrast to his skin, which was nearly as black as Reza's armor.

"This is President Nathan," they told him.

"Why," Reza had asked, perplexed not by the man's color or garments, which he knew were diverse among humans, but by how he had been addressed, "does the president have a name, and is not simply the president for always?"

This, in turn, confused them. "He – or she, as the case may be – is not president forever," one of the scientists had replied, deeply curious as always at anything he said or asked, "but only for the time he has been elected by the people, the voters. Then he is replaced by someone else, again selected by the people. That is the way a democracy works."

"And his spirit lives on in whoever follows, to help guide... him, or her?" Reza had asked.

At this, the researchers began asking him questions that he could not answer for fear of revealing more than he was able of the Way and his Empress. The researchers were intensely interested in all his beliefs learned while among the Children of the Empress, but there was little he could tell them. He fell silent, his own question unanswered.

Had Jodi or Braddock, or especially Father Hernandez, been at hand, Reza was sure they would have answered without expecting information in return as the scientists often seemed to. Of all the humans he had met so far, those three and the red-headed one called Sinclaire were the only ones he trusted, for their hearts were true, if strange in their own way. But they all had been barred from him for reasons he did not understand.

But now, he thought, he would be able to see the president himself.

"This way, sir," one of the four Marine warriors who attended him said, gesturing to the left, down yet another corridor in the great building that was the ruling place of the "government," another concept that he had vaguely understood as a child, but that now eluded him entirely. The Kreela had no similar thing, only the Empress and Her will.

Now, approaching the great wooden doors to what could only be a throne room, it was time to see the essence of that for which he had given up all that he cherished and loved, to his very soul.

The Marines stopped abruptly and stood to the sides of the door. The commander of the guard, a highly decorated staff sergeant, opened the door, then stood aside.

"Please, sir," he said, motioning Reza through the portal. He was to meet the president without a formal guard.

The president was a man of courage, Reza thought. Perhaps, a man of honor.

He stepped over the threshold into the main Council chamber, the same room where the closed-door session had been held several days before. Now, as then, it was full of people, all of them staring silently at Reza as he stepped into the room.

Uncertain, he stopped a few paces from the doors, sensing them closing behind him. He did not feel threatened, only uncomfortable, as might a tiny scree lizard, cupped in curious hands.

Reza knew, however, that he was far more powerful than such a tiny creature, and in this knowledge he drew comfort.

He surveyed the room and drank in the strange mix of emotions that floated here like the smoke from Braddock's cigarettes. He sampled the unfamiliar smells of different perfumes, was amazed at the dazzling array of colorful clothing. Standing in his armor and weapons, having stolidly refused the flimsy human garments endlessly pressed upon him, he felt as if he were the only solid, tangible object in the room. Everything else before him was as much an illusion as had been the small holograph of the president.

Suddenly, as if on an unseen signal, the assemblage in the room stood and turned to face him. A female whom he had never met before stepped forward.

"Welcome, Reza," she said, beckoning him to come closer, to the center of the raised semicircular dais at which the human elders sat, observing him closely. "My name is Melissa Savitch, and I'll do what I can to help you communicate with the others." And keep you from being thrown to the wolves, she added silently to herself. Rabat had been outraged that Savitch should suggest – demand – that she herself be by Reza's side during what Savitch knew was in all respects an interrogation, but Savitch had held firm. Without her to keep the less constitutionally scrupulous at bay, she knew that Reza would soon find himself strapped to a table, an electronic probe sticking out of his skull. "Mr. President, members of the Council," she said, turning to face the elders, "may I introduce to you Reza Sarandon Gard of Hallmark."

And there, standing but a few paces away, was the president himself.

"Welcome home, young man," he said. President Nathan had wanted very much to have himself and the entire Council down there, on the floor, to welcome Reza in a more personal fashion. But the Secret Service had been adamant that they remain separated, and more than a few of the senators had voiced their own personal objections. An unknown quantity, armed and known to be extremely dangerous to his opponents, Reza posed an incalculable threat to the core of the Confederation government at close quarters; the Council was quietly protected by an invisible force field immune to any attack Reza could make. Or so the Secret Service hoped. "I bid you welcome home to the Confederation, on behalf of all of humanity."

"My humble thanks, my president," Reza replied formally as he knelt and brought his left fist over his breast in salute. "My sword is yours to command."

This caused a few raised eyebrows and hushed murmurs in the audience.

"Young man," President Nathan said, "you need not kneel before me. I am not your king, your lord, or your emperor. I am chosen by the people of the nation of humanity to serve and to lead. Yet, I remain but a citizen myself. Please, be at ease."

Reza relaxed slightly from his position of subordinate humility and looked at the dark man, who smiled.

"Sit, and be comfortable," he said.

Finding no skins laid out on which to sit, only the awkward and uncomfortable human-designed furniture, he simply knelt on the shiny wooden floor right where he was, resting his armored hands on his knees.

For a moment, he thought he had done something wrong. The elders suddenly seemed confused, as if some form of vital protocol had not been adhered to.

But the president quickly resolved the matter. Smiling with good nature at Reza and the others in the room, he said, "Ladies and gentlemen, let us all be comfortable in our own way." Reza heard some laughter at that before everyone sat down.

The woman who had first spoken to him appeared again beside him, awkwardly sitting down on the floor with her legs pressed close together and folded beneath her, as if she were afraid of showing the parts of her body beneath the tube of fabric she wore from her waist.

"I guess where you come from they don't use chairs," she said, smiling.

"No," he answered, noting the sense of genuine concern this woman held for him. "Animal hides are much more comfortable."

"I'll see what I can do," she replied in a whisper as the president cleared his throat.

"Are you sure you want to sit on the floor, Miss Savitch?" the president asked amicably.

"I'm fine, sir."

"Very well, then," Nathan said, nodding. "Reza," he went on, his voice deepening in pitch with the gravity of his words, "your return to human space has posed a number of very complex challenges for us. While we would like to think otherwise, that we are wise enough and powerful enough to know all there is to know about anyone or anything, there are some questions that only you can answer for us. Unfortunately, these questions are the most serious of any we have had to consider in your case.

"Fundamentally, Reza, we are concerned about your loyalties after so many years in the Empire. For example," he held up a yellowed piece of paper, the one Wiley Hickock had written so many years before, "you presented this to military representatives of this government, offering it as proof of citizenship and declaring your interest in joining the Confederation Marine Corps. Further, while you have been extremely cooperative in most instances, in not one case have you divulged a single scrap of information about the Empire, a fact we have found most disturbing."

Nathan paused a moment to look at Reza carefully, assessing for himself if the young man understood the importance of what was being said. If he did not make some kind of showing now, Nathan would have little choice but to give in to the increasing pressure by certain members of the Council and the High Command to use more serious methods of interrogation.

All he received was Reza's unnerving alien stare.

"Reza," Nathan said, "as most who know me understand, I am not one who enjoys long speeches with great fanfare, and I also do not wish to tax your understanding of our language on so critical an issue as this. But you must understand that a great deal – your future, and perhaps ours, as well – rests on what you say and do now, here in this room. I realize that once more you must find yourself in a strange new world with strange customs, and have had to relearn your native language in but a very short time. But these people," he gestured with his arms, indicating the senators sitting to either side, "indeed all of the Confederation, need some reassurance that your presence among us is of your own free will, and that your loyalty now is – and always will be – to this Confederation of Humanity."

The room became deathly silent except for the occasional creak of a chair as someone unconsciously leaned farther forward in their seat, the better to hear what words Reza might utter, or to see what he might do in response to those of the president.

"Take your time answering, son," Nathan said quietly.

"Reza," Melissa whispered beside him, "think carefully before you answer; but, whatever you say, it must be sincere enough to let these people understand that you're with them, that you're one of them. If you feel you need help of any kind, ask me – that's why I'm here with you now." That really was all she could say. The president had laid the ground rules, and the ball was deep in Reza's court. It was now up to him to play out the game.

"Mister President," he began slowly, his deep voice resonating in the hushed room with the accent of the language in which he dreamed – the Old Tongue – heavy on his words, "there is no secret to why I am here. I am neither the devil some see, nor a god. When first I came to the Empire as a boy, I promised myself that I would never fight against those born of human blood. This was a promise I have kept for all of my life." Reza looked at each of the senators sitting around the dais, his green eyes boring into each of them with a look of such uninhibited animal power that several of them had to turn away. "You ask me why you should believe my allegiance to this Confederation, why you should accept and value my honor, why you should trust my words and my silence. In answer I tell you this: everything dear to my heart, all that made my life worth living, all that I suffered for, have I sacrificed to return to this realm, to serve you with my sword rather than slay you. I can offer you nothing of substance in proof, for there is nothing I can give save my word and my life."

He withdrew the knife that had once graced the palm of the Empress, and had since bound his life to Esah-Zhurah's.

There was a collective gasp from the audience, and several Marines and Navy officers rose from their seats, reflexively reacting to the potential threat, but none were quite ready to challenge the armored figure sitting quietly before the dais. President Nathan did not flinch or change expression.

"You ask me why you should trust me," Reza said quietly. While he hardly understood anything about these people and the culture they had built around themselves, he realized that only the greatest sacrifice would prove to them that he was not a "traitor," a term for which he himself had no reference from living among the Kreela. He would die, but at least his name would not be held in contempt, and his honor would be preserved among humans as well as his sisters in the Empire. "I tell you that you are all I have now," he said, "that there is nothing for me but to serve you, to offer you my life. I can never return to the Empire, for my Way there is finished, my bond to Her Children severed." He held the knife in both hands as if it were a platter, offering it toward the president. "You ask for proof of my honor; I offer you my life."

"No," Melissa gasped as Reza turned the knife's glittering blade toward his throat. She grabbed at his arms in an attempt to thwart his suicide, but her best efforts had as much effect as if she were grappling with a giant redwood.

The room broke into a pandemonium of unfocused noise and movement as those who could see what was happening leaped out of their chairs with cries of astonishment, and those behind them acted similarly because they could not see what was taking place. Those seated at the dais were on their feet, with the president trying to calm both Reza and the panicking assemblage, but his words were lost in the din. To the left, opposite the doors through which Reza had entered, a troop of Marines burst in, weapons at the ready.

Reza took it all in calmly, absorbing both the words and feelings of those around him as he might take a breath of air before diving deep under water. He fastened his mind upon the image of Esah-Zhurah that never left him, that caused his blood to boil in his veins, and prepared for the final leg of his journey. He steeled himself for the frozen emptiness that awaited his soul like the river in which he had once almost lost his life.

It is time, he told himself, and the blade that Pan'ne-Sharakh had crafted long before he was born shot toward his throat, aimed at the flesh that lay exposed above the collar that bore his name. In his mind's eye, the gleaming metal traveled ever so slowly, and the panicked humans slower still. There was yet a lifetime to ponder things that had once been, and things that might have been...

"Reza."

The blade stopped just as its tip touched the skin of his neck, drawing a small bead of blood. It was not the cry of his name that had stopped him, for the sound of the voice was lost among the many others echoing about him. It was the feeling behind it, the wave of empathy that crashed upon him so unexpectedly, with the force of desperate love.

And there beside him, where the one who had called herself Melissa had been, knelt a woman whom he had never before seen, a stranger who was yet oddly familiar to him. She wore the black dress uniform of a Navy officer, with gold trim around her sleeves and crimson piping down the sides of her perfectly tailored pants. The almond brown eyes, caring and frightened, seemed on the verge of tears. Her face was perhaps nearly his age in human time, but somehow seemed so very, very much younger. It was as if hers was a face from the past, from a time that came to him only in odd dreams now, when he once knew her as...

"Nicole," he breathed, the sound of her name, unspoken for so many years, startling him with its sudden familiarity.

"Yes, Reza," Nicole whispered hoarsely as she touched his face with a trembling hand. "Oui, mon chère, c'est moi... it is I."

As everyone watched in silent amazement, Reza let the ornately inlaid knife slide to the floor as he embraced the woman who had returned for him from the past to help him step into the future.

SEVEN

"This is madness, Job, sheer madness," Senator Borge declared to his longtime friend and political rival. Ice cubes clinked in the tumbler that was now nearly empty of the expensive Scotch that President Nathan kept especially for his friend and opponent. The president's personal living quarters, built on the site of what had once been the United Nations building in Old New York City, were sparsely but tastefully decorated with priceless original silk batiks depicting the rise, decline, and eventual rebirth of Nathan's native Masai tribe.

Strom Borge detested the room. "It's completely irresponsible of you as Commander-in-Chief to allow such a thing. Over twenty billion people have died in this damned war. And here you are, worried that we might be infringing on one person's rights, for the love of All."

Looking out the enormous pane of plastisteel that served as the room's east wall, facing forever into the rising sun, Job Nathan sighed in resignation. He was tired of arguing, but he was not about to alter his decision. "We've talked about this enough, Strom. And don't play your guilt trip scenario about war casualties, either. Believe me, my friend, as much as you might like to believe otherwise, I have felt each of those deaths as if they were members of my family. Unlike your hero of twentieth century Eurasia, Joseph Stalin, I don't accept those figures as simple statistics; they are all human beings – every single one of them. And making Reza Gard another statistic is not going to help the war effort." He turned away from the window, his face creased with age and the strain of leadership. "We're losing this war, Strom, as I am sure you are well aware. It may take a number of years for that to become clear to the general populace, but the fact remains that we cannot replace our losses as fast as they are incurred. We don't trade planets with the Kreelans; they take them from us after bloody fighting, as if there is no end to their resources, which maybe there isn't. They never give us a chance to return the favor. And our losses have been accelerating over the last few years."

He turned to look out the window again, his eyes taking in the ocean waters that once had been poisoned, but that had in the centuries since been restored to sufficient purity that the water once again was teeming with life. "Reza represents what may be our only chance, Strom, and our decision now must be the right one, and not simply for his sake. If I were confident that your methods were the best for the situation, I would have acted upon your suggestions and those of General Tensch. I would sacrifice one life, a thousand, a million to end this war. But that is only wishful thinking, and I will not punish someone who has committed no offense – other than being in the wrong place at the wrong time as a child – for the sake of fantasy."

"So," Strom said quietly, watching the president with an almost predatory gaze, "you are confident that Reza is actually going to pan out as a Marine, then?"

Nathan shrugged. "I think it will be an interesting experiment in culture shock," he said. Borge smiled politely, but obviously was not amused. Going on in a more serious voice, the president said, "General Tsingai has taken responsibility for getting Reza prepared for Quantico and overseeing his training there, and Zhukovski's recommendation to have Mackenzie and Carré assigned there as temporary duty instructors was accepted by L'Houillier, with my endorsement. As for how well he will adapt to his new environment – or it to him – who can say? The most important thing is that the matter is settled unless or until something untoward happens."

Strom Borge looked at his friend with an expression that was calculated not to show his true feelings. "You realize, Job, what will happen if you're wrong, if Tensch, the others and myself are vindicated?"

"Yes, my good senator," Nathan replied coolly, raising his brandy snifter in a mock toast. "I will be slated for early retirement, or worse. Would you have me thrown in prison? Shot, perhaps? Then you, Strom Borge, will be the next president of this Confederation."

Borge smiled thinly. *That will only be the first step*, he thought to himself as the last of the scotch slithered down his throat.

* * *

General Tsingai and his newly acquired special aides – Carré and Mackenzie – had done their best to prepare Reza for his introduction to the Marine Corps at Quantico. Quantico was the Confederation Marine Corps' primary training facility, located almost five hundred light years from Earth and the North American city after which it was named. Tsingai, a veteran of many campaigns, was the post commandant. It was a far more significant assignment than it had been on Earth, for Tsingai's domain encompassed not only the planet of Quantico, but the rest of its star system, as well.

Despite the tremendous resources at his disposal, however, Tsingai remained somewhat at a loss as to how to deal with his latest, and in many ways most significant, challenge. Reza had been among other humans for several months now, but unlike most humans who came to live in a culture different from the one into which they had been born, humanity had made virtually no cultural impression on him at all. He could speak the language well, he understood the things he was being taught, but he consistently failed to adopt anything that would have made him a bit more human. Even the best efforts of Carré and Mackenzie, who appeared to be the only two who could draw anything at all from him, failed to get him to open up to human ways and loosen his tongue about his experiences in the Empire.

"Well," Tsingai said to both of them as they all stood watching the induction about to begin in the massive courtyard below, "I guess we've done what we can. Now we wait to see if he sinks or swims."

"He will be all right," Nicole said quietly beside him.

"Yeah," Jodi added. "It's the others who had better watch it."

Tsingai grimaced inwardly. "You're sure that he understands that he is not to act like some warlord down there? We're risking a lot of lives by letting him keep his weapons. If he harms anyone…"

"He will harm no one who does not threaten him with death, General." Nicole strained to see the dark figure in the crowd below, but could see nothing but a mass of bodies, slowly aligning like iron filings trapped in a magnetic field. "This he promised me, and it is a vow he will keep."

Frowning, Tsingai watched the crowd of inductees as the drill instructors, the DIs, began forming them up. He hoped the two women beside him did not notice the white knuckles of his clenched hands.

Somewhere down below, they heard a DI bellow.

* * *

"Line up on the white lines, NOW!"

Reza stood like an ebony pillar among the crowd of inductees who filled the courtyard outside Quantico's main in-processing building. The other would-be Marines favored him with wary, sometimes frightened, glances and quiet mutterings. He wore his armor and weapons, and carried his few precious belongings in the hide satchel that had accompanied him as a gift from the Empress, for it contained all the few material things he treasured, besides his weapons. He had politely refused the general's request to adopt some form of human dress after learning that what little off-duty time he had would be his own; he would proudly wear the uniform of the Corps, but he found the civilian clothing unattractive and ill-fitting. Most difficult for the general to accept, of course, had been Reza's refusal to surrender his weapons to anyone, for any reason. He was a warrior, and his weapons were a part of his body, his soul. He also refused to cut his hair, but never explained why. General Tsingai had grudgingly agreed to these unusual accommodations, but only after very intense arguments from both Jodi and Nicole.

Reza looked at the men and women around him. They ranged from a youthful seventeen to a trim forty, of all different colors, shapes, and ways of life. They were clothed in a bewildering variety of clothes that Reza found somewhat comical and completely alien to the ways of the Kreela. But the diversity in clothing only underscored the fact that Quantico, and the other installations like it, served as temporary melting pots to even out the gaps inherent in the regimental system.

Apparently, Reza was perhaps more diverse than some of his companions could handle. He met their stares, could sense their unease like the predatory animal he was. These were the same feelings he had encountered from almost everyone he had met so far in the human sphere, most especially from those in the high council chamber in which he had been judged, and apparently found worthy. Part of him wanted to reach out to those around him, to tell them that he bore them no ill will, that he had come to fight for them, with them.

He was jostled from behind, and he reacted instantly and instinctively, whirling about with the claws of one hand ready to slash at the eyes as his other hand went for the blade of the short sword that had been a gift from Tesh-Dar.

"I'm sor–" a young inductee, a gangly boy about the same age as Reza, apologized before his face blanched and his eyes bulged from their sockets with surprise and fear at the whirling apparition before him.

Reza stopped his defense and counterattack, relaxing his body instantly. He regarded the young man quietly, noting the complete lack of threatening feelings from this mere child. He noticed the sniggering that took place in the row of people behind the boy, and understood that they had pushed him into Reza to see what kind of reaction they could get.

"Really really I'm sorry I didn't mean to bump into you I–" He was babbling in a steady, fearful stream.

"What is your name?" Reza asked quietly of this young human who evidently had volunteered to be a Marine. While military service was compulsory, service in the Marine Corps was rarely enforced by draft placement; the Corps had all the volunteers it could handle. What courage might lay beneath the surface to make this timid creature want to seek his Way in the Marine Corps?

"Uh... Eustus... Eustus Camden. Look, really, they pushed me I didn't–"

"Be still, Eustus Camden," Reza said, and the boy instantly quieted. Reza watched and felt the emotion's of the young man's tormentors, gauging their reactions. What courage this boy may have, he thought, was ten-fold what they possessed. "I was told that trainees may choose their room-mates," Reza went on, fighting through the accent that he physically could not suppress from his speech. "I choose you." Ignoring the stupefied gasp of his new human tresh, Reza turned back around toward the front rank.

Behind him, Eustus Camden turned to the three recruits behind him – his tormentors since childhood – to give them his best version of a withering stare, but they sniggered and made faces at him.

"Looks like you got a new buddy, Eus," one of them hissed.

"Go to Hell, you bastard!" Eustus spat in reply.

"You there!" a voice burst through the ranks. "I MEAN YOU, BOY!"

Eustus felt like shrinking into a tiny ball and evaporating as a DI that looked like a human fireplug with a built-in PA system instead of vocal chords stormed up to him and began berating him for talking in formation.

Dear Lord, Eustus thought. What have I gotten myself into?

As the DI reviewed some fascinating aspects of Eustus Camden's heritage, a ripple of excitement went through the crowd. The doors to the in-processing building had been thrown open. It was time.

Things had changed little over the centuries in how new blood was brought into the military. Each rank was filed in with mechanical precision, aided where necessary by the DIs and a liberal application of psychological pressure that would become all too familiar to the recruits over the next sixteen weeks.

The lines filed into the front of the main administration building quickly and in good order. Almost all the trainees had several months of prior training conducted by local training centers. Some, mostly those who were coming from Territorial Army units to join the Corps, had considerably more.

Reza soon was lost in the flurry of questions, computer scans, and the rest of the modern paperwork required to become a Marine. Most of the forms, Reza had to leave blank or nearly so. Nicole and Jodi had anticipated this and had researched what they could to help him fill in the information. He meticulously wrote in the names of his parents, which he had been unable to remember but that Jodi had discovered in his mother's service records. And then, something that meant a great deal to him, Nicole had thought when she coached him through it, he signed his name, Reza Sarandon Gard.

Next was the physical exam. Every recruit bemoaned it because they had all gone through at least one in the previous months and were tired of being scanned, probed, and poked.

"Strip!" shouted a short Filipino sergeant major with a face like parched leather and a voice that pierced the group's ears like a squawking parrot. The group of about a dozen recruits, which included Reza, was already undressing. Men and women were examined in the same room at the same time, for the war had left little room for the modesty of earlier periods; it did not take into account race, creed, color, or sex, nor did the Corps.

After seeing what the others were doing, Reza began to unclasp his armor, carefully putting the pieces in the plastic bins provided for the purpose. While he had refused any medical examinations while on the Aboukir, Nicole and Jodi had said this was required to become a Marine, and he had decided to allow it. Only his collar and its pendants remained as he slipped the last of three bins into the wall lockers where they would stay until the in-processing was finished.

"In the name of God," Eustus uttered from behind him. He was staring at Reza's back, his mouth hanging agape, as was everyone else's who could see.

The nearby recruits took a few steps back, shocked speechless by the tendrils of scar tissue that undulated across Reza's body.

"Looks like he got caught in a tiller," quipped a dark-skinned woman who appeared to be quite unimpressed.

"Gross," hissed a woman with blond hair cut nearly down to her skull. She turned away, making a face of disgust.

"C'mon, goddammit," growled the sergeant major. "None of you are any better looking!"

Putting away their feelings toward Reza in hopes of avoiding any more serious action by the sergeant major, the recruits slowly shuffled to the exam booths set up around the room. The ones who had to stand in line waiting for the medtechs continued to gawk at Reza.

When he came to the head of the line at his station the female medtech carried out the requisite tests with hardly a look at any part of his anatomy other than what happened to be of immediate clinical interest. He watched her intently, intrigued by the compact high technology equipment with which she worked.

His interest made her nervous. The unblinking stare from his sharp green eyes was beginning to upset her, but she did not become really upset until she saw the results of his gene and DNA scans on the computer. This was the first time that Reza had allowed anyone close to him with medical probes, and it appeared that the machine had decided that he was not really human, delivering a message proclaiming "species unidentified."

"Stay here," she ordered tersely. She got up to speak with the sergeant major. "This is all wrong," she told him quietly, glancing nervously at Reza. "And I know there's nothing wrong with my equipment. I just calibrated it this morning."

"I know, corporal," the sergeant major replied. "Just log the results and pass him on to the next station. The... discrepancy was anticipated."

The medtech hastily finished the remaining details and let Reza go with the others, relieved that she no longer had those predatory eyes burning into her.

The naked recruits gathered up their things and followed their Filipino chaperone to the next stop, the quartermaster. There, each was measured and fitted for the camouflage combat uniforms they would wear for the duration of their stay. They would not receive a dress uniform until graduation. That was the first and only official function – other than a possible court-martial or two – that they would attend during basic training.

Reza received his uniform with a mixture of curiosity and apprehension. He was intrigued by the weave of the fabric, yet he was concerned at how little it offered in the way of protection. His armor was a second skin to him, and he was not enthused by its replacement.

They finally got to their last stop before the noon meal was to be served: billeting. In this one respect, things had perhaps become more civilized, less regimented, in that there were only two trainees to a room. In active duty units the troops often lived in open bay barracks, usually with thirty or forty men and women to a bay, but Quantico had been laid out differently at its inception for reasons no one quite remembered, and the quarters had never been updated. But one thing that both the Quantico dorms and open bay barracks had in common was that they were entirely coed. The women were billeted with the men, whether they were in barracks or semi-private rooms. This often caused a stir among the troops from the more conservative worlds, but it could not be helped. The time of sexual equality had, more or less, finally arrived.

"Gard, Reza!" called the Marine sergeant handing out the billeting assignments. Reza stepped forward, still chafing at the feel of the training center uniform he now wore. He carried his armor and satchel in his arms.

The young man handed him a key. "Room 236. Across the courtyard, second floor, turn right."

"I wish to specify Eustus Camden as my roommate," Reza said.

The Marine glowered at him. "Move out!" he shouted.

Reza left as the man called out the next name, assuming that the sergeant had granted his request.

As luck would have it, he did.

"Remember, people, chow at twelve-hundred. That's twelve o'clock for you civilian and Territorial Army pukes!" someone shouted from the room behind him. He assumed that "chow" meant food, but he was not sure. Shaking his head in puzzlement, he joined the stream of new recruits making their way to the rooms they would be sharing for the next six weeks.

* * *

"Battalion, ten-HUT!" The Filipino sergeant major brought the recruits in the auditorium to attention. "Listen up, trainees," he began. Reza frowned to himself. He had a terrible time understanding the man's accent; he was not alone. "Your first week is now over," the sergeant major continued. "It was easy. You had a day to rest. That was easy. Now you will begin to learn how to be real Marines, not just boys and girls in ugly Quantico uniforms." He smiled, his perfect white teeth blazing from his rawhide face. "That will be very hard. Not all of you will make it. Some of you might even get yourselves killed, and more than a few will cry for their mommies and daddies." There were a few nervous laughs in the captive audience, but the sergeant major was quite serious. "But whoever finishes will be worthy of the uniform you will receive when you graduate. That will be a real uniform, not the toy soldier costumes you wear now.

"You already met your classroom instructors last week. Most of them are officers or NCOs who are on a break between combat assignments. You will see some of them again during your advanced courses. Providing you make it that far." Aquino's flawlessly polished black boots clicked on the polished wood of the stage as he strutted to the side that held a podium bearing the Marine Corps emblem, a galactic swirl overlaid by crossed sabers. He was so short he would have almost disappeared behind the podium had he been speaking from it, but the medals on his khaki uniform dispelled any notions about his size affecting his combat abilities. "Instructors, POST!" he barked.

Five people marched out onto the stage and assumed parade rest facing the trainees. The sergeant major gestured toward the screen behind him that held the new week's schedule. "Starting tomorrow, you will do PT for three hours, starting at oh-six-hundred. Every day." The trainees groaned. "Captain Thorella will be your primary instructor."

An ox with arms and legs instead of four hoofed feet stepped forward from the line of instructors. His uniform was specially cut to accommodate his enormous frame of hardened muscle. He snapped his hands to the creases of his trousers as he came to attention, a fierce grimace on his face.

The trainees groaned again.

"Oh, no," Eustus muttered beside Reza. The good captain was already well known to everyone in the group, and Eustus and Reza had become two of Thorella's personal favorites during their break times between the intro week classes.

"Pipe down," Aquino ordered. "If there's anyone out there who's better qualified, step up." He glared at the trainees. The moaning abruptly ceased. No one came forward. "In combat," Aquino continued, "there is no substitute for proper physical conditioning. Captain Thorella will ensure you are ready."

Thorella smirked at his new victims. "See you at The Bridge tomorrow, ladies and gentlemen," he announced to more groans and muffled curses before he stepped back into line. The Bridge was a log across a creek where Thorella "instructed" trainees in the arts of gravity and physical humiliation. It was well-known from its brutal reputation.

"You will have two instructors in common skills and small unit tactics," Aquino went on. "Staff Sergeant Taylor and Gunnery Sergeant Walinskij." The two stepped forward. "Common skills will be every other day for three hours during block one of your training. Small unit tactics will be on the remaining days during the same time period. Short duration deployments for field exercises to try out what you have learned will be announced later.

"Light weapons training will be by Gunnery Sergeant Grewal Singh." Singh broke the tradition of the preceding cadre by smiling as he stepped forward. Singh was well versed in the fine art of being an asshole, but he preferred other, more palatable methods of getting his points across to his students whenever possible.

"And, a special guest to Quantico, Navy Lieutenant Jodi Mackenzie will see to your close combat needs." She snapped to attention, stepped forward exactly seventy-five centimeters, and stomped her right foot down at her new posting. She did not smile, nor did she scowl. Her face bore the neutral calm of a complete professional. Someone in the audience whistled. Mackenzie paid them no attention. She would undoubtedly find out who it was during hand to hand exercises. They would not be whistling then. "While Lieutenant Mackenzie is by trade a fighter pilot, she has the benefit of recent experience during the Rutan campaign, where she fought with and eventually came to command the 373d Marine Assault Regiment."

The sergeant major did not have to mention that Nicole Carré was a classroom instructor, whose instruction blocks included military history and battlefield automation. The recruits had already gotten a dose of her curriculum, and most of them were still reeling. She was sitting in the back row of the auditorium with the other instructors who had already been introduced to the recruits.

The sergeant major nodded, and Mackenzie resumed her place in line. "All of the instructors here have at least one full year of combat experience. Carré, Thorella and Mackenzie have received Silver Stars in the line of duty, and the rest have received citations for gallantry. Some of you out there have combat experience. I expect you to put it to use here. If there is a point of contention between you and an instructor, I will moderate it myself. If you have an idea to improve our tactics or training," he paused and looked directly at Reza, "I want to hear it. We are training you not only to fight, but also to complete your mission, whatever it may be, and hopefully to survive. You are no good to the Confederation dead; make the Kreelans die for their Empire instead.

"But I don't want any pissing contests," he went on after a slight pause and a less-than-surreptitious glance at Reza to see if his earlier words had gotten any reaction, which – somewhat to his disappointment – they hadn't. "You are here to train. If you knew it all you would be in the Fleet Admiral or Marine Commandant's chair. You aren't. Remember that. Are there any questions?" He looked about the auditorium. "No? Good. That concludes the morning brief. Drill sergeants," he called to the DIs interspersed through the hall, "take charge of your platoons and get them to their training..."

* * *

The next day, at The Bridge, Eustus stood in a momentary daze as the blood from his broken nose pattered into the water that slowly passed under the log on which he and Thorella were standing. Each held a pugil stick, a pole about a meter long with a bulbous pad at one end and a padded hook at the other.

"Awww," Thorella said theatrically, "what's the matter, recruit? You need mommy to wipe your nose for you?" He laughed as the younger man's face set itself into a mask of venomous ferocity. "That's better, you queer," Thorella sneered as Eustus came toward him. "It's nice to see you show some balls for a change."

Thorella had been the king of The Bridge since his arrival at Quantico. He loved it. He was a towering mountain of a man, his flexing biceps larger around than most of his contemporaries' thighs. His face was molded in a permanent grin that would have made his face very attractive except for the black, darting eyes that were without depth, without feeling. He was cunning, intelligent. He was a killer, and he enjoyed his chosen profession. No matter what the prey.

This was the first day on The Bridge for this batch of recruits, the morning after Sergeant Major Aquino's briefing. Thorella requested the cadre put Reza up first, but they had opted for tradition. Thorella took his place as King of the Bridge and waited for voluntary opponents. If no one came forward to challenge him, names were called alphabetically. Two of the recruits voluntarily came up to try their hand at knocking Thorella from his perch, but both wound up with soaking uniforms and splitting headaches.

In a short time he had worked his way through the trainees to Camden, who now stood on the opposite end of the bridge.

"Take it easy on me, kid," he smiled, his little obsidian eyes glittering with anticipation. He had something special planned for this one.

"Fuck off, sir," Camden hissed through his bloodstained teeth. He did not know how to swim, and even though he knew the water below was not deep and there were instructors standing by to pull people out, he was not thrilled with the prospect of being knocked down – semiconscious, undoubtedly – into the cold stream. He gripped his weapon tightly, hoping to anticipate Thorella's moves.

Thorella waited casually for Eustus to come within range before feinting a blow to Eustus's feet, then he hit him in the face just hard enough to split his lip, but not so hard as to send him spinning from the log. As Eustus fought to recover, his face now streaming with blood from his violated nose and now his mouth, Thorella slammed him hard in the stomach, driving the wind out of him.

Gagging and dripping blood, Eustus fell to his hands and knees, barely retaining his grip on his useless weapon.

"C'mon, recruit," Thorella complained, "you're disgracing my uniform by even wanting to call yourself a Marine. Some blue-skin is going to use you for a tampon if you fight like that. You'd probably like it, just like your buddy Gard."

Eustus did not take Thorella's last insult lightly. His family had been raised on a very small outpost settlement not far from Quantico 17. Too small to support even a single regiment, it more than made up for its small size by the devotion to duty of its inhabitants: the Camden name had appeared proudly on a succession of Marine uniforms. Eight gold stars now hung in his widowed mother's house for his father and the sisters and brothers who had died in the line of duty. Only Eustus and his youngest brother, Galan, remained, and his little brother would volunteer for service when he turned seventeen. That was the way things were. And when Galan finally finished school and left to join the service, his mother intended to finish her days helping the sons and daughters of other families in the sector military hospital. She expected to outlive her two remaining sons, but that would not stop her from continuing her contributions to the war effort.

His heart in a cold rage now, Eustus lunged into a fierce but technically uninspired attack that the captain easily defeated. Drawing Eustus into the trap, Thorella moved very close to him, first driving the hooked end of the stick into Eustus's crotch behind the screen of his body. As Eustus gagged and began to sag to his knees, Thorella hit him in the face again with the padded end, bruising his right cheek.

As the young trainee toppled backward, Thorella snagged his left foot with the hook and yanked it toward him. Eustus hit the log with a loud crack; had he not been wearing a helmet, he probably would have fractured his skull.

Grinning like a death's head, Thorella contemptuously kicked Eustus's unconscious body off the log, sending him tumbling into the water below where he was retrieved by two waiting trainees who had already taken their plunge.

The sergeant major frowned slightly, but said nothing. He held his silence not because Thorella was an officer – Aquino's power as senior enlisted man in this camp on Quantico far overshadowed the captain's – but because he believed that a bloody nose here and there helped to toughen his trainees for the deadly fighting that awaited them among the stars: if they couldn't handle this, they would never be able to handle combat. The captain had overstepped the bounds somewhat with Camden, but not so far that any action could really be taken against him. But Aquino would be watching. And he wished that Thorella did not appear to enjoy himself so much.

"Buddha," Reza heard someone whisper in the silence that fell over the trainees who waited their turn with the troll who guarded the bridge. It was the first remark of a hushed torrent of resigned commentary: "This is bullshit." "I can't believe they're letting this guy get away with this." "Oh, man, we're going to get our asses creamed."

And, what Reza understood to be the classic epithet: "Oh, shit."

He considered their comments, as well as what he had just seen. He himself was not overly impressed with Thorella's method, as it was trivial gameplay in terms of his own experience. What offended him was the reasoning behind Thorella's tactics: it was not to instruct or inspire, to make the trainees more competent in battle. Even in Reza's first days in the kazha, while the tresh were often cruel, they did not spar with him without useful purpose. No, he thought, Thorella's actions were born of his personal hatred and contempt for those around him. More specifically for Eustus and, as he was well aware, for himself.

Thorella made a theater of yawning and stretching before he called out, "Who's next? Darman! Get out here. I–"

Before the young woman, who was clearly trying to mask her fright, could step up, she felt Reza's hand on her arm, gently pushing her aside as he stepped forward.

"I request the honor to fight you, captain," he said formally. Reza had decided that a lesson in humility was in order.

"You understand the rules, trainee?" the sergeant major said before Thorella could reply to Reza's challenge, but it was more a statement than a question. He did not want a bloodbath on his hands, regardless of who started it. Thorella was much bigger than Reza, but he was not sure that size and the captain's appreciable skill would make up for the unknowns that presented themselves with the younger man.

"I believe I understand Captain Thorella's rules, Sergeant Major Aquino," Reza replied carefully. "I shall obey them."

Aquino's eyebrow arched. Captain Thorella's rules, he thought. This should be interesting. "Very well. Continue."

"All right, you little slime-bag half-breed," Thorella whispered under his breath. "Let's see just what color blood you've got."

Reza ignored the stick one of the other trainees offered to him.

"Take your weapon, Gard," Thorella ordered.

"I have no need of it," Reza replied as he stepped onto the log. He felt clumsy in his combat boots and exposed wearing the flimsy camouflage uniform rather than his armor, but he thought he would be sufficiently agile for the job at hand. He waved away the helmet one of the trainees offered him.

"This is more like it," Thorella said, impressed, as he removed his own helmet, tossing it aside. Even if Gard was a loser, he thought, at least he knows how to go down right. But he was also eager to see how Reza would look after the unpadded grip of the metal bar had been smashed across his shoulder blade. Or the side of his exposed skull.

Reza walked about a third of the way out onto the log and stopped, his eyes never leaving Thorella. His scarred, tan face was calm, his callused hands hanging at his sides.

"Well, come on, freak," Thorella said, his mouth a cruel smile that split the lower half of his face like a crevasse.

Reza offered him a hand gesture that he had seen used by some of the other trainees. He did not know what the extended middle finger meant, but understood that it was entirely offensive in nature.

"You arrogant little prick," Thorella said as he made a lightning-quick thrust at Reza's midsection. Had it connected, he probably would have broken some ribs.

But Reza had somehow disappeared, and Thorella found himself flying through space, propelled by the enormous force he had put behind his own attack. "Shit!" he hissed as he fell, face-first onto the log, scrabbling desperately for a grip before he fell into the water. The hooked and padded stick slipped from his grip and disappeared into the stream with a splash, accompanied by a series of gasps from the watching trainees.

Quickly regaining his feet, Thorella found Reza standing casually a couple meters away, behind him, watching with that stare of his. But now he also wore a slight smile – something he had relearned from Jodi – on his face.

Thorella was incensed, but he kept it well beneath the surface, in the same place he kept all the feelings that seethed within him that could not be exposed to the light of public scrutiny. "Not bad, punk," he said amicably as he flashed a wolfish smile at the onlookers. I'm going to tear your guts out for that, he screamed to himself.

Reza said nothing as he waited.

Thorella moved forward cautiously, his body fluidly transitioning into his favorite hand-to-hand combat stance, edge-on to Reza, his arms raised to their strike/defend positions.

Aquino was growing concerned. Thorella's stance was not one he wanted to see practiced here: the technique he was intending to use was for killing only, and was only learned and practiced under very carefully supervised conditions. Still, he hesitated to say anything. Just as much as everyone else, he was curious as to what Reza would do.

Thorella was nearly within striking range. He was not planning any feints or drawn-out sparring contests. He wanted to hurt Reza, hurt him bad, hurt him now–.

Thorella's cruel smile vanished, to be replaced with the feral snarl of a rabid animal. He darted forward with agility amazing for so bulky a body, making a vicious thrust at Reza's midsection with his left hand, closed in a rock-hard fist.

Reza deflected the blow without discernible effort and stepped aside, his booted feet solidly balanced on the sloping side of the log. He felt it roll slightly and compensated for it; the log was not fixed in place. A few chips of wood fell into the running water below.

In this way Reza entertained Thorella for a while, parrying the larger man's thrusts while allowing himself to be pushed toward one end of the log, ostensibly cornered.

"Stand and fight, you bastard," Thorella snarled. "You've got nowhere else to run, now."

The fist that lashed out like a knife toward Reza's throat would have killed or crippled him had it found its mark. Instead, it found the wall of Reza's palm, his fingers closing around Thorella's larger hand like a vise. The sound of the impact echoed over the streambed like a rifle shot. Thorella tried to pull away, but quickly discovered that to do so was impossible: it was as if his hand had been set in concrete with reinforcing steel around it. He had never encountered a grip so strong.

"What is wrong, captain?" Reza inquired politely. He began to increase the pressure on Thorella's fist, simultaneously canting it at an angle that began to force the captain to lose his balance on the log or risk having his wrist broken.

"If you let me go now," Thorella whispered threateningly, "I'll let you off easy. Otherwise..."

"Do not threaten me, child," Reza said contemptuously. "Your lack of honor and courage disgrace your bloodline, your peers. Were I not bound by my honor to the strange laws of your people, I would slay you as the beast that you are. Beware, captain."

Thorella's eyes bulged with outrage. "Why, you little motherfu–"

He did not have enough time to finish the sentence as Reza flicked him from the bridge as if he were no more substantial than a wad of paper. Howling obscenities, Thorella flew through the air until he hit the water, throwing up a tremendous splash that would be the subject of delightful recounting among the trainees for weeks.

There was another collective gasp among the recruits. Thorella had never been dropped by anybody, and Reza did it his first time on the bridge. With his bare hands. For a moment, there was total silence.

Eustus was the first to react, clapping and whistling his approval. "Way to go, Reza!" He was quickly joined by the rest of the trainees.

"What a belly-flop!" someone exclaimed amid the chorus of laughter from the trainees. Some of the instructors smiled. The little leather-faced Aquino nodded, impressed, and that did not happen very often.

"You mean to tell me that somebody finally got that asshole?" Reza heard a voice in the group ask, incredulous.

"Couldn't have happened to a nicer guy," said another.

Thorella suddenly burst from the water, sputtering with rage. He slapped at the surface in impotent fury at having been bested. When he finally contained himself, he looked up to where Reza stood on the bridge, silently watching him. Thorella put on his smile again, the lower half of his face smeared with blood from his tongue where he had bitten it as he hit the water. The blood made him look like the water had washed away the skin of his face to expose the red muscle tissue and ivory skull underneath. He pointed a finger at Reza in warning. "Watch your back, freak," he hissed. "Watch your back." He winked like they had a mutual secret, and then he moved off toward the shore.

The hatred Reza saw in the man's eyes left little doubt as to the future. He knew that someday he would probably have to kill him.

* * *

"What's the matter, Marine?" Thorella sneered. "Can't you take it?"

Ever since Reza had tumbled him from the bridge, Thorella had made even more of an effort to make their lives completely miserable. Sometimes he enlisted other officers and NCOs – and even some trainees – to aid him in his mission, but mostly he preferred to administer his harassment personally. The post command staff, while conscious of his singling out Reza and Eustus for special attention, generally made no move to interfere as long as Thorella kept his actions within the unwritten limits of cadre deviltry. For the most part, he complied. Grudgingly.

Eustus cursed to himself as he tried to keep from collapsing into the gravel. He had been doing pushups now for five minutes straight after a grueling five kilometer full-pack run with the rest of his platoon, and his traitorous arms were shaking like the bass strings of a harp, about to give out. His hands were bleeding from the jagged rocks under him, the edges of the sharp granite shards of The Pit doing their best impersonation of razor blades. He looked up at Thorella's square face.

"No pain, no gain, sir!" he huffed in a less than respectful voice.

"Yeah, Camden, but in your case it's no brain, no pain." Thorella got down, right into the younger man's face, so close that a drop of sweat from Camden's nose trickled onto Thorella's. "You drop out on me, you start eating gravel, and we're gonna take a nice long run through the bogs to warm up your legs, Camden. A nice long run." The bogs were a notorious hell for the trainees, a series of ankle deep patches of soft ground and reeking standing water that made running more of an excruciating experience than it normally was. Thorella knew without a doubt that Camden wouldn't be able to hack it after everything else he had been through that morning.

"Fuck off, sir!" Eustus hissed enthusiastically through clenched teeth.

"Keep it up, dickhead," Thorella warned quietly, the ubiquitous smile etched onto his face. Eustus wanted to barf right between his eyes, but he didn't have the strength to spare. "Let's see how your buddy's doing over here."

Reza was as solid as stone, Thorella noted despairingly. The big captain looked around for some sandbags or something to pile on the smaller man's back, but he could find nothing nearby, and it wasn't worth the effort to go looking too far. He might miss something. "How do you feel, freak?" He tugged on Reza's hair like he might an animal's tail. Someday he was going to cut it off and put it with the other trophies in his collection, he thought smugly.

"I am well, Captain Thorella." Reza refused to call him "sir".

"That's good, freak. Know why? Your buddy over here's starting to look a little tired, and I was thinking you might want to help him out. Camden!" He barked. "Recover and get your ass over here!"

Eustus heaved himself up and staggered to attention in front of Thorella.

"Stand on his back," Thorella ordered. Eustus just looked at him, his face a question mark. "I'm talking to you, trainee dickhead. Mount up. Now."

Eustus opened his mouth to tell Thorella just where to take it when Reza interrupted.

"Go ahead, Eustus."

"No way, Reza. This is totally–"

"Just do as I ask of you." He looked up. "Go ahead." Eustus shook his head and did as he was told, placing his booted feet carefully on Reza's back. He threw a look at Thorella that left few doubts as to his thoughts. The captain only smiled more.

"All right, Marine. Start knocking 'em out. I'll count cadence, trainee dickhead here will count repetitions. In cadence, exercise! Oooooooooone..." Reza lowered himself to the ground, his arms like hydraulic pistons. "Two..." He raised himself back up. "Threeeeeeeee... four."

"One," Eustus spat, enraged that this kind of thing was allowed to go on. He looked around, careful not to upset Reza's balance. No other instructors were in sight. Unless they wanted to fight Thorella – he had no doubt that Reza could hammer him to the ground, but they would both get tossed in prison – they were stuck.

The pushups were brutal, a slow count down, a pause at the bottom, and a fast push up to be in time for the next repetition. If you got behind, you found yourself starting from zero all over again.

"Thirty." Eustus was amazed at Reza's strength. He was lifting most of his own body weight, plus the additional eighty kilos Eustus boasted. He imagined that someone as big as Thorella could maybe do something like that, but Reza was almost half the larger man's size.

Thorella was beginning to get impatient, but he reminded himself of the old adage that good things come to those who wait. His smile became a toothy grin in anticipation. "Ooooooooone... two... threeeeeee... four."

Reza made it, but he was beginning to slow down. His pace was just slightly off. "Thirty-one."

"Bullshit," Thorella snapped viciously. "It's zero, trainee. Zero."

Eustus snarled and was about to leap for Thorella's throat, damn the consequences, when another voice joined in.

"That is enough, Thorella!" he heard Nicole bark. "Camden, get off of him! Reza, on your feet." Greatly relieved, Eustus stepped down. It was like getting off a sheet of spring steel. He leaned down to help Reza get up.

Reza nimbly got to his feet, not even breathing hard, as Nicole stormed across the field like a miniature whirlwind, her normally neutral expression distorted with a very unprofessional look of anger. "What the hell is going on here? Reza, are you all right?"

"Yes, ma'am." The lactic acid that remained in his muscles was already dissipating. But he was ravenous from the temporary change he had made to his metabolism. He would be making several passes through the mess hall line this afternoon.

"I'm not through here, ma'am," Thorella tried to bully her. The only time the two of them came in contact was over Reza and Eustus, and then it was a clash of the titans, at least from Eustus's point of view. "If you recall, I am in charge on this field."

"Not anymore, captain," Nicole snapped. "If anything like this ever happens again, I will put you up on charges."

"Well, well," Thorella chuckled, not the least bit intimidated. He stepped closer to the petite Navy officer, his bulk looming over her like a freight train beside a bicycle. "Not only is she going to pull rank on me, she's going to write me up next time. Maybe I'll get a spanking, too?"

Sadly, his intimidation was not having the desired effect. Nicole did not budge.

"You can do whatever the fuck you please. Ma'am," he told her, finally giving up on simple intimidation. "But on this field, I am in charge, regardless of what you say. And if you interfere in my business again, I'll write you up." He rendered her a mock salute and stomped away like a prehistoric beast, screaming at other gasping trainees doing grass drills, ordering them to recover for a quick run through the bogs before they hit the showers.

Nicole saw the blood on Eustus's hands, then took one of Reza's hands in hers, looking it over. She was shocked at how callused it was. The gravel had not made any indentations in the skin. "Both of you, I want you to go to the infirmary and get checked out. And I want you two to stay together so you can protect one another. I do not trust him."

Reza did not trust him either, but he did not understand the depth of emotion Nicole felt. Perhaps, he thought, it is only a protective instinct. He turned back to her, his eyes blazing with a cold fire that had been ignited under an alien sun. He made an expression that might have been a smile except that his teeth appeared poised to tear something apart. "Do not worry, commander."

"What a shithead," Eustus mumbled as they walked back toward the compound. Reza frowned at his friend's description, trying to conjure up a suitable image in his mind. After a moment, he smiled.

EIGHT

"C'mon, Reza, I can't believe you're not going to take this pass." Eustus watched him with disapproving eyes, hands on hips. He had fashioned himself into a credible ersatz younger brother in only a few weeks.

Reza shrugged as he pulled on the black undergarment over his naked body. His skin tingled with delight as the smooth material glided on. He was always tempted to dress and undress several times simply for the pleasure of the sensations, of the memories that it evoked. But not now. "Thank you for your concern, my friend, but it is not how I would spend my free time."

His roommate threw up his arms in frustration and sat down on Reza's bunk, watching him dressing in his Kreelan armor. No matter how many times he watched Reza do it, it never failed to give him the creeps to see him change so totally into an alien.

"Look," Eustus pleaded, shaking off the thought, "you've got to get out and see something of the universe around you, Reza. You've got to learn to have a little bit of fun instead of being so morose all the time. We've got a chance to go to town! Don't you realize what that means?"

Reza smiled. "'Booze, babes, and booze,' as I heard someone say. Some others said 'Booze, beef, and booze.' I believe I would prefer the latter. The mess hall does not know how to prepare meat correctly. Perhaps the town has good beef, but I prefer to hunt my food myself."

"No, no, Reza," Eustus said impatiently. "That isn't the kind of beef they're talking about. They're talking about beefcake."

"And what is wrong with that? Can you not still eat it?"

Eustus shook his head, blushing. He was raised in a liberal home, but public talk of any kind about sex still embarrassed him. The thought of Reza and "beefcake" together in the same context was too much. "It means guys, Reza, guys! Men, not animal meat. It's, well, a kind of reference to, uh, manliness, I guess." He sighed. "Look, never mind. You just ought to come with us. You might enjoy yourself for once. All the time you're sitting with your nose at the vidscreen or down in the armory messing with the weapons or just sitting in here in some kind of a trance. You never have any fun, Reza.

We could have a few drinks, maybe see a kino or even a live show. We might even meet some girls or something. That'd be kind of nice, wouldn't it? I mean, the female trainees are nice, but..."

He trailed off as he saw Reza stiffen and shudder slightly, almost dropping his breastplate.

"I have no need for females," Reza whispered hoarsely. He recovered quickly, fastening the armor into place with a vicious snap.

Eustus panicked. He had never considered the possibility that Reza might be homosexual. While he did not care for it personally, it was a widely accepted practice in many parts of the Confederation. "Reza... I mean, uh, if you like guys, well, I guess that's okay, too, but..."

"No." He turned to his friend, smiling weakly. "I am not that way. I just need to be alone."

Eustus saw tears welling in his friend's eyes. "Hey, are you okay?"

Reza shook his head. "No, but there is nothing to be done about it. And I will speak no more of it." With a quick yank of a leather strap, he secured the short sword to his back. "I wish you a good time, my friend. I will see you when you return."

Then he padded silently out of the room without turning back.

Eustus watched him go, wondering exactly what was bothering his friend so much.

* * *

While Eustus and most of the other trainees were piling into the buses that would take them to the nearby towns, Reza was running through the forest as fast as his legs would take him, which was far faster than any human being had ever run. He whispered between the trees, faster than the wind, taking in the scents of the forest animals and trees, all descended from Old Terra after Quantico had been terraformed. He smelled a rabbit, several squirrels, and some larger predators: a fox and two wolves. The sun had set and it was time for them to hunt. Like them, Reza's vision in the darkness was as keen as those born of Kreelan flesh: another gift of the Change.

He opened his mind, going beyond mere sight and smell. He could sense the birds overhead in their nests, the strange creatures that burrowed underground that he had never seen but knew were there, the insects that clung to the ground and the leaves of the trees.

At last he reached a spot that suited his spirit, a deep cove of trees with a small creek running through it. He knelt next to a rock and became one with it, thinking nothing, sensing everything. Time passed...

When the sky was completely dark, Reza stirred. He wanted to see the stars. He lay down on his back, wondering at the countless points of light that brightened the night sky.

"Where is she?" he asked the sky in the Old Tongue. There were so many questions he wanted to ask, but there was no one to answer. He had made the only decision his Way allowed, thereby damning himself to an eternity of spiritual solitude and Esah-Zhurah to... what? He prayed to the Empress to carry his love to Esah-Zhurah in her dreams. At this moment he would have given anything to be with her, but even the Devil that Father Hernandez so feared would not be lured into making such a bargain.

Sleep finally carried him to the faraway land he had once called home.

* * *

Dawn came.

A deer neared the creek, thirsty for a drink. Reza rose silently from his sanctuary and approached it. It did not run away, for it sensed nothing to fear; he appeared only as an insubstantial shadow, no more a threat than was the mist. That was how Reza preferred it. He wished the animal no pain. Death, when it came, was instantaneous.

This was the first time he had been able to make an unhurried hunt since leaving the Empire. Reza constantly craved meat, but there was no accommodation to be found in the mess hall. Instead, he was forced to hunt in the occasional spare hour or so that was not taken up by training or commander's call. He knew his abnormal need for meat was a result of the Change, but it was one he welcomed; it was another means of preserving in his mind the heritage he had earned, the love he now missed.

He cleaned the deer carefully and stripped it of meat, cutting it into strips to carry back with him, where he would dry and salt it. What little was left of the carcass he carried away from the stream, that the other animals could have their share, and that the water would not become fouled.

He laid out the hide and began to cure it, fortunately a swift process using the methods Esah-Zhurah had taught him long ago. Getting the proper ingredients had been very difficult, but he had finally convinced a pharmacist at the hospital to make up what he had requested. When asked what Reza was going to use the concoctions for, he had told the man, explaining the process in halting Standard, the technical terms of curing a hide not coming to him easily. Strangely, the man had not believed him, but had indulged his request anyway, the ingredients being harmless ones. Reza shook his head in silent wonder at how humans so often mistook the truth for deception.

In any case, Reza was eager to have a skin to sleep on again, even one as thin as this. The human-fashioned bed in his room was unbearable.

* * *

"Hello, mon ami," Nicole said as she leaned against the entryway. Reza had left the door standing open to let fresh air flow through the room from the window. "May I come in?"

"Of course, commander," he said, coming gracefully to attention. He had been sitting on the deerskin, reading another technical manual. He had felt her approaching long before she reached the door, but he reacted as if he had not known this. He had discovered that certain of his abilities unnerved those around him, and he had gotten into the habit of screening himself with more human reactions, difficult as they often were to emulate. "You are always welcome here."

"Please, Reza," she said as she stepped into the room, quietly closing the door behind her, "we are off duty now. You can relax and call me by name."

Reza nodded, noting her clothes and the light makeup that adorned her face. She was dressed in a close-fitting scarlet blouse of pure silk, skin-tight black pants, and a gold sash tied around her petite waist. A slim gold chain hung around her neck, and her feet were wrapped in soft black leather boots.

"I thought you had gone into town with the others yesterday, when I did not find you here," she said casually, knowing full well that Reza would not have gone. This was the first and only free weekend the trainees would have during their basic training. Very, very few chose to pass up the opportunity to go into one of the nearby towns and get their fill of booze, gambling, and sex before returning to the discipline of the barracks. Jodi had begged Nicole to go, but she had refused, insisting that Jodi go on with some of the other instructors for an outing probably every bit as wild as those the trainees had in mind, Nicole claiming she had some work to finish that could not wait.

While she did not say so, Jodi had suspected otherwise.

"No," Reza said lightly, smiling as he shook his head. "After Eustus explained to me the merits of 'booze, babes, and booze' and the controversy over 'beefcake,' I decided to forego such pleasures for simpler pursuits." While Eustus was sometimes an awkward young man, his vigor in any endeavor he set his mind to was not to be underestimated. "No, Nicole," he said, his smile fading slightly, "I have no need of these things. I went hunting instead."

Nicole sat down on Eustus's bed, and Reza folded back into his sitting position opposite her, his legs resting on the freshly cleaned and cured deerskin that lay atop a collection of blankets that he had scrounged from somewhere. He had removed the bulky bed frame, having found it intolerably uncomfortable. Along with his long, braided hair, it was written off as an acceptable – barely – deviation from the norm, and therefore exempt from inspection as long as it was kept orderly and neat, which of course it was.

Nicole shook her head. Very few things he did now surprised her. Or so she liked to think. "It looks very comfortable," she said, silently wondering what the animal fur might feel like against her skin. She felt the stirrings of heat in her body and a flush rising to her cheeks, and she quickly changed the subject, groping for a more delicate way of approaching him.

"I have spoken several times with Eustus," she said as she compared the two sides of the room. Eustus had the maximum number of allowable personal effects displayed: a holo of his mother and father, another of his whole family – so many children! – and a real photograph, tastefully framed in luminous black metal, of a famous singer with the woman's autograph.

But on Reza's side, there was nothing but bare wall and – she stopped. That was not quite true. The silver crucifix she had given him when they were children hung from a pin directly above his bed. It made her flush with a combined sense of pride and guilt, of conflicting duty and impatient desires.

"He thinks the world of you, Reza," she told him. "And, from what the other instructors have said, not only he but your whole platoon has been performing and learning better and faster than the others, thanks to you."

"All of them have the warrior spirit," Reza said, proud that others had thought and spoken well of him. It was a far cry from what they had said in his first days among them, and there remained those who would never trust him because of his unusual heritage and the collar he wore. "They simply have not yet learned to use it and control it. But this shall come, in time."

He looked at Nicole, who seemed to be studiously examining the portrait Eustus treasured. "Nicole," he said quietly, sensing the turmoil within her, "what is wrong?"

"I am afraid, Reza," she said, still averting her eyes. "There are things I would like to say, to do, but I..." She shook her head, a bittersweet smile on her face. "I am so silly, Reza," she told him. "I have waited all this time to have you alone to myself for a while so that we could... get to know one another again. I thought it might be good to talk of things other than the war, or what you can tell us of your time in the Empire. To get away from all the things of official interest. But now I find my courage has gone. I do not know what to do, what to say." She looked up at him then, her brown eyes brimming with tears. "Would you hold me?" she whispered.

Reza held his arms open for her, and she knelt next to him, wrapping her arms around him in a fierce embrace, her head against his shoulder.

"What is it in the world that could frighten you so?" he asked softly.

"Oh, Reza," she whispered. "Ever since the day that I found out Hallmark had been destroyed, I knew that you had not died. I simply could not accept it. You were... special in my heart. I had dreams that someday we might... be together. Something in me knew that you would come back, that you would be with me again. Years passed, and still I waited for you. There were times... there were times when it seemed that the thought of your return was all that sustained me.

"But I have not always been faithful to your memory. I know we were only children then, but it seemed more real than anything I have since felt, as foolish as that may sound." He felt her quiver in his embrace, holding him tighter, drawing him closer. "I sometimes listened to the advice of others and the wants of my body; I slept with a few men, but it was never right for me. Never." She brought her face close to his, her eyes glowing with a passion he suddenly realized no one else had ever witnessed. "May God forgive me, Reza," she whispered, "but I love you. I have always loved you."

He felt the sudden heat of Nicole's lips pressing against his, parting for the velvet tongue that yearned to touch his own. He felt the strength of her emotion, was almost overcome by it as she pressed herself against him, the warmth of her breasts burning through her flimsy silk blouse, searing his own chest with the heat of her need.

"Nicole," he managed before she pulled him to her again.

"Make love to me," she whispered urgently between kisses as she pulled him down on top of her. Her hands began to work on the bindings of his clothes. "There is nothing in the world I have ever wanted so much as I want you now."

Confused and alarmed, his nervous system afire with sensations he was powerless to control, Reza somehow managed to gently disengage himself from her embrace. "Nicole, please, I cannot do this," he said softly as he rolled over, gently pushing her away.

"Reza, what is wrong?" she asked, her voice trembling. "You do not want me, do you?"

Reza sat up, an expression of pain and misery on his face. "Nicole..." He shook his head, his mind swirling with confusion as his blood began to burn with desire for the one his heart held most dear, and whom he could never again hold close to him, could never again touch. It was physical agony.

"Nicole," he rasped, fighting against the roaring pain that surged through him, "I love you as a friend and kindred soul more than any other, for who you once were in my eyes and my heart, and for who you are now. But I cannot give you the love you seek, the true love of my heart, for that forever belongs to another."

Nicole felt like she had been stabbed through the heart, and Reza felt her pain in his own. "Who?" she asked, bitter and angry, not at Reza, but at fate. Why? she cried to herself. Why must it be like this, after waiting so very long? "Who is it? One of the trainees? Jodi?"

Reza shook his head slowly, rubbing the scar in his hand where Esah-Zhurah had shared her heritage with him, consummating their love with blood. "No," he replied. "No, if only our lives were that simple, but it is not so."

Nicole watched the skin of his face tighten as his jaw set. His eyes closed, and his head bowed, as if a heavy burden had just been dropped upon his shoulders. He was in pain, terrible pain. She sat up next to him, her sudden anger at his rejection overtaken by concern. She put a hand to his face simply to touch him, to reassure him. His skin was on fire, almost too hot for her to touch.

"Mon Dieu, Reza," she gasped, "are you... are you all right? You are burning up."

"It shall pass," he whispered fiercely as he fought to control the trembling that swept his body. "I get this way when I think of her. It has been... the most difficult thing for me to deal with. Her face is seared into my brain, and my blood burns at the mere thought of her."

"Who is she?" Nicole asked again softly.

Reza's hands tightened into fists of iron. "Her name is Esah-Zhurah," he whispered. It was the first time he had uttered her name aloud since leaving the Empire.

"A Kreelan," Nicole whispered, incredulous.

"Yes," he said mournfully, opening his eyes again to face her. "She has the key to my heart, but I shall never see her again. I am banished from her, as I am from the Empire."

"Tell me about her," Nicole asked quietly as his skin began to cool under her touch. She wrapped her arms around him, holding him close. "I want to know who this... woman... is, what she means to you. Please. I know you have sworn not to reveal the secrets of the Empire, but this is very important to me. I must know."

How to tell her? Reza wondered dazedly, acutely aware of her body against his. How could he share with her what he had been, what he had known, what he had felt then and now? He was not concerned with staining his honor with words spoken of the Empire where Nicole was involved; he was worried more about how to convey to her all that made the love he had shared with Esah-Zhurah what it was.

Then he knew. Perhaps he was wrong to even think what now ran through his mind, but he could imagine nothing more fitting. And the more the thought took hold, the more he knew it to be the right thing, almost as if some unknowable power had suddenly dictated this course in his life. "Will you trust me, Nicole?" he asked. "Will you trust me with your spirit and your life?"

A chill ran up Nicole's spine at the sound of Reza's voice. It was not malevolent, not chilling, but held a note of power and understanding that seemed ages beyond his years. The intensity of his gaze proclaimed it as a challenge, daring her to follow where no others of her kind save the man kneeling beside her had gone.

"Oui, mon ami," she said evenly, trying to keep the sudden surge of excitement out of her voice, "I trust you."

Moving away from her, Reza turned to the precisely arranged stack of his Kreelan things and withdrew a particularly beautiful and deadly looking knife. Nicole suddenly wondered what Reza was going to do, but she had given him her trust, and was not about to take it back.

"Give me your hand," he said, holding up his own in the space between their bodies as he had done before with Esah-Zhurah. He put the knife between their joined hands, the blade now flat and cold against their palms. "This is one of the most ancient and sacred rituals among my people," he said, his soft voice a marked contrast to the sparkling fire that danced in his eyes. "In our blood lies our spirit, our honor, our soul. In sharing our blood," Nicole suddenly felt the warmth of blood upon her skin as Reza drew the knife across their palms, but she felt no pain, lost now in Reza's eyes and the lilt of his voice, "we share ourselves with one another, that we may become one. In Her name, let it be so."

Nicole felt Reza's hand close tightly with hers, and she silently wondered at what a silly thing this was, for what could come out of pressing two bloody wounds together? Surely blood did not really flow from one to the other? But why did she feel no pain, for surely the knife had cut her deeply?

"Reza," she gasped as a tingling began in her hand, a warm, prickly feeling the likes of which she had never before felt. The feeling raced up her arm like an incoming tide, then spread through her body like the warmth from a glass of good brandy on a chill evening. "I feel... dizzy," she said, watching as Reza's face began to swim before her, and the light in the room faded toward darkness.

"Come," she suddenly heard him say in a language she had never heard before, but somehow understood. "Come with me."

He stood there, waiting for her, dressed in the gleaming armor that she recalled had once disturbed her, had found threatening somehow. But now it seemed normal, as if that is the way he always had been, and always would be. Behind him she could see a great city of stone and spires, with a brilliantly colored moon hanging in the sun-filled magenta sky. She stopped and stared in awe at a world that no human had seen and survived except Reza. He held his hand out to her, and she took it, barely noticing the talons on her hands and the blueness of her skin, for that was the way she had been born, a daughter of the Empress. And within her, she felt the endless chorus of voices that sang the melody of Her will and love. She felt the power of her own spirit there, a tiny but wondrous drop in an endless ocean of souls.

"Our Ways again are one, my love," she said, feeling as if sunlight bathed her heart, as if the Empress had caressed her soul with kindness.

"In Her name, may it always be so," he said, tenderly kissing her on the lips. "Yours shall my heart always be, Esah-Zhurah."

She smiled as he spoke her name, and walked with him toward the great gates and the wonders that lay beyond.

* * *

"Nicole!"

Nicole sat up at the vaguely familiar voice, blinking at the light that illuminated her surroundings. She fought to say something, but her body did not understand the words her mind wanted to form. Her lips moved, but no sound came.

"Nicole," Jodi said urgently, "are you all right?"

Nicole? Was that her name? She looked at her hands, at the rest of her body, confused by their pale color. Where were her talons? My name is Esah-Zhurah. No, she thought again, as the dream rapidly faded, that cannot be. My name is Nicole. Nicole Carré, not Esah-Zhurah. That name belonged to another. She frowned, unable to remember who the other woman might be.

"Nicole?" Jodi asked again, her hands on her friend's shoulders, her eyes wide with concern. "Say something, will you? Do you need the surgeon?"

"Non," Nicole rasped, finally locating her voice. "I... I am all right." She managed a weak smile that did nothing to reassure her friend.

"You look like hell, Nikki," Jodi said, reluctantly releasing Nicole to sit up on her own. "My God, you were having some kind of wild dream, woman, let me tell you."

"Did I say anything?" Nicole asked, her mind still in a deep fog. She caught fleeting glimpses and sensations flashing across her memory that seemed totally alien, yet somehow familiar...

"The only thing I could understand was when you said Reza's name," she replied quietly. "The rest was gibberish as far as I could tell." God, Jodi thought, and I thought I had a wild time last night. What had Nicole been doing? She had been crying Reza's name over and over, as if she was never going to see him again. Well, she thought, somewhat bitterly, at least her suspicions were confirmed: Nicole was in love with him. Even if she was risking a lot by fraternizing with a trainee, Jodi conceded that at least Nicole had managed to fall for a decent guy this time.

Nicole looked at her palm. Where there should have been a bloody gash from the knife there was only a scar that looked as if it had been there for a long, long time.

"Jesus, Nicole, how did you get that?" Jodi yelped, taking hold of Nicole's hand to get a better look at the scar. She knew her friend's body fairly well from living together for so long, and knew that this had not been there the day before. But if that was so, she thought, confused, how could there be a scar now? They didn't just form overnight.

"A long time ago," Nicole mumbled noncommittally, pulling her hand away. She was still dazed, confused, and wanted only to be alone to think. She looked at the clock. It was almost oh-seven-hundred. Time to get up. She groaned, feeling as if she had run a full marathon. No, she corrected herself. She felt as if she had lived a lifetime in a single night. The only problem was that she did not remember now whose life it had been. "A long time ago," she repeated absently as she pushed herself out of bed and headed toward the bathroom and a long shower, wondering silently what had really happened last night.

"A long time ago?" Jodi murmured after Nicole had closed the door between them. "Bullshit."

* * *

"Reza," Eustus puffed as he ran with his friend through the obstacle course that took up nearly three hours of their morning every other day, "you know Commander Carré, right?"

"Yes," Reza replied as he led Eustus over a water obstacle. Both of them cleared it with room to spare. They were almost halfway through the course, with about half their classmates ahead of them. Reza chose to pace Eustus, for he himself had never found the obstacle course particularly challenging. He was breathing now only slightly faster than normal, which was practically not at all. "I knew her when we were children. She was... special to me then. And she is a good friend now."

"Oh," Eustus grunted as he leaped up and heaved himself over a ten-foot wall that shook as if it was undergoing a perpetual earthquake. Scrabbling like a rat, he gripped the top and hurled himself over and down the other side, rolling as he landed.

Reza was already on the ground waiting for him, as if he had simply walked through the wall. "Why do you ask?" he said.

"Well," Eustus breathed as he fought to keep up with Reza's relentless pace, "I heard some of the instructors talking when I was passing by their table in the mess, when the commander wasn't around." He paused as they navigated a series of barbed wire mazes. They were very primitive, but very effective for focusing one's attention on one's surroundings. "They said she's been acting a lot different than she normally does."

"How so?" Reza asked, curious. The training schedule had been so busy that he and Nicole had not had a chance to speak to one another since she had come to his room three nights before. Sharing himself with her had somehow released him from the horrible pain that came with thoughts of Esah-Zhurah, the furious burning in his blood. He had not realized what agony it had been until, later that night, after he had led Nicole back to her room and put her to bed, he had dreamed of Esah-Zhurah in his sleep. He had awakened in tears, longing for her, but the pain was no more than a dull throb, as if Nicole had taken away the bulk of the pain by sharing his burden. Nicole, in her turn, had seen and felt the world he would forever call home, voyaging through Reza's spiritual memories as Esah-Zhurah, viewing it as she might, knowing his love for her. But those memories would only visit her in her dreams – she would never be able to relate them to another soul.

Eustus blushed slightly, not knowing how Reza would take what he had overheard. How did you tell someone like Reza that one of Nicole Carré's colleagues said she was acting "like she'd found a really good lay"?

"Well," Eustus said, searching for a somewhat more tactful phrase than the original version, "I guess she seems abnormally cheerful and outgoing, like she's suddenly taken normal pills and stopped being so, you know, aloof, I guess." The two of them sprinted across a worn wooden log laid over a mud-filled bog. "They think she's sleeping – you know, having sex? – with someone, but they can't figure out who it is." He cast a sideways glance at Reza. "It wouldn't happen to be you, would it?"

Reza did not answer, instead throwing himself and Eustus to the ground as the brush nearby erupted with a volley of liquid "bullets" fired by patrolling robots at the trainees running the obstacle course. Any trainee having the telltale red stain on his or her fatigues at the end of the course was in for remedial reaction training and two dozen pushups per "hit." The technique was an effective attention-getter.

Satisfied that Reza and Eustus had reacted properly by quickly rolling into the nearby foliage after hitting the ground, the two rovers moved out of their temporary hiding spot and further back down the trail in search of other victims.

"Damn, but I hate those things," Eustus muttered, again thankful that Reza usually ran with him. He always seemed to know exactly where the lunatic machines were. Eustus only worried about what would happen in combat, when Reza probably would not be by his side.

They went on running, gaining speed for the next set of obstacles – the surprise set – that was different every time and lay around a few more bends in the trail, still out of sight.

"You haven't said no," Eustus said, trying to pick up where he had left off.

"I have not had sex with Commander Carré," Reza replied quietly, almost toying with the truth. While their bodies had never touched in that way, the cache of memories she held in her subconscious included the times he had lain with Esah-Zhurah. In her dreams, Nicole would remember them as had Esah-Zhurah herself after they had been joined in blood. "She is a friend and superior officer, but she is not my lover, nor has she ever been." He smiled to himself, hoping against hope that his touch had brought her some happiness, that perhaps she no longer would have to live her life as the cold and quiet Ice Queen. While he had not touched her body, he had touched her heart, and had found it tender and warm, wanting but afraid to love. She, in her turn, had granted him release from much of the pain he felt merely at the thought of Esah-Zhurah. What magic this was, he did not know. All he knew was that his heart had been lifted and that he could fulfill whatever destiny awaited him. "If she has found freedom in her heart," he went on, "I rejoice in her happiness."

Eustus smiled at his friend's words, not because of the stilted way in which Reza often spoke, but because everything he said was sincere. Eustus, who would have given his eye teeth to have the attentions of someone like Nicole Carré, could not help but admire Reza's complete lack of jealousy toward whomever Carré's lover might be.

"You're such a sap sometimes, Reza," he said lightly as they rounded the bend and saw the set of obstacles that Thorella and his minions had devised for them today. "Oh, shit..."

* * *

With few exceptions, the sprawling Quantico headquarters compound was asleep. The command and communications watch centers, deep below the planet's surface, maintained their vigils, humming with matters of insignificance and importance both. Above, trainees pulling guard duty at their posts stamped their feet to keep warm in the chill night air, waiting impatiently for their watch to be up so they could return to their bunks and the religious comfort of sleep. Overhead, no stars showed through the solid cloud cover. The sweet smell of rain, creeping in among the reek of ozone and bitter oil of sleeping war machines, promised an early morning downpour.

Only a few lights were visible throughout the complex. The warning strobes on communications towers blinked on and off, warning away any incoming ships. Guardhouses located along the roads leading onto the base glowed softly. Then there was the bright pink neon sign over the post's premier NCO club. It was a gaudy aberration that somehow had survived long enough to become an icon of the Corps. And, of course, there were lights illuminating the entrance to the bunkers where the post's weapons and equipment were kept.

Many considered the lights a danger, believing that they would only serve as an added target signature in case of a Kreelan attack. This argument was countered by the belief – demonstrated in many drills – that without the lights, it took a great deal longer for the trainees and Marine Corps regulars who staffed the base to get to their assigned bunkers in the massive confusion of an attack. Moreover, in all the years that humans and Kreelans had been fighting, never once had any Kreelan ships even ventured near Quantico, let alone attacked it, despite the fact that the base was on well-established transit routes between colonies that had repeatedly fallen under attack over the last several decades. Some thought it was almost as if the Kreelans were intentionally avoiding the base and its young warriors-in-training.

Now, under one of those lights next to the yellow and black striped blast door that served as the entrance to bunker 175, a red indicator showed on the entry panel: the bunker was occupied. Inside, through the second set of blast doors and the man-sized inset hatch that now stood open, the interior was dark, save for the light of a single hand-held lantern. Carefully balanced on one of the armorer's worktables, its narrow beam was focused on one of the many suits of heavy combat armor that was the primary item in this bunker's inventory. The armor, different from the light armor that Jodi had become accustomed to during her time on Rutan, was of far sturdier material. Completely airtight and equipped with its own maneuvering system, and combined with the heavy armament it allowed the wearer to carry, the armored suit transformed a single human being into a weapon of awesome firepower. Their expense and complexity made them a rare item outside of Marine fleet units.

Not coincidentally, the trainees of Reza's company were to use these very sets of armor in an upcoming exercise that served as the final exam before they received their regimental assignments. Combining all of what they had been taught here, with a great deal of "ingenuity enhancers" thrown in, the final exercise – or "ENDEX" as many called it – was more than a canned field problem that everyone was expected to pass: in ENDEX, failure often meant sudden and violent death.

That was exactly what the sole occupant of bunker 175 was concerned with, although not in nearly so generic a sense. The man smiled as he worked with gloved fingers that seemed far too large for the nimble work they were engaged in now.

Almost finished, he thought placidly as he fitted the auxiliary access panel, about the size of his palm, back to the right thruster pack that bulged from the armor's backplate. Beneath the panel lid, amid the extremely complex but solidly reliable jet control system, a pair of circuits had been slightly altered, their metallurgical and electronic properties not quite what they had been before. When the thrusters had been used a preset amount of time, about half as long as it took for a Marine to hit the ground from an exo-atmospheric combat drop, the right side thruster would fire at maximum burn until it had exhausted its fuel supply. And the left would be disabled, useless. The wearer, faced with a hopeless asymmetric thrust situation, would be left falling, helpless as he spun like a top into the ground. Any remaining fuel and the few live weapons the individual would be carrying would explode, eliminating any physical evidence of tampering.

That was the first modified circuit's intended function: to cause the failure. The second one was somewhat more devious: it sabotaged the miniature telemetry system through which the suit's functions could be monitored by Navy ships or other Marines tied into the same data net. It, too, would fail, just before the thruster fired for the last time. There would be no indication of what had gone wrong.

"A terribly unfortunate accident," he murmured to himself as the panel clicked into place and sealed.

Replacing the heavy armor on its storage rack, he shone the light over it to make sure that nothing appeared amiss. No, he thought, no one would notice a thing. The light paused a moment on the name that had been written in temporary stencil on the armor's breastplate.

"PV-0 GARD," it read.

Happy landings, he thought as he left the bunker, closing the doors and reactivating the alarm and access recording system behind him. Even the computers would not know he had been there.

Whistling a tune he had made up himself, he briskly walked the almost two kilometers back to his quarters, noting with pleasure that the trainee sentry there, ensconced in the warmth of the tiny lighted cubicle outside the officer cadre's quarters, had fallen asleep. Passing up the spontaneous urge to berate the young woman for her dereliction of duty, the man silently passed on, unheard and unseen, to a sound sleep and pleasant dreams of what was soon to come.

NINE

To an untrained eye, the hangar deck was the epitome of confusion as would-be Marines in full combat gear poured from the ready rooms and into the cavernous launch bay of the old auxiliary carrier, their feet hammering an urgent tattoo as they double-timed their way into the waiting drop ships. Overhead, klaxons bleated and eerily calm voices issued instructions and warnings over the ship's PA system as the launch sequence began. But the apparent chaos was an illusion: every movement, every order, had been rehearsed for days before the recruits had set foot on the ship.

Inside Boat 12, Reza's platoon was settling in, securing their weapons and themselves into the dropship's harnesses for the bumpy ride that doubtless lay ahead. Dressed in powered assault armor that made Reza feel more like a trapped animal than a human killing machine, they were about to do what Confederation Marines got paid for: taking the fight to the enemy. Only this time, the enemy would be human, fellow trainees from another battalion, and the energy bolts would not hurt them. Too much.

"Stand by for launch," Nicole told the trainees in Boat 12's cargo section. Then she reported in to hangar deck launch control. "Pri-Fly, this is Delta One-Two, standing by."

"Roger, Delta One-Two," the controller replied. "You're first up. Launch on green." Outside Nicole's viewport, a series of lights that a race car driver might have found familiar cycled from red to amber. "Launch," she heard the controller say as the light went green.

Even with the little ship's gravity and acceleration controls, the catapult launched the boat with enough force that Nicole could sense it. Ahead of her, the catapult tube seemed to peel away to reveal the stars. As the boat was released from the launch field, she took control and smoothly maneuvered it toward their target, one of Quantico's continents that had been established as a massive training range.

"Delta One-Two, this is Eagle One," came Thorella's voice through the comm link. He was flying ahead of them in a fighter that had been modified to carry the assault group coordinator and an assistant, in addition to the pilot. Today, Thorella was serving as assault group coordinator, with

Sergeant Major Aquino observing. This jump, the last before graduation, was going to be their toughest – in training, at least – and Aquino wanted to be there to see it.

Jodi, as usual during the exercises of the past few weeks, had the great misfortune of being Thorella's pilot.

"Delta One-Two," Nicole acknowledged.

"Delta One-Two, you are point for first wave. Note that local target defenses are active; no deep-space systems or fighters noted." That meant that Nicole's ship probably would not have to worry about being seared out of space by any simulated enemy weapons, but nearer the ground the Marine trainees would have to contend with flak. The Kreelans were never known to use anti-aircraft fire, as they preferred their opponents to get to the ground in one piece. But it never hurt to train for the unexpected.

Thankfully, Thorella had chosen not to throw any enemy fighters into the scenario. Yet, at least.

"Did you copy, Reza?" she asked.

"Affirmative," he replied through the boat's intercom. During each exercise, trainees would be chosen at random from within each platoon to fill the leadership positions in the company. Reza had drawn the position of "platoon guide" for this drop; not being qualified NCOs or officers, the designated trainees were ostensibly unfit to be termed "leaders." Be that as it may, in his distinguished post Reza was tied into the drop group's command nets and was responsible for the orders and reports that concerned his platoon.

Reza looked at Eustus, his acting platoon sergeant, who nodded vigorously, eager to get on with it.

"We are ready, commander," Reza reaffirmed.

Nicole could not help but smile at his voice. Despite Thorella's best efforts, his endless harangues and futile attempts to provoke him, Reza had excelled during his training, and was now ranked at the top of his class.

Behind and to either side of Nicole's boat, eight other similar vessels now flew, carrying the first company of Reza's trainee battalion, one of thirty active at any given time on Quantico. In a real drop, the Marines normally deployed in battalion or full regiment strength, and there would be hundreds of ships – assault boats, gunships, fighters – swarming toward the surface.

For the trainees, however, the exercises focused on platoon and below training and tactics. Training for anything more was deemed a waste of time for men and women who likely would either be dead or out of the service before they reached company command or higher, and who needed now only the basics of how to survive in combat. Besides, many a trainee had noted wryly, it would have been too expensive to mount such exercises on a continual basis for a Confederation that had been surviving economically on good-faith War Bonds for nearly half a century.

Reza surveyed his command with a calculating eye. While the Way was one of glory through individual combat, Her Children were not unfamiliar with the tactics and strategies that accompanied mass warfare. Her blood united them, eliminating the need for the complex command, control, and communications – "C3" – systems that the humans relied on for relaying orders and reports between those doing the fighting and those who were directing the battle. Reza had tasted that uniting force for but a fleeting instant in the span of his own lifetime before being severed from that spiritual lifeline; now, among humans, he had only his wits and training such as this to guide him, and he found that it was a poor substitute.

He clicked over to the platoon's command net, reserved for the platoon guide (or leader) and the platoon "sergeant," and asked Eustus, "Did Scorelli replace the loose ammunition feed housing on her weapon?"

"She should have," Eustus said through his suit's external speaker. Unlike Reza, everyone else already had their helmets on. "I told her to, anyway." He glanced back at the nervous looking woman who clung tightly to her weapon, one of the platoon's four auto pulse rifles, very similar to the one a soldier serving under Reza's father's had used a lifetime before.

Reza smiled. "I can hear it rattling, my friend," he said. More than anything else, the other trainees had learned from Reza how valuable the art of stealth was. An enemy that could not be heard, could not be seen, and could not be found, was extremely hard to kill.

"Sorry, Reza," he said sheepishly. Reza did not have to remind him that, as platoon sergeant, he was responsible for making sure that the platoon leader's directions were actually carried out. Eustus shook his head, disgusted with himself. Over the muffled roar of the dropship's engines, he had heard nothing. "I'll take care of it."

Eustus clicked over to First Squad's net and quietly, without making a scene, corrected the deficiency. Scorelli hurried to oblige.

"Suit up, Reza," Nicole said from the cockpit, looking at the telemetry displays for her passengers, which showed his suit helmet still not attached. She knew how much he hated the armor, but there was no getting around it: they were almost at the drop point.

Grimacing, Reza did as he was told, hefting the helmet from where it sat between his feet and jamming it on his head. He heard and felt the hiss of air as the suit brought its own environmental systems on-line, isolating him from the universe beyond its layers of flexible ceramic and fibersteel. Of all the things he could say he loathed, being confined in this suit was one of the worst. In his Kreelan armor, he was completely free, the leatherite and Kreelan steel conforming perfectly to his body and its motions. His eyes and ears, his nose and tongue, were all free to tell his mind of the physical world around him as his spirit sought out things that lay far beyond. But in the suit, there was only the bitterly dry air and the tasteless water held in the recycling system, which also required pure distilled water, and could not tolerate the waters from the streams from around the base with which Reza had become familiar and now cherished. Worse, although there were packets of dried and salted meat in his external pouches, there was no food within the suit for him to eat; he found the concentrates simply intolerable, inedible. If he were forced to remain in pressurized armor for the entire exercise – a full week – Reza would be very hungry indeed. Simply ducking out of sight for a quick bite to eat was not only unthinkable to Reza as a form of cheating, it was also a technical impossibility. The telemetry data links that tied every set of Marine space armor to anyone able and interested in receiving the information would know if a suit had been opened. And that certainly included the exercise umpires.

In front of his eyes, his helmet, the power to it now enabled, glowed in a panorama of virtual reality, displaying his environment in a user-selected palette of shades and colors that rendered the differences between dark and light, rain and smoke, completely immaterial. While the virtual reality systems, tied into sophisticated suit sensors and able to receive external inputs from other suits or vehicles – even ships – did not have limitless range in a tactical environment, they gave the human soldier a distinct edge against a Kreelan opponent. When the suits were available.

But even that technology, Reza added silently and with a note of personal pride, was not equal in battle to a Kreelan warrior priestess... or priest.

He examined the projected drop zone again, just to confirm that what he held in his memory was perfect, for when they reached Quantico's surface they probably would not have the advantages of the space armor indefinitely, and he refused to rely on the computerized battlefield intelligence systems. The general plan was to make the initial landing and assault, and then hold a critique of the operation, while armorers prepared the suits for the next class cycling through. From there on in, the trainees would fight their mock battles with the kind of basic armor that Jodi had used on Rutan, and which was the mainstay of Marine personal armor everywhere.

"This should be a lot easier than the last one," Eustus commented, tapping into Reza's view of the terrain. The drop zone was in an area of rolling hills, dotted with tree groves and covered with knee-high scrub, and promised few landing injuries, although it left little in the way of cover for the attackers. "Landing in that rocky stuff last time really stunk."

Reza nodded grimly. There had been fourteen injuries, two of them serious, in their previous landing in the training area's desert zone, a wasteland of sharp, irregular granite rock formations that had been a literal hell to jump into and then fight out of. Reza's battalion had lost nearly two-thirds of its strength – on paper – by the time the administrative critique was given. It had not been a glowing one.

In only a few more minutes, the appointed time had arrived. "Prepare for drop," Nicole announced from the flight deck. An illuminated bar that ran the length of the cargo compartment suddenly turned red. "Two minutes."

Unlike many ships and atmospheric craft, Marine dropships had no designated jump- or loadmaster. That was the responsibility of the senior man in the jump group. There was simply too little room aboard to spare.

"Stand up!" Reza bellowed as he moved aft toward the jump doors that had now cycled open. Beyond the eerie blue sheen of the force fields that kept the air in the compartment from exploding into the vacuum beyond, Reza could see the cloud-shrouded outline of the target continent. A blinking red cursor in his helmet visor informed him of the drop zone's exact location in the middle of an enormous expanse of green vegetation.

The men and women of his group unharnessed themselves and checked over their equipment and themselves one last time. Once they had stepped through either of the two doors at the rear of the compartment, they would not get another chance before they hit the ground. And mistakes made now could make that one long, hard step.

"Sound off!" Reza barked.

"First squad, ready!"

"Second squad, ready!"

"Third squad, ready!"

"Heavy weapons, ready!"

Eustus nodded inside his helmet, the movement invisible to anyone outside. "That's it then," he said.

"Reza," he heard Nicole's voice one more time on the platoon command channel, "thirty seconds..." She paused. "And please, mon ami," she said quietly, "be careful."

"Roger," he replied. "And I will."

"Don't worry, ma'am," Eustus's lighthearted voice broke in. "I'll keep his butt out of trouble."

The flight status strip above their heads turned from a mournful red to a brilliant green.

"Go!"

In twos, the Marine trainees shuffled out the doors and fell into the infinite void of space.

* * *

"There they go," murmured Jodi as she saw dozens of new blips appear on her sensors. Normally, the countermeasures devices on all the ships and the suits themselves would be active, trying to erase their signature from any electronic or thermal detectors. But even here at Quantico, some small compromise was made for safety. Each suit had a beacon built into it to make finding the trainees easy. The only combat jump Jodi had ever made was when she ejected over Rutan, and that had been enough. "Bon voyage, guys."

"Cut the chatter, pilot," Thorella snapped from the seat behind her. "Come to course three three two mark eight seven and reduce your throttle to station-keeping. I want to stay close to them during descent."

"Sure thing, Markus," she replied casually. While he was the acting group coordinator, he did not outrank her. She was senior to him in time in grade, and it amused her to goad him by addressing him on a first name basis.

Sergeant Major Aquino remained silent.

* * *

Reza maneuvered slightly to his left to get a better view of his platoon's dispersal. A series of four wedges representing each of the squads under his command was spread over a few kilometers now, with one squad ahead of him and the rest behind. Eustus, the platoon sergeant, was between the third and last – heavy weapons – squads. Behind and above his own silently falling formation, five hundred and twelve other figures in space armor floated and jetted about as they sought to reach their individual falling stations within the battalion's designated thousand cubic kilometer maneuver zone.

For once, Reza was thankful for the computers that calculated where everyone should be on the way down. Exo-atmospheric drops were always a challenge in geometry: extra distance between individuals and units was better when they were still high up, to keep losses to a minimum in case the enemy brought any heavy weapons to bear on them. But later, as they entered the atmosphere – if there was one – and neared the ground, their formation needed to tighten up considerably if they were to maintain vital unit integrity. A combat unit that landed together and intact could fight. One that did not was nothing more than meat waiting for the Kreelans' swords.

That, Reza told himself, we are not. This would be their best jump, he thought, and his blood began to sing at the devastation – simulated though it might be – they would inflict on their enemies waiting below. His comrades, while lacking many of the benefits of a martial upbringing such as his own, nonetheless would prove worthy opponents for Her Children when the time came. For a species intellectually dedicated to the pursuit of peace, humans were finely adapted for the art of making war.

The altitude display on his visor continued to unwind toward zero as they approached their target, the miniature field generators of the suits deflecting the friction heat of the upper atmosphere as they plummeted downward. With a little more than eighty kilometers of altitude to cover, and a slant range to the drop zone of about one hundred and fifty, they only had a few minutes of flight remaining.

High above, the drop ships were returning to the carrier to bring down the next battalion that was scheduled to jump. Only the group coordinator's fighter remained with them, its rakish hull barely visible to Reza's naked eye.

He clicked down to the platoon's common net, listening for any idle chatter. There was none. There were only a few clipped words as people maneuvered to keep position, informing their neighbors they were moving, and where to, with their actions echoed in their helmet data displays.

Reza smiled. It was going very well. Their training was paying–

The thought was torn from his mind, as he suddenly felt crushed within his suit and a shrieking roar filled his skull. The planet rushing up at him suddenly began whirling, faster and faster, until it was nothing more than a kaleidoscope of color that alternated with the black of space and the shining stars. He heard voices calling to him on the comm link, but he could not make out the words over the roar of what he realized must be his suit's maneuvering jets. Worse, he himself was unable to speak, the air crushed out of his lungs by the induced g-forces as he spun out of control. His arms and legs felt like they were about to rip out of their sockets as he spun around and around, faster and faster, and his vision began to narrow to a tiny tunnel, then vanished into a gray mist.

In only a few seconds, Reza blacked out.

* * *

"Reza!" Eustus cried as he watched his friend's suit spin crazily out of control, one of its thrusters firing like a roman candle. He desperately

clicked over to the emergency frequency, biting on the control so savagely
he caught his tongue. A sudden taste of salty copper filled his mouth.
"Mayday! Mayday!" he shouted. "This is First Platoon. Reza's suit looks like
it's had a malfunction. He's heading down and out of control!"

"I've got a lock on him, First Platoon," Jodi's controlled voice came
back. "Moving to intercept."

"Negative," Thorella's voice interjected coldly. "I've got over five
hundred other people out here to watch over, and this ship isn't capable of
making a pickup. We don't have suits on."

"Then what the hell—"

Another voice, accented by his native Tagalog, broke into the
conversation. "Camden, designate someone to take over your platoon and
break formation forward of your group," Sergeant Major Aquino ordered
tersely. "Pilot, rendezvous with Camden as quickly as possible."

"Roger," she said thankfully. Fuck you, Thorella, she thought.

In about fifteen seconds she had Eustus in sight. "Now what?" she
asked.

"Camden," the sergeant major said, ignoring her, "what I have in mind
is going to take some guts. Can you handle it?"

"We're wasting time, sar-major," Eustus replied quickly. "Let's have it."

Aquino nodded to himself. The boy had dedication. And a set of brass
balls. "Behind the cockpit is a recess that you should be able to squeeze
yourself into. It is outside the fighter's gravity control system, so you will
have to hold up to the gee's we pull. Understood?"

"On my way." Eustus was already jetting toward them. In a few seconds,
Jodi heard him clambering over the hull behind them. "I'm here, sar-major.
Let's go."

"Find Gard, Lieutenant Mackenzie," Aquino ordered before he told
Eustus the rest of what he planned. He did not tell either of them that his
interest in Reza was far more than academic. He was an old friend and
confidant of one Admiral Zhukovski, who had provided Aquino with
information that someone within the cadre was going to try and kill Reza.
Where he had gotten such information, he would never say. However,
Aquino was almost sure it was Thorella, although there was certainly no
shortage of other likely candidates. But he had no evidence. Yet.

Jodi rammed the throttles forward, momentarily forgetting that Eustus
had no protection. "Shit," she hissed to herself as Eustus yelped, and she
dropped the thrust back to something she thought he might be able to
handle. "Sorry, Eustus," she said. "You still with us?"

"Barely," he breathed, his fists clenching even harder to the recessed handholds. Had it not been for the augmented strength the suit gave to his own body, he would have been left behind the leaping fighter. That was close, he sighed to himself.

Scanning her instruments, Jodi picked out Reza's tumbling form. "Reza," she said over the comm link, "do you read me? We're coming to get you. Hang on."

Not surprisingly, he didn't answer. Jodi bit her lip, wondering if he was even still alive. As puny as the thrusters were on those suits, they were still plenty powerful. At least it had finally burned itself out of fuel, she thought bitterly, wondering how such a thing could happen. The armored space suits the Marines used were probably the safest pieces of military hardware next to the common rock. While a thruster lighting off like that was not impossible, it was sure damn unlikely.

Behind her, Captain Markus Thorella sat silently.

The short time it took to close on Reza's spinning form passed like hours, and their time was quickly running out. "Altitude, ten kilometers," her ship's computer reported in Nicole's voice.

"I know, goddammit," she hissed, trying to keep the fighter stable in the increasing buffeting from the atmosphere. She followed the little blip on her head-up display like a bloodhound, but she could not yet see Reza visually, and she could not go much faster for fear of losing Eustus. "C'mon, Reza," she whispered to herself "Where the hell are you?"

There! A tiny speck became visible right off the fighter's nose, tumbling against the backdrop of the rapidly approaching ground as Jodi dove straight down toward the planet surface.

"Got him in sight," she said, easing the throttles forward a little more, but not too much: if she was going too fast when she reached him, her ship would overshoot, and there would not be time for a second pass before Reza hit the ground. "Stand by, Eustus."

"Any time," Eustus breathed. He was getting sick from being bounced around while hanging onto the fighter's back like a parasitic insect, and his hands were beginning to cramp from holding on for dear life to the thin bar aft of the cockpit, even with the suit augmentation.

"Altitude, five thousand meters," the computer warned. "Warning... warning," it went on as a steady warbling tone sounded in Jodi's headset. If she did not pull out soon, she never would.

Steady, now, she breathed to herself as she crept up on Reza's windmilling form. Now!

"Go, Eustus!" she shouted.

Without hesitation, Eustus flung himself into the air stream screaming around the fighter, trusting that his suit's screens would keep him from being smashed into jelly against the ship's hull. At the same time, Jodi separated away in the opposite direction, leaving him tumbling in her wake.

"Holy Jesus," Eustus breathed as he felt himself being grabbed and pummeled by the atmosphere. A beep was going off in his ear. Altitude. Quickly righting himself with his thrusters, he pointed himself like an arrow at Reza's inert form and shot toward him, closing the dozen or so meters between them in only a few seconds.

"Gotcha!" he huffed triumphantly as he grabbed one of Reza's flailing arms. Pulling his friend to him, he linked their suits together at the waist with the built-in safety tethers. Then, fumbling at Reza's sides with his hands, he fought to separate the bulk of the equipment attached to Reza's suit. If he could not get rid of it, they would be too heavy for his own suit's jets to put them safely on the ground. "Come on," he muttered angrily as the altitude warning tone sounded faster and faster. When the tone become a continuous sound, the suit's thrusters would not have enough time to slow them to an acceptable landing velocity, and the most elementary laws of physics would take over. They would be splattered like eggs over the ground below.

With a sudden snap, the molded combat pack and the fifty or so kilos it represented popped away.

"Burn!" Eustus shouted into his helmet, initiating the preprogrammed firing sequence that Aquino had told him to use. Canted at a ridiculous angle to account for the asymmetrical thrust condition imposed by the weight of Reza's body, the two jets of Eustus's suit flared and fired at their full thrust.

Grunting at the force of the suit's thrusters, Eustus kept his eyes glued to the suit visor and the scene beyond as he and Reza continued to plummet toward the ground. "Please, Lord of All," he hissed through clenched teeth over the roar of the straining jets and all of six gees, "Come on... come on..."

The whirling numbers that indicated their descent velocity gradually slowed as the jets fought against the force of Quantico's gravity. They flashed through one thousand meters, still falling like a rock. The trees and hills below, so beautiful from higher up, held all the beauty now of a trap of sharpened bamboo stakes.

Through his faceplate and his rapidly dimming vision, his blood drawn away by the force of the thrusters, Eustus caught a glimpse of Jodi Mackenzie's fighter nearby as she brought it down in a matching spiral descent.

Well, he thought with a detached part of his panicking consciousness, they won't have long to wait.

At five hundred meters, the fuel caution warning began sounding in his ears. The jets were going to run out of fuel before they hit the ground. "Shit," he muttered bitterly. He closed his eyes.

A few seconds later, the jets flared one final time and died. Eustus felt himself seized by the sickening sensation of free-fall. They weren't going to make it–

With a roar of snapping branches, he found himself tumbling through the middle of a stand of trees, their limbs tearing at his arms and legs, hammering his back, and whip-cracking against his helmet. Before he had any time to react, he found himself in a short free-fall again.

He hit the ground. Hard. The wind was knocked out of him like a child who had fallen from a swing, and Eustus fought back tears of surprise and pain.

But he mostly felt relieved. He was alive.

* * *

"How's your head?"

Reza blinked away the stars that clouded his vision, only to see Eustus's concerned face.

"Fuzzy," he answered quietly as he took stock of his body. Obviously, they had survived their fall. "What happened?"

"I don't know, exactly," Eustus said as he removed the palm-sized mediscanner from Reza's forehead. It did not register any damage more serious than a very mild concussion and some hellish bruising. "It looked like one of your thrusters went berserk and sent you tumbling. Sergeant Major Aquino came up with the idea of me hitching a ride on Lieutenant Mackenzie's fighter to come pick you up. And, well, here we are." He smiled sheepishly.

"I owe you my life, my friend."

"Stow it, Reza," he said, smiling more brightly now. "I promised Commander Carré I'd keep your butt out of trouble, remember?"

Reza nodded, tried to smile at his friend's humor. "What are we to do now?"

Eustus snorted. "Well, I already reported that you looked like you were going to be okay, at least according to this thing," he held up the scanner. "Captain Thorella said that unless you needed a medevac out of here, we're supposed to move our butts back to the battalion op zone or we'd have to E & E through Second Battalion when they land." A wry smile curled his lips. "A mere forty klicks away, and through Second Battalion's training lanes."

Reza frowned. "E&E" was better known as escape and evasion, a convenient acronym for one of the most hellish aspects of Marine training. As part of the ENDEX, all of the trainees would have to go through a ten-kilometer long stretch of "enemy territory," doing whatever they could to keep from being captured by the mock enemy forces that would be gunning for them. Not surprisingly, very few ever made it through without being bagged. Everyone who was caught had to spend the remainder of the E&E exercise in a mock prisoner of war camp, undergoing unpleasant but harmless "torture" and lectures on how to do better next time, in the real world. The best motivator, however, was the fact that the Kreelans did not take prisoners. In combat, anyone who was caught was killed. Period.

"I take it then," Reza said slowly as part of his mind began directing his body toward repairing itself as rapidly as possible for the long travel ahead, "that we had best move quickly and soon?"

"That would seem the prudent thing to do, if you're up to it." Despite the reassuring signs the mediscanner gave him – apparently enough to satisfy Aquino, as Thorella could not have cared less – Eustus was not at all sure Reza was really up for this. They had a long way to go.

"Do not worry, my friend," Reza said, sensing Eustus's mood as he collected up his rifle – which miraculously had survived undamaged – and other gear. The now-discarded armored suits would be left where they were until one of the dustoff crews came to pick them up. "Come, Eustus. We are wasting time, and have far yet to go."

* * *

"They've finally decided to get a move on," Thorella muttered to himself as he watched the two icons representing Eustus and Reza move off toward their battalion's drop zone. He frowned to himself as he stood up from the display and stretched his cramped back muscles. Aquino had gone back to the main base in a shuttle after determining that Gard was all right. Thorella knew that the little Filipino bastard was going to try and pin something on him, but there would not be anything for him to find. In the meantime, Thorella had to play out the game as it was scripted. It would not do to call too much attention to himself by trying to take Gard out again. For now.

"You know something, Thorella," he heard a silky voice behind him, "you're a real fucking sleazeball."

"One of these days, Mackenzie," he said just loud enough for her to hear, "I'm not going to have to take that from you anymore." Unfortunately, Thorella did not have control over the cadre roster. Mackenzie seemed forever glued to him, a thorn in his side. But someday...

"Is that a threat, you ox?" she challenged in the comparative silence of the empty command post. Only she and Thorella were on duty right now, the rest of the cadre out wreaking havoc among the struggling trainees. She knew Thorella could probably beat her in a hand-to-hand match, but not by much. She was good, and had had a good teacher. She wished that Tony Braddock were here with her now. "You know, I just don't understand why Tsingai doesn't just send you to the rock pile where you belong. You hate your own people as much or more than you hate the Blues, and yet they just keep bailing you out of all the trouble you seem to make for yourself. Now, why is that?" She didn't expect more than an epithet in reply.

But Thorella obliged her with what she had to consider an intellectual tour de force, at least for him. "There are a lot of things I wouldn't expect you to understand, Mackenzie," he replied calmly. "But I would think that the fact that our race needs people like me to survive against an enemy like the Kreelans would be self-evident, even to you. The trouble is that you're soft and malleable, like wet clay. I realize that people like you would like nothing better than for the rest of us to just roll over or turn the other cheek as the Kreelans send in their seed to poison us, but that's not how it's going to be." He turned to face her, his face a cold mask of hatred. "There are a lot of people who never wanted that half-breed to contaminate our population, to disgrace the Corps, and I'm one of them. Where there's one, there's more, and pretty soon we'll be overrun with half-breeds spreading their ideas and their genes through our population." He leaned closer to her. "And I'll do anything I can to stop that from happening."

Thorella's use of "half-breed" was not lost on her. With black skin and blue eyes, her own racial lines were far from any measure of purity people like Thorella seemed to find acceptable. But her own personal anger took second place to her growing suspicions that Reza's mishap had not been an accident. "Does that include murder, captain?" she asked quietly, waiting tensely to see if Thorella would attack her.

Slowly, he smiled. "I don't know what you mean, lieutenant. And if you accuse me of anything, I certainly hope you have a lot of evidence to back it up. Because if you don't," the smile evaporated, "you can kiss your career goodbye."

"No," Jodi said as she casually began to step away from him, "just wondering." He's insane, she thought. But his warning struck a chord of truth in her. How had he managed to stay out of trouble, despite the numerous allegations of disgraceful conduct that had been levied against him, all of which eventually were dismissed? He must have some sponsorship from higher up the chain. The question was, how high? And could they get away with trying to kill Reza, or anyone else, for that matter? "I think I'll just go and check on my ship, if you don't mind."

"Not at all," Thorella said flatly.

Watching her go, he knew she would have to be taken care of. When this little exercise was over, he would have to talk to his mentor again. He would know just what to do.

Smiling like the Dark Angel, he busied himself with the exercise unfolding around him, seemingly oblivious to Reza and Eustus. One of them he hated, the other was simply in the way.

* * *

Senator Strom Borge's face was a mask of contemplation. It was the face he often wore while jousting with his colleagues over the many issues of state and war the Confederation Council faced each day. The men and women he secretly loathed. They were weak and foolish, leading the Confederation into genocide at the hands of the blue-skinned alien horde. But he knew better, and worked diligently each day to set things right, biding his time until the day that he would no longer feel compelled to conceal his true goals, his real ambitions. Power was his sole reason for existence, and to exercise unlimited power was his ultimate goal. Someday, he thought. Someday soon.

A small sheaf of genuine paper slipped from the slender fingers of his hands as he gazed out the window that took up the entire wall of his office suite in the Confederation Plaza, as his thoughts wandered among the myriad lights that shone in the evening darkness outside. The paper contained a message from his protégé in the military, Markus Thorella, requesting guidance as to how to pursue the matter of dealing with Reza Gard. Thorella's initial attempt at quashing their unsuspecting enemy, while imaginative and seemingly foolproof, had nonetheless been thwarted, and the senator was not willing to put Thorella at risk again. At least, not yet.

Tapping a finger to his lips, an idea came to him. "Maria," he said.

"Yes, senator," the disembodied voice of his secretary outside answered immediately from unseen speakers in the room.

"Inform General Tsingai that Reza Gard is to be assigned to the Red Legion," he told her, "on order of the Chairman of the Confederation Council's Military Oversight Committee."

"Immediately, senator," she replied.

He sat back, smiling. Tsingai would protest, of course, but he would not press the issue after he, Senator Strom Borge, threatened to expose his little ongoing extramarital affair in public. Borge knew everything about everyone, and considered no one beyond his reach or influence.

Outside, his secretary carried out his instructions, silently wondering at the terrible fate that awaited Reza Gard.

TEN

The day Reza had looked forward to as a boy, and then again when he rejoined humanity, had finally come. He stood at parade rest, hands clasped behind his back, alongside his peers. The four companies of the graduating training battalion stood in mass formation on the parade ground as the post commandant gave his graduation speech, but Reza paid him little attention. His thoughts focused on the single stripe now on his sleeve that, lowly in rank as it was, signified that he was worthy to be a Confederation Marine. He had made good Wiley Hickock's faith in him from those bittersweet days that he had once forgotten. Past that, he thought of the future, of the time – soon, now – when he would be cast into battle and his blood would again sing in time with his sword.

The pomp and ceremony of graduation finally came to a close, the last comments and speeches rendered. It was now time for the trainees' last act as a battalion.

"Battalion..." he heard Eustus's voice boom over the field. He had been chosen as battalion trainee commander for this final day, and had loved every minute of it.

"Company..." each of the trainee company commanders echoed.

"Atten-SHUN!" Over five hundred pairs of boots stomped the ground, heel to heel, as the battalion came to attention.

"Dismissed!" Eustus's final command was drowned out by a sea of jubilant cries as the former trainees voiced their thanks that the hell of the last weeks was finally over. Hundreds of hats flew into the air, and the once orderly formation broke down into a riotous mob that surged toward the barracks area to prepare for whatever Fate had in store for them.

No longer old or young, man or woman, rich or poor: they were Marines.

* * *

Reza's platoon stood at attention before Sergeant Major Aquino in what they knew was a private ceremony he conducted for every platoon that graduated under his tutelage. Out in a far corner of the post, arrayed before an abandoned storage building that was away from any prying eyes, he began the ritual.

"Listen up, Marines," he bellowed in the tinny, heavily-accented voice that they had all come to respect, a note of pride in his words that he was no longer addressing recruits, but young warriors ready for battle.

"Some of you now will be going on to more training, to be specialists of some kind. The rest of you will be going straight to a combat regiment somewhere. But all of you, sooner or later, will be out in the fleet. And in the fleet there is no room for petty personal problems or grudges. Life, as you will soon find, is too short for that, and there is no room for it on a warship or in battle."

He held up an electronic notepad that they already knew was their unit roster. "When I read your name, you are to go into the building," he nodded to the door behind him, "and wait. Then anyone who wants a piece of you will get their chance, and all of you can get any hard feelings out of your systems now and leave them here, where they belong. We want you to take out your aggressions on the enemy, not on each other." He paused, surveying his audience, looking for squeamish faces. He saw none. Good. "When you're done, come back out and take your place in formation, then we will go on to the next one. I will observe to make sure no one gets carried away. Any questions?"

There were none. While the ritual they were partaking in was officially prohibited, it was a longstanding tradition that would survive anything less than outright murder, and Aquino was not about to let anything like that happen on his watch. "Very well," he said, focusing on the roster. "Alazarro!"

Jose Alazarro broke ranks and double-timed into the building.

"Anyone want a piece of him?" Aquino challenged. Four Marines nodded. "What are you waiting for?" the sergeant major snapped. The three men and one woman hustled through the door, followed by Aquino. There followed a few minutes of muffled grunts and groans, after which all five Marines, three of them with bloody noses or lips, returned to the formation. Together.

And so it went.

Reza stood in the building after his name was called, wondering about this strange practice as he took his turn being "on the spot," as some of the others called it. Eustus, called long before him, had cleared up some things with the young men who had once bullied him, and who now had broken noses and bruises, plus some respect, for their one-time scapegoat.

But such things held no interest for Reza. He loathed some of his companions – he did not consider them peers – disliked a few more, was neutral toward most, and genuinely liked a very small few. Despite any negative feelings he held for any one of them, however, he had no reason to assert himself. He was a priest of the Desh-Ka, and any matters of import would not be settled to his satisfaction outside of the arena and the clash of sword and claw. And this, to be sure, was not the arena.

He turned as two figures entered the building, their footfalls soft on the stained concrete floor. He nodded at Aquino, who took his place to one side in the role of officiator to make sure things did not get too ugly, and the older man nodded back gravely. Reza understood that his situation was somewhat different than that for the others. He would have to meet a higher standard of "satisfaction." Reza would be happy to oblige. His only real challenge would be to prevent himself from seriously injuring or killing his challenger.

Washington Hawthorne stepped forward. A towering pillar of ebony muscle, Hawthorne made a mockery even of Thorella's imposing form.

"I don't have anything against you personally, Reza," he said, "but I wanted to know if I could take you on man to man, without all the usual bullshit. You understand?"

Nodding at the man's candor, understanding him perfectly, Reza stepped up to meet him. Hawthorne's motives, while not particularly wise, were nonetheless honest and understandable, at least to Reza. He made a note that this was a man who might someday make a valuable ally and friend.

"When you are ready, Marines," Aquino announced.

Hawthorne nodded, happy not to be disappointed. He had not worked very closely with Reza, but he had heard about how great he was supposed to be in close combat. He wanted to find out for himself without wearing all the protective gear and playing by all the stupid rules the instructors sometimes – but not always – required. He raised his fists like a pugilist and moved in, anxious to see how Reza would react. Reza was a lot smaller, probably more agile than Hawthorne, but he was certainly a lot more vulnerable to any blow that the larger man could deliver. Hawthorne smiled.

The contest began as a black fist the size of a cantaloupe shot toward Reza's face with all the force and speed of a jackhammer...

Reza gave Hawthorne the feeling of a real fight without really offering him one. He easily dodged the larger man's blows, and only when Hawthorne began to feel frustration and anger at not being able to get a solid hit against his opponent did Reza finally bring the match to a close. Dodging another of Hawthorne's Herculean strikes, Reza nimbly stepped forward to deliver a carefully placed blow to the larger man's solar plexus, dropping him without doing any damage. Reza was hardly using his true combat skills, but Hawthorne was not an enemy.

"Son of a bitch," Hawthorne gasped as he collapsed, doubled-over with the pain that had exploded inside him. After gagging and choking for a few moments, effectively paralyzed from Reza's single strike, he looked up through tearing eyes to find a hand extended toward him.

"You fight with spirit, my friend," Reza said, "and shall prove a worthy opponent for your true enemies, whom we shall face together. Come, let us leave this place."

Nodding slowly, his curiosity satisfied at the expense of a slightly bruised ego, Washington smiled as he took Reza's hand, allowing the smaller man to help him up. "I just had to find out for myself, Reza. I'm just glad you're on our side."

Together, the two of them headed back outside where they would await the completion of their platoon's unofficial farewell party.

A much-relieved Sergeant Major Aquino followed them out.

* * *

The newly appointed Marines stood in murmuring groups in the main hall, waiting for the harried cadre officers to post their orders. One after the other, they were called forward to the rows of tables at which the officers and NCOs sat, presenting and explaining each trainee's first official orders. There was no reason for people to be doing this, of course: the trainees could have their orders posted just as easily by electronic mail, and very few actually needed anyone to explain orders. But the Corps had developed a tradition of seeing their people off to their first assignment with a human face and a word of encouragement, rather than a sterile electronic beep followed by an equally lifeless form letter.

Nicole and Jodi stood beside Reza as they all waited for Eustus to return with his orders. Nicole was nervous, Reza could tell, and also touched with sadness. She did not want to leave him again.

Eustus came running back, weaving his way toward them through the throng of fellow Marines, some of whom were cheering at their orders, others groaning with dismay. He held them clutched in his hand, the slender plastic seal still unbroken.

"Well, dummy," Jodi blurted, "where are you going?"

"I want to see what Reza's say first," Eustus panted excitedly. "I've been... well, kind of hoping we'd get assigned to the same unit."

"Don't hold your breath, bucko," Jodi told him seriously. "The fleet's a big place, and the Corps is spread all through it and on hundreds more planetary garrisons besides. The chances aren't too good."

"Yeah, but I figure that we're probably going to be assigned to an orphan regiment, right? I mean, my homeworld never had any regiments of its own, and Reza technically doesn't have a homeworld for regimental assignment. So that makes the chances of us being in the same orphan regiment that much greater, right?"

Jodi looked at him skeptically. "Orphan" regiments were so named because the homeworld that originally raised them and kept them supplied with recruits had either been decimated or destroyed by the Kreelans. When that happened, the regiment's colors and organization remained intact, but it got whatever replacements could be sent to it, regardless of the source. Planets that did not have enough people to raise a complete regiment of its own and did not have an agreement with another world to supply replacement personnel had their Marines put into orphan regiments as replacements, fresh blood. While this was not a problem in most cases, in some it could be disastrous. In one case, an entire regiment had to be forcibly subdued after the military personnel – MILPO – office had unwittingly assigned a large block of replacement Marines to it, not realizing that the fresh troops, from a conservative Muslim colony, were likely to clash with the regiment's indigenous Hindus. It took three other regiments to put down the resulting insurrection and mutiny.

"Well," Jodi said, "I'll give you an A-plus for imagination. But I still wouldn't get your hopes up too high."

Eustus looked to Nicole for support, but she only shrugged. She did not know either. She had asked, of course, but the MILPO officer had stonewalled her for some reason, and she suspected that Thorella probably had something to do with it. "I do not know, Eustus," she said simply.

"Gard, Reza!" one of the NCOs shouted over the low din in the room.

"Hurry up, Reza," Eustus said, anxious to find out if they would get their assignment together.

Reza made his way forward and came to stand at attention before Sergeant Major Aquino, who had taken Reza's orders packet from the sergeant at the table and now held it in his hands. The older man looked up at him with his piercing black eyes.

"I am not surprised that you made it this far, Gard," he said as he handed Reza his orders, "in light of what you went through before you came to us here. I hope you go far in the life you have chosen, and in the Corps." He gestured to the sparkling new Marines around him and said quietly, "I wish all of them were half as good as you." He stuck out his hand. "Good luck, Marine."

Reza nodded as he shook the smaller man's hand. He had always liked Aquino. "Thank you, sergeant major. I shall do my best."

"That is all I ask. Carry on."

Reza quickly walked back to where the others were waiting, the orders burning in his hand. He wanted to get out of this world of "discipline" and make believe combat and into the world where he belonged, where his sword would sing with honor to Her glory, even though She no longer saw him in Her heart. The thought depressed him until he saw Jodi, Nicole, and Eustus. They and the Corps were his family now, and he would do his best to bring honor to them all.

"Well?" Eustus asked. "What is it? Where are you going?"

Reza opened his orders and scanned them. "I have been posted to the 1st Battalion of the 12th Guards Regiment," he told them.

"That's the Red Legion, isn't it?" Jodi said, shocked. Nicole's mouth dropped open. The Red Legion was infamous throughout the Corps as being a dumping ground for every undesirable individual and bloody mission in the service. It was the High Command's garbage disposal. "My God, Reza, that unit's a meat grinder!"

Eustus tore his orders open. "Dear Father," he whispered. He looked up at Jodi, then Reza. "What is it they say about not wishing for something, because you might get it?"

"You received the same assignment?" Nicole asked, aghast. "This is absurd! There must be some mistake–"

"There's no mistake, commander," a familiar voice spoke from behind. They all turned to find Thorella standing there, an angelic smile on his face. "Those orders came from on high, or so I hear. I hope you enjoy your duty stations, gentlemen. Now, if you'll excuse me–"

"You fucking piece of shit," Jodi snarled. "You know they don't deserve that. Even you can't hate them that much. The Red Legion isn't anything more than a marching coffin."

"My, my," he said, shaking his head theatrically. "You Navy types do have a way with words. I know you won't believe this, Mackenzie, but it actually wasn't my idea. But you're right: the Red Legion is a meat grinder, although it isn't listed as such. But that makes it all the more fitting for a traitor and his sidekick."

Eustus made to step forward, his fists clenched, but Reza held him back. "No, Eustus," he said before turning to Thorella. He stepped close to the larger man, and was rewarded with the sharp tang of fear that suddenly erupted from his pores. "There will come a day of reckoning for you, Markus Thorella. And I pray I am there to witness it."

Thorella snorted derisively, but Reza could tell he was still afraid. "Say your prayers for yourself, half-breed. You and your little buddy here will have your hands full as it is." He looked at Eustus. "I was thinking of getting you a jar of petroleum jelly for when you get there, Camden. I hear the NCOs in the Red Legion don't like their little boys dry."

"That is enough, captain," Nicole hissed. Her anger had called forth an unfamiliar burning sensation in her body, as if her blood was on fire. Her conscious mind was afraid that if Thorella did not shut up, she would find herself lunging for his throat. "Leave us. Now."

"Yes, ma'am," he sneered. He threw a mock salute, turned on his heel, and sauntered away through the crowd.

"Motherfucker," Jodi called quietly after him.

Nicole turned to Reza and Eustus. "I will see if I cannot get in to see General Tsingai about this," she said. "He may be able to—"

"No," Reza said firmly. "At least, not for me. I thank you for your concern, Nicole, but I have received my orders, and I shall do my best to carry them out." Jodi opened her mouth to protest, but Reza silenced her with his eyes before he spoke. "I do not do this purely out of respect for orders which, I suspect, are not entirely legal. But I have also heard of the Red Legion, and perhaps – for me – it is the best place. I believe that I probably would fit in better with a group of misfits than I would in a regular unit." He held up a braid of his long hair to illustrate his point. He was the only Marine any of them had ever seen whose hair was not the regulation crew cut. And that was the least of his differences.

Jodi scowled furiously, the normally crystal smooth skin of her forehead wrinkled like aged parchment. "What about you, Eustus?" she asked.

"I'll go with Reza," he said decisively, pocketing his orders. "A Marine's job is going to be tough no matter where he is. And I figure that sticking with Reza makes my chances of staying alive and doing my job well that much better." He had glanced at Reza's orders and compared them to his own. They were slated for the same company, and he could only hope that they would be assigned to the same platoon.

"Oui," Nicole said resignedly, trying to keep the sadness from her voice. Not only was Reza leaving her again, he was probably going to be sacrificed as undesirable cannon fodder on some rock in space that had nothing more than a number for a name. "I guess that is that, then."

They all stood there for a few minutes, as if not quite sure that the play they were acting out was real or only a bad dream.

It was Eustus who finally broke the spell. "Well," he said, "I guess we'd better get packing. The transports start loading at fourteen-hundred, and we've got a long trip ahead of us." The Red Legion was scattered over a sector of space nearly two months' hyperlight travel from Quantico.

Nicole held back her tears as she walked with her friends toward the barracks, wondering if a year from now any of them would still be alive to remember this day.

ELEVEN

Six Years Later

Captain Reza Gard sat at a nondescript desk in the small cubicle that served as his company's CQ and administrative office, trying valiantly to deal with the paperwork that he could not in good conscience leave for his adjutant, Corporal Alfonso Zevon. Zevon, who only recently had been transferred to A Company, 1st Battalion of the 12th Guards Regiment (Red Legion), had transformed the company's paperwork, which Reza considered to be a small slice of Father Hernandez's Hell, from an unqualified mess into a real system. It was a gift that Reza was endlessly thankful for, especially since Zevon also happened to be an expert marksman and a good fighter. What terrible thing he had done to earn himself a posting to the Red Legion, Reza did not know, and would never ask.

He looked up as his First Sergeant poked his head through the door. "Reza," Eustus said, "there's a message coming in for you on channel five. It's from Nicole."

Reza's skin tingled at the sound of her name. It had been months since he had last heard from her, but he had felt recently that something was different in her life, something good had happened. He felt it in his blood, the blood he had shared with her. "Thank you, Eustus. I'll take it in here." Eustus smiled and ducked back out.

Reza shook his head as he thought about his friend. Eustus had insisted on staying with him in the bloody machine that was the Red Legion, despite receiving several offers to be posted to other, more "reputable," regiments. He had also received several offers – strongly supported by Reza – to go to officer candidate school, but that, too, he had refused. "Why would I want to become an officer?" he would ask, seemingly perplexed. He had risen through the enlisted ranks on his own merit, and now served as the senior enlisted man in his company. He was honored to serve Reza, and Reza was equally honored to have him.

Washington Hawthorne, too, had joined the Legion – by choice, amazingly enough – two years after graduating from Quantico. He had survived long enough to become Reza's executive officer, and would soon be up for command of his own company, an event that Reza awaited with anticipation and pride in his friend's abilities.

As for Reza himself, his start in the Legion as a much-maligned rifleman who had spent nearly as much time fighting his fellow Marines as he had the Kreelans had changed five months after his arrival to the unit. At the Battle of Kalimpong, half of their battalion was wiped out in an ill-planned attack against a Kreelan mining operation that had been discovered in the system's asteroid belt. Reza had managed to rally the survivors in time to beat back a fierce Kreelan counterattack that had come very close to destroying their ship, the old cruiser Pegasus (which not long after, Reza lamented, had been burned into vapor by a Kreelan battlecruiser). For that action, Corporal Reza Gard had won the Confederation Medal of Honor and a trip to Officer Candidate School, where Nicole pinned on his gold second lieutenant's bars three months later. He had returned to his battalion to take over A Company's 1st Platoon, and ten months later had assumed command of the company itself after the acting company commander and executive officer were killed in action. Four years ago, that had been. Four years. A lifetime...

Gratefully shoving aside the data pad that been monopolizing his time, Reza turned his attention to Nicole's message. "Play," he ordered the console. After a short pause, Nicole's face appeared in the screen, and his heart warmed at the sight of her. She looked as beautiful as always, and was – he was not able to describe it exactly – warmer, somehow, more vibrant. Happy, he thought. For perhaps the first time since they were children, she looked happy.

"Mon ami," she began, almost hesitantly, "I hope all is going well for you, that you are safe there on the Rim. Jodi and Father Hernandez are fine, and asked me to say hello to you; I am sure that you will soon receive messages from both of them, but I told them to wait until I had brought you the news.

"Reza..." she paused, unsure how to continue, and he found himself leaning closer to her image, as if he could somehow sense something from the electronics in the console, "I do not know how you will feel about what I am going to tell you. I hope you will not be angry with me for not talking with you about it before, but these messages are often delayed – I can only pray that you receive this one in time – and I could not bring myself to wait any longer to make a decision." She looked down at her hands, obviously nervous. It was a state he had never seen her in before. She looked back up. At him. "Reza, Tony Braddock asked me to marry him. I told him yes."

Reza felt his mouth drop open in surprise. Jodi had sent him a message some time ago, saying that Braddock had been medically discharged from the Corps after receiving a near-fatal wound in combat. He had then turned up on Earth as the Council Representative from Timor, of all things, and quickly made something of a reputation for himself on the Confederation Council. Nicole had met him through Jodi, and – Reza now surmised – one thing had led to another. Jodi had gone on to say that Braddock had asked Nicole out on several dates – with Jodi watching over them like a zealous parent – but that was the last he had heard over the last several months. Until now.

"Mon chère," Nicole went on, "I can only hope that you receive this in time, because I want more than anything for you to be here, to be with me when I take the vows. It has been two years since you last went on leave, when we last saw each other for but two days on Solaris. I know that it may not be possible, for this is war, but if you can, my brother, please come. With my father gone, I would like for you to be the one to walk down the aisle with me, to give me away to Tony. Please."

Reza's chest tightened as he saw Nicole brush away a tear. She wanted so much for him to be with her. This is what he had been feeling in his blood for the last couple of months. It was the song of her happiness.

"There is a file attached with everything you should need to get here, transport schedules and so on. I do not know how, but Jodi found enough priority-one transit vouchers to get you from the Penlang La transit station on the Rim back to Earth." She forced a smile, and he could imagine her fears that he would never receive the message, or get it late, or not be able to come back to Earth. Or be dead. So much could go wrong over distance and time, through bloody war. But his blood burned brightly, his spirit calling to her, to reassure her that her message had found its way to him.

"Take care, Reza," she said. "Je t'aime." The screen faded to black.

* * *

Jodi waited alone at the crowded spaceport terminal. Nicole and Father Hernandez had wanted to come, but Jodi had insisted that they stay and get ready for the wedding that was to take place this evening. She had arranged Reza's transport schedule as well as she could, but getting people from the Rim to the Core Worlds on any kind of real schedule was impossible. Jodi was nervous, worried that Reza wouldn't make it, because he had not appeared on any of the earlier flights today, and the shuttle coming down now would be the last one scheduled before the wedding was to start. They were cutting it awfully close.

To add to her consternation, the trash-hauler (a less-than-affectionate name most pilots held for the ugly little orbital shuttles) was late, as usual. To make matters worse, she had no idea if Reza was on it, or even if he had made transit aboard the transport the shuttle was now returning from. She had tried to find out two dozen times over the last week if Reza was on the rosters of any of the seven different ships he had to board to get from the Rim back to Earth, and she had drawn a blank on all of them. The harried transportation people had tried to be helpful, but it hadn't changed the fact that she knew no more now than she had a month ago.

"Trying to track things down on Rim transits," one of the agents had told her with a shake of her head, "makes finding a needle in a haystack look easy." Jodi had no idea what a haystack was, but she'd gotten the picture. She decided to just go to the terminal and wait, because if Reza wasn't on this shuttle he was going to miss the wedding, anyway.

Finally, the transport arrived, its squat shape heaving into view while it jockeyed for position next to the extending boarding tube. The repeller field shimmered against the ground as the gaily painted – in red, white, and blue, no less – shuttle settled on its seven landing struts.

After what seemed to Jodi to be an interminable wait, passengers began to trickle from the gateway. She tried to get closer, but a solid wall of babbling people prevented her from seeing anything more than bobbing heads.

"Goddammit," she muttered in annoyance as a Navy commander pushed past her to embrace a squealing woman from the shuttle. The two of them, oblivious to the rest of humankind, solidly blocked the aisle with their wet and sloppy reunion. Jodi thought she was going to gag.

"Pardon me, please," a deep voice said from among the debarking passengers trapped behind the commander and his bimbo. The request had been gentle, but was nonetheless the voice of one accustomed to being obeyed. The babbling among the nearest waiting friends, relatives, and others suddenly ceased as the man, now revealed as a Marine captain in dress blue uniform, stood silently, waiting.

The commander released his significant other and gave Reza a hard stare. "Aren't you forgetting something," the commander said, pointing to the three full gold rings around his sleeve, "captain?"

"Not at all, commander," Reza replied, returning the man's stare. He pointed to the single ribbon – a cluster of white stars set against a field of azure blue – that made up its own row above the seven other full rows of combat decorations, five more rows than the Navy officer could boast, that adorned his uniform.

The Navy officer stared at the ribbon for a moment, before slowly lifting his right arm in a salute. While he outranked Reza, centuries-old tradition dictated that a bearer of the Medal of Honor was entitled to a salute first by his or her fellow service members, regardless of their rank. In the war against the Kreelans, there had been many Medal of Honor winners; unfortunately, since most of them were awarded posthumously, pitifully few recipients survived to enjoy the courtesy that tradition granted them.

"Good day to you, sir," Reza said pleasantly as he smartly returned the salute and stepped past the man and his open-mouthed companion.

"Reza!" Jodi cried, throwing herself into his arms, burdened as they were with his two flight bags. He didn't even have time to utter her name before she covered his mouth with hers in an unexpectedly passionate kiss. Reza could not see, but behind him, Jodi made sure that the Navy man saw the three stripes on her sleeve as she put her arms around Reza's neck. When they made eye contact, Jodi gave him a wink. A moment later, she drew away from Reza, who still stood there, stunned.

"Jodi!" he breathed, his face flushed with – mostly, he knew – embarrassment. "What are you–"

"Just welcoming you home, is all," she said, a devilish smile lighting up her face as she took him by the elbow and led him into the main terminal.

"Commander Mackenzie," Reza said with a smile as he sensed the Navy officer behind him fuming in embarrassment and not just a little bit of jealous envy, "you are a bloody liar."

Jodi laughed. "No doubt. But hey, let's get a move on – we're late and we've got a long way to go."

* * *

"So," Jodi said when she had gotten him settled into her skimmer, "how was your trip?"

Reza grunted. "Long. Boring. And I am convinced that not one single galley in the entire human fleet – outside of my own ship, of course – can properly prepare meat for a Kreelan warrior."

Jodi laughed. "Well, don't get your hopes up here, either. Tony bought one of those silly barbecue contraptions not long ago. I guess he didn't like the processor food, and now he's convinced himself that he can cook with the thing." She shook her head. "I guess you can eat anything if you put enough of that weird sauce of his on it, though."

Reza made a face. "I will cook," he said with determination.

The skimmer shuddered lightly as it pulled away from the ground. A moment later, the landing gear retracted and Jodi turned the craft southwest. Reza watched the ground fall away. The spaceport complex soon faded from view as the skimmer gained speed and altitude.

But his mind was not on the lush trees and velvet green landscape rushing by below. He was thinking of Jodi. The happiness that had bubbled from her at the spaceport seemed to have evaporated. Beneath the crumbling veneer he saw fear and, more than that, a growing mountain of loneliness. There was silence between them for a time, but Reza could feel her pain, and it reminded him of the wound that still bled within his own heart.

"What are you going to do, Jodi," he asked quietly, turning to her, "after Nicole is wed?"

"I... I don't know, Reza," she said, trying to keep her voice even as she switched on the autopilot. "I know that three's a crowd, but I haven't had any brilliant flashes of insight as to what I'm going to do with the rest of my life. Not after... not after she leaves me."

"They would let you stay–"

"Yeah, right," Jodi interrupted. "Come on, Reza, what am I supposed to do? Be the live-in nanny for the kids they want to have? How about Tony's public relations rep? Or maybe Nicole's manicurist. Yeah, I can see that one: Jodi Mackenzie, shoots down alien fighters by day, does nails by night." She was silent for a moment, and then hammered a fist against the flight console. "Fuck it," she shouted angrily. "Just fuck it all to hell!"

She made to pound on the unoffending console again, but her fist found only Reza's palm, which gently enveloped hers. He drew her to him with irresistible strength and held her as the tears came.

"I know that she doesn't want me," she said as she fought against the painful tide in her heart, "but in my mind I kept thinking that, maybe someday she'd come around. I mean, not even to sleep with me – I knew from the first that that was always going to be just a fantasy. But I thought that maybe I could be her companion, someone she could share her life with." She closed her eyes and buried her face against Reza's chest, her tears streaking his uniform. "But now, it's all over. Sure, we can still be friends," she said bitterly. "And what the fuck does that mean, Reza? That maybe she'll remember my name after the first tour we have to spend apart? That maybe we can squeeze in a quick lunch now and then – if we happen to be in the same star system – so she can tell me all about Tony and their oh-so-wanted kids? It's not enough for me, Reza," she choked. "It's just not fucking enough."

She shuddered against him, holding him tighter, and she could not see the tears in his own eyes as he thought of Esah-Zhurah. He had never stopped thinking of her. Never. The pain was not so great as it once was, but it ebbed and flowed like the tide.

After a while, her sobbing eased, then stopped. Her arms loosened slightly from around his chest, but only a little. "I doubt I'll be lucky enough to grow old, Reza," she whispered, "but if I get that chance, I don't want to grow old alone."

"Jodi," he told her, "the loneliness you fear is what has filled my heart since I left the Empire... since I left behind the woman who owns my heart. The only things that have sustained me since then have been my memories of her and the friendship I have been shown, by you more than any other. You are right when you say that it is not enough, to just be friends when your heart cries out for something more. But sometimes it has to be enough. Fate is neither kind nor fair; it simply is. But no matter what happens, remember that I will always be there for you. No matter how many stars apart we may be, I will always be there..."

* * *

Tony Braddock did everything he could to resist the urge to pace back and forth before the altar. The patient beauty of the chapel that had been the gleaming centerpiece of the otherwise bland Ridgeway Military Reservation was in stark contrast to the anxiousness he felt. The chapel had stood on this spot for over four hundred years, silent witness to countless baptisms, weddings, and funerals. But to Tony, waiting for the remaining members of his tiny wedding party to arrive so he could finally marry the woman he loved, the last forty minutes had seemed every bit as long as the chapel's four centuries.

"Where can they be?" he wondered aloud for what must have been the tenth time. He glanced yet again at his watch before looking out at the guests who now filled the many pews behind him. Neither he nor Nicole had many friends here, and they originally had wanted a small, private ceremony. But by the time they had invited their few real friends, Nicole's squadron-mates, and finally made the obligatory invitations to members of the Council – plus the spouses of all of the above – the chapel had been filled to capacity, with nearly five-hundred people in attendance.

Such an event, of course, also drew the attention of the media. Nicole's combat record, and her current score of nearly two hundred kills, was well known, and Tony was a member of the Council. While their wedding was not exactly considered the gala event of the year, there was a healthy interest in getting some shots of the bride and groom, plus any other notables who might pass before the lens. Besides, the editors had reasoned, there might always be the odd opportunity to gather a bit of smut in the process. In any event, two junior but competent reporters had been dispatched to take in the scene. One was from the Confederation Times, the other from the Navy Journal. They had already circulated amongst the guests for interviews and any tidbits they might pick up while people were still arriving. But right now the two were standing at the back (there was nowhere for them to sit), looking much like everyone else was at the moment: impatient.

Father Hernandez, too, looked around worriedly. While the people here seemed good-humored and were certainly willing to put up with certain inconveniences, there was always the question of how long was too long. Jodi was to be the maid of honor, and Reza was to play a dual role, giving away the bride as well as being Braddock's best man. As such, their absence constituted something of a problem.

He sighed heavily. "Well, I will see what your bride wishes to do," he said.

Braddock watched him disappear through one of the doors that let onto the dais that held the altar, trying not to feel silly as he stood there alone, waiting.

"Jodi," he muttered under his breath, "I'm going to strangle you..."

Meanwhile, Hernandez bustled back to the room where Nicole had been getting ready. Knocking on the door, he called, "Nicole. They have not yet arrived. What do you want to... do...?"

At that moment she opened the door and stepped into the corridor. She wore a white wedding gown that made her look like a princess from a fairy tale. The porcelain skin of her face glowed beneath the veil she wore, and her eyes glittered like jewels, showing no concern, only joyful anticipation.

"They are coming now, Father," she told him. She could always tell when Reza was near, always knew how he felt. "Trust me," she said after he gave her a look of acute disbelief.

"Now, child," he began, "I know you're nervous on this magnificent day, but you should not let your imagination–"

A door swinging open at the end of the hall, followed by the sound of running footsteps, interrupted him.

"Oh, Jesus – oh, shit, sorry, didn't mean to say that, Father – Reza's shuttle was late and we..." Jodi's explanation tapered off when she saw Nicole standing there next to the old priest. "Nicole," she breathed. "God, you look so beautiful."

"I only wonder if the good councilman will be able to properly appreciate such beauty," Reza said with a smile from behind Jodi. "It is good to see you again, Nicole."

They embraced, Nicole putting her arms around Reza's neck as he lifted her from the ground, holding her tightly against his chest.

"Reza," she breathed as she kissed his cheek, "I am so glad you could come. I knew you would."

"All the warriors of the Empire could not have kept me away," he told her. "I am so happy for you, Nicole. I only wish... that I had more time to be with you than we have had over the last few years." Almost unwillingly, he lightly set her down again. "But–"

"Do not speak of it, mon ami," she told him, putting a finger against his lips. "You are here now. That is all that is important. Nothing more."

Hernandez cleared his throat. "Nicole," he said, "I think perhaps that it is time to begin."

* * *

The music was not traditional; Nicole's concession to tradition had been her wedding gown. Nonetheless, the chapel's ancient pipe organ – bringing to life a composition by Jules de Clerc, from Nicole's native La Seyne – declared the occasion one of joy. Everyone was now standing, turned toward the rear of the chapel. The time they had spent waiting for this moment was forgotten as the moment of truth – and beauty – arrived. Tony Braddock stood nervously at the head of the maroon carpet that would guide his bride to him. Father Hernandez stood by the altar, his eyes beaming.

Jodi came down the aisle first, bravely holding back the tears that were at once a sign of joy and sorrow. Her dress whites sparkled in the sunlight admitted by the chapel's two-story high windows as her feet made a precise seventy-five centimeter stride toward the altar. She took her place just to the left of where Nicole was to stand. She smiled at Tony's happily anxious face, and the two of them waited for the bride to emerge.

The music changed tempo, slowing slightly, the major chords now as bright as the sun outside. As one, the guests turned toward the rear of the chapel, expectation plainly written on their faces.

Reza, his dress blues a vivid contrast to the regal white of Nicole's wedding gown, led her arm-in-arm down the aisle. He ignored the sudden murmuring of those who noticed the Kreelan collar he wore and the length of his hair; in fact, he ignored everyone except the woman who walked beside him and his friends standing at the altar. He rejoiced at the happiness he could feel in her heart and in Tony's, and the pride he felt in Father Hernandez's. Inside, though, he wept at the pain he felt in Jodi's heart, pain that was so much like that in his own. But on his face he wore the mask that he showed to the world when he did not wish to show the truth inside.

Nicole glanced over at him, a cloud of concern flashing across her face. She momentarily felt a pang of guilt at the pain she could sense deep inside him, a melancholy chord that ran through her blood. She felt as if she was abandoning him by marrying Tony. But she had offered herself to him long ago, she had wanted to love him, but he had gently turned her away. Their eyes met for a moment, and their minds linked for just that fraction of a second.

It is my Way, Reza's eyes told her. Yours is upon a different – I pray happier – path.

Is it indeed, my brother? her own eyes replied, echoing the doubt in her mind.

Reza turned away. Nicole wanted to hold him to her, to force him to look her in the eye once more, but the moment was gone and the altar now stood before them. What had gone unspoken was lost now forever, she understood sadly. She could feel the rhythm of his soul in her blood like faint sighs in the night, but she knew that from this moment on he would never open himself up to her as he once had, would never let her look into his eyes like that again. Not because he was jealous or angry about the vows she was about to take, but because he loved her, and did not want to endanger the happiness she might find with another, with the man she was about to marry.

"I love you, Reza," she whispered.

Reza stood in silence beside her as the music drew to a close; they had reached the end of their journey to the altar.

"Good people," Father Hernandez said, standing before them, "let us pray." Among the guests heads lowered and eyes closed. Reza, respectful of but untouched by Hernandez's God, silently studied the figure of Christ hanging from the cross upon the wall over the altar as Hernandez offered a prayer to Him:

"Holy Father, we have come together this day to seek Thy blessing for this couple who would be married in Your house, with Your love. Father, dark are the times in which we find ourselves. The demons run rampant upon the field of stars that shine in the night sky. But we ask Thee to smile upon these two who stand before You now, to protect them and let their love grow in your heavenly light for all the days of their lives. In Jesus' holy name we pray, amen."

"Amen," echoed the gathering.

"Please, be seated." Hernandez waited until they had settled themselves in the pews before he continued. "Brothers and sisters, we are gathered this day to witness the ceremony that, among my priestly duties, has without exception been my favorite to administer. To unite two hearts, two souls, in the eyes of God is like presiding over a new creation in His Universe, playing a hand in the birth of something unique and wonderful.

"In the case of the man and woman who today have come forward to declare their love for one another through the bond of marriage, I must say that I am especially pleased. I have known Nicole Carré and Tony Braddock for years, not as warriors and servants of the Confederation, but as friends. And it is now with great gladness that I would ask them to step forward to take their vows before the Almighty."

With a nod, Reza released Nicole's arm, and she stepped forward to where Tony stood waiting. They turned toward each other, shyly, like children about to experience their first kiss, and Tony carefully lifted her veil and smiled at her lovely face. Together, they turned toward the elderly priest.

Reza took a place two paces to Tony's right, mirroring where Jodi stood next to Nicole. He met Jodi's eyes briefly, and they both tried to smile, but it was all either could do to hold back their tears: Jodi for what she was about to lose forever, and Reza for all he had lost long since.

"Anthony, with the Lord as your witness and the love of Christ in your heart, do you take this woman, Nicole Carré, to be your wife, to love her and nurture her, to entwine your soul unto hers, to become one with her for all Eternity?"

"Yes," Tony said, his voice carrying through the chapel like a bell, "I do."

"Do you offer this woman a token of your love, Anthony, and of your devotion to the vows you take this day?"

"A ring, Father," Anthony said. He turned to Reza, who deftly placed a wedding band in his hand. But it was no ordinary ring, and this was the first time that anyone but Reza had seen it: it was made not of gold or silver, but Kreelan metal that Reza had fashioned for her. Sparkling like diamond but far stronger, it bore an intricate pattern that he had managed to fashion in the short time he had to work on it before leaving for Earth. The design was based on what Pan'ne-Sharakh had created for Esah-Zhurah's tiara many years before; it was Reza's homage to his old mentor, and to his love.

"Reza," Tony gasped, "it's beautiful." He had a backup ring in his pocket that he would have used had Reza not made it to the wedding, but it could never compare to what he now held in his hand. The ring Reza had fashioned glittered and shone as if it were alive; and, in a way no human would ever understand, it was.

Reza only nodded, gratified at how wide Nicole's eyes got when she saw it, sensing the surge of joy in her heart.

Smiling, Tony passed the ring to Father Hernandez, who held it in one of his age-spotted hands as if this, made of the strongest substance known, was but a fragile flower.

"And you, Nicole Carré," Hernandez continued, "with the Lord as your witness and the love of Christ in your heart, do you take this man, Anthony Braddock, to be your husband, to love him and nurture him, to entwine your soul unto his for all Eternity?"

"I do," she answered softly, her voice nearly gone from nervous anticipation.

"And do you offer him a token of your love, and of your devotion to the vows you take this day, Nicole?"

"Yes, Father, a ring," she said, turning to Jodi and holding out her hand.

Jodi felt her face go slack. The ring! What did she do with it? Where could it–

She suddenly sighed with relief as she felt a small object pressing against her left breast. She had put it in the inside uniform pocket over her heart. With an embarrassed grin, she reached into her coat – after undoing two of the buttons – and got the ring for Nicole, who only smiled and shook her head. "I love you," she mouthed silently.

She had no idea how those tacit words pierced Jodi's heart.

Hernandez took the ring – a plain but thick gold band – and held both rings up so the well-wishers could see them. "The ring," he said, his voice filled with wonder, as if this were the first time he had ever uttered these words, "is a symbol of life, without beginning, without end. It is a symbol of perfection to which we may aspire in our love for one another, and all the more so between husband and wife. It is a covenant of love between you; shall it never be broken or cast aside." He handed the Kreelan metal ring back to Tony, the gold one back to Nicole, and they placed them on each other's wedding finger, and remained holding hands.

Hernandez looked out upon the audience, his eyes beaming, yet perhaps with a trace of fire. "Is there one among you who would come forth to speak against this marriage, that it is unjust in the eyes of God?"

Jodi felt a sudden mad urge to scream, to shout, "Yes! Yes, damn you! I don't want her to marry him!" But she held her tongue and smiled, and after a moment the giddy feeling passed.

Hernandez nodded, pleased. It rarely happened, but there had been times when objections were raised, and of course that had upset the course of the ceremonies in question.

"Very well, then," he said. "May this union as witnessed by God and Man never be broken." He looked down at Tony and Nicole, spreading his arms wide as if to catch the drops from a spring rain. "I now pronounce you husband and wife." With a huge grin on his face, he leaned toward Tony. "Well, what are you waiting for, young man? Kiss the bride!"

The two of them embraced and kissed as if they were auditioning for a movie love scene, and the onlookers – even the two jaded reporters – whistled and cheered their approval...

* * *

Jodi was not sure how many hours might have passed since the end of the reception, since the new Mrs. Nicole Braddock had been whisked away with her adoring husband in a sky-limo to a week-long honeymoon on the beaches of the old French Riviera. Actually, now that she tried to think about it, the only thing Jodi was really sure of was that she was totally, utterly drunk.

"Drunk right off my little black ass," she chuckled humorlessly to herself as she took another swallow from the half-empty bottle of champagne. Two empties already lay on the floor beside her like spent lovers. Which, she supposed in the hazy realm that had become her thoughts, was probably about as close as she was going to get to true love. "Too bad they don't make 'em with batteries." She laughed at the thought until she cried, but there were no more tears to be shed. Her body had none left to give.

Jodi couldn't recall much about what happened after the wedding, even when she really tried to. Nicole had been happy, smiling and chatty as a teenage girl after being asked to the prom by the school hunk, which was totally out of character for her. She was so happy. And Jodi had found herself drifting away to the far side of the room, trying to keep her pecker up, as they say, but also trying to shield the world from the fountain of jealousy that had sprung up within her. And that, of course, had only made her feel worse, because she loved Nicole and she adored Braddock. When the two of them had left the reception, Jodi knew that Nicole had been looking for her to say good-bye. But Jodi had hidden herself away in one of the hotel's anterooms until Nicole and Braddock had finally had to leave. Jodi simply couldn't bear to talk to Nicole just then, because she knew that she would do something, say something, that she would regret for the rest of her life. So she had made herself disappear. She had chickened out on her best friend in her hour of glory.

But not Reza, she remembered with sudden clarity. No, not poor Reza. She knew that he was trapped in his own little hell, letting himself be ripped apart by memories of whatever life he had known before, thoughts of the woman and the love he himself had left behind somewhere in the Empire. But he had let none of it show. No, not him. Not the Kreelan warrior priest trapped in flesh that was all too human. Jodi was sure he must have ground his teeth to nubs in his effort to mirror the happiness of his friends, dutifully playing out the role he had drawn in this particular play. He had even treated the two curious reporters with something like respect as they barraged him – this strange Marine who wore a Kreelan collar and had long braided hair – with questions, hoping to find some kind of interest angle in an otherwise smut-free VIP wedding.

No, she thought ruefully, Reza had been a pillar, while she had melted and flowed like sullen lead. At least he had been until Nicole and Tony departed and he had been left alone in a crowd of strangers, mingling like oil in water until the revelers headed home or to another stop on their party venue.

It was after they had all gone that Jodi had finally returned from her coward's hideaway. She found Reza sitting alone in a corner of the great reception hall, with no company other than the cleaning bots that were disposing of the evening's detritus. He was clutching a mug – no doubt filled with that evil brew he sometimes concocted – in his hands, and was staring silently into some other time, some other place. His face, which had never seemed to age since the first time she had seen him in Hernandez's musty room in the church on Rutan, was now drawn, haggard. It seemed that he had aged fifty years in the course of an evening. His strong shoulders were rounded, as if he had been whipped, beaten into submission. Defeated.

He must have known that she was standing there, watching him, but he did not acknowledge her presence any more than he did the cleaning bots. Jodi was just about to walk over to him, to try to say something, anything, when he absently set the mug down and then staggered out of the hall. Jodi could not believe her eyes: Reza was drunk, or at least he acted like it.

After that, she surmised wearily, she must have gathered up some bottles of booze from a nearby table and wandered back here to her room. Fortunately, she and Reza were in the same hotel where the reception had been, so at least she had not had to publicly embarrass herself by finding some form of public transportation. Her private disgrace was quite enough, thank you very much.

She took another deep swallow, spilling champagne down her uniform, trying to make it all go away, trying to drown out reality. But her conscience was nagging at her enough now that the alcohol was no longer providing the yearned-for numbing effect. It just tasted bitter.

She slammed the bottle down in frustration, ignoring the fountain of foam that suddenly spouted from it like a gleeful ejaculation. She turned to the comm panel and ordered the ever-patient computer to connect her with Reza's room.

"One moment, please, madam," responded a pleasant automated female voice.

"Hurry the fuck up," Jodi grated, not knowing how much longer her courage might last.

"There is no answer, madam," the computer finally replied.

"Is Reza Gard in his room?"

"The room is currently occupied," the machine answered, refusing to give out any other information on who might be there.

"Try again."

"One moment..." There was a longer pause this time. Jodi figured the computer must have been programmed to try and accommodate idiots like her by trying longer the second time. Jodi wasn't going to bother with a third. "There is no answer, madam. Would you like to leave a message?"

Jodi didn't bother answering. She was already halfway to the door, a full bottle in hand.

She hadn't bothered to check the time, partly because she wouldn't have cared, and partly because she was too drunk to think of such a thing. But she was happy that it was late enough for the hallways to be empty. She knew she must look like hell – her uniform jacket gaping open, champagne spilled all over her blouse, her hair going wild – but she couldn't have cared less. In fact, had she encountered someone who would have made so much as goo-goo eyes at her, she probably would have tried to whack them over the head with the bottle that she was working on even as she shuffle-staggered toward Reza's room. They were on the same level, but in different towers, and it took her a while to realize that she had already passed his room twice.

"Christ, Mackenzie, you couldn't find your ass with both hands and a compass," she muttered to herself as she finally reached his room, number 1289. She pounded on the door, eschewing the more polite method of using the call panel. "Reza!" she shouted, heedless of the people in four adjacent rooms whom she had just succeeded in waking up. "I know you're in there! Open this fucking door!"

She waited. Nothing. She was about to pound on the door again, when a sudden flash of inspiration brightened her alcohol-shrouded mind. She pressed her hand against the access panel, hoping that Reza had keyed her into his room's access list.

Apparently, he had. The door hissed open to reveal nothing but darkness. Jodi staggered inside just as someone two rooms down poked his head out into the hallway to see what the fuss was about. The door whispered closed behind her.

She stood there a moment, leaning against the wall of the foyer, fighting against the sudden sense of vertigo that was a gift of the alcohol coursing through her system and the total darkness of Reza's room.

No, she thought, it wasn't totally dark. Toward the far side, through the ridiculously large – at least, it seemed that way to someone used to a warship's spartan accommodations – living room suite, she could see some faint points of light: stars in the sky, showing through the sliding clearsteel door that led onto the balcony outside.

"Reza?" she called. No answer. The room was totally, almost unnaturally, quiet. "Reza, are you here? Answer me, dammit!" She groped forward in the darkness, not thinking to turn on a light. The silence in the room was unnerving, and she felt little pricks of fear along her spine. It didn't feel as if no one was here, she thought. She just wasn't sure who was, and suddenly she thought that she had made a bad move by coming here.

Her shin suddenly came in contact with something very hard-edged and quite unyielding, and she let out a yelp of pain that she was sure had somehow given her away, as if her earlier shouting had not.

She was just about to turn around and bolt for the door when, out of the corner of her eye, she saw him. At least, she thought it was him: a dark figure kneeling in the middle of the expansive balcony. He was in his Kreelan armor, its black surface mirroring the stars in the sky above. But his head was not turned toward the stars; it was bowed as if in prayer.

"Reza," she said quietly as she stepped onto the balcony, ignoring the throbbing pain in her shin where she'd hit the coffee table, "are you okay?" She still felt a tingle of fear, and she now knew why: the Reza she was looking at was a Kreelan warrior priest, not merely a captain in the Confederation Marine Corps. That is why she had felt so strange just a moment ago. Something inside her had known that he had let slip his human mask.

She shook the feeling off, trying to concentrate as she knelt beside him. "Honey, what's wrong?" she whispered, tentatively reaching out to touch his arm. It was so hot that it was painful to her touch.

"I... I cannot go on," Reza rasped through gritted teeth. "The pain, Jodi... I thought I had banished it forever with Nicole's help, but the pain has returned. My blood is fire, my heart an angry wound, for I cannot clear the memory of my love's face from my mind. I would rejoice for Nicole's happiness, but it has brought back too many memories. Molten steel sears my veins... it is too much."

It was then that she saw the knife that he held with both hands. It was the weapon he was most fond of, a beautiful but deadly dagger that she had never known him to let out of his sight.

"So what are you going to do?" she asked bluntly. "Just kill yourself and be done with everything? Is that how Kreelan warrior priests get out of tough spots – just ram a knife through their throats?"

Reza turned to glare at her, and without the booze she might have wilted under such a withering assault from his swirling green eyes, but not now. Not tonight.

"Let me tell you something, tough guy," she went on, moving closer to him, their noses only a hand's breadth apart, "you don't have a monopoly on heartache. How do you think I feel after watching the only person I've ever really loved marry a good friend? And how do you think I feel about being jealous as hell of him, so jealous that I couldn't even bring myself to say goodbye to either of them before they left for their honeymoon? And I was her maid of honor! What a fucking joke that is!" She tried to laugh, but strangled on a sob as she reached out and grabbed him by the shoulders, ignoring the heat that burned its way into her palms from the metal armor and his searing flesh beneath. "So I don't want to be hearing any of this shit about how your heart is tearing itself to pieces, Reza, because mine is, too, and I need you now, damn you, I need you so much, you're all I've got left. You promised me you'd be there when I needed you, Reza. You promised me, dammit! Don't you leave me, too. Don't you dare…"

Then she reached for him, wrapping her arms around his neck as if she were drowning, just as she had when he had pulled her from the river on Rutan so many years ago, and he was honor-bound to save her. Careful not to tear her clothing or skin with the talons on his gauntlets, he drew her to him, shielding her with his arms as he commanded his body to cool while fighting a savage battle with the loneliness that burned in his blood. The knife he laid carefully beside him. He still longed for its cold metal touch, for the release from the hell that his existence had once again become. He was so happy for Nicole and Tony, but what he felt reminded him too much of his life with Esah-Zhurah, as if he had been forced to relive it. And with those thoughts, those feelings, once again had come the burning agony of loss that was as powerful as when he had first left the Empire.

Silently, he cradled Jodi in his arms as she cried, doing his best to isolate himself from the past, closing off the universe beyond this woman, his friend, to whom he owed a debt of love.

Jodi didn't realize that she had fallen asleep until she noticed that she no longer felt the hot steel of Reza's armor pressing against her. Instead, her body was nestled against something warm and firm, but made of flesh, not metal.

She opened her eyes to find herself still out on the balcony with him, but he had taken off his armor and gathered her up to lay beside him in a padded chaise built for two. He had one arm wrapped around her, holding her to him, with her head resting on his powerful shoulder. The night air was warm enough that she didn't need a blanket, Reza's body providing all the warmth she needed. Above her, the stars still shone, and she guessed – hoped – that only a little time had passed, and that the night had not yet begun to wane toward morning.

"Reza," she whispered, "are you awake?"

"Yes," he replied, instinctively holding her just a bit tighter. "I have not yet found... sleep."

Peace, she thought he meant. He had not found the peace he was looking for, and probably never would. Just like her. A thought, quite alien to her way of thinking, began to uncoil in the back of her mind, stretching like an awakening lion. She reached out and touched Reza's face, much as he had done to her on the day that he had first appeared before her like an unholy apparition in Father Hernandez's rectory. How lonely he had been then; how lonely they both were now. "Tell me about her," she said, gently turning his face toward hers, "tell me about the woman you love."

Reza hesitated, but only for a moment. What does it matter? he told himself through the red haze that had settled over his mind like the acrid smoke that is all that is left after a fierce battle, one that leaves no one alive, no victors, only the vanquished. Telling her of his love was certainly no betrayal to the Empire. And, perhaps – just perhaps – sharing his pain with her might in some way help rejuvenate the emotional shield that Nicole's blood in his veins had provided him over the years, that now had failed him in the face of an onslaught of memories that he could not control.

"Her name," he said, forcing his tongue to work within the numbed orifice his mouth had become, "is Esah-Zhurah..."

Jodi listened intently as Reza wove the tale that had been his life with an alien woman whom he had once hated, yet had finally come to love with all his heart.

He and I have so much in common, she thought in the depths of her mind. There is so much in common between us, and yet so little in common with those around us. She realized then that she wanted Reza to heal her, just as she wanted to heal him. She wanted the pain to be gone, if only for a moment, for both of them.

In that moment she did something that she never thought she would do: she kissed a man. Not as a friend, or as a stunt, but with passion, with desire. She thought she could only want a woman, but Reza was so different from all the other men she had ever known, and that difference somehow made it seem right to her. She pressed her lips to his as she pulled him against her, wrapping her arms around his neck, entwining her fingers in the braids of his hair.

"Jodi," Reza rasped as he tried to pull himself away, "I cannot..."

"I don't want to have to explain this to you, dammit," she sighed as she again pulled him to her, harder than before. "I need an escape, Reza, and you're it. Just pretend... pretend that I'm Esah-Zhurah. I don't want you to fall in love with me. I just want you to hold me, to be... a part of me for a while. To take the pain away. And let me do the same for you. Just for a little while..."

Reza suddenly shuddered against her, as if he were fighting off a terrible fever.

But then she sensed a change in him, perhaps a kind of acceptance of what was, what he wished could be. Their lips met again, but this time it was Reza who kissed her. Her body tingled as she felt his powerful hands touch her, tentatively at first, but then with growing confidence as they sought out the catches to her clothing.

Jodi sat up to help him, straddling his waist as she did so, and she could feel the heat rapidly building within her as she took off her uniform, throwing it carelessly aside. Her heart began to race and she bit back a sigh as Reza's hands tenderly cupped her now-exposed breasts. She fought to pin him down, wanting to tear away the black Kreelan clothing from his body so she could feel his skin against hers, but her efforts had no more effect on Reza than if she had been trying to restrain a volcano. She gave up completely the instant that Reza's mouth closed over one of her nipples, and she cried out in surprise and delight as an orgasm unexpectedly swept through her like a rogue wave upon the ocean, coming from out of nowhere and carrying her away. My God, she thought, just before her body went into convulsions of delight, he didn't even have to touch me anywhere else...

Reza felt his lover climax, and sensed his own body soaring toward those heights as the woman he held – he knew it was Jodi, but in his mind, behind his closed eyes, he could only see and feel Esah-Zhurah – finished her own pleasure and had set about bringing him his. He felt her unsure but eager hands at work upon his manhood, stroking him, teasing him into involuntary sighs of pleasure. And then... and then he was inside her. In no time he felt himself tearing upward through the sky as his body suddenly melted away, dissolving in a geyser of passion that had come to claim him from the hard bitterness of reality.

Later, Jodi smiled at Reza's sleeping form. Pulling up a blanket she had retrieved from inside to cover their nakedness, she thought that things had worked out just fine. Her eyelids grew unbearably heavy as she snuggled next to him, her head on his shoulder, and her last thought before sleep took her was echoed by her lips.

"Thank you..."

* * *

She awoke to the sun and a gentle morning breeze. She stretched her body, remembering the night before with a sharp but pleasant tingling between her legs. She suddenly wondered if Reza was up to another bout of lovemaking.

But that hope evaporated as soon as she opened her eyes. Reza was no longer next to her, and she knew that he would not be found in the suite behind her, either. His shuttle wasn't due to leave until around noon, but she knew instinctively that he was gone.

That, however, was a disappointment she was prepared to deal with. Last night they had given each other something that both had desperately needed. It was something she could always feel good about, could always look back on to help warm her heart.

With a sigh of resignation, she rolled over, and was confronted with something she had not expected. A single red rose, the most perfect and beautiful she had ever seen, waited for her upon a small stand that Reza must have placed next to the chaise that had been their bed last night. Gingerly, careful to avoid the thorns, Jodi picked up the rose and smelled its fragrance.

"Be careful, Reza," she whispered to the sun that was yet rising over the city. "And remember that I'll always be there for you."

* * *

Hernandez was waiting for him in the transit lounge, as Reza knew he would be. He felt a pang of guilt at not having spent as much time with the old priest as he would have liked, but the same could be said for all of his few other human friends, save Eustus, who served beside him. There had never really been enough time for friends in this age of war, and he knew there never would be, least of all for a warrior like himself. "Peace" as humanity fought and died for was a concept as alien to him as was the blue skin of the Kreela to them. And in that, he thought, perhaps they had found a higher purpose than he himself could ever aspire to, for the Kreela fought only to bring glory to Her, while the humans fought for their future, and the future of their young. It was a novel concept, but clearly one that he did not fully appreciate.

Father Hernandez, still as animated as ever, was nonetheless losing his battle with age. He rose unsteadily to his feet with the help of a walking staff – he had steadfastly refused anything so elegant as a cane, and certainly would not accept any "modern medical hocus-pocus" – and made his way from the chair where he had been waiting.

"Greetings, my son," he said warmly as he grasped Reza's outstretched hand with fingers that could yet make one's knuckles pop.

"Hello, Father," Reza replied, trying to ignore the sudden resemblance in spirit between this man and Pan'ne-Sharakh, now long dead, but not forgotten to Reza's heart. "You did not have to come to see me off. It is much too early in the day for such a late sleeper to be roaming about."

Hernandez scoffed at Reza's light humor. Both of them knew full well that Hernandez had risen before the sun every day of his life, on Rutan or any other of the several worlds he had visited since leaving his old parish, no matter how many or how few hours were in their days. "Well, young man, I had to make sure that someone would be here to get you on the proper shuttle. The Lord indeed knows that even Marines need a shepherd, and most especially you!"

"Indeed you are right, Father," Reza told him with a smile. In the background he heard the sterile female voice of the starport announcing that his flight would be boarding in five minutes.

Hernandez scowled at the voice. "She sounds like my mother," he muttered. Then he turned again to Reza, seriously now. "You won't be seeing me again, you know. I'm an old, old man, and by the time you get back from your next adventure, wherever it may be, I fear I shall be long gone."

"Father–"

Hernandez held up his hand, cutting Reza off. "You know it is true, Reza, and that is the way of things; it is how things should be. And, believe me, after seeing the likes of this world, I cannot but yearn for the next.

"And that brings me to you, young man. While I haven't learned everything about you that I would have liked, I do know that you are troubled spiritually, and even if you had never given me a clue in words, I could tell from your eyes. You offer the world around you the eyes of a hunter, Reza, but I see something deeper: I see fear. Not fear of anything living or dead, and not even fear of Death itself; you are afraid of what comes after, of what becomes of your soul when your body turns to dust."

From the suddenly haunted look on Reza's face, Hernandez knew he had been right.

I only wish that I had had more time with this one, he complained to his God. Over the years they had never really had a chance just to sit down and talk, and for the most inane of reasons, it seemed to Hernandez now. But he could not turn back the clock, and his own time among the living was swiftly winding down. No matter, he thought, I will make do with what is given me.

"Reza, tell me. Let me help you reach for what lies beyond that threshold. If you are willing to open your eyes and your heart, Salvation awaits you."

"Father, I have studied your God, and the gods of many other religions. But salvation for me lies with none of them, for I am merely a part – painfully separated – of a greater being, the Kreela. Perhaps the Empress answers to your God, for in truth I do not know if I consider Her to be 'the Creator,' as you believe of your God. All I know is that Her blood is in my veins, and for a short time I could hear Her voice, and the voices of the billions of Her Children, singing in my blood, in my heart. We were one as I never was before, and have never been since. She commands the living and the dead of Her people, Father – all who have ever lived and died with Her blood in their veins."

That, indeed, was a revelation to Hernandez, but he had no time to contemplate its meaning. Behind him, the cool female voice announced, "Shuttle APX-954, now boarding for transit to C.S.S. Hera. All passengers are to report to Gate 73B..."

Reza gathered his flight bag and a smaller one that contained gifts – souvenirs and chocolates – for Eustus and his troops.

Time! Hernandez cursed. Would you not give me just a few precious minutes, Lord? No, of course you wouldn't!

"Reza," he said hurriedly, stepping closer and dropping his voice slightly so as not to be overheard by the passengers streaming by toward the gate, "in my profound ignorance, I once accused you of being the Antichrist, of being Satan's instrument. I know that I was terribly wrong, but now I must wonder if you are perhaps the opposite. Many think of angels – even Christ Himself – as being always kind and peaceful, menacing toward none. But that is not really true. Some of the angels are warriors, Reza, and the Prince of Peace has powers of destruction that defy imagination." He looked Reza in the eye, knowing this would be the last chance he would have in this life to try and understand this miracle/curse that had changed his simple existence forever. "What are you, Reza? What are you really?"

"I am no angel, Father, nor am I your Messiah. If anything... if anything, you may think of me as Adam without his Eve, cast out of the Garden with no hope of ever returning." Reza smiled the best he could and extended a hand to Hernandez. "Take care, Father," he said, "and may your God smile upon your soul."

Hernandez watched him as he left, swallowed up in the slogging torrent of military and civilians who were still crowding onto the shuttle. "Goodbye, my son," he said sadly. "You shall always be in my prayers."

He stood there, alone, and waited until the shuttle lifted its squat bulk into the sky. As its contrail finally disappeared from the sky, it struck him that perhaps Reza's words were truer than the young man had himself believed.

"An Adam without his Eve," Hernandez muttered as he shuffled toward the far distant exit to the terminal. He stopped then, turning his attention again toward the sky and the invisible stars beyond. "Or the prodigal son who is yet to return home?"

TWELVE

Over a year after Nicole's wedding, Reza found himself in a predicament whose resolution eluded him, and he did not have either Nicole or Jodi from whom he could draw strength. In what Reza considered a wretched twist of fate, his company, reinforced with a battery of artillery and a tank platoon, had been ordered to Erlang on a "civil unrest" mission. His job was to ensure that the flow of metals and minerals from the planet's mines to Confederation shipyards continued uninterrupted. He had been briefed that the two major political and demographic factions on the planet had been having troubles getting along for the last few years, but recently tensions had risen sufficiently to arouse Confederation concerns, enough to sponsor the mission Reza found himself stuck with. Since it was an undesirable duty and the Red Legion happened to be in that area of the Rim, it was assigned to them. And, since "shit rolls downhill," as Eustus was so fond of saying, Reza's company got the job.

Civil unrest, Reza thought acidly, a growl escaping his throat. No one had bothered to tell him that the planet was about to erupt into open civil war, with him and his Marines trapped in the middle. On one side there was the Ranier Alliance; on the other, the Mallory Party. Both seemed very similar at first glance, but as with many things human, it was the underlying details that led to disagreement, bitterness, and – eventually – bloodshed.

From what Reza had been able to piece together from the wildly diverging accounts of the colony's existence that he had extracted from the library database, a colonizing expedition led by one Ian Mallory had landed on Erlang nearly two hundred years ago. The colonists numbered over fifty thousand men, women, and children from the Grange Cloud asteroids. They had decided to risk all they had for the prospect of something better and had pooled their money to buy an outdated ore hauler from a bankrupt Grange mining firm. They refitted it themselves for the seven-month voyage that would take them to the Promised Land. Reza was not an expert in the art of starship construction, but he had to marvel at the courage of these people, that they had traveled so far in what was no more than a hulk awaiting the breaker's torch.

But they paid a steep price for their dream. The old ship's engines were not as reliable as the colonists had hoped, and by the time they finally made planetfall over a year after they left the Grange, nearly five thousand of them had died of starvation and disease.

Abandoning the ship in a stable orbit from which it later could be tapped for raw materials and its few remaining supplies, the colonists descended into their Eden in the landing barges they had brought for the purpose. Miraculously, all but one landed safely.

Unlike so many similar expeditions, which often suffered countless hardships only to meet with ultimate disappointment and, in many cases, death, the Mallory expedition had truly found the Garden of Eden. A sister to what Earth must have been in the age before homo sapiens, their new home – Erlang – was a priceless and beautiful gem of blue skies and green valleys, of towering mountains and seas teeming with life. Despite the losses of their loved ones and the nightmare of the long voyage, the Mallorys had found their dream, and over the years their colony grew and prospered.

Some three hundred years later, the Raniers arrived. Unlike the Mallorys, Therese Ranier and her fifteen-thousand followers were upper-class descendants of the shipbuilders of Tulanya who had decided to emigrate to a newly-discovered world, even farther-flung from the human-settled core worlds than Erlang had been.

Unfortunately, their ship, despite being generations newer and designed from the outset to transport a colony expedition, had an engine mishap that fortuitously left no permanent casualties in its wake other than its primary stardrives. By no small miracle, they happened to be close enough to Erlang's system to make it there in a few months on their auxiliary drives. Had the stardrives failed much before or after they did, Ranier and her group surely would have perished in the vast wasteland of space that separated Erlang and her closest neighbors, for there would have been no ships nearby to heed their distress calls.

The arrival of the Ranier ship signaled a change in the peaceful agrarian life of Erlang's inhabitants. It did not take the newly arrived minority long to determine that the Erlangers – the Mallorys, as they eventually came to be called – knew and cared little for the capitalistic concepts in which the Ranier group had been raised and took for granted. When they came, the Raniers found little more than a barter economy, with virtually nothing in the way of industry except for textiles and the manufacture of basic farming implements. And while they deeply appreciated the Mallorys' open invitation to make Erlang their home, the new arrivals knew that they had not invested so much and traveled so far simply to work the land like the simple peasants they took the Mallorys for. Regardless, their decision, after a suitably short debate, was unanimous: they would stay. Of course, with their ship disabled they had no other choice at the time, but Erlang offered too much profit potential for them to pass up.

Over the next century or so, the two groups worked to mold Erlang into the vision of what each thought it should be. Unfortunately, their visions and plans for their bountiful world soon diverged. The Mallorys were content to live with what they had, celebrating the anniversary of their landing each year with a feast and the knowledge that they had been saved through divine grace, no matter which divinity one chose to believe in. They were farmers and hunters, whose only profit was for their children to grow up strong and well on a world that would provide for all their needs for as long as any of them could imagine.

The Raniers, on the other hand, saw the enormous potential of Erlang as an economic power in this far-flung sector of space, and soon saw the Mallorys as a key ingredient in their budding plan for exploiting the planet. It did not take long for the newcomers to begin opening shops and businesses, to establish the roots of a real economy in the various Mallory settlements. And in but a few years, the Raniers had discovered the minerals that they knew would someday make them rich. It was hardly surprising that most of the backbreaking labor was later to be undertaken by Mallory hands.

Many years had since passed, and the dreams of Therese Ranier had come true in more ways than she could have imagined had she stood among her people today. With the first visits by enterprising merchant ships, Erlang quickly became the leader of a loose economic coalition of rim worlds. Her mineral wealth had put her very close to the top of the list as a resource for everything from gold and diamonds to the many ingredients that went into constructing starships, starships that soon came to visit the planet with reassuring regularity, despite Erlang's remote location. And those families who had invested in this vision of the future – virtually all Raniers – had grown rich beyond the wildest dreams of their predecessors.

But there was a darker side to Erlang's success. Only a hundred years after the Ranier ship had arrived, the way of life that had been cherished by the Mallorys was all but gone. The simple but effective system of barter and goodwill that had seen them through the many winters since their forebears arrived had been replaced by the specter of the bank and the company store. When once a person only had to turn to their neighbor for help or food, now they had to pay for it with money they often enough did not have; and if they did not, they had to find work from a Ranier, usually in the mines. At first, work in the mines, being paid for it, seemed like a good thing, a way to better their families' lives. After all, many of them had thought, did their forefathers themselves not make their way in the mines?

But they had forgotten the hardship and eventual abandonment by the owners of the mines that had forced their forebears to seek out Erlang in the first place.

Worse, the Mallorys quickly lost their political power in a new system that the Raniers had promised would give one person one vote. Unfortunately, they neglected to inform the Mallorys that the only votes that really counted would be from Raniers, who in later generations became classic practitioners of the Golden Rule: whoever has the gold makes the rules. This was an alien concept to the Mallorys as a group, as they had practiced the most basic kind of democracy since they landed on Erlang: anything that impacted on the whole colony was voted on by the whole colony, and on any part by those who stood to be affected. It was a tradition that had stood the test of time in many years of hard living.

But now most Mallorys lived in poverty, engaged in hard labor in the mines or cutting down their once pristine forests to make barges and ships to haul minerals to the Mallory spaceport. Exhausted from their daily fight to stay alive, they had lost the battle for civic equality, if not their pride. And their pride is what sustained them, along with a burning will to survive and overcome. It was the same strength that had carried their forefathers across light years from hopeless despair to find God's gift. And their sons and daughters vowed that they would someday reclaim what they somehow had lost.

Then, of course, the war with the Kreelans had come. While Erlang had never itself been attacked, the planet had nonetheless felt the impact of the war as the newly formed Confederation – of which Erlang had unanimously become a member – sought to tap the resources, human and material, of its constituent worlds. Erlang was not yet large enough to raise a combat regiment of its own, but the Confederation sponsored it with equipment to form a powerful Territorial Army and Coast Guard to protect its vital mineral wealth. Virtually all the Territorial Army personnel were drawn from Ranier families, a slight that the Mallorys fought to overlook in the best interests of their world. Then, fifty years later, the first regiment was raised for the Marine Corps for service on worlds that no Mallory and few Raniers had ever seen or heard of; the enlisted ranks were filled by the sons and daughters of Mallory families, the officers all drawn from Raniers. And so the Mallorys saw their children bleeding and dying under alien suns, but weren't trusted to serve in defense of the world that was their home.

It was the final insult, the spark that ignited their long-suppressed rage into open violence. A series of strikes and riots ensued that were quickly and savagely put down by the Ranier-controlled Territorial Army and police forces, and thereafter the Mallory townships had lived under virtual martial law.

The emergence of outright oppression, however, only fueled the determination of the Mallorys to overcome the domination of the Raniers. Mallory township elders and activists set about organizing themselves into a political underground that became known simply as the Mallory Party. The party was illegal in the Houses of Parliament that were dominated by the Raniers and puppet Mallory leaders who made up the Ranier Alliance. But the Mallory Party had gradually gained strength in numbers and weapons until its leaders felt they could force the Ranier Alliance to accept it as a viable political entity and return some sense of equality to Erlang. The Mallorys had hoped that the Confederation would assist them in their efforts to achieve political equity on their homeworld. But the Confederation government, preoccupied with an endless war and besieged with the pleas of worlds under attack, had little time to deal with what the Council saw as little more than petty political squabbling.

This, of course, did nothing to make the Mallorys – or the Raniers, for that matter – any more receptive to Reza's newly arrived Marines. As he always did before landing his people, Reza had made a reconnaissance of the spaceport where he had intended to land his troops. He found that it was encircled by two rings of people, each invisible to the other. On the inside were police and Territorial Army troops facing out toward the landing zone's electrified perimeter; on the outside, facing in, hundreds of people Reza could best describe as partisans lay in wait, as if planning an ambush for the incoming Confederation forces. Reza reached out his mind to them, and his initial observations were confirmed. Armed with hunting rifles and homemade bombs, the civilians hiding in the forest had every intention of attacking the spaceport in hopes of driving the Marines away before they could become established.

Reza was impressed by their courage. Even if there had been no Ranier troops between the waiting Mallorys and the incoming Marines, any battle would have been swiftly decided. There would have been many dead Mallorys, and his Marines would still have landed.

Realizing that the landing could not go as planned, Reza had decided to make a tactical landing on a ridge overlooking Mallory City and its spaceport, about five kilometers distant. The colony's president, who had sponsored a welcoming parade for the first Confederation Marines to visit

Erlang in nearly ten years, had not been happy about the unannounced change in plans.

"What in blazes are you doing, captain?" President Belisle's voice crackled over the comm link. "You are only cleared to land at the spaceport, not–"

"Forgive me, Mr. President," Reza cut him off quietly, "but I believe a more neutral location would serve my purposes better. I apologize for ruining your welcoming plans, but it cannot be helped. I will be in contact with you again as soon as we have completed our landing." He disconnected just as the president's reddening face contorted with a reply.

That had been two hours ago. He watched the holo tactical display that had been set up in a large room of an abandoned equipment building as his troops finished deploying into a defensive perimeter. Until Reza could sort out who their enemies were and who were their allies – if indeed there were any – he would trust no one. The landing boats and the carrier that had dropped them here had already left orbit and jumped into hyperspace. The Marines were on their own.

"We're ready, sir," Hawthorne reported from where he hovered over the company's command and control console, monitoring everyone's progress while Eustus walked the perimeter outside, making sure everything was being done right. "Everyone's in place, and the arty's sited behind the ridge." For this mission, they had received a battery of six multiple rocket launchers – MRLs – that Reza had targeted against the local Territorial Army garrison and the city's three aerospace defense sites. Just in case.

Hawthorne paused a moment, nodding to someone who was speaking into his headset. "Walken says he's ready when you are." First Lieutenant Rudi Walken commanded the mechanized detachment: one platoon of armored skimmers and one of tanks that Reza had been given from the regiment's armored battalion. Like the artillery, it was a choice luxury that filled Reza with suspicion. Such units were very precious, especially in the Red Legion, and were not allocated without a great deal of forethought by regimental command. While the detachment was small in size, there likely were few weapons on Erlang that could destroy the armored skimmers, and nothing that could touch Walken's five tanks.

"Very well," he said, grabbing his helmet and rifle. While officers were supposed to only carry sidearms, ostensibly to force them to lead the fight instead of acting as another rifleman, Reza carried both. Sometimes having an extra rifleman made the difference between victory and defeat. As always, the Empress's dagger clung to his waist, while the Desh-Ka short sword given him by Tesh-Dar lay sheathed at his back. "You have the con, captain."

"Aye, sir," Washington acknowledged. While the exchange was a Navy tradition, Reza had become fond of it and had adopted it for when he delegated his authority to one of his subordinates to take command of the company in his absence. "Good luck."

Reza frowned. He feared that they would need it. "Come with me, Zevon," he said as he passed the younger man, who stood at attention for his commander.

"Sir," he said, following at Reza's heels. In his left hand he carried the plastisteel case that contained the computer interface and the other materials he needed to keep the administration of the company together, as well as some more mundane items with which he took notes and drafted messages for his commander. In the other hand, he carried his rifle. While at any given time he was the company clerk, commander's adjutant, or one of a hundred other things as needed, he was a rifleman first and always.

Outside, Reza quickly surveyed his company's positions. As he knew it would be, all was in order. "Captain," Eustus said as he met Reza beside the armored skimmer that would carry him into the city, "be careful."

Reza suppressed a smile at his friend's words. Eustus had turned out to be what some of his troops had termed a perfect mother hen.

"We will be back before dusk," Reza said. Eustus nodded and stepped back as Reza and Zevon squirmed through the skimmer's hatch, Zevon closing it behind them.

"Rudi," Reza said through his helmet's comm link as he folded himself into one of the skimmer's seats, fighting the claustrophobic reaction he always suffered when he had to ride in armored vehicles, "it is time."

"Roger," Walken replied. The convoy was made up of the skimmer carrying Reza, Zevon, and a rifle squad, sandwiched between the two tanks of the tank platoon's light section. The other three tanks and seven skimmers would remain here with the company. Content that everything was in order, Walken spoke into his helmet microphone. "Convoy Alpha, this is Alpha One. Move out."

The heads of over two hundred Marines swiveled in unison to watch the little convoy depart. The air crackled and the ground shook as the two tanks lifted on their anti-gravity screens. Titans of surface warfare, each massed over two hundred tons and carried enough firepower to level a small city, with armor that protected them from all but the most horrendous weapons the enemy could bring to bear. A legacy of mankind's self destructive age, the modern tank had no equal in the armory of the Kreelans, and it was behemoths like these that had turned the tide in many a battle from disastrous defeat to life-preserving victory. Alas, their great power came only at an astronomical cost in labor and resources, and there were never enough of them to go around.

As the two turreted monsters began to move forward, the bottoms of their armored hulls borne a meter from the ground, the much lighter and more agile skimmer lifted and quickly took its place between its larger cousins, its thinner hide protected by their bulk and potential menace.

* * *

"They're coming down The Lane, now," Mallory City's mayor, the Honorable Crory Wittmann, said from the balcony as he watched the Marine vehicles thunder down the main thoroughfare of the city, which fortunately was wide enough for the tanks. People had poured out of buildings at the noise, thinking perhaps that an earthquake was in the making. Such was their surprise when they saw the house-sized shapes rumbling past their shops and apartments, the camouflaged flanks of the vehicles adorned with the seal of the Confederation followed by the word MARINES in tall black letters. "God, look at the size of those things!" he said excitedly, like a young boy seeing his first parade.

President Belisle glowered from his chair, his face a cherry red that reflected the anger still boiling inside him. What else could go wrong? he thought acidly to himself as he considered berating Wittmann for being such an impressionable imbecile. The Ranier Alliance was in trouble, big trouble, and people like Wittmann were too stupid to see it. First the Mallorys began to think they were equals instead of just the laborers they had always been, holding strikes and forming their own underground political party, as if any of the brutes understood what politics was really all about. Then the Territorial Army, which Belisle and his predecessors had gone to great lengths to maintain as a club to keep the Mallorys in their place in the mines, had begun to mutiny in the provinces after having to carry out a few jobs against the workers there. No bloody stomach for it, Belisle thought savagely, cursing the weaklings who had been in charge. A few summary executions had settled that issue – for the moment, at least – but Belisle and the Alliance were no longer content to rely on the Territorial Army outside of the colony's major population centers, including Mallory City.

He pursed his lips as if he had just sucked down a lemon. Mallory City. The name made him want to spit, but it had been a necessary compromise when it had been chosen. Bloody beggars.

All that was bad enough, he thought. But being snubbed by an arrogant Marine – a captain, no less! – was far, far too much. He was going to send good Senator Borge a very choice set of words as thanks for the support he had promised. The cargo ships that streamed through Erlang's ports to carry away their loads of metal and minerals for the Confederation must not be worth very much to the man and the Council if they could only spare a niggardly company of Marines to help keep the Mallorys at work. Taking into account the ships that carried away cargoes for personal consumption by certain political figures, the tiny contingent he had been apportioned made little sense, indeed. Belisle's face tightened, his mouth compressing to a thin line. The Marine captain was going to learn a lesson or two about how to deal with the sovereign leader of Erlang.

The Marine tanks took up station on opposite ends of the square in front of the parliament building. The skimmer pulled up to the steps of the Assembly Building in front of an assemblage of shocked legislators who had been awaiting the arrival of a ceremonial procession, not a tactical deployment.

Three stories below the balcony on which Wittmann stood, four heavily armed and armored Marines emerged from the skimmer and took up deceptively casual positions beside the vehicle, their weapons at port arms, their eyes in constant motion, alert for any sign of trouble. Reza and Zevon followed them out and silently returned the gaze of the speechless legislators until Reza finally spoke.

"Will you take me to President Belisle, please?" he asked a man in a dull gray woolen suit that passed for high fashion in Erlang's capital city. The man looked around for a moment, as if expecting someone to come to his aid. After no one made any sign of addressing the situation, he turned back to Reza.

"Er, this way... captain," he said, resigned to the fact that he had been charged with the irritant that had enraged the president, and Belisle was not known for his kindness toward bearers of bad news.

"Thank you," Reza said with as much courtesy as he could muster in what struck him as an intolerably arrogant atmosphere. He did not need his special senses to tell him this was the case. It was plainly written on their faces.

Leaving the rest of his escort with the skimmer, Reza and Zevon (who reluctantly left his rifle in their vehicle) followed their unwilling guide through the gawking crowd, whose mood had soured to the point of outright surliness. Zevon shot a deadly glance at someone who muttered something about his parentage. The man shut up and turned away.

After leading them upstairs, their unwilling guide paused at a set of enormous and outrageously ornate doors that looked entirely out of place in the building's modern architectural style of whites, grays, and blacks, of classic geometric shapes. Two nervous Territorial Army soldiers stood guard outside.

"The president is through these doors," their guide said curtly. "You will, of course, excuse me if I don't accompany you." As if afraid that he was going to be physically beaten for some unnamed transgression, the man quickly disappeared down the hall, leaving Alfonso and Reza looking at each other.

"Sir," Zevon announced quietly, "these people give me the creeps."

Reza's only comment was an arched eyebrow. "Let us meet the President of Erlang, then, shall we?"

Ignoring the two soldiers, Reza opened the massive door and entered the room beyond.

"Captain Gard, I presume," Belisle's voice boomed from behind his desk, situated in the middle of a room as large as some flight decks Reza had been on. Directly overhead was a crystal chandelier that must have weighed at least five hundred kilos and cost more than some colonies had in their vaults. The walls were adorned with shelves of books that climbed to the ceiling, which itself was glorified with a painting that appeared to depict the taming of Erlang's forests. "So nice of you to join us."

"Mr. President," Reza said formally, as he and Zevon crossed the two dozen paces to Belisle's desk. "I offer my apologies for spoiling your plans, but–"

"But?" Belisle interjected hotly. "But what? I should have you charged with reckless navigation and wanton destruction of government property, your Navy ships and Marine vehicles tearing up Helder Ridge. You were sent here to do what I want, what my government wants, and so far you aren't measuring up very well. You're supposed to keep the mines open, and keep those damned Mallorys at work!" The older man rose from his desk, his face redder than ever, his eyes narrowed into dark slits.

Wittmann, who had come over from the balcony with the intent of shaking Reza's hand in welcome, shrank back behind the one individual on Erlang who wielded very close to absolute power.

"I ask for a regiment and men to do the job," Belisle spat, "and what do I get? A stinking company of misfits!" He walked around the desk, coming face to face with Reza. The two men were about the same height, but Belisle was much paler from never having worked in the sun. His hair, gray from age, was full and perfect, perhaps too much so. His body was in good shape, although a far cry from Reza's near-perfect form. When Belisle opened his mouth again, Reza was assaulted by the strong smell of cognac. "Who the devil do you think you are, mister? Captain Gard, I have half a mind to strip you of your rank and take your men and equipment for the Territorial Army."

Reza's eyes narrowed. Beside him, Zevon could feel the sudden heat from Reza's body, and his hand lowered just enough that his palm touched the butt of the blaster that hung at his hip, his trusty rifle's temporary replacement. Without moving his head, his eyes scoured the room for any trace of treachery.

"To attempt such a thing would be most unwise, President Belisle," Reza said, his voice masking the sudden flames that had erupted in his blood. "As you well know, you have no direct authority over me or my Marines, and any attempt to do what you are suggesting would be met with the stiffest resistance. Further," he took a step closer to Belisle, until their noses almost touched, "you do not seem to understand my orders, sir. They are to ensure that the flow of material from Erlang is disturbed as little as possible. They do not say to oppress the Mallorys or support the Raniers. I have been given complete authority in how to proceed." One minor and ironic advantage of being in the Red Legion, Reza thought: unless at least an entire battalion was participating in an operation, subordinate commanders detailed to missions like this one were given a free hand in determining its outcome. It was only natural, since many officers and units did not survive the tasks assigned to them, anyway.

"Is that a threat, captain?" Belisle hissed.

"No, sir, it is a statement of fact. I wish to cooperate with you, but I will not be coerced or browbeaten. I am a Marine, my people are Marines, and we will not be used as a political tool by either you or the Mallorys."

Belisle laughed, a coarse bark belonging to a heartless predator. "Big talk for a man who only has a couple hundred people behind him," he sneered. His voice turned cold. "Let me tell you something, little man. I make the rules on this world, and people either play by them or they get hurt. Badly. The Mallorys would love to get their hooks into a bleeding heart do-gooder like you, but I'll warn you now against it. You were sent here to help me to keep the mines open, and that's what you're going to do."

"I believe we are agreed that keeping the mines open is the objective," Reza said, "but what if I do not 'play' by your rules to do that, Mr. President?"

Belisle smiled like a hyena. "Captain, at the snap of my fingers I could have ten-thousand troops on that mountain where your beloved Marines are, and they wouldn't be up there just to pick mushrooms. Your people wouldn't stand a chance."

Wittmann watched in wonder as a smile crept upon Reza's lips.

"The view from your office is truly magnificent, Mr. President," Reza said admiringly as he moved past Belisle and out onto the open balcony, a structure that extended a dozen meters to his left and right around the curved face of the building. His eyes scanned the view for a moment until he had found what he was looking for. "I see that your people have a fondness for history and remembrance," he said, gesturing toward a tall mountain directly to the east of the capital that bore the inscription in enormous numbers of the dates on which the Mallorys and Raniers arrived. Below the dates, carved into the mountain face years ago, was the first scar of what was to be a giant likeness of Belisle. Today, fortunately, no workers were there. "Perhaps you also have a fondness for the future."

"What's that supposed to mean?" Belisle growled. He did not hear Zevon whispering something into his helmet microphone, but Wittmann did. "Karl," he stuttered, using Belisle's first name, "they're going to–"

Whatever the mayor had intended to say was to go unsaid forever as the mountain face suddenly erupted into a boiling mass of exploding rock and burning dust, the result of a single bolt fired from one of the tanks in the Marine encampment. It took ten seconds for the sound of the detonation to reach the capital, and it was still so loud that it shook the building like rolling thunder in a gale wind.

By the time the sound had died away, the mountain lay shrouded in a black cloud of dust and smoke.

"A great pity," Reza said, genuinely sad at having to destroy part of what had been a magnificently beautiful mountain, even after human hands had immortalized their own conceit with hammer and chisel. When the smoke cleared, there was only a smoldering crater where Belisle's likeness was to have been.

He turned back to Belisle, who was now as pale as the inside of his mistress's thighs. "Do not threaten me or my people again, Mr. President," Reza said quietly, his deep voice cutting through the city's sudden silence like the fin of a shark in dark water. "You will think on these things this night, on how you wish to solve your problems here, with or without my assistance. We will speak again tomorrow."

He and Zevon departed, leaving Belisle and Wittmann to contemplate the ramifications of what they had just witnessed.

* * *

"I tell you, Ian, our time has come," the man said passionately. "Surely it was a sign we saw today, that the days of the Raniers are numbered!"

There were nods of assent from people around the crowded room, visible in the low lamplight through air choked with pipe smoke and the salty smell of sweat clinging to bodies that had been laboring hard only hours before. Numbering one hundred and thirty-eight souls, they were the elected cell leaders of the Mallory Party, each of whom represented the interests of thousands of people.

But this meeting was not a normal one, by any means. It was the first time in over five years since representatives of all the groups had gathered to discuss the future of their people. The last time they had met, they had been betrayed by a young fool with a loose tongue, and many of their number, including the speaker's father, had been arrested, tortured, and then executed as traitors by the prefecture police and Territorial Army. No event since then had warranted the risk of another such meeting. Until now.

"Perhaps the mountain was not a warning to us," the man went on, "but to the Raniers. Perhaps the Marines–"

"They are here to help the Raniers!" a woman with a face of angry leather shouted from the other side of the gathering. They were men and women of all ages, tall and short, but all with the callused palms of those who labored for a living, and the hollowed eyes of those who lived in despair but who dreamed with hope. "Our first plan was best, to kill the Confederation dogs before they set foot on our soil. Now they'll turn their weapons on us, on our children, to keep us in the mines, digging like rats! I say we walk away from these damned pits. Blow them up. Collapse them for good. If they want the lode, let them dig it out themselves, and their Marines be damned!"

There were angry murmurs and more nods. Some were from different people than before, and some from those who had earlier agreed with the man's words. They were afraid, angry, and confused by the events of the day. They had known the Marines were coming, and had done their best to lay an ambush for them, believing that they were here to act as a whip for Belisle. But after the Marine ships suddenly diverted to the ridge, and then destroyed the site of Belisle's effigy in stone, the Mallorys' original determination to openly rebel had wavered. The seniors had called a meeting, and every group from every province had managed to get a representative here by nightfall. It had been a terribly dangerous gamble, but was considered worth the risk. But until the meeting ended and they were all safely away, more than one wary eye would be fixed on the approaches to the hideout, and local Mallory agents were in contact with spotters outside the nearby mines, watching for trouble.

"No."

In unison, all eyes turned to the owner of that voice. Enya Terragion, all of twenty-three years old, had not been with the Committee very long, but had early on won its respect.

"We must fight the wrongs we have suffered with right, with justice, not with spite," Enya told them. "Yes, we could destroy the mines, but where would that leave us? The Raniers would take their fortunes and themselves and leave us behind to rot in poverty worse than we know now."

"Fine, then!" someone shouted. "Good riddance to them!"

"We don't need their damned money to live!" added another.

"No, we don't," Enya said, her voice rising above the shouting. "But consider this, all of you: we remember stories of what it was like when the first Mallorys came here, how Erlang provided for them, how they carved their lives from the soil and the forest. But we can't go back." Her words hung like rifle shots in the suddenly silent room. "We can't go back. Look at yourselves: to right and left, and across from you. Who do you see? Do you see someone who can hunt in the forest, till soil and plant grain, spin wool into yarn and weave, someone who can provide for so many of us?" Many eyes dropped to the floor, many fists clenched in frustrated realization of the truth. The years had taken away their skills and given them a population that could not be sustained by a simple economy. "When was the last time any of you had something to eat or wear that did not come from the company store? How many of you have a plow, or know how to make one?" Her challenge was met with a resentful but contemplative silence. "And even if we could go back to the old ways, do we want to go back, when we could go forward? My father could not read, but he saw to it that I could, and I vow that any child of mine shall also. Gerry's boy," she nodded to a woman who sat a few seats down, "was born blind, but the doctors at Kielly's Hospital gave him his sight. Are these, and so many more, things we want to give up?" She paused again, her deep brown eyes touching each face in the crowd. "You all think that the lives of our first blood on this world were grand and full of joy, and for them they were. But that was their world, their time. This is our time, and we must make Erlang our own world, with our own vision, and not that of our forebears."

"So what do you suggest, girl?" a man who wore a patch over one eye and had a mass of scar tissue over the right side of his skull said sarcastically. "That we just say 'pretty please' to President-By-God's-Holy-Right Belisle and ask him to give us our lives and freedom back? We've tried that approach, many times, but it doesn't work. These people only understand what comes out the end of a gun, and we've got enough now to give it to 'em."

"What about the mountain?" Enya said over the chorus of agreeing voices. "Do you think our tiny, outlawed hunting rifles are a match for their pulse guns? Will our gasoline bombs stop their tanks or thwart their artillery?"

Silence.

"Good people," she said, "even should the Kreelans never show their terrible faces on this side of the Grange, we have many an enemy in our own kin, in the Raniers who oppress us, in the Confederation Council members who rob our world of its riches for their own gain. We are a remote world, far from the center of human consideration. It is time we sought out some friends, if we can, and show them that we are not the mindless brutes the Rainiers claim we are."

"Regardless of the cost?" the leather-faced woman asked.

Enya shook her head slowly. "No. But at least we can find out the price before we pay in blood, perhaps needlessly."

"And you think these Marines may help us?" Ian Mallory, a direct descendent of the original Mallory, said. He held his position solely through due democratic process in his ward and through his own abilities, not by his name. Longest surviving member on the Committee, he served as its leader.

"All of you heard earlier what Milan told us of Wittmann's horror at what happened to the mountain today, at what the Marines did to it," she said. Milan was the Mayor's servant and a Mallory spy. "Whoever these Marines are, whatever they came to Erlang for, it was not to be solely for Belisle's pleasure. Will they help us? I do not know. But I am willing to wager my life that it is worth the risk to find out. And if my way does not succeed, no other alternatives are closed away from you."

Ian Mallory nodded, his gray beard slowly bobbing against his barrel chest. He was a strong man, and proud, but held out little hope for a successful armed rebellion of his people against Belisle's Territorial Army. It had been tried before, and failed. As then, many Mallorys would be slaughtered, and Erlang would still remain under Ranier control. More than that, his people would be driven inextricably from their roots, from their heritage of honest work for an honest wage, the helping hand of a neighbor, a government that said "yes" to its people, not "no." He hoped beyond hope for a settlement that would restore his people to their rightful place in an environment of forgiveness and of looking to the future, where perhaps Raniers and Mallorys could someday simply call themselves Erlangers. But it was a difficult road. The past held so much bad blood, but his heart grew weary from the burden of hate that it bore. His wizened eyes sought out the gaze of his friends, his people.

"The time has come for talk to end," he said. "Does anyone have anything else to say on this matter, over what has already been spoken?"

No one did. Unlike many committees convened over the ages, the Mallorys did not have the luxury of talking and not acting. Every meeting ended in a vote and action.

"Then it is time to have a show of hands. All in favor of letting Enya speak to the Marines on our behalf, raise your hand." Roughly two-thirds of those present, some after a moment's hesitation, raised their hand above their head. "All those against?" The remainder raised their hands. There were no abstentions in a Mallory Committee vote. The right was too precious to waste.

"And what if she fails?"

Ian frowned. It was an unpalatable prospect, but an all-too realistic one. "If that happens, we'll have no choice but to destroy the mines and fight the Raniers and the Marines face to face." And die, he thought grimly.

THIRTEEN

"Captain," Zevon said from the dim red glow of the command post, "a personal message just came in for you from Tenth Fleet. I thought you might want to see it."

"Thank you, Alfonso," Reza said, instantly awakening from a restless sleep. He was not tired, particularly, except that dealing with the unfathomable intricacies of human politics drained him terribly. He would never become accustomed to a dark art that was unutterably alien to him and the ways of his people. His other people, he chided himself.

Reza took the proffered electronic notepad from Zevon, who immediately turned away and left him in privacy, closing the curtain of thick canvas between Reza's personal area and the company HQ.

Keying in his personal code, Reza was rewarded with Tenth Fleet's emblem and a video message. It was from Jodi.

"Hi, Reza," she said warmly, her face as beautiful as ever. It had been over three years now since he had last seen her or Nicole in the flesh. "I know I only wrote you last week, and you probably get sick of me sending these things all the time." Reza smiled. While the two of them had religiously exchanged letters every two weeks for years, only half of them ever got through. Looking at the date, he saw that this message had been posted three months ago. Electronic miracles, indeed, he thought sourly. "But I had some news for you, and I'm afraid it isn't good." Reza could see a veil of sadness fall over her face. "Father Hernandez died two days ago in Rome, here on Earth. I guess he was on another one of his trips between Rutan and the Vatican to tie things up with the Church again when his heart finally gave out. From what Monsignor Ryakin said – he called me this morning – Father Hernandez died in his sleep." She paused as she brushed away a tear. "I know you won't be able to come to the funeral or anything – it'll probably be long since over by the time you even get this – so I ordered some flowers for the ceremony in your name. I hope that's okay with you."

Of course it is, my friend, he thought sadly. He had liked Father Hernandez a great deal, and often thought how good it would have been to spend more time with him. But that was not part of Reza's Way. He only hoped that Hernandez had found whatever it was in life that he had been searching for, and that his God would look after his soul as Reza wished the Empress might, but could not, after he himself died.

"Well, now that I've got you depressed, I can at least say that there's some good news. Tony and Nicole are doing great. Big surprise, huh? Nicole's in charge of one of the training squadrons at the Red Flag range now (I'm her exec), and it seems that Tony's been making quite a splash as a member of the Council. Seems like he hasn't forgotten to be a Marine, anyway, the way he gives some of those candy-ass senators a good tongue-lashing.

"Anyway," Jodi went on, her recorded image taking on a smile that was radiant despite her evident sadness at the changes time had brought, "all three of us will be going to Father's funeral, along with some of the others in your old welcoming committee. Even that stupid Rabat bitch loosened up enough to say she was going. Probably some kind of publicity stunt, I suppose.

"So, I guess that's it for now." Her piercing blue eyes turned serious. "Please, Reza, take good care of yourself. Tony says he's going to write you soon, too. And Nicole... well, Nicole seems to know when to write, so she'll do it when it's time. Tell Eustus I said hello, and Nicole promises to send him some more chocolate from Paris next month. I miss you, Reza. All my love to you." She blew a kiss at him. "Bye until next time."

The transmission ended.

Reza sat in the dark, alone with his thoughts. He wondered what would happen to him when all his friends were gone. Because he was so different from the others of his chosen kind, it was very difficult to make even friendly acquaintances, let alone meet someone with whom he could share a deeper relationship. Most of those in his graduating class at Quantico toward whom he had felt any kinship had either died or received medical discharges. Those to whom he was closest – except for Nicole and Jodi – were here with him, and had miraculously survived the perils they had faced over the years. But that could not last forever; they were stunning aberrations beside the Red Legion's massive casualty statistics.

A sudden surge in the activity beyond the canvas drew him away from his melancholy reverie.

"Captain," Hawthorne, his executive officer said, pulling the makeshift door aside with one tree-trunk sized arm. "Sir, you'd better come check this out. We've got a visitor at the perimeter."

"Show her in." Reza had sensed the young woman approaching the encampment some time ago.

Hawthorne only nodded, registering no shock or curiosity that Reza knew it was a woman who had come to visit them. He had long ago learned that his commander's seeming lack of curiosity about elaborating information did not mean he was not interested; it was just that somehow he already knew. "Yes, sir."

As Hawthorne relayed the orders, Reza put his uniform on over the silken black Kreelan garb he had worn every day of his adult life, the collar of his heritage and standing among humanity's enemy prominent above the neckline of his battle dress uniform. Carefully positioning the ancient dagger at his side, he went out into the pale yellow light of the command post.

* * *

"You don't understand, senator," Belisle said urgently, desperately restraining his growing fury as he spoke to the life-size holographic image of Senator Borge. "This man destroyed one of the capital city's landmarks, and threatened the entire colony with destruction if we didn't deal with him."

Borge's face took on a fatherly look that Belisle found maddeningly patronizing. "Karl, Karl, please, calm down. It is not that I doubt you, old friend. It is just that I find it difficult to believe that the people I dispatched to Erlang would do such a thing. The orders I laid down were very specific, and the command personnel chosen were, shall we say, of the highest reliability. I can only assume that there was a breakdown somewhere in the military chain. Please, rest assured that your interests are my interests, and I'll do everything in my power to rectify the situation."

Belisle nodded. Borge was a man of his word, as well he should be. He had profited enough from Erlang's riches. "What do you intend to do, then?"

"Well, first I need to know the unit that's causing you all the trouble, so I can track down where things went wrong and fix the problem." He smiled like a wolf, except wolves did not smile with malevolence. "And if you could provide me the name of the officer in charge, I can... effect a change in his career development profile, as it were."

"A summary court-martial and execution would be nice," Belisle muttered.

"That could be arranged, I suppose. Now, who are these people?" Borge's effigy motioned for someone to take a note.

"I don't know what unit it is. They never bothered to tell me." His mouth puckered momentarily in a sudden fit of anger, then he went on,

"But the officer in charge is a Marine captain by the name of Gard. I don't know his first name."

For a moment, Borge did not speak, but his eyes widened perceptibly. "You said 'Gard?' Did he have long, braided hair and a Kreelan collar around his neck?"

Belisle thought about that a minute. "Yes," he said, suddenly feeling like an idiot. He had been so angry when Gard arrived that he had not noticed any obvious oddities. Perhaps because of the helmet he had been wearing? "Yes, by the Lord of All, he does. How in the devil did you know?"

"Never mind," Borge said grimly. "Karl, this man is extremely dangerous to our plans, and it is only the worst of luck that put him in charge of the Marine contingent I ordered to help you. I'll be sending help immediately. In the meantime, do whatever you have to do to cooperate with him. Make whatever concessions are necessary."

"But that would mean—"

"Just do it, Karl. Remember that it is only for as long as it takes for me to repair this misfortune. Any compromises you make can be undone easily enough. Am I right?"

Belisle thought about it a moment. Giving in to the Mallorys would not be an easy thing, even for a short time. On the other hand, if he agreed to a "compromise," he just might be able to lure their leaders out into the open and finish them off for good, an opportunity he had missed only by a hair five years ago. His mouth curled into a satisfied smile.

"Yes, of course, Senator," he said. "And this may give me the opportunity to finish some other long overdue... housecleaning."

"Good. I'll have someone on this right away, and they will be in touch with you regarding the plans as soon as they are in motion." Borge's projected face nodded once in farewell, then the image faded into random sparks and disappeared.

His spirits lifted, Belisle went to bed and his waiting mistress.

* * *

"Please, sit down," Reza told the young woman standing between a pair of his Marines who, while no taller than she, appeared enormous beside her in their combat gear. He nodded to them, and they quickly and silently left the command post.

"Thank you, captain," Enya said, having difficulty taking her eyes off him. He was so different from what she had expected. A tall man, lithe and strong, his body was well-muscled, yet sinewy like a cat's. He would not have seemed that much different from many in his company were it not for an alienness that clung to him. She saw the collar around his neck and his long braided black hair, but was taken most with the jade green eyes that seemed to swirl with color in the dim lamplight. Groping for the chair that was poised across the table from where Reza stood, she nearly tripped and fell as she sat down.

"You have nothing to fear here," he told her, as he sat down on another of the simple folding field chairs. "You have come representing the Mallorys." It was not a question.

Enya could only nod. Having seen the arsenal that lay in this camp, and now the quiet power in this man's eyes, she suddenly understood the seriousness of what she was undertaking. If these people were to turn on hers, no Mallory would ever again know freedom. The fear that welled up within her at the thought only served to fuel her determination: she must not fail.

"Yes," she said, taking a deep breath and staring Reza right in the eye, which took much more willpower than she had imagined it might. Not to look at him, but to occasionally look away. "I am Enya Terragion, a member of the Mallory Party Committee. I am empowered to speak with you on their behalf."

"You are the ones who sought to ambush my troops at the spaceport?" Reza asked, curious to know if she would speak the truth. If she did not...

Enya did not hesitate. "Yes. We feared that you had come to further oppress us, and the Committee decided to try and defeat you before you could add your firepower to that of the Territorial Army."

She heard a quiet snort off to one side, and turned to see a hulking black man who looked quick as a tiger, shaking his head as he turned back to whatever he had been doing.

"I believe Mister Hawthorne is saying that you were very... fortunate, Enya Terragion," Reza said, "that such an incident was avoided."

Enya nodded somberly. "We realized that today, when you destroyed the mountain. All of our people near the spaceport would have been killed, would they not?"

"If not all, probably most," Reza said simply. It was a fact beyond dispute. "I am glad things turned out differently." He smiled. With his eyes.

Enya blinked, trying to break the mesmerizing hold he seemed to have on her. "What do you intend to do here on Erlang?" she asked quietly. "Will you help Belisle herd us into the mines?"

"That depends on you," Reza said as Zevon, as if on cue, poured coffee for Enya. Suspicious that it was a trick, she only looked at it. Reza reached over and took a sip to prove it was safe, forcing the bitter liquid down his throat. He had always hated coffee. He set the cup back down on the table.

"My orders," he said through the bitter aftertaste, "are to ensure that the flow of minerals from the mines to Confederation shipyards continues without interruption. As I am sure you are aware, Erlang is virtually irreplaceable to the shipyards in this sector." He looked at her pointedly. "Those are my orders. How I carry them out is largely up to President Belisle... and you."

"Meaning what?" she said coldly. She pushed the coffee away. "That Belisle calls your superior and orders you to do his bidding, and we are worse off than ever before?" She shook her head. "Do not play games with me, captain. We are willing to talk with you, but we will not sacrifice everything for which we have lived and suffered without a fight. We know that you blew up the mountain to frighten Belisle, and perhaps us; you succeeded on both counts. But what are we to do now that you have put the fear of God in us all? Our only real weapon is our willingness to work the mines, and it is a weapon we are ready to use, and will use – to the death, if necessary – if it is forced upon us."

Reza's brow furrowed in thought for a moment before he spoke. "I pledge to you, as I have pledged to my Marines, that we will not turn upon your people, no matter our orders." Not surprisingly, disobeying orders was almost a Legion tradition, and it did not grieve Reza to ignore orders that conflicted with either his instincts or sense of rightness, corrupted with Kreelan influence as some thought it was. Good fortune, however, had seen to it that he had only rarely had to act in such a fashion. "My people are warriors, not murderers, and I will be perfectly honest with you: my mission cannot succeed without cooperation from both your people and Belisle."

Enya twisted her face into a scowl of skepticism. "And how," she said, "are we to go about doing that?"

His green eyes fixing her like a deer in a beam of light, he said, "Your people and Belisle will negotiate, and quickly. The plans you make shall be your own. I will guarantee neutrality. You will do what all humans seem to love to do: you will talk. You will reach a consensus."

"And if we don't?"

Reza shrugged. "Then you both shall suffer. If your workers strike or destroy the mines, you destroy Erlang's greatest defense against the Kreelans, which is providing raw materials to the shipyards for building warships that can protect you. As rich as your world is, by colony standards you have almost no ground defenses against a fleet assault. Worse, your Territorial Army seems more adept at police actions than waging war against the Empire. You would also push Belisle to vengeance, and his wrath would drive him to murder. The Territorial Army would be unleashed to slaughter Mallorys on a scale that I could not prevent." He shrugged. "On the other hand, Belisle has every interest in keeping the mines open, regardless of the cost. Erlang's economy and his own wealth depend on it. More than that, he cannot leave here with such blood on his hands. He will be exposed as a petty tyrant, a criminal and – if it comes to it – a mass murderer. No planet in the Confederation would take him."

Enya shook her head. "Belisle will never agree to it, no matter how little or how much we ask of him. The lines of hatred run too deep."

"He has no choice."

And what choice have we? Enya thought. What Reza said, while glossing over a great many smaller issues, was essentially true. If the Marines protected the Mallorys from punitive action by the Territorial Army and the police, and if enough changes could be made quickly...

There was hope, she decided. There was terrible risk, but no more than they faced already. Mallorys had already placed charges on all but the smallest mines, enough explosives in the right place to collapse the shafts and destroy much of the equipment. But if the mines were destroyed, there would be no limits to Belisle's retribution. And the outcome of a civil war between the Mallorys and the TA was not worth a moment's contemplation.

"On behalf of my people," she said formally, "I accept your offer of neutrality and negotiations with Belisle. What are we to do?"

* * *

To his visitors, Belisle appeared furious, yet resigned to the fact that the time for change had finally come. Having arrived in one of the armored skimmers, again escorted by two of Walken's tanks, the Mallory representatives had walked into the president's conference room and taken their appointed seats opposite their Ranier counterparts. Reza stood at the end of the table.

"I wish to make perfectly clear my position in this matter," he said. "I now act as an impartial third party mediator to your dispute until the proper authority has arrived from the Confederation Government."

"And who might that be?" Belisle asked, smugly thinking that he already knew the answer: a full regiment of Marines who would answer to him.

"Someone who is much more adept at these matters than am I," Reza said. "General Counsel Melissa Savitch."

Belisle's mouth hung slack as the blood drained from his face. "That's not possible," he squeaked.

The Mallorys, as well, were stunned.

"Isn't she the senior Confederation Counsel?" Enya asked incredulously. "Flattering as it is, why would she take an interest in this matter? Because of the mines?"

"No," Reza said, shaking his head. Melissa had stayed in touch with him over the years, and had become a welcome and cherished face in his small circle of friends. She had risen steadily until she had reached the pinnacle of achievement in her chosen field, now designated the highest-ranking member of the Confederation's judicial wing. "It is because I asked her to come, and she agreed. It is good fortune that she was on a visit to Nathalie when my message reached her. She will be here in five days. I am acting local counsel until she arrives."

"You bastard," Belisle suddenly spat. "You bloody freak."

"You test my impartiality, sir," Reza said coolly, but the look in his eyes was close to what Belisle had seen just before his own likeness on the face of Haerding Mountain had disappeared.

For a moment, Belisle did not know what to do. But then he remembered what Borge had told him before about anything done being undone easily enough. Let the good counselor come, he thought icily. He was sure that something fitting could be arranged. "Get on with it, then," he said in only a slightly more cordial tone.

Reza looked at him suspiciously, his mind ringing with alarms of intended treachery. But until Belisle exposed his intentions, Reza could not be sure, nor could he act. He decided that he would be very careful with this slippery serpent.

"Mr. Mallory," Reza said to the leader of the Mallory Party who represented two-thirds of the souls on this planet, "please, sir, begin."

Slow and rocky though it was, they took their first steps upon the road toward a true democracy.

FOURTEEN

"Are you sure you wouldn't like to come along with us, captain?" Enya asked. "It's a truly beautiful place."

Looking up from the paperwork Zevon had forced upon him, Reza shook his head. "No thank you," he told her, smiling. "I appreciate your offer, but I have much to do here." He knew quite well that she fervently hoped he would say no, for purely personal reasons of her own. "Perhaps another time."

"Are you sure, captain?" Eustus asked valiantly, also hoping against hope that Reza would say no, but he felt honor-bound to ask. "Zevon always has you doing too much paperwork crap, you know."

Reza fought to keep from smiling. Sometimes, he thought, being able to sense the emotions of others must be more interesting than actually reading their thoughts. Eustus was helplessly, hopelessly in love with the young woman standing close beside him, and Enya felt the same about Eustus. The Marines had only been planetside for two weeks, but the changes had been little short of miraculous, especially after Counselor Savitch had arrived to oversee things. Sensing something malignant in Belisle's mind, Reza had assigned two of his best Marines to be her bodyguards, despite Savitch's vehement protests. They went with her everywhere, including the bathroom (both Marines were female). He had since gotten the sense from Belisle that whatever he had been plotting would not be put to the test, but there was something else about him that Reza was missing, something the man knew that fueled an inner fire of arrogance and patient vengeance. But what?

"That crap, as you're so fond of saying, First Sergeant," Zevon said tiredly, interrupting Reza's chain of thought, "is what keeps all of us paid, fed, and loaded with ammo. If you want me to cut your paycard loose—"

"No, no! Not that!" Eustus cried with mock horror, raising his hands to his face as if to ward off some nightmarish creature.

"First Sergeant," Reza said formally.

"Sir?" Eustus asked, suddenly confused by Reza's tone of voice.

"Dismissed."

Smiling, relieved, Eustus saluted. "Aye, sir," he replied.

"Captain," Enya said, bowing her head.

Watching the two of them leave together, Reza felt a sudden weight upon his heart. Where was Esah-Zhurah now? What was she doing? Was she thinking of him? Was she even still alive?

But there were no answers to his questions. He pushed her beautiful face from his mind and forcibly immersed himself in the jumble of paperwork that Zevon pushed at him to sign.

Outside, Eustus and Enya mounted the horses that waited patiently near the command post. Riding through the company compound, Enya smiled at the Marines who went about their daily routine. Some exercised or practiced hand-to-hand combat, others washed or shaved, several groups were clustered around the gigantic tanks that now lay in great pits dug into the ridge, working noisily on some mysterious mechanism inside the huge vehicles. Yet others, those who were off-duty and on free time, simply lay in the sun, getting tanned and doing what soldiers often loved above all else when granted the time: sleeping. Still others, whom she did not see here, had passes to go into Mallory City and take advantage of whatever hospitality offered itself.

Eustus had chosen to spend his two-day pass entirely with her.

Once outside the perimeter, Enya took them to an easy trot, leading Eustus into the woodlands that had once provided all the needs of her people. They rode on, paying no attention to time, but taking in the sights, smells, and sounds of what had to be one of the most beautiful worlds in the Confederation, if not in all the galaxy. They spoke in the language of those who knew they were in love, but had not yet confessed it to one another. Idle banter, mostly, that avoided hinting directly at what they felt inside. The day was warm, the air clear as it always had been for as long as any human had known, and both were having some of the happiest days of their lives.

At last, they came to Enya's favorite place, a small crystal lake, surrounded by majestic conifer-like trees that lay next to a sheer rock face that rose hundreds – perhaps thousands – of feet above them, its top hidden in a wreath of clouds.

"My father used to bring me here all the time," she explained as they dismounted and left the horses to graze in the hardy grass. Brought by Therese Ranier's settlers as pets, the horse had been their single greatest positive contribution to the lives of the Mallorys, who kept stock of their own in the forests beyond the Raniers' reach.

"Enya, this is absolutely fantastic," Eustus said in awe as he looked up at the rocky face. It soared up... and up... and up. Finally looking down into the water, he only saw the rock face again, this time reflected from the water's smooth surface, for there was no wind, not even the slightest breeze. "I've never seen anything like this in my life."

Enya smiled, taking his hand and leading him along the shore of the lake. "We were told as children that this is a magic place," she said as she plucked off her shoes so she could walk barefoot in the cool, wet sand along the water's edge. "Sometimes you can hear voices, my father used to tell me. I've heard them, too, singing in the rock. They always sound so sad."

Eustus looked at her skeptically. "Voices in the rock?" he said.

Enya smiled, tossing her head playfully, her silken hair brushing Eustus's shoulder. "I know it's only the wind moving through some kind of tunnels or something. But when you hear them... it... it doesn't sound like the wind at all. They sound like sirens in mourning, or maybe lamenting a lover's loss."

Eustus stopped, conscious of the warmth of her hand in his. "Sounds romantic," he said as she stepped close to him, her breasts brushing his tunic.

"Yes," she breathed, "it does, doesn't it?"

The kiss, when it came, was all that Eustus had anticipated, and more. They held each other for what seemed a long time, and when their lips finally parted, Enya silently led him by the hand to a bed of soft grass, pulling him down to lay on top of her.

"Are you sure...?" Eustus breathed between her increasingly passionate kisses.

"Stop procrastinating," she whispered in his ear just before her lips and teeth began to work their way down his neck, her hands unfastening the clasps of his uniform.

Eustus raised himself up enough to bring his fingers to bear on her blouse. Cursing his own clumsiness, he finally exposed her breasts and their erect nipples, and Enya sighed as his lips made contact.

They continued to wriggle out of their clothes like two butterflies, struggling to emerge from cocoons that were bound together, their frantic breathing echoing across the still water and the towering rock beyond.

"Ow!" Enya gasped, rolling over so quickly that Eustus toppled over onto his back beside her, his pants shoved down around his knees.

"What's wrong?" he asked, terrified that he had done something to hurt her. "Did I–"

"No, no," she said, shaking her head. A scowl on her face, she reached underneath herself with one hand, feeling around until she had found what she was looking for. She held up her hand to Eustus and smiled. "Just a dragon's claw."

"A what?" Eustus said, taking the object from her hand. It was the length of his index finger and really did look like a claw, curved and pointed, except that it was flat and completely black. The surface was fairly smooth but pitted, like a piece of rock or metal that had been sandblasted or weathered with age.

"A dragon's claw. People have found them all around here. Nobody knows exactly what they're made of. Some kind of weird rock, I guess. They're supposed to bring good luck." She paused as Eustus looked at the scythe-like piece of rock. "Do you feel lucky?" she whispered huskily, one of her hands stroking Eustus's flagging erection back to life.

"Yes, ma'am," he said, his eyes alight with renewed desire as he tossed the dragon's claw aside, "I surely do."

* * *

The warmth of the sun and the heat of their lovemaking made for two sleepy lovers, and Eustus had fetched the blanket Enya had brought. "For a picnic," she had told him. Now, lying awake on the soft flannel, Enya's head resting on his shoulder, his mind and heart skirmished over the future.

I've done my three required combat tours, he told himself. While that was not enough to retire from federal service, it was sufficient to get himself a posting to a non-combat position or Territorial Army assignment. He could stay here, he thought. With Enya. While he had only known her these two weeks, he felt as if he had known her all his life. He had known infatuation before, but never like this. He loved her, he admitted to himself. He had never really loved anyone before; there had never been time. But here...

Beside him was the crumpled heap that was his uniform, and the crimson dragon of the regimental insignia stared at him as if saying, "Traitor." The men and women of the company beside whom he had fought and lived, whom he had helped to survive and who had helped him – how could he simply walk away from them? They were not the riffraff they had once been. No matter what the raw material, they were the best Marines in the service. Reza had seen to that.

Reza. He almost groaned to himself. What of him? How could he turn his back on Reza? Deep inside, he knew that Reza would understand the burning in his heart, the desire to stay with this woman who was now a part of him. Eustus had served him well, and they had long been close friends; more than that, they had developed the bond that only those who live through times of extreme hardship know, the knowledge that they can rely on each other, no matter what.

But that only seemed to make things worse. Reza would go on and on, until finally he was alone. And alone he would die, with no one to watch over him, with no one to be there for him, to remind him that he was human and not the half-alien beast that so many believed he was.

His thoughts sinking to despair, he turned his head to look at the cliff that soared into the noon sky. A glint of light from the ground nearby caught his attention, and he reached out and retrieved the dragon's claw from where he had dropped it. Turning it over in his hand, he examined it closely in an effort to push thoughts of the future from his mind. One of his fingers slipped, rubbing across the curved edge of the "rock," and he saw a line of red appear on his finger.

Some lucky charm, he thought sourly as blood began to seep from the half-inch long wound that was like a huge paper cut. He set the rock down carefully, avoiding the edge on which he had cut himself, and sucked on his finger to get the bleeding to stop. He knew that rocks and minerals of various types could be sharp either naturally or with a little help from busy hands, but the dragon's claw Enya had given him seemed to have an extraordinarily good edge.

As he thought about it, checking his finger to see if the bleeding stopped, something about the dragon's claw nagged at him. There was something vaguely and disturbingly familiar about it, but he could not put his finger – which by now had stopped bleeding – on it.

One of the horses suddenly looked up from where it had been contentedly stuffing its face with grass, its ears pricked forward. The other one did the same. Both of them began snorting, their nostrils flaring and eyes widening in alarm.

Eustus had been with Reza long enough to trust his own instincts and those of others, especially animals.

"Enya," he said, rousing her from sleep, "wake up."

"What is it?" she said, her eyes snapping wide open. She was a deep sleeper, but when she woke up, she was fully awake almost instantly. She sat up beside Eustus, drawing the blanket up to cover her breasts.

"The horses are spooked," Eustus said quietly, reaching for the blaster that normally hung low on his thigh, but was now nestled in the pile of clothing beside him. The feel of the weapon, nearly as long and large around as his forearm, steadied and comforted him. No predator of the forest could survive its firepower. He raised his nude body into a wary crouch, his eyes scanning around them, a tingling sensation running up his spine as his scrotum contracted, drawing his testicles into a less exposed position. He looked at the horses. They were staring straight across the lake, their eyes fixed on the cliff. "Something over there is spooking them," he whispered, "but I can't see any–"

And then he heard it, a keening sound that appeared at the uppermost range of his hearing and slowly moved down the scale.

"The sirens," Enya whispered excitedly. "The horses heard them before we did."

Eustus's blood chilled at the sound as it evolved into a chorus of haunting voices that alternately boomed and whispered over the lake, the sound reverberating between the cliff and the trees around them.

"Jesus," he whispered, but the name of the Christian Savior was swept away on a melody of sadness and mourning that was like nothing he had ever heard. The song evolved into a complex harmony that would have been the envy of the most accomplished chorus, the notes washing over Eustus and Enya like gentle but urgent waves upon two tiny reefs.

And then, as rapidly as they had come, the voices ebbed away, their mournful song fading into notes so low that Eustus and Enya could no longer hear them. The two sat, transfixed, until they noticed that the horses had resumed their eating, the sound no longer audible even to their more sensitive ears.

Eustus swallowed, then sat back down, the strength drawn from him as if someone had sucked it out with a straw. The blaster slipped from his numbed hand to fall harmlessly onto the blanket.

"I told you," Enya whispered into the sudden silence as she pulled herself close to him, wrapping her arms around his chest. "Isn't it incredible?"

"That's hardly the word for it," Eustus said, wincing at the sound of his voice, as if it were an unworthy intrusion to his ears after what he had just heard. "Come to think of it, I don't think there is a word to describe it."

Enya nodded. "That's the third time I've heard it. The first was when I was nine. The last time was five years ago. And it's different every time, as if you're hearing different parts of the same song."

"Has anyone ever tried to find the caves or whatever it is that makes the sound?"

"People have tried to find the source for a long time," she said, "but I've never heard of anyone finding anything except little caves and such that didn't lead anywhere, and had no strange acoustic properties that would account for the sound."

He looked at her. "Care to do some exploring?"

She eyed him slyly. "Why? Haven't you done enough cave exploring for one day?"

He pulled her close and kissed her, feeling his body react to the warmth and softness of her skin, the smell of her body. "You're right," he said as he lay down, pulling her on top of him, her legs straddling his waist. "Maybe I should get some more experience here first."

"Excellent idea," she breathed as he slid inside her.

* * *

Eustus trailed behind her as she made her way along the rock ledge like a mountain goat. Extremely agile himself, the result of Reza's training more than any intrinsic ability on his part, he still felt clumsy as he watched her fluid movements.

"Watch your step here," she warned, pointing to a spot on the ledge that was crumbling. Enya easily stepped over it, seemingly oblivious to the fact that they were a hundred meters or more above the lake.

Eustus peered down quickly, then up, before he stepped over the crumbling part of the ledge. While it had looked sheer from their earlier vantage point, the cliff face had an undulating series of ledges that was almost like a secret staircase, wide enough to walk comfortably without turning sideways against the cliff.

"Are you sure that the place you saw was this far over?" Eustus asked, silently cursing himself for not bringing his binoculars so they could have gotten a better look at the mountain before they started up.

"Yes," Enya told him. After they had decided to abandon – temporarily, at least – their amorous pursuits, she had taken a good look at the cliff and noticed a dark spot where there should not have been one. Below it were streaks of dust and debris, as if part of the cliff face had sloughed off, revealing... what? "It shouldn't be much... Eustus!"

"What? What is it?"

"We found it," she said, her voice alive with childlike excitement. "It's a cave, just like I told you!"

Coming up behind her, Eustus saw it: a ragged opening that looked just big enough to crawl through. The ledge they were on, he saw, ran just to the edge of the hole. The rest of it had been taken down by the loosened rock that had fallen to expose the cave, and now lay somewhere under the lake's placid surface far below.

"Enya," he asked seriously, "do you think this is safe? I mean, whatever caused the rock to fall might happen again."

She paused a moment, considering. "They were doing some blasting at the MacCready mine not too long ago – that's on the far side of the mountain. I imagine that's what must have caused it. But Ian told me they weren't going to be doing any more explosives work for a while." She frowned to herself. Unless Belisle betrays us, she thought. "It should be fairly stable, as long as you don't go firing off your gun or something."

Eustus grinned. "I already did that."

She laughed, then began to move toward the cave entrance. Eustus, concentrating hard now, followed close behind her.

"Let me have your light," she said.

Out of long habit, Eustus carried a variety of essential items on his pistol belt everywhere he went when dressed in his combat uniform. His blaster, of course; but he also carried a handheld light, comm link, basic medical kit, and his combat knife. Unclipping the light from his belt, he handed it to her. "Be careful," he cautioned.

Nodding, she turned on the light and shone it as far as she could down the cave mouth. "Well, it's not just a pocket, anyway." She turned the light off and clipped it to her pants. Then, judging the distance carefully, she half stepped, half jumped from the end of the ledge into the low mouth of the cave.

Eustus followed quickly behind her, willing himself not to look down as he crossed the small gap. Enya took his arm and steadied him in the low opening. Crouching down, they made their way forward in a duck walk, Enya shining the light ahead of them. After a few meters of scrabbling over rough rock, they emerged into what seemed like a larger tunnel, big enough for them to stand upright with plenty of room to spare.

"Look at this," she said, shining the light around the tunnel. "This looks like it's been bored out."

Eustus looked back at the section that led outside. The walls there were much rougher and rocky, almost as if someone had pressed a cap of debris into the main tunnel. "Could it be an old mine that your people dug out some time ago?"

"And be covered over with rock like that?" Enya shook her head. "No. I know we could bore a hole up this high if we really wanted to, but it would be bigger than this. A lot bigger. Besides, the rock that was covering this up looked like part of the cliff, not just debris pushed back down the shaft. If that were the case, this cave would have been filled with rocks and dirt, but it's not. It's too clean."

"An airshaft?"

"With no opening to the outside?" She shook her head. "And it's so smooth." She knelt down and brushed away some of the dust on the floor. "It's almost like glass. Our boring machines are good, but nothing like this."

Eustus frowned. None of it made much sense. It's almost as if someone had bored out the tunnel almost to the cliff face from the inside, he thought. "Well, I guess there's only one way to find out what it is," he told her.

Enya leaned over and kissed him on the cheek. "I love a man with a sense of adventure," she told him.

Wondering what they were getting themselves into, he followed her into the cave.

"This is unbelievable," she said after they had gone about three hundred paces into the tunnel.

"This thing's as smooth and straight as a pipe," Eustus said quietly as he followed the slight downward angle of the floor. The echo inside was becoming increasingly eerie, and he had to fight back the urge to grab Enya and head back toward the rapidly fading light behind them. "Has any evidence been found of any other sentient races having lived on Erlang before your people arrived?"

She shook her head as she walked onward, following the white beam of light from the flashlight.

"No, nothing. People have looked, of course." She did not add that only the Raniers had had the time and money for archeological pursuits. "But only animal bones and such things have been discovered. No paintings, carvings, pottery, or any of that kind of thing, and certainly no tools or other signs of a sentient race."

Eustus frowned. His brain knew something, he could sense it, but he just could not quite make out what it was. I've got all the pieces, he thought, I just can't put them together right.

Something hard and sharp in his pants cargo pocket rubbed against his leg.

The dragon's claw.

A tunnel made neither by human hands, nor by nature.

The dragon's claw. A weird rock that was sharp enough to draw blood.

"Oh, my God," Eustus groaned as he shuddered to a stop, the hair on the back of his neck standing at stiff attention.

"What?"

"Give me the light, Enya!"

Her eyes wide with concern in the pitch darkness, she handed the tiny torch to him.

Grabbing it from her, he shone it on the dragon's claw he had carefully extracted from his pocket. "Oh, shit," he murmured. "I knew I'd seen this before."

"Eustus, it's just a rock," she told him with utter conviction.

He looked up at her, his face creased with fear, something she had never seen him show before. "No it's not, Enya. It's Kreelan metal, a blade from what Reza calls a shrekka, the most lethal blade weapon the Kreelans have. They can penetrate armor that'll stop a pulse rifle cold. You said these things have been found all around here?"

Enya nodded. "Yes. I mean, it's not like thousands have been found, or anything, but all the ones that I know of – probably a few dozen over the years – have been picked up around the valley outside. Eustus, are you sure?"

"Yes, I'm sure. Once you've been tagged by one of these, or seen someone else get hit with one, you don't soon forget. I would've recognized it sooner, except that it's in terrible condition, and the center hub is missing." He thought about that for a moment. "Enya, this thing must have been here for a long time. An incredibly long time. Kreelan blade steel is the toughest material known. It lasts forever and stands up to practically anything. Some metallurgists are even convinced that it's some kind of quasi-organic material, able to reshape itself, to maintain its edge and balance without any kind of sharpening." He looked at her. "We've never been able to duplicate or reforge it." He looked down at the blade he held gingerly in his hand. "This thing must have been here for thousands of years." He looked up at her. "Maybe longer."

Enya was very quiet for a moment, until the eerie silence in the tunnel made her afraid not to speak, just so her ears could hear something. "So, you think this tunnel was made... by them?"

"That would seem to fit," he said quietly, turning the shrekka blade over in his hand.

"Then what is this place?" Enya asked. "And if there were Kreelans here at one time, where did they go? Why did they leave?"

"I don't know. But I guess nobody can say anymore that the Kreelans have never ventured beyond the Grange. Because they were here, all right. At least they were when our ancestors were still learning how to finger-paint on cave walls."

"Could... could they still be here... down there?" She tilted her head toward the darkness of the tunnel.

Eustus shook his head in the reflected light, but with less conviction than Enya would have liked to see. "If there had been any still alive here, I'm sure your predecessors would have met up with them. I've never known Kreelans to be particularly shy around humans."

"What should we do?"

"I think we should go back and get Reza. He's the only one who could make any sense of this, and–"

He broke off as Enya collapsed. Her hands covered her ears, her mouth open in a silent scream of pain. Even as he made a motion to help her, the sound erupted in his skull like an explosion, knocking him to his knees. The flashlight fell from his hand, went out as the switch hit the smooth rock, plunging them into darkness.

The voices had returned. The keening wail rapidly grew and multiplied into the chorus that he had heard outside, but in the tunnel it was so loud that his teeth rattled.

"Come on!" he screamed into the gale of sound, his words carried away as they left his lips. Staggering to his feet, he felt in the darkness for Enya, suddenly terrified that something had happened to her. But his desperately groping hands found her arm, and frantically he seized her and pulled her to her feet. Dazed and deafened by the sound that was now so powerful that it seemed to be jarring his insides loose, he ran through the tunnel, dragging Enya behind him, trusting his feet to guide him down the center of the curved floor, running toward the distant light.

The sound only grew stronger, until he was sure that his eardrums must burst.

"Not much farther!" he shouted to himself, even though he was unable to hear his own voice.

Suddenly, he stumbled and fell sprawling into thin air. "What–" he cried. The fall was not far, less than a meter, but the rock he fell upon struck him a stunning blow, and Enya landed right on top of him. The two of them lay there, dazed, as the voices ebbed and flowed, then slowly died away into silence.

After a few moments, he finally had enough strength to do more than hold his eyes open. "Enya?" he croaked. He was struck with surprise at being able to hear his own voice through the ringing in his ears. He thought he would be totally deaf.

"Here," came the muffled reply. She was lying beside him now, breathing steadily.

"Are you all right?"

"I think so," he managed. His head hurt like hell, he had a split and bleeding lip, and he might have twisted an ankle, but nothing was broken. "You?"

"I'm all right. But there are better ways of getting me to fall on top of you in the dark. Where are we?"

Now there was a good question, Eustus thought, smiling at her humor. She was tough. He liked that. "I don't know. I thought I was running toward the entrance. I could see a light. But... I guess I must have run the other way, deeper into the tunnel."

Pause. "You saw a light? At the far end?"

"Yeah. But now that I think about it, it wasn't the right color. Too cool, not yellow like the sun. Bluish, sort of." He found her face with his hands, held her to him. "I guess the tunnel just ended here... wherever here is."

"Where's the light?" she asked. She kissed his hands, glad they were both alive, but increasingly curious about where they were. What was this place?

"Dropped it in the tunnel. We should be able to find it on the way out."

Still trembling from the force of the voices – or whatever it was – that had struck them, Enya raised herself to her knees, trying to orient herself in the darkness.

But it was not completely dark. Somewhere in front of her, it was impossible to tell just how far, she could see a dim bluish glow like a smudge of watery blue paint on a black canvas. "Is that the light you saw?"

Eustus turned over so he could look where she was, orienting himself with her body. "That must be it, but it was a lot brighter when I saw it. It was a point of light, like a star, not like it is now."

"What could it be?"

"Some kind of fire, like methane burning? That burns with a blue color, doesn't it?"

Enya shook her head in the darkness. He felt her hair brush against his hand. "No, we should be able to distinguish the flame clearly. This looks like the light is being diffused, or something. I'm going to see what it is."

"Wait," Eustus said, digging into his utility pouch. "We don't have the light, but we can still get some light in here. I don't smoke, but this is too handy an item not to carry. Here, use this."

Enya heard a clicking sound, then saw Eustus's bruised face in the yellow light of the tiny flame of his cigarette lighter. Behind him, she saw something else. She pitched backward, screaming, her eyes wide with terror.

With reflexes honed through years of combat, Eustus drew his blaster, rolled in the direction of the threat, and fired three times. Only after the crimson energy bolts flashed from the weapon did he get a glimpse of what he was shooting at.

A Kreelan warrior.

He fired twice more for good effect before he noticed that there were others, all around him. His nerves jangling with dread, he reluctantly took his finger from the trigger. If they had wanted to kill him, he would have long since been dead.

"Give me the lighter," he said in a shaking voice, still holding his pistol at the ready. His nose filled with a strange odor from the work his blaster had done, but it was not the customary stench of charred meat. It was more like burned dirt or dust, with a tang of molten metal.

Enya reluctantly surrendered the tiny lighter, then scrambled to her feet, following Eustus as he stepped closer to the warrior he had killed.

They saw immediately, however, that she was already dead. Long dead.

"Lord of All," Enya whispered as she stepped around Eustus, kneeling beside what remained of the corpse. "It looks like a mummy."

The skin, where it showed through the extensive armor the Kreelans wore, was desiccated and shrunken over the bones. The eye sockets were empty, the silver-flecked orbs that had once filled them long since shriveled to nothing. The hair, still meticulously braided after all this time, clung tenaciously to the skull. The hands were skeletal, making the talons look all the more deadly.

"Let's look at that one," Eustus suggested, interested in examining a whole specimen. The one he had shot was missing its entire torso, and the smell, while not terrible, was very unsettling.

"Why are they still standing?" Enya asked quietly. As far as the light could reach, there were corpses standing at attention in what looked to be a circle, facing inward. Facing what? "Did someone somehow prop up the bodies?"

"From what I've seen, they were probably this way when they died," Eustus said. "I'm sure no one touched them after they were dead. Kreelan anatomy's a lot different than ours. It could be that their skeletal structure is more durable after they die, breaks down slower, maybe." They sure seem that way on the battlefield, he thought. "Besides, Reza told me once that the Kreelans remove the collars from their dead, kind of a last rites thing. These ladies still have their collars on."

"Except, my love, that these aren't ladies," Enya said.

"What? Of course they—"

"Look at the breastplates," she said, pointing to the dust-covered armor of the nearest intact warrior. The dark metal followed the contour of the massive rib cage that once must have supported a formidable mass of muscle, but the form was clearly that of a male. "No breasts there."

"Hold this," Eustus said, handing her the lighter, his heart pounding with excitement. Humans had never encountered a male Kreelan, even a dead one.

"What are you going to do?"

"Check this guy out," he said, taking his knife from its sheath and cutting away the armor from the mummy's waist. "I'll be damned," he breathed. "Will you look at that. This Kreelan has an honest-to-goodness mummified pecker. The Confederation Academy of Sciences is going to love this."

"What does it mean?" Enya felt slightly embarrassed, looking at the alien's exposed genitals, shriveled though they were. Remarkably similar to a human's, this one must have boasted a penis in life that would have been any man's envy.

"Well, for one thing, we might be able to figure out how the Kreelans reproduce and how often. Kind of give us an idea of the Empire's demographics, I suppose." He shrugged. "Hell, I don't know, except that it's something no one's ever seen before."

"After seeing what you've got, I'm not very interested in an alien mummy's privates," Enya said lightly. The knowledge that they had found a potentially very important piece of the answer to the puzzle posed by the enemy thrilled her beyond the fear that still nagged at her from being in this strange chamber.

"Yeah," Eustus quipped, "especially since mine's a first sergeant."

They both laughed, shedding some of their fear in the process. They were on an archeological dig now, not running for their lives from some unknown terror.

Now that they knew their would-be enemies were dead and crumbling with age, incapable of attacking them, Eustus held the light up and turned around slowly so they could see what else lay in the chamber. "Look at that," he said, pointing to what looked almost like a tapestry of Kreelan runes that ran from the chamber's floor to disappear in the darkness beyond the light's reach. "We've got to get Reza in here. He could read this for us."

"Eustus," Enya said, thinking aloud, "have you ever read much about Terran archeology?"

"No," he admitted.

"My father made me read things on every subject he could find a book on," she told him. "He had me read them to him aloud, because he wanted to learn, too, but he did not know how to read himself." Another legacy of the Raniers, she thought bitterly. "In one of those books," she went on, "there was something about the old Egyptians on Earth, and what they called the pyramids. That's where they buried their royalty, in big chambers inside the pyramid, usually with everything the priests thought the king or queen would need for the afterlife. Food, clothes, everything. And I think some of them even had soldiers, or replicas of soldiers, buried with them to protect them, or something. I can't remember it all anymore." Those days were a long time ago, before the police murdered her father during a "routine" interrogation.

"That's what you think this place is? Some kind of burial vault for royalty or something?"

"Well, it has the right feel to it. I mean, who – or what – would be important enough to the Kreelans that all these warriors would stand around it, guarding it, I guess, until they themselves died?"

"But then," he asked, "what happened to the others, the ones who brought these warriors here? There must have been some, right? And why did they leave?" He thought for a moment. "Wait a minute. Maybe not all of them did. If pieces of shrekkas were laying around, maybe there was some kind of battle here?"

"But then who are these people? The winners, or the losers? Or maybe someone else?"

"Who knows?" Eustus said. "But we haven't found your king's – or queen's – body, yet."

"Let's move toward the center of the room."

"Okay, but be careful."

With Enya still holding the light, the two of them slowly moved toward where the center of the chamber should be, at least according to the facing of the long dead Kreelan sentinels. There were a lot of them, probably hundreds.

"This room is really big," Enya whispered as they moved through the darkness to a point where nothing was visible around them but the floor, which had been inlaid with colored stones or tiles that had remained like new, polished and free of any trace of dust. The lighter's flame, tiny though it was, cast enough light that they could no longer see the blue glow that lay somewhere in front of them. "How long will this thing last?" she asked about the lighter.

"A few hours," Eustus said. "I fill it up every time I use it. It runs on some kind of high-tech..."

Enya did not have to ask why his sentence abruptly ended. It didn't matter, anyway. She would not have been paying attention. She had seen what had cast Eustus into sudden silence. "What is that?" she whispered.

Before them lay the treasure over which the ancient male warriors had been standing silent guard for countless centuries. Atop a spire of something resembling clear and slender glass sat what looked like nothing so much as an opaque crystal in the shape of some living thing's heart. And at its center shone a faint blue glow.

The two of them stood there for a moment, transfixed by what they saw, by the simple but undeniable elegance and beauty of the structure before them, which itself stood only as high as Eustus's shoulder. The crystal heart itself was a bit larger than a man's fist.

"This is where the light was coming from, then," Eustus said quietly as he moved closer. "The color's right, but it's so much weaker now. You can hardly see it at all."

Looking more closely at the glassine pillar on which the heart was poised, Enya said, "I don't know much about the Kreelans, but they must have incredible artisans. I'm not much of an art expert – Mallorys aren't even allowed in the few good museums here – but my personal opinion is that there was an incredible talent and genius behind whoever made this."

"So, this is our – what did they call them? – pharaoh, a piece of sculpted crystal with a blue glow in it. A radioactive isotope maybe?"

"Cherenkov radiation?"

"What kind of books did your father let you read, anyway?" Eustus asked, smiling. "I thought you were supposed to be a dumb miner or something. Cherenkov radiation... I don't know, maybe."

Enya stepped closer to the spire, the light now playing crazily through the glass. "What could it be?" she whispered to herself as she extended a hand toward the crystal heart.

"Enya," Eustus warned, "maybe you shouldn't–"

It was too late. As her fingers brushed the crystal's surface, Eustus's ears were filled with the crackle of electricity and his nose with the smell of ozone as the crystal heart suddenly pulsed with light, a blue flame so bright it left spots swirling in his vision.

"Enya!" he shouted, grabbing her by the shoulder and whirling her away from the crystal that had begun to pulsate erratically. "Are you all right? Answer me!"

She only trembled in his arms, as if she were in a state of shock. Her eyes were wide open, staring at the crystal, her lips trembling but mute.

Eustus half dragged, half carried her back toward the entrance. He noticed in the sudden explosion of light that there were six other tunnels leading down here. He was not confused as to which one to take because of the pile of smoldering bones that was the Kreelan warrior he had shot, whose shattered remains now served as a gruesome trail marker.

Behind him, the crystal heart began to pulse more rhythmically, and the light coming from it grew with every beat, so intense that Eustus did not need any other source of light as he frantically made his way down the tunnel.

Something is going to happen, his mind screamed at him. They had to get out...

"Eustus," he heard Enya rasp.

"I'm here," he told her as he propelled her along, ignoring the pain in his foot from when he twisted it entering the chamber. "We're getting out of here!"

His ears began to tingle, and he realized that the voices were coming again. And he suddenly realized what the sound really was: it was the voices of the warriors standing guard over that thing. Eustus did not believe in ghosts, but he knew with absolute certainty that what they had heard was not the sound of wind through caves, or anything artificial. Those dead mouths back there might not be moving, but that's where the sound originally came from. Where it came from now, he did not know, nor did he wish to find out.

The light continued to brighten, much faster now, and Eustus was almost blinded even facing away from it. Worse, he felt like his neck and arms were getting sunburned.

It's some kind of bomb, he thought suddenly. That only made him move faster.

The voices, when they finally came, were every bit as loud as before, but Eustus was ready for the pain, at least psychologically. What he was not ready for was the song itself. No longer a mournful dirge, the voices seemed to be elated, filled with joy at something that Eustus probably would never understand.

Behind him, even as the voices rose, he could hear the snapping and popping of flames as the mummies began to burn in whatever supernatural flame Enya's touch had sparked. He could hear the air crackle with heat, a wind rising in the tunnel as the heated air sought freedom outside, rushing up behind them like a frenzied locomotive.

"Eustus, what is it?" Enya cried. "What is happening?"

"I don't know," he screamed over the rising chorus of the dead warriors and the crackling hum growing behind him like a rapidly approaching storm. "Hang on!"

With a final leap, they hurled themselves into space, falling from the cliff face through the afternoon air toward the lake. They hit the water just as a stream of blue light, bright as any sun, exploded from the shaft and into space.

Far below, Eustus and Enya struggled toward the shore of the lake and sanctuary from the power of the alien beacon that now reached out toward the stars.

* * *

Reza stood in the company headquarters, thinking, waiting. Suddenly he felt a tingling at the base of his skull, unlike anything he had ever felt before. A warning?

"Alfonso..." he said to Zevon before getting to his feet and going to the door. Opening it and looking outside, he noticed nothing amiss. All was as it should be. Freeing his spirit, he searched around the encampment for any threat to his people, his mind's eye scouring every rock and tree.

"Sir?" Alfonso asked quietly, his rifle at the ready to protect his commander. He knew Reza probably did not need it, but that would not keep him from being prepared.

"I do not know," Reza said as he completed his mental sweep of the area. Nothing. But the tingling continued, grew stronger. "Something feels... wrong? Different? I am not sure."

Zevon scanned the area, as well. He happened to be looking at the enormous mesa a few kilometers away when seven streams of electric blue light erupted from it and shot through the sky.

"Captain! Look at that!" All around the bivouac, Marines were leaping to their fighting positions, regardless of what they had been doing.

But Reza did not hear him, nor did he see the blazing blue lances Zevon was frantically pointing out to him. He did not have to. At the instant the beams erupted from the ancient cavern, Reza felt as if a set of electrodes had been inserted into his brain and an invisible switch thrown.

Convulsing but a single time, Reza's eyes rolled up to expose the whites before he collapsed to the ground.

* * *

Eustus fought to keep his footing as Enya helped him run through the forest and Hell erupted behind them. He still couldn't believe they had managed to survive the fall from the blazing tunnel into the lake. They had struggled to shore and started running for their lives.

"Look!" she shouted above the roar of the cataclysm behind them.

Turning his head just enough to peer back through the canopy of smoldering trees, Eustus could see that the shaft of blue light behind them had changed its position. Sweeping slowly in a horizontal arc through the mountain, the beams – he could see others now, too, lancing toward the horizon – were slicing the rock apart, as if they were consuming the upper half of the mountain. Sheets of flame and rock, molten and vaporized to plasma, shot out and upward. The lake was now a boiling pit, the trees at its edge bursting into flame from the heat of the ash and rock that spewed from the disintegrating mountain. Beneath them, the ground shook with the force of an earthquake, the trees around them swaying precariously over their heads.

"Come on!" he shouted, pushing her forward, "We've got to get out of here!"

"Where are the horses?" she cried.

"Long gone, if they've got any brains at all. Run!"

They staggered onward, forcing steadily hotter air into their lungs. Eustus felt like the steam that was now roiling from the doomed lake was poaching them. Above them, he could hear the crackling of the treetops as they burst into flame. And everywhere was the rain of ash and glowing blobs of molten rock.

Behind them, the great beams continued to circle the mountain, faster now, grinding and burning it away to expose the pulsing core that Enya had somehow brought to life.

"Look out!" Enya screamed as she shoved Eustus aside, both of them toppling over a rock outcropping. A huge chunk of burning rock smashed to the ground where they had just been, burning a hole into the earth. "What are we going to do?"

Eustus didn't have a good answer. The smoke-filled air was so hot it was almost searing their lungs, and flaming debris was raining all around them. As slow as he was moving now, limping along on his injured ankle, they didn't stand a chance of escaping the fire.

"Enya," he pulled her close so she could hear him shouting, and also so that he could feel her next to him one more time, "I'm not going to make it. Can't run fast enough. You've got to go on alone, try to–"

"No! I'm not leaving you! We both go or we both stay!" The look in her eyes left no room for argument as her hands tightened in his.

He turned away, not wanting Enya to see the look of hopelessness on his face. He expected to die in the Corps, but he never thought it would be like this. And not with the woman he loved beside him.

He looked up to the sky, now so clouded with smoke and ash that the sun was no more than a dim disk in the darkness, searching for inspiration. Instead, he saw salvation.

"Look!" he shouted, pointing at the glinting metal shape that was rocketing toward them. "They've found us! They must've homed in on my comm link!" Eustus had tried to call the company and warn them of what was going on, but could hear nothing over the din crashing all around them.

Weaving through the flaming treetops, the hail of liquid rock spattering dangerously on its lightly armored sides, the "jeep" – one of a dozen light utility skimmers in the company – settled half a meter above the ground beside them, the troop door already open. Eustus saw a fully armed and armored figure with the name ZEVON stenciled on the helmet, frantically gesturing for him to get on board.

"Get in!" he shouted at Enya, who needed no further prompting. Zevon hoisted her aboard with one arm, his other still clutching his rifle, aiming it out beyond Eustus. With a grunt of effort, Eustus threw himself in after her, slamming the hatch shut just as a shotgun blast of debris hit the outside of the door.

"That was close, Top," Zevon said through gritted teeth as the jeep's pilot raced upward and away from the burning forest as fast as the little vehicle could take them. The debris outside sounded like hammers were being thrown at the skimmer, and Eustus's nose filled with the smell of charred clothes, skin, hair, trees, rock, and metal. "What the fuck – sorry ma'am – happened?" Zevon asked.

Eustus and Enya exchanged a strained look. "We don't really know," Eustus said as he took a long drink from the canteen Zevon handed him. He gave another to Enya.

"The Kreelans have been here," Enya told him. "It was a long time ago, probably hundreds or maybe even thousands of years. There was what looked like a tomb or something deep in the mountain." She cast her eyes down. "I think I touched something I shouldn't have."

"Yeah," Zevon said, looking worried, "looks like it."

"Back off, Zevon," Eustus warned. "It wasn't her fault."

"It doesn't matter to me, Top," the younger man replied. "But you two are going to have to explain to the XO why the company commander is in a coma."

"What the hell do you mean, he's in a coma?" Eustus demanded. "What happened to him?"

"He got some kind of funny feeling just before those beams lit off," Zevon explained. "Said he felt like something was wrong or different, but he didn't know what. We went outside to look. A minute later, all hell broke loose back there where you were, and the next thing I know the captain stiffens like someone hit him with a cattle prod, and he falls to the ground like a sack of potatoes." Zevon was silent for a moment. Reza had been like a father to him, and he was not able to deal with the situation as well as he would have liked. "The medtechs have been working on him, but all they know for sure is that he's in some kind of coma."

Eustus closed his eyes. "Sweet Jesus, what have we done?"

Enya leaned close against him, tears in her eyes.

"Eustus, I'm so sorry. It was stupid. I–"

He put a finger to her lips. "It wasn't your fault. There was no way for us to know. I should have dragged us out of there the instant we figured out it was Kreelan, and gone to get Reza."

The jeep emerged from the cloud of smoke and spiraled in to land at the Marine firebase, now fully alerted to a disaster the magnitude of which had yet to become apparent.

Fifteen

Lieutenant Josef Weigand sipped at a cup of scalding, bitter coffee as he struggled to stay awake and alert.

Lord of All, he thought, how I hate this job. He almost laughed at himself. He thought the same thing at least a hundred times a day, but he had refused every opportunity to give it up.

He took a moment to look through his ship's forward viewport, giving his eyes a rest from scanning the battery of instruments that surrounded the command console, as if he would notice anything before the computer did. Outside lay a seemingly endless nebula of swirling gas and dust that danced to a rhythm measured in millennia, giving off light and radiation in brilliant displays that surely could have been the inspiration for Dante's Inferno. This was why he always decided to sign on for yet one more tour, one more mission as a scout: the bloody view.

Weigand was one of eight men and women crammed into a tiny ship that only had a number, SV1287, for a name. At least that is how she appeared on the Navy's ship registry. But to her crew, she was the Obstinate, a name that applied equally well to her maintenance and operation, as to her defiance in the face of the enemy.

Defiance, however, was not the mission of Obstinate's crew. A scoutship, she was a specialist in the fleet, packed with every passive scanning instrument her tiny hull could accommodate. Her unarmored skin bristled with dozens of telescopes and antenna arrays to pick up the faintest trace of the enemy without betraying her own position. She carried no weapons, and the only time she activated any radiating sensors or shields was when she was in friendly space or in the direst emergency. Her job was to watch and listen, but to be neither seen nor heard herself. The only contact she had with human space was through the secure tight-beam communications gear she used to communicate with the STARNET intelligence network and fleet command.

Another benefit of scout work, Weigand thought wryly as he refocused his attention on the signal monitors. There was no brass to worry about, no additional duties to drive a junior officer crazy, no ass-kissing. Nothing but him, his little crew, his ship, and the stars. And if the Kreelans wanted to find him... well, they'd have to catch him first. Obstinate was one of the fastest ships in the human fleet, and with her big ears and eyes, she would know long in advance about any Kreelan ship coming her way.

He heard a few muffled moans coming from the back and smiled. Stankovic and Wallers again, he figured. With eight people crammed into a tiny tin can for three to six months at a time, some allowance had to be made for romance. Or outright lust. Whatever. At least that's the way Weigand looked at it. As long as things didn't get out of hand and jeopardize their mission – which he did, in the end, take seriously – he let nature take its course. Personally, he preferred to remain celibate while on patrol, not out of any lip service to some mythical superior morality, but because it was simply too complicated. People who thought they loved one another or just wanted to play grab-ass one day all too often hated each other the next, and the last thing a scoutship commander needed was an overly neurotic crew. And the crew could not afford a commander who was a few newtons shy of full thrust mentally, or involved in some emotional skirmish with one or more crewmembers. The possibilities for disaster were simply too great out here, all alone. Among the crew, he had his ways of straightening things out, just as long as he didn't get involved himself.

No, Weigand preferred looking out the viewport to wrestling under the covers, at least until port call and the mandatory month-long crew stand-down. With a sigh, he chose to exercise his only viable option: he would have to make do with the ship's coffee. It was a poor trade for months without sex and a decent drink, but there was nothing to be done about it.

More moans, louder this time. Buddha, he thought, didn't these kids ever sleep?

Then he heard the thunk of a boot against a bulkhead panel and another voice admonishing the young lovers to keep it down in language that was far from romantic.

Here we go again, Weigand thought. The other seven members of Obstinate's crew were all in the crew section, trying to sleep – or whatever – through the transition shift. Weigand preferred to have his little crew rotate shift partners periodically, to keep anyone from either getting too attached or too hateful of any one person. The transition shift was when he made them all eat, sleep, and crap on the same schedule for twenty-four hours until the new cycle came up and they switched partners. He took the twenty-four hour duty himself, while the crew battled it out in back. It was his favorite part of the cruise: he got to be alone for a whole day, to sit and watch over the computer as it sniffed through the thousands of cubic light years around them for traces of the enemy.

He glanced at the main intel display, which presented the computer's slow-witted human controllers with an easily assimilated visual representation of the space around them, and whatever it had found within it. Scouting was a lot like fishing, he thought, checking out each fishing hole in turn to see if you got a bite. He had been on some missions where they had not spotted a single Kreelan ship or outpost in three months. Other times, they had to extend the tour weeks on end to wait out Kreelan warships that prowled the scout's patrol area. But most patrols were somewhere in between, with Kreelan activity present in some spots, and absent at others.

In this case, a few light years into the QS-385 sector – a quaint name for a zone of space that no one otherwise cared about, far beyond even the human-settled Rim colonies – Josef Weigand the interstellar fisherman had gotten more than a nibble. After jumping into the nebular cloud to conceal her arrival, Obstinate's sensors had immediately picked up three separate sets of Kreelan activity, all within a radius of about fifty light years. Two were clearly warship flotillas by their rapid movement across the sector, apparently en route to the third, which appeared to be some kind of outpost or settlement with vessels already in orbit. This was the kind of find that the crews of other ships like the Obstinate hoped to discover. Fleet command was keen to go on the offensive somewhere – anywhere – in hopes of drawing the Kreelans away from human settlements, following the maxim that a good defense comprised a good offense. With that in mind, "indigenous" Kreelan outposts such as this one were at the top of the list. Several such worlds had been found, but most were too far away or too well-defended (as far as the scoutships could determine) to be attacked without taking too much from defensive campaigns on human-settled worlds that already stretched Navy and Marine resources to the limit.

From the looks of it, Weigand thought dejectedly, this world fell into the same category. While the computer had only been able to identify three of the dozen or more ships out there by class, what it told Weigand was depressing: they were all dreadnoughts. Battleships, and big ones, too. Even if a human fleet could get here, he told himself, they would have a hell of a fight ahead of them before the jarheads even hit dirt.

He watched another display in silence as the computer busily worked away at identifying the remaining ships, comparing their signatures with known Kreelan ship profiles and playing an extraordinarily complicated guessing game for those that did not fit. Unfortunately for Confederation

Navy analysts, the Kreelans did not build their ships in classes – each comprising one or more ships of similar construction and characteristics – like the humans did. It was as if they hand-built every ship from scratch, tailoring it to serve some unknown purpose in an equally mysterious master plan. Some tiny ships carried a tremendous punch, while a few of the larger ones were practically defenseless. And so, the analyst who needed to categorize the Kreelan ships as something settled for a generalization: fighter, corvette, destroyer, cruiser, battleship, super-battleship, and so on. The only advantage to their ships being unique, of course, was that once identified, they could be tracked just as men in ships and submarines on long-ago Earth had tracked one another, using the unique sonic signature produced by each vessel.

None of these ships, however, matched any of the thousands of entries in the computer's database. More depressing news, Weigand thought. More ships we've never even seen before. More ships to fight.

The display flashed three times to alert him that it had completed another identification, showing him everything it had determined about the ship and its postulated class.

"Oh, great," he murmured. "A super-battleship this time. Isn't that special." That made it two battleships identified in one flotilla, plus another battleship and this super-battleship in the second. He pitied the human squadron that ever had the misfortune of running into either of these groups. And the Lord of All only knew what was in the squadron orbiting the outpost.

"Well," he said, reluctantly setting down his coffee in the special holder someone had glued to the console, "I guess it's time to phone home and tell mommy and daddy the bad news." Super-battleship sightings qualified for immediate reporting, regardless of where they were or what other activity was going on. Short of invasion alerts, they were the Navy's highest priority.

He was just calling up the STARNET link when an audible alarm went off.

"Warning," the computer said urgently in the sultry female voice Weigand had programmed in, "radical change in profile for targets Alpha, Bravo, and Charlie. Vector analysis initiated."

Weigand ignored the flashing STARNET access screen, alerting him to the fact that he was accessing a controlled military intelligence link, and that any unauthorized use could result in fines, imprisonment, or both. "Highlight profile changes," he snapped.

The main holo display split into three smaller holos, each zoomed in on one of the three Kreelan targets. "Targets Alpha and Bravo" – the two maneuvering flotillas with the battlewagons – "are executing near-simultaneous course changes toward a similar navigation vector. A new maneuvering target is separating from target Charlie; designating new target Delta. Target Delta is accelerating rapidly along a similar vector as Alpha and Bravo."

Weigand watched as the two designated flotillas hauled themselves around in what he could see was more than a casual maneuver: the ships were cutting the tightest circle in space that they could. The third flotilla, coming out of orbit, was accelerating at what must be full thrust to get far enough away from the planet's gravity well to jump into hyperspace.

"Warning," the computer bleated again, "Targets Alpha and Bravo have executed hyperspace jump. Calculated time for target Delta is thirty-six seconds."

Those ships were going somewhere and fast, Weigand thought. He hit the ship's alert klaxon. Stankovic and Wallers would have to finish their little party some other time.

"Crew to general quarters!" he snapped over the intercom.

Golda, his exec, was in the seat next to his before the klaxon finished its third beat and automatically switched off. There was no need for big-ship sounds in a scoutship. "What's going on, Josef?" she asked as she strapped in and scanned her console.

"Alpha and Bravo just hauled around to similar vectors and jumped," he told her as he started the computer feeding information to STARNET while he began composing a manual report for the intel types on the other end. "A new crowd came zipping out of orbit–"

"Target Delta has jumped into hyperspace," the computer said, "at time nineteen thirty-seven-oh-four Zulu."

"Computer," Golda said, ignoring the bustle of the other six people on board who were now cramming themselves into their respective positions throughout the tiny vessel, "can you project navigation vectors to potential targets?" Unlike in "real" space, where a ship could alter course at will, in hyperspace it was restricted to linear motion along its last vector until it dropped back into the Einsteinian universe. That being the case, the ship's vector just before it jumped could be used to plot potential destinations. Of course, there was always the chance the ship would drop out of hyperspace somewhere, maneuver onto a different vector, and jump again in a completely different direction.

"The only human target along projected axials for all three target groups is Erlang, trans-Grange Sector," the computer said immediately.

"What's on Erlang?" Weigand asked as he watched the computer pump information into the STARNET buffer before it was sent in a subspace burst to a receiver many light years away.

"Population one point five million. Terran sister world. Responsible for seventy-five percent of strategic minerals and metals for trans-Grange shipyards."

He and Golda shared a glance. "Estimate the probability of Erlang vector being initial course only, and not the final destination."

The computer was silent for a moment. "Probability is non-zero."

"What the hell is that supposed to mean?" Golda asked.

Before the computer could reply with its own explanation, Weigand said, "It means that whoever's on Erlang is going to be hip-deep in shit."

* * *

Those were the same sentiments of the young Marine STARNET watch officer. Buried in the special STARNET processing and analysis center two kilometers beneath the surface of Earth's moon, she glowered at the reports from three different scoutships. They were in far flung regions that read the same except for numbers and types of ships: a massive Kreelan battle fleet, probably the largest ever seen during the entire war, was headed for Erlang.

"Send a FLASH to Tenth Fleet," she ordered the yeoman sitting at the fleet communications station, "and get confirmation that they have this information."

While the analysts behind her were busy piecing together what information they had, she turned to her own console and hit a particular button. After a moment when all her screen said was "Call in Progress: Line Secure," a bleary-eyed but alert face finally appeared.

"Admiral Zhukovski," she said, "STARNET is declaring an impending invasion alert for Erlang, in the Trans-Grange sector."

A man all too used to these calls in the middle of the night, Zhukovski's expression hardened, a reflection of his soul as it readied itself for more bad news, the announcement that yet more human lives were about to be lost.

"Brief me, captain," was all he said before he sat back, his good eye fixed on her image as he listened to her report, his good hand clenched tightly out of view of the monitor.

Sixteen

Enya sat quietly in the semi-darkness of the hastily completed command bunker, shielded from the ops section by a blanket hung over a cord strung between two walls. She was maintaining a vigil over Reza. Three days after she had touched the crystal and started the mysterious reaction, Reza still lay unconscious. His heart beat very slowly, his breathing slower still. In fact, were it not for the sophisticated medical instruments available to the company medics, they probably would have thought him dead.

In the meantime, the rain of ash from the disintegrating mountain had finally stopped, most of it consumed by the cutting beams originating in the center of the mountain. Finally spinning so fast that the beams became a nearly solid disk of energy, they began to sweep upward, forming a rapidly narrowing cone of brilliant cyan that quickly destroyed what was left of the mountain. They swept the debris up and away into the upper reaches of the atmosphere where it formed a cloud that easily rivaled the one on Earth after the explosion of Krakatoa centuries before. The area around the mountain had experienced horrendous winds that had done much damage to Mallory city and the nearby townships. But those, too, had finally subsided, leaving amazingly few casualties in their wake. After the beams had done their work clearing away the mountain top, they also disappeared, leaving behind a perfectly smooth bowl, a gigantic crater, that now radiated a ghostly blue glow, much less intense than the cutting beams, from its center into the dark heavens above.

"Any change?" Hawthorne asked quietly.

Enya shook her head. They had kept Reza here in the company firebase instead of moving him to the hospital in Mallory City mainly because Washington Hawthorne seemed to trust Belisle even less than the Mallorys did. Besides, Hawthorne had figured that it would not make any difference. A Mallory General Hospital neuro specialist had come and examined Reza, but could not make heads or tails of his vital signs and the basic changes in his physiology that had been wrought in the Empire. He wanted to run a quartermaster's list of tests on him, but Hawthorne had politely refused and thanked the man for his time. He knew that the tests would only help satisfy the surgeon's curiosity, and not help Reza to recover.

"No," she said quietly, shaking her head dejectedly, "no change yet." They had assured her that this was not her fault, but it was. If only she had not touched that... thing.

Washington put a massive hand lightly on her shoulder. "Don't worry," he said. "Reza's a tough bastard. He's breathing. He'll be okay."

"Oh, Mister Hawthorne," she asked, "what have I done? What is that thing out there?"

"Your guess is as good as mine, probably better, because you seem to know something about most anything, or so Eustus tells me." He smiled to make sure she knew it was intended as a compliment, and not sarcasm. She only managed a weak parody of a smile in return. "Look, why don't we take a break and get some coffee? Eustus'll be back pretty soon from checking on Counselor Savitch in the city, and I'd feel awful bad if he had to see you like this."

"Thank you, but–"

"Enya, give it a rest. You can't take the whole universe on your shoulders. Please, trust me. He'll be all right. Erlang will be all right. I promise."

She knew that he could not possibly keep such a promise, but his saying it seemed, for now, enough. "All right. I'll take you up on it. But only if you find me some tea; your coffee is terrible."

Hawthorne laughed quietly as he followed her out of the tiny cubicle and into the red and green glows of the equipment in the ops section.

* * *

"What is thy name, child?" a voice softly asked from somewhere near, somewhere far away, speaking in the Old Tongue.

"Reza," he said, wondering if he had somehow been blinded by whatever had struck him. All around him was darkness, cold. And then he realized he had no eyes. No body. He floated in Nothingness, a spirit without form. "Where am I?" he asked, strangely unafraid. Thus has Death come, he thought.

"You are... here," the voice said. "You are with Me."

"Who are you?" He could sense the spirit that spoke to him as his feet sensed the earth: he could judge only that it was there, but not how great it might be.

"I am She," the voice began with a flare of pride and power before it faltered. "I am... Keel-Tath." Reza sensed time beyond his understanding in the brief pause that followed, time that spanned millennia. "Long has it been, my child. Long have I waited for you, for The One."

Reza felt a spark of excitement, a tremor of fear. The One, who was to fulfill The Prophecy. "Keel-Tath," he thought/spoke Her name in awe.

"Yes," She said. "Yes, that is – was – my name before the Ascension, before... the Darkness." He felt Her touch as might two clouds brushing against one another in the sky, their forms distinct, yet one. "Lonely have I been, My child, waiting for you to come, to awaken Me, with only the songs of the Guardians to keep Me company here, in this place of mourning." Her spirit shimmered against him, a touch of leather, a touch of silk. Power. Curiosity. Love. Sadness. "But that time is past," She said, Her spirit brightening as the sunrise over a tranquil sea. "You and I shall become as One, and all shall be forgiven."

"My Empress," Reza whispered, his spirit electrified by Her touch, and terrified of revealing the truth to Her, "I am not the vessel to bring you forth once again into the world."

Curiosity again, so intense that he shrank back in fear, but there was nowhere for him to retreat to, for She was everywhere, everything; She was the Universe itself. "You were not born of My womb, yet you are of My blood," She said as the eyes of Her spirit probed to his very core, all that he was and was not laid bare before Her inquisitive gaze. "You wear the collar of My honor, yet you are shunned by the peers. You are of the Way, yet you are apart, lost to the love of She-Who-Followed... and to She-Who-Shall-Come. A warrior priest of the Desh-Ka, the greatest order that ever was, that ever shall be, and who never again shall see his temple. You are The One, child."

He felt her curiosity continue to swarm over him like a mass of inquisitive insects, hovering, darting, drawing out all that lay within his heart, his mind. He cried out in fear and pain, anguish and rage at what could have been, but would never be. He begged for Her to hold him, to comfort him against the pain. He begged for Her to destroy him, to cast him into the pit of Oblivion and the darkness of the damned.

At last Her curiosity was satisfied, for She knew of him all there was to know. "Child," she said, enfolding him in warmth, "you need not fear My wrath, for your heart and courage are worthy of My love, and the lonely melody of thy blood is joy to My ears, a song that shall forever live in My heart. I know the measure of thy Way, and that the time of My return draws near. You are The One who shall redeem the sins of others, and who in turn shall return to grace."

She held him in Her heart that he would know Her love, and told him, "Do not fear the Darkness, My child. For while in this lonely place My eyes are blind to what is, to what will be, there shall come a day when I again will open My eyes to the light of the sun of the world of My birth, and smell the scents of the garden of the great palace that was built in My name. And on that day, My son, shall you be saved."

Reza would have spoken then, but She held him, stilled him. "Until that day, you must live according to the Way you have chosen, for the glory and honor of She-Who-Reigns."

She withdrew from around him, fading into the Nothingness from which She had come, into the voices of those whose spirits had comforted Her mourning heart through the ages. "Rise, My child," she commanded from afar. "Awaken."

Seventeen

"President Belisle, I demand an explanation." Counselor Savitch was more than furious. She was outraged.

"I'll be honest with you, counselor," Belisle said, a sneer on his face as he looked out the closed French doors onto the still ash-covered balcony of his parliament office. The two of them were alone. Despite their protests, Savitch and Belisle both had insisted that her Marine bodyguards remain outside the door. "Your coming here was, shall we say, an unpleasant surprise," he told her. "I had asked the Council for Marines to help the cowards in the Territorial Army keep the Mallorys in their place, but no one ever counted on getting a half-breed traitor like Reza Gard and that motley band of thugs in Marine uniforms." He grimaced. "That was a mistake that no one was able to foresee."

Melissa Savitch shivered at the hatred in the man's voice, wondering what anyone could ever have done to him to make him so completely devoid of compassion toward a fellow human soul. But he didn't think of Reza as human, did he? she thought.

"Yes," he went on, almost as if to himself, "he really took me by surprise, and calling you in made it a damned bleeding liberal party." He turned from the glass doors to face her, a sly, serpentine smile on his face. "But that's all in the past, let me assure you."

"Just what is that supposed to mean?"

"It means, counselor, that your services are no longer required," a new voice said. Behind her, the door to one of the three anterooms adjoining Belisle's office had opened, and a Marine whom she had never seen before silently stepped into the room.

"I'd like you to meet Colonel Markus Thorella, commander of the First Guards Marine Assault Regiment," Belisle said as he began backing away from her.

She was about to say something when her eyes caught sight of the dark metal shape in Thorella's hand.

"Sorry, counselor," he said. His voice did not sound particularly apologetic.

Thorella's predatory smile was the last thing she saw before the blast from his pistol vaporized her skull.

* * *

"Sir!" shouted the comms technician from her console. "We've got trouble!"

"What now?" Washington Hawthorne growled, covering the distance to the lance corporal's position in three great strides.

"Sergeant Bayern radioed 'Black Watch,' then she went off the air," the comms tech said as her fingers flew over the console's controls. "I haven't been able to raise her again. No contact with PFC Morita, either."

Hawthorne's face grew tight, his fists clenching tight. "She didn't get out what it was?"

"No sir," the comms tech told him. "But I heard what sounded like firing, pulse guns." She paused. "Two shots. I think Bayern was already hit when she called in."

Hawthorne's blood ran cold with anger. "Goddamn," he hissed.

"What happened?" Enya asked quietly, afraid of what she might hear. "What is 'Black Watch?'"

Hawthorne turned to her, his eyes angry white orbs in his black face. "That's a shorthand code for what we call a losing proposition, when Death has you by the collar and you've only got time to get out a word or two. Two Marines, and probably Counselor Savitch, are gone. Dead."

"My Lord," Enya whispered, getting unsteadily to her feet. "Why? What could have happened?"

Hawthorne turned on her, his voice savage not because he wanted it to be, but because he needed the truth, and fast. "Were any of the Mallorys planning anything against Belisle or Savitch? Anything?"

Enya shook her head, shocked that he would even consider such a thing. "Of course not," she said angrily, her own fears boiling up inside. "We had everything to gain from the Counselor's intervention, and literally nothing to lose. None of the Mallorys, even the farthest fringes, planned anything but cooperation with her. We did not trust Belisle – as I see now was wise – but we were not planning anything against him. We have suffered too much and waited too long for what the counselor promised to deliver. Only now it looks as though it was all in vain."

Hawthorne nodded, relieved. "I'm sorry Enya, but I had to know."

She nodded that she understood. "What will you do?" she asked.

"I'm not sure yet," he said, uncomfortable with the situation. His choices were extremely limited. It had been bad enough sitting a few kilometers from some kind of Kreelan-induced cataclysm, the full effects of which they could not even guess at. Now he had to deal with what appeared to be treachery and murder on the part of fellow humans. "It looks like we'll have to send a recon patrol in to find Savitch, but–"

"Reza!" Enya suddenly exclaimed as she saw the Marine captain emerge from behind the curtain that separated his sick-bed from the ops center. His face was extraordinarily pale, even in this dim light. She ran over to help him as he began to slump against the wall. Hawthorne was close behind. "You should be in bed!" Enya told him as she helped him up. "You look terrible."

He shook his head, a look of impatience on his face.

"Captain," Hawthorne said as he took over from Enya in helping Reza, wrapping one tree-trunk of an arm around his commander's waist.

"Washington," he rasped as his exec settled him onto one of the metal chairs clustered around the tactical display, "we are in grave, grave danger."

"What do you mean, sir?" Hawthorne handed Reza a canteen, from which Reza drank greedily. He was soaked with sweat, dehydrated.

"First, tell me exactly what happened when I passed out."

Hawthorne turned to Enya, who guiltily explained everything that had happened in the mountain and since then. Reza listened in silence, his eyes focused on the wall, on something only he could see.

"What does it mean?" she asked when she was through. "What will happen to us? To Erlang?"

"Very likely," Reza said, "this world will be destroyed." They sat in stunned silence as he went on. "You have stumbled upon something that has been lost to the Empire for over one hundred thousand years, something that they value over all else in the Universe: the tomb of the First Empress. She was the most powerful of their kind who has ever lived." He paused for a moment, taking another drink. "I have no doubt that every available Kreelan warship within hundreds of parsecs is heading here at this very moment."

"Can we capture or destroy it?" Washington asked, groping for some kind of leverage, something he could fight the enemy with when they came. "Maybe even take it hostage?"

Reza shook his head. "You cannot take a spirit hostage, nor can it be captured or destroyed." He nodded toward the wall display that showed a panorama of the outside and the glowing bowl that once had been a mountain, and was now only a reflector of the crystal heart's mysterious aura. "Anyone or anything who is not of the Blood and ventures into that light will perish as surely as if they had set foot upon the face of a star."

"And if you think that's good news," Hawthorne said grimly, "you're going to love this..." He told Reza about what had happened to Bayern and Morita, and his suspicions that Savitch was dead.

Eustus suddenly appeared through the tunnel entrance to the bunker, his back soaked with sweat: the air conditioner in his skimmer was not working.

"Reza!" he blurted. His eyes were wide with relief that his friend and commanding officer was alive. But his enthusiasm dimmed when he saw the look on everyone's face. It was the expression of the Damned. "What's wrong? What the hell is going on?"

"Eustus," Enya said, coming to embrace him openly in front of his fellow Marines, something she had promised him she would never do, "I fear I have killed us all."

"What–" He never got a chance to finish.

"Captain," the corporal at the comms console interrupted, her face ashen, but for a different reason, "Sir, I think you'd better come over here."

Reza did as she asked, walking unsteadily the two meters to her position. "Yes, corporal?"

"It's a call for you, sir," she said, stepping away from the terminal.

And there on the visual display was the grinning face of Colonel Markus Thorella.

"Well, well, well," he said, "if it isn't my favorite captain." The smile grew wider, more menacing. "It's been a long time, Gard."

Reza's blood trilled with fury at the man's face, Belisle just visible behind him: the mysterious deaths of his two Marines had just been explained.

* * *

The two men glared at one another for a long time, Reza struggling to restrain the fire in his blood, Thorella smiling with unconcealed smugness.

"What did you do to my Marines?" Reza asked in a voice as cold and empty as the depths of space.

"I was just going to ask you about that, captain," Colonel Thorella said conversationally. "It would appear that the civil authority here," he nodded to Belisle, "seems to think they got a little out of hand. What was it you said, Mr. President?" he asked rhetorically. "Ah, yes. Murdering Counselor Savitch. I'm afraid my troops and I weren't quite fast enough to keep your troops from committing that heinous crime, but we were able to prevent Erlang's lawful president from coming to harm." His smile became the hard-mouthed frown Reza had learned to be wary of during his time on

Quantico. "And then there's this fascinating incident with the mountain, or what's left of it. I'm afraid you've got some explaining to do, captain."

"And what of the Mallorys in the Parliament Building?" Enya blurted out from behind Reza.

"Ah," Thorella said brightly. "You must be the young and witty Enya Terragion. I'm terribly sorry, my dear, but your friends have been arrested as accomplices to murder. Even as we speak, the rest of your illegal council is being arrested. But don't worry. We'll be by soon enough to take care of you, too." He turned his attention back to Reza, who stood shivering with rage. "And you, captain, should not have been so stupid as to try and be the great righter of perceived wrongs," he said as if he were speaking to a child who had done something wrong, but who should have known better. "You were foolish to the last, and now you're going to pay the price. Hawthorne!"

"Sir," the big man said, reluctantly moving toward the screen. He knew what was coming.

"So nice to see you again, Hawthorne. It's too bad you didn't choose another regiment, though. You might have one day made a good regimental commander. As it is, you'll go no higher than your friend." To whom he turned his attention once again. "Captain Gard, as senior Marine officer on Erlang, I hereby relieve you of your command. Hawthorne, you are now in command of your company. Do you understand me?"

"Yes, sir," he rasped, his eyes narrowed to angry slits.

"That's good, because I have orders for you. First, you are to place Captain Gard and Enya Terragion under arrest and confine them until representatives of my regiment pick them up for holding pending court-marital for the captain and civil arraignment for Ms. Terragion on charges of conspiracy to commit murder. Second, you will order your company to stand down and prepare for immediate transport off-planet, as per President Belisle's fervent wishes. You've done enough damage here already. We don't need any more. Is all of that crystal clear, captain?"

"Yes, sir."

"Good. Carry on." And the screen went blank.

It was a long time before anyone said anything. It was Enya who spoke first.

"Reza," she whispered, placing a hand on his still-shaking arm. "I am so sorry."

"That murdering bastard," Eustus spat at where Thorella's image was no more than a memory. "Can't we send a message to Fleet?"

"And say what?" Reza asked quietly. "Whom do you think they will believe? A captain raised by their enemies, a man who is largely hated by his own kind, or a regimental commander of excellent standing who obviously has tremendous political force behind him?" He shook his head. "No, my friends, there will be no help from outside. But we are overlooking the real problem."

"What's that?" Hawthorne asked.

"The Kreelans," Reza replied. "They are on their way."

* * *

"I can't believe they will cooperate so easily," Belisle said after Hawthorne had radioed back that Thorella's orders had been obeyed. "That bunch is like a cult of personality focused on Gard. They won't give him up so easily."

Thorella smiled and waved his hand dismissively. "My dear president, don't be so apprehensive. I hate that half-breed traitor with all my heart, but I do have to admit that he does have a sense of honor, to a fault. He realizes that he's in a box, and the only way his company can get out unscathed is if he cooperates."

"You're going to just let them go, then?"

"Of course not. But their cooperation will simplify their demise. One assault boat can hold all their personnel. We'll have them leave the vehicles and heavy equipment behind, as I'm sure the Territorial Army could always use it." He shrugged as he stepped on a spot of blood that had once belonged to Counselor Savitch, the coagulated liquid having penetrated deep into the office's huge genuine Persian rug. "I hate to lose a boat and the flight crew, but it's a price I'm willing to pay."

Belisle nodded, satisfied. He liked this man, and was beginning to think that he might just request Borge to have Thorella posted here permanently.

"Now," the colonel mused as he stepped toward the glass doors that looked out onto the glowing crater, "we'll just have to find out about this little puzzle, too, won't we?"

* * *

"They're here." Eustus turned away from the tactical display, his face pale and drawn. Outside, the skimmer from Thorella's regiment that had come for Reza and Enya had just touched down.

Reza emerged from behind the blanket that served as a door to his impromptu quarters. Enya, who had been sitting beside Eustus while they waited, not holding hands but wanting to, gasped.

The Marine uniform was gone. In its place he wore his Kreelan ceremonial armor, the great rune of the Desh-Ka a flame of cyan on the black breast plate. The talons of his gauntlets gleamed blood red, reflecting the crimson light of the tactical display. The great sword given him by

Pan'ne-Sharakh was sheathed at his back, and at his waist hung the short sword Tesh-Dar had entrusted to him, along with the most valued of all his possessions, the dagger that had been his gift from Esah-Zhurah. On his upper left arm clung three shrekkas like lethal spiders.

"Do not be frightened," he said in a voice that none of them had ever truly heard before. It was not the voice of a company commander. It was the voice of a king.

"Why... why are you dressed like that?" she asked. He looked exactly as the warriors in the tomb must have before they died. She shivered involuntarily.

Reza smiled thinly. "I have worn the Marine uniform with honor for years," he told her. "I will not wear it while I am under suspicion of such acts as I have been accused, for that would be to disgrace all who wear it honorably." He looked at the others. "Thorella has always treated me as the enemy, as a Kreelan warrior. I do not wish to disappoint him."

"Isn't there anything we can do, Reza?" Hawthorne asked quietly as the command post guard shouted that Thorella's people were waiting.

Reza turned to him. "Get our people off this planet if you can, my friend. But do not trust Thorella. He will try to destroy all of us to eliminate the evidence pointing to his crimes."

"What about Enya?" Eustus asked, in a way ashamed of his concern for her when he had an entire company of his own people to look after. But he could not help it any more than he could still his own heart.

Reza put a hand on his shoulder. "I swear that no harm shall come to her from Thorella's hand, my friend. I cannot make the same promise for when the Kreelans come, but Thorella shall not harm her."

"And what of my people?" Enya asked quietly, bitterly. "Belisle will murder them, finish what he tried to do five years ago."

"I cannot see the future," Reza told her softly. "But we shall do what we can."

He looked around him then, at the people who had been his friends and fellow warriors for so long. "Go with honor, my friends," he said simply. There was no more time for good-byes.

After a quick embrace and a last kiss from Eustus, Enya turned to follow Reza through the dark tunnel to the even darker world beyond.

EIGHTEEN

"What is that thing, Gard?" Thorella asked as he stared at the blue glow streaming from the crater, pouring its light forth into space. He could see the movements of his regiment's skimmers and tanks as they took up their positions around the city and partway up the ruined mountain. He and a few of his most trusted troops had come in first to deal with Gard and Savitch, landing over the horizon and coming overland in a skimmer to avoid detection. The rest of the regiment had been landed soon after Gard had been taken into custody. Thorella would have liked to kill him straight away, but his sponsor had convinced him that a gory show trial, followed by Gard's execution, would be much more satisfying.

Reza remained silent. He would kill Thorella, no matter what the cost, he had decided, but the time had not yet come. He had also decided to kill Belisle, as well. Despite Nicole and Jodi's best efforts to educate him that society alone was best left to judge the crimes of others, he knew that it was not always so. These two men had committed murder and would continue to do so with impunity unless he stopped them. Too much power lay behind them, power that lurked in the shadow of the pillar civilization had built to Justice, power that crushed its victims without remorse, without compassion; the laws of society could not reach them. For Bayern and Morita, killed by fellow Marines; for Melissa Savitch, who had answered his call for help and died for her trouble; for the Mallorys who had died and those who would soon die, he would kill Thorella and Belisle. He was the only instrument of Justice that might prevail. He alone could avenge the fallen.

"You know," Thorella said quietly, "you could be a bit more cooperative. I would hate to see Ms. Terragion accidentally abused during her interrogation."

Reza said nothing, but kept staring at Thorella, who sat behind a wall of armorglass. Reza retained his weapons because no one dared challenge him for them, and Thorella was content to let him have his way, as long as he himself was safe.

So you believe, Reza thought, imagining the look on Thorella's face if Reza stepped through the wall, as he easily could. Part of his mind was with Enya, who sat in a large interrogation room downstairs with a number of her friends. If Thorella decided to go ahead with his threat, Reza's period of waiting would be over.

"No," Thorella said after a moment's consideration. "The only women you ever cared about were Carré and Mackenzie, the frigid bitch and the dyke. Maybe I'll make Ms. Terragion my mistress while I'm here. That would make Camden happy, I know. At least, until it comes time to execute her." He smiled. "You're going to the gallows, Gard. You know that don't you?"

"I shall not go alone."

Thorella laughed. "No," he said, ignoring the implicit threat, "no, rest assured that you won't. There will be plenty of Mallorys swinging beside you. But that's beside the point." He leaned closer to the glass. "I just want to know what that thing is out there, that could chew up half a mountain. We've probed it and run drones around it, and it doesn't even register. Some kind of Kreelan energy source?"

You could say that, Reza answered silently. "I have nothing to say to you, Markus Thorella."

"Guards!" Thorella suddenly barked. Six of Thorella's best men, Reza's guard force, stepped forward from where they had their weapons trained on Reza's back. "Put him with the others. If he tries anything, kill them all." That was what Thorella believed would be an effective tool to enforce his will on Reza: the threat of death to the others.

As he turned to leave, Reza glanced again at the unearthly glow of the mountain.

Soon, he thought. Very soon.

* * *

"We're starting over it now, sir," Emilio Rodriguez reported as he began to turn his skimmer over the top of the glowing crater. He had been circling it for ten minutes, gathering more information – which meant no information, he thought sourly – before actually flying over it.

"Hurry it up, Rodriguez," Major Elijah Simpson, the regiment's intel officer, snapped. Many said that his intelligence was directly proportional to his patience. He was a very impatient man.

"What an asshole," Lauren Nathanga, a tech from the regiment's intel company who was Rodriguez's passenger, said over the intercom.

"No arguments here," Rodriguez sighed.

Their little jeep crossed over the lip of the crater about one hundred meters above the glass-smooth rim.

"This is really incredible," Nathanga said. "The power it must have taken to do this, and yet we don't have a single reading except some residual heat from whatever cut through the rock."

"Anything yet?" Simpson interjected.

"Still scanning, sir," Nathanga replied, shaking her head. "We're... What is that?"

"What's going on?" Simpson demanded over the radio, but neither Nathanga nor Rodriguez heard him.

The two explorers had suddenly found themselves encased in a web of blue light that seared their flesh. They thrashed and writhed, screaming in agony as their skin began to burn, as if they had suddenly been cast into a furnace. The last thing Lauren Nathanga saw was Rodriguez's smoking body bursting into flame. Then Nathanga was herself consumed by the cleansing fire.

Back at the command post, Major Simpson watched and listened in horror to the screams and the nightmarish video coming back across the comms link. First Rodriguez, and then Nathanga suddenly exploded into human torches, burning so bright and hot that the jeep's control panel must have begun to melt, because the video abruptly cut off. Thankfully.

Simpson got exactly two paces across the regimental command post before he retched on the floor amid the other shocked members of the intel section.

Undamaged except for the crew compartment that lay smoldering from the flames that had left only husks of carbon where once there had been human beings, the skimmer continued on its way across the crater, eventually crashing into the ocean over two hundred kilometers away.

* * *

"So," Nicole said, "what you are telling us is that we will be too late."

The Gneisenau's chief intelligence officer nodded grimly. "I'm afraid that about sums it up, CAG. Even if the Kreelans don't have any ships heading to Erlang that might be closer than the ones our scouts have detected, the estimated on-orbit time of the first enemy battle group will still be at least an hour ahead of our own ETA."

The faces around the table, real and projected, frowned. That meant the Kreelans would have time both to start their assault on the planet and array their ships in a defensive posture for a Confederation counterattack that they knew must be coming. While the humans still had some degree of tactical surprise on their side, it probably would not be enough to make a difference. While the Tenth Fleet task force – of which Sinclaire's Gneisenau was the flagship – had eleven battleships, two carriers, and a host of cruisers and destroyers, the Kreelan defenders would hold most of the cards in what was shaping up to be the biggest fleet engagement in decades.

If only we had more bloody ships! Sinclaire cursed to himself. "What do you think, Nicole?" he asked her. He hated calling Fleet Captain Carré "CAG" – Commander, Aerospace Group. He respected the position and the tradition, but to him the acronym sounded like some kind of affliction.

"It all depends on what we are up against," she said, noting the Hood's CAG nodding agreement. Nicole and Jodi had only recently completed their tours as instructors at the Fighter Weapons School on Earth, and had both accepted combat assignments on the newest fleet carrier, Gneisenau. Jodi had taken over one of the new ship's squadrons, finally accepting the responsibility and grade that she had so long avoided, while Nicole had assumed the post of senior pilot and aerospace group commander. "We have one-hundred sixty-three fighters and attack ships on Gneisenau ready to fight, plus another one-hundred and thirty-five on Hood. But we have no idea what the enemy will show up with other than the seven capital ships – two in the superdreadnought category – that STARNET was able to confirm before the Kreelans jumped. And we do not know, out of those, how many carry only guns and how many carry guns and fighters both."

"I would venture to say," said Captain Amadi, Gneisenau's commander, "that we should expect the worst. There is some compelling and unknown reason why the Kreelans are going to Erlang. They have never done this before, spontaneously converging on a colony from so many different quadrants. I suggest that we go in with the fighters and destroyers screening forward, followed by the main combatants in wedge abreast, and the attack ships and cruisers held in reserve to the rear."

Sinclaire nodded. It was a standard tactical formation, and for good reason. It would give them a lot of flexibility in an unknown situation, meaning that they could bring a lot of power to bear in any quadrant very quickly. Or retreat with a minimum of losses, he thought grimly. "Comments?"

"What about sending a recon in ahead of the van?" the captain of one of the destroyers, a young woman who was always looking for a fight with the enemy, said.

Sinclaire smiled at her eagerness. She was a good destroyer captain, aggressive and fearless, one of a breed that was increasingly hard to find. Destroyer captains and their crews did not usually live very long. "Given that we know little of what we'll be facing," he said, "I don't think we can afford to give the enemy the least advantage over us, more than they have already. Surprise is all we've got right now, and I won't surrender it without good reason. Maybe next time, Captain Dekkar."

The woman frowned, disappointed, but she nodded understanding.

"Have we been able to contact the colony yet?" someone else asked.

"No," the intel officer answered. "The comms people believe that the subspace signals are being blocked by an ion storm that came up within the Grange cloud. Until we're past it, we won't be able to reach them."

"Any other ideas? No? Then that's it. We'll go with the overall attack plan as suggested by Captain Amadi. The flag ops officer will issue formation and launch orders to your commands by twenty-two forty-five Zulu for the jump in-system at oh-five seventeen tomorrow." He looked at the chronometer on the wall of the conference room. "That gives us a tad over nine hours from now until we arrive at Erlang, people. Let's not waste a second of it."

* * *

"Brooding isn't going to help," Enya said.

Reza opened his eyes and looked at her. He seemed utterly calm. "I am not brooding," he said quietly, offering her a gentle smile. "I am thinking." He looked to Ian Mallory, who sat against the wall across from him. Mallory's left eye was swollen shut, his split lip still bleeding slightly. The Territorial Army contingent that had arrested him and the other seniors of the Mallory Council had beaten them badly. "We must find a way to get a message to your people," Reza told him. "They must get out of the cities and towns, away from anywhere the Territorial Army or Thorella's troops might stand and fight the Kreelans."

"What difference would it make?" the older man said quietly, his open eye blazing with anger and bitterness. "They'll be slaughtered either way. I'm not like most of this flock," he said, gesturing with a hand that boasted two broken fingers. "I've been off-world. I've seen what happens during a Kreelan attack. The TA has oppressed us for many years, but I can't justify asking our people to abandon the only hope they may have for survival. The Territorial Army troops are the only defense any of my people have."

"Listen to me, Ian Mallory." Reza said urgently. "If they do not leave, if they are anywhere near troops who will fight the Kreela, you condemn them to certain death. The Kreela do not come to your world now to fight as they usually do, seeking to honor the Empress in battle. They come to take the First Empress home. Any resistance will bring instant devastation. There will be no landings or ground battles. Kreelan warships will simply obliterate every defensive position on this planet from orbit, and every defended human settlement will be annihilated. This is more important to them than any other event in the last hundred thousand years, and they will take no chances. They will spare nothing, no one, who raises a hand against them."

"And they'll spare unarmed people?" someone scoffed. Reza had noticed that the mood of the Mallorys had changed dramatically since he had appeared in his Kreelan garb, the aura they projected verging on open hostility. Only Enya's word and their own fears of what he might do in retaliation held them in check.

"If you do as I say, yes, your people will be spared." He looked at Ian. "But there is a price that must be paid."

"I knew there must be a catch," Ian grumbled. "How much blood need be spilled?"

"Seven hundred," Reza said. "If you wish your people to live, you must find exactly seven hundred souls who are willing to fight and die for the rest. Men or women, it makes no difference. They must assemble in a single line upon the plain on the far side of the mountain of light, with no weapons other than those that may be hammered in the forge or carved from wood."

"Why seven hundred?" Enya asked. "And what are they supposed to accomplish other than satisfying Kreelan bloodlust?"

"There must be seven hundred because that is the number of the host that accompanied the First Empress here after she died, after her spirit inhabited the vessel, the crystal heart that was awakened by your touch," Reza explained. "The Seven Hundred who brought her here were the ones you found in the burial chamber, the Imperial Guard. The number will not be lost on the warriors who are coming here; they will understand." He looked around at the others in the room. "As for what your volunteers are to accomplish, they will fight for your world," Reza said, "against an equal number of Her warriors, similarly armed. Theirs shall be a sacrifice for the rest of your people, those who survive the destruction of the cities."

"We could not hope to win against trained warriors," Ian said.

"It is not a battle that is meant to be won, Ian Mallory. It is a sacrifice, a showing of the honor of your people, that the Kreela will understand and respect."

"I take it, then," Ian asked darkly, "that the seven hundred who go forward onto the Plain of Aragon may all expect to die?"

Reza nodded. "It is the only way."

The room was deathly silent. As they spoke, the others of the Council had gathered around the trio, the uninjured helping those who were. Even imprisoned and under sentence of death without a formal trial, the Mallory Council still held the future of their people in their hands.

"I say we put it to a vote," Enya said, looking at Ian. "We've got nothing left to lose, except the lives of everyone on this planet, Raniers and Mallorys alike."

"Let the Raniers die!" someone hissed like acid eating through metal.

"Don't say that!" Enya retorted. "Not all of them are like Belisle. There are–"

"You cannot save them," Reza said quietly. "If you give them warning, Belisle will find a way to turn it against you. He would confine the Mallorys in the cities where they would be killed, and evacuate the Ranier families to the forests, although that would not save them in the end. Only those who choose to fight on the plain have the power to save your world, but the Raniers must also bear their share of the price of your planet's survival; it is they who shall be sacrificed to the guns of Her warships."

The faces around him were grim. Even the most hardened of the Mallorys here knew that there were innocents among the Raniers, people who had helped them in some way, or who simply had no control over the planet's course as Belisle led them through tyranny. Men, women, children, they would all die in the cities. They would have to, that the rest of Erlang's people might live.

"I say do as he says," growled an older woman who had suffered more hardships than she cared to recount. "Better to make a stand than to just wait and get shot, either by the aliens or by our own."

Ian nodded respectfully. Her words were well thought of in this circle. "And you, Markham?"

"Aye," a big man, an equal in physique to Washington Hawthorne, said easily, as if he made these kinds of decisions every day. "I'll raise an ax and a little Cain any day. All the better that it be for a good cause."

"Waverman?"

"Aye."

And so it went, around the room. The vote was unanimous. They would fight.

"Does that meet with your satisfaction?" Ian said to Reza after the last of the council had nodded her head. "Will that be enough blood for you?"

"Ian!" Enya said, dismayed. "He offers us a way to survive, after trying to help us against Belisle. You have no right to treat him that way."

"We're the ones who'll be dying, girl. He has no stake in this."

"You are wrong, my friend," Reza said gently. He could feel Ian Mallory's pain and trepidation, and was not resentful that he was the focus of the man's anger. Mallory did not – could not – understand the Way or the fulfillment of the Prophecy. But there was no other course for them to take.

"How's that?"

"Because I am the one who will lead your people into battle."

Ian only looked at him.

"Why you, and not one of us?" someone else demanded.

"Because only one who wears the collar of the Empress may declare such a combat," he explained.

"How much time do we have?" Enya asked in the silence that followed.

"I do not know exactly," Reza said, "for I do not know where the closest Kreelan warships might be. But I would say that we only have a few hours to act."

"A few hours isn't enough time," Ian said pointedly.

Reza fixed him with a stony gaze. "It is all that you have."

* * *

The next step, getting the Council's instructions out of the Parliament building and to the Mallorys outside, was not as difficult as Thorella or Belisle would have liked. One of the guards was a Mallory sympathizer known by Ian to be trustworthy, and he was passed a message in code, written on a stained sheet of paper that had once been a shopping list for the company store in Laster, a town far to the north. The guard, in turn, passed it to the servant of Mallory City's mayor, who passed it to someone heading out of the building. In less than an hour, the instructions had been transmitted over the inter-city communications networks to every village on the planet.

The orders were viewed with incredulity by many, but there was no mistaking Ian Mallory's coded signature, and they knew that he would die long before he revealed it to Belisle's minions. While there were a few who refused to believe it, thinking either it was a trick or that the Council simply did not know any more what it was doing, the vast majority of Mallorys did as they had been instructed.

It was fortunate that the message had been sent late in the evening, for it gave the Mallorys the cover of darkness to carry out their instructions. Evacuation plans were on hand for every township, and in the darkness the Mallorys began their exodus, taking with them only a prescribed bundle of things essential for survival – a few tools, a good knife, some food – to avoid arousing too much suspicion from the periodic Territorial Army patrols. Since most of the townships were ringed by forests that the villagers had known since childhood, finding their way to the designated rendezvous points was not a problem. Moving in silence, carrying the very young and the old or infirm who could not walk or keep up, the Mallorys disappeared by the thousands from their homes.

By first light, when the horns blared at the mines signaling the start of another twelve-hour shift, only the Ranier shift supervisors had appeared, wondering what had happened to all their workers. In the meantime, the miners who were streaming from the mines headed quickly toward their ramshackle homes... and then vanished.

NINETEEN

"What the devil do you mean, 'No one's showed up to work?'" Belisle shouted into the comms terminal.

The man at the other end shrank back. "Just what I said, Mr. President," he stammered. "There was no one at the gates except the supervisors, and the miners working the night shift practically ran home. We tried to find them, even sent in TA patrols, but there wasn't anyone there. Anywhere. The whole township's empty."

"That's impossible! People can't just vanish into thin air! Where did they go? Surely you idiots can find a few thousand people wandering about!" He stabbed at a button on the comm link, and the man's image disappeared.

"I'm afraid it's worse than that, Mr. President," Wittmann, the mayor, said quietly behind him, as if afraid he would be beaten for bringing more bad news.

"How can it?" Belisle snapped angrily, his mind unconsciously figuring the monetary losses for every hour that even a single mine lay idle.

"I just got a report from the chief at Promontory Mine," Wittmann said uneasily. "He reports the same thing. The Mallorys are all gone. They just vanished into thin air. Food still on the tables, fires burned cold in the kitchens with pots still hanging over them. That sort of thing."

Belisle just stared at him. Promontory Mine. That was Erlang's most productive source of income. Even the time that they had spent standing here talking had cost them over a million credits. "Find them!" he yelled. "Find them and get them back to work, or you and your family will be down there breaking rock!"

He turned to Thorella, who sat casually in one of the office's chaise lounges, a look of contemplation on his face. "They've finally gone and done it," Belisle said, spittle flying from his mouth. "They're openly rebelling. What are you going to do about it, colonel?"

"Well," he said casually, scrutinizing the nails of one hand, "there's not much we can do with your miners until they've been found." He smiled in spite of himself. The planning it must have taken to allow hundreds of thousands of people to disappear overnight under the nose of the Territorial Army was indeed impressive, even to Thorella. Hunting them down would be a real challenge, he suspected, which was something he always enjoyed. "But we can certainly inquire among your friends in the basement about the matter, as I'm sure they have something to do with it."

"That's impossible," Belisle spat. "The cell they're in is impossible to breach. They couldn't get out a whisper."

Thorella frowned. This man could sometimes be so ignorant. "You underestimate your opponents, my friend. I'm sure your staff has its share of sympathizers. I reviewed some of the recordings of the goings on in the cell not too long ago, and discovered that certain portions had been... edited. And whoever did that could just as easily get a message out to warn the Mallorys." His frown grew deeper. "The question is, warn them of what?"

"Retaliation by the Army and police, of course," Belisle said impatiently, thinking Thorella an imbecile for not coming to that conclusion right away, and also wondering who on his staff could possibly have betrayed him. It was unthinkable. "And rightly they should be afraid. There will be reprisals."

"But would that be cause for evacuating the whole Mallory population?" Thorella thought aloud. "And if they were openly rebelling, wouldn't they have tried to destroy the mines? Why did the miners just disappear?" He was not concerned about Belisle's threatened reprisals. That was a job for which the Territorial Army was well suited, and did not concern him or his Marines. But was there some other threat, of which he and the Raniers were unaware?

There was one way to find out. "I think, Mr. President," he said, "that we need to ask your Mallory friends some questions." He turned to the guard who stood nearby, a Territorial Army sergeant. "Have Ian Mallory and Enya Terragion brought up here immediately."

"Yes, sir," the sergeant replied, saluting before he left the office to carry out his mission. Thorella had no way of knowing that the man was a Mallory sympathizer.

"Sir," Thorella's adjutant called from where he had installed himself in one of the anterooms, "Major Simpson's on the line. He has an emergency – the recon of the crater."

Now what? Thorella wondered, annoyed, as he went to take the call and learn about the disastrous reconnaissance mission over the glowing crater. Could nothing go right today?

* * *

Thorella and Belisle had been counting on the explosive device set in the holding pen to be a deterrent to any unwanted actions by Reza or the others. It was a sophisticated device, and might even have worked, had Sergeant "Pippi" Hermutz not disabled it earlier, leaving the arming light glowing threateningly to reassure anyone who took an interest that the device was still viable. He was also responsible for destroying the recordings of their vote to evacuate the Mallorys, as well as sabotaging the surveillance gear for the rest of the short time it would matter to anyone.

"Wait here," he told the other guards as he keyed open the outer lock to the cell. "I'll bring them out."

He went inside, waiting for the outer door to close before he opened the inner one. He immediately picked out Ian and Enya, sitting close to Reza in the group of thirty or so, all of whom got to their feet as he entered. Until he had carried out the message Ian had drafted, none of the others had realized he was one of them, even though his heritage was Ranier. He was simply one of a growing number of people who had grown tired of Belisle's kind of leadership and oppression of others. He noted the tension in their faces. They wanted to know if their families were safe.

"Everything seems to have gone according to plan," he whispered to Ian. "I don't know about the rest, but at least Promontory and Sheila townships were evacuated all right. And Charlotte" – a woman he only knew by her code name – "told me that the volunteers you asked for are in place and with the equipment you said to bring." Charlotte had not bothered to tell him that it had been inordinately difficult to send only seven hundred to the plain: nearly every man and most of the women who heard of the chance to stand and fight had wanted to go.

"Thank you for your help, Pippi," Ian breathed. "We all owe you a debt we probably will never be able to repay."

"It's just nice to feel like I'm doing something right, for once," Hermutz sighed. "Belisle and his kind are no friends to anyone but themselves. But that's for another time." He looked at Enya, then back to Ian. "That Marine colonel, Thorella, wants you and Enya for interrogation. Belisle thinks the Mallorys are gone because they're afraid of reprisals, but Thorella suspects something more. What should we–"

Reza visibly stiffened, his eyes widening slightly.

"What is it?" Enya said, putting a hand on his armored shoulder, feeling him quiver beneath it.

"They have come," he told her. He could not sense those of the Blood, ever since the Seventh Braid, his link to the spirit of his people, had been severed the instant before the Empress exiled him from the Empire. But he had cast his mind's eye upward, into the human ships that orbited overhead, and had heard their cries of surprise as the first of the Kreelan battle groups converging on Erlang had arrived in-system. Those cries soon turned to screams of panic and pain as the great Kreelan warships began the devastation above that would soon begin here, on the surface. He focused on Ian. "We have no more time," he told him. "We must leave at once, or we will be caught in the coming holocaust."

"I might be able to get a few of you out," Pippi said, glancing over his shoulder to see if the other guards were becoming suspicious. They were looking through the viewport. Pippi waved. "But there's no way I can get everyone out. The parliamentary guard force would cut you all down before you got a foot past the cell block doors."

Reza thought for a moment. No matter what powers he had, he would not be able to kill every guard before the shooting began. Some, or many, of those with him now would be gunned down. "Then take Enya and Ian with you," he said. "I will see to the rest."

"But–" Enya began.

"Go now," Reza said. "I will meet you on the knoll that overlooks the plain. Go."

Reluctantly, Enya and Ian let themselves be prodded out of the cell. As the door closed behind them, Markham, the man who could have been Hawthorne's twin, said, "So, Gard, what are we supposed to do? Just sit here until the Kreelans start shelling Mallory City?"

Reza looked at him, a grim smile on his face. "Yes," he said.

Markham did not think it was funny.

* * *

Pippi Hermutz could not get away with escorting the two prisoners by himself, he knew, and there were no other sympathizers here who could help him. So, out of necessity, he chose a man he knew to be a strong supporter of Belisle to help him. It would make killing him a little easier on his conscience.

After the four of them crowded into the elevator that would take them upstairs to the president's office, Pippi turned to his Territorial Army colleague and subordinate, Hans Miflin, and shot him between the eyes with a low-power pencil beam from his blaster. Just strong enough to penetrate the man's skull, it turned his forebrain into bloody steam. Twitching like a pithed frog, he collapsed to the floor of the elevator.

Enya jammed the STOP button. Ian and Pippi propped up Miflin's body beside the door in a sitting position so it would be harder for someone outside the elevator to see him.

"My God, Pippi," the elder Mallory breathed. "How can we kill one another like this?"

Pippi looked at him as if he were a child. "Too easily, Ian. But at least he was armed. Most of the people he's killed in his lifetime weren't. Keep that in mind the next time you feel like shedding a tear for the likes of him." Checking that none of them had any blood on their clothes, he said, "Take this." He handed Ian his blaster, and then picked up Miflin's gun, handing it to Enya. "Keep them hidden unless you need them. Go straight out the back door, through the kitchens on the first level. You can't miss them. Someone should be waiting for you there with transportation."

"What about the others?" Enya asked.

"Reza will have to deal with that," he said impatiently. "I've done all I can."

"What about you, Pippi?" Ian said.

He nodded at the blaster in Ian's hand. "You have to shoot me, to make it look like an escape. Injure me enough to make it convincing."

"But aren't you coming with us?" Enya asked, incredulous. "Pippi, the Kreelans are coming!"

"I have to think of my family," he said. "I can't leave the building before my shift is up without drawing notice to myself. And if Belisle or his people ever find out that I've helped you, my wife and children..." He shook his head. Sympathizers were treated far more harshly than Mallorys. His entire family would probably be imprisoned, and he would be executed. "You owe me this, Ian."

Clenching his jaws, Ian raised the pistol, aimed as carefully as his trembling hand allowed, and shot Pippi in the head, through his helmet. Their rescuer collapsed, and Enya quickly knelt and put a hand to his neck.

"He's still alive," she whispered as the stench of smoking flesh turned her stomach. She had to get out of here or she would vomit.

Ian carefully placed Pippi's body on the other side of the door in a position similar to Miflin's. "Thank you, my friend," he whispered, a hand on the man's shoulder. He knew there was no way either he or his family would make it out of the city alive when the Kreelans came. He should have saved him the pain and simply killed him, he thought sadly. Standing again, he turned to Enya. "It's time."

Nodding, she pushed the RUN button, and the elevator lurched upward toward the first floor.

It stopped and the doors swished open. Ian had been praying fervently that there would be no one standing there when it did. Thankfully, no one was.

"This way," Enya said, leading him to the left, behind the twin staircases that were the centerpiece of the foyer. This early in the morning, few of the

Parliament's bureaucrats and other functionaries were about. They saw two guards, but they were half asleep, inattentive.

Turning down a long corridor, Enya saw the silvery doors that led to the main kitchens. In the job she had once held as a runner for one of the more moderate Ranier representatives, she had often come down here to get him food to satisfy his compulsive eating habits, his only vice.

There were three cooks getting ready for the morning meal service in the main dining room, but they did not see the two refugees as they stole past a row of gleaming copper and stainless steel cookware along the far side, away from the steaming urns.

The back door loomed ahead. Enya opened it, only to find a Territorial Army uniform blocking her way.

"Hey!" the man said, raising his rifle.

Enya shot him in the chest.

But that was not the end of their troubles. Ten meters away stood a big Marine transport skimmer and a group of camouflaged, armored figures with their weapons pointed directly at them.

"Don't," Ian said as she raised her pistol. "It's useless," he said, defeated.

Tears of frustration in her eyes, Enya threw down her weapon and raised her hands. Ian did the same.

Suddenly, a familiar face peered out through the skimmer's personnel door. "Don't just stand there," Eustus shouted. "Get in!"

"Eustus!" Enya cried as the Marines bundled her and Ian into the troop carrier, hiding the Territorial Army soldier's body in a nearby trash bin and retrieving their weapons from the pavement before someone noticed something amiss, unlikely as that was in the darkness of this early hour.

Inside the vehicle's armored hull, Enya and Eustus kissed and embraced. "What are you doing here?" she asked.

"One of your people came and tipped us off to your little breakout," he told her. "But let's save that for later. Where are Reza and the others?"

"They're still being held," Ian told him.

"We've got to get them out of there quickly. Belisle and Thorella are expecting us for interrogation, and they'll be getting suspicious."

"Well," Eustus said, "we should be able to do something about that. But I'm not sure what we're going to do afterwards. We don't really have anywhere to go, and we'll have Thorella's entire regiment on our ass."

Ian and Enya looked at each other. "What about the plain on the far side of the mountain?" she asked.

Eustus looked at her blankly.

"The messenger didn't tell you?" Ian asked. "That the Kreelans are coming?"

Eustus's eyes widened. "They only told us that you guys were going to make a break and that you'd need help getting away. Nobody said anything about Kreelans."

That would figure, Ian thought. The courier had only told them what he had been ordered to; his cell leader would have given him only the information he absolutely needed for that specific task.

"When, where, and how many?" Eustus asked.

Quickly, Enya and Ian explained what was about to happen to their world.

* * *

When the door to the cell whined open, Reza and the others were ready and waiting.

"It is good to see you again, my friend," he said as Eustus came through the doorway.

"You, too, sir," Eustus said as he ushered some of his Marines forward to help with the people who could not move on their own. Some of the interrogations had taken more of a toll than others. "But I wish I'd known about the Blues being on the way."

"The squadron in orbit is already nearly finished," Reza told him. He had drawn away his mind's eye from the carnage above. He had seen more than enough. "Did you get a message to Hawthorne?"

"Aye, sir. The company's volunteered to stand on the plain. That should give the Kreelans a bit more–"

"It cannot be so, Eustus," Reza told him as they led the group to the bank of elevators, past the limp bodies of the guards whose only sign of injury was the lack of a pulse. "Only Erlangers and myself may stand upon that field. You and the company must stand aside."

"And just what the hell are we supposed to do?" Eustus said angrily. He was not about to leave Reza to die with a bunch of miners who had never been in a battle bigger than a beer hall brawl. "We've got a boat, but if the squadron upstairs is catching it, where does that leave us? We may as well fight and do some good." He thought of how Thorella had ordered them into that boat, and how amazed Eustus had been at the number of ways Hawthorne had found to stall him. While they would never know it for sure, he knew that Hawthorne's tactics had saved all their lives. They figured Thorella was going to plant an explosive among their equipment for a convenient accident, but it had never come to pass. And never would.

"More of our forces are on the way," Reza told him. "Nicole is coming." He could feel her, just barely. She was preparing to do battle, and her Bloodsong, faint though it was, rang clearly in his heart. "They will arrive soon. And when they do, you and Hawthorne must take the company to safety. Just remember: you must not fire on any Kreelan forces or you will be destroyed. If you offer no resistance, they will not attack you." If all goes well, he thought.

"I'm not leaving you," Eustus said stubbornly as they filed through the kitchens to the back door, the cooks staring at them wide-eyed. The Parliament's Territorial Army guards had been no match for Reza's Marines, who now moved quickly to get everyone out before a more general alarm was called.

Reza pulled him aside by the arm. "I leave you no choice, Eustus," he said. "There are... rules to the engagement I am planning that forbid me to allow any but those who have lived in the shadow of the mountain to fight for their right to remain. If those rules are not obeyed to the letter, the battle is forfeit, and every soul on this planet shall perish." Eustus turned away, unable to look him in the eye. "I shall not forget you, my friend," he said gently.

"You're not planning on coming back, are you?" Eustus asked hoarsely.

"No," Reza said. "I have no illusions about what is to come. The Mallorys, for all their courage, cannot win. They will die, and I with them. But perhaps that will be enough to spare the rest." He glanced up at the parliament building. "Besides, there is some personal business I must attend to first that would make my future service to the Confederation... awkward." He smiled solemnly. "I have put away the uniform of the regiment forever, my friend." He pointed to the armored skimmer and Enya's face peering intently through the still open door, past the two Marines who stood warily on guard. "There is the best reason of all for you to go," he said. "Her love is true. You would be wise to ask her to be yours. Take her with you, Eustus."

"Reza–"

"Go." Reza's voice turned to steel. There was no more time. "That is an order, First Sergeant."

"Yes, sir," Eustus rasped, standing tall and rendering his commanding officer and best friend a sharp salute.

Reza returned it as a Kreelan warrior, his left fist against his breast. He watched as Eustus clambered into the heavily loaded skimmer after the watchful Marines, the door hissing shut behind them.

As the carrier sped away, Reza went back inside, bearing the long sword that was inscribed with his name before him like a flaming torch to ward off the darkness.

* * *

"No one answers downstairs, sir," the Territorial Army orderly said matter-of-factly.

"What?" Belisle snapped. His mind was on the brink of raving insanity after receiving report after report of vanished Mallorys and idle mines. Virtually every single worker had disappeared on him, and none had yet been found. "Don't tell me the guards have vanished into thin air, too?"

"You may inspect their bodies, if you wish," Reza said from an alcove in the far wall. There was no door behind him. "Yours shall join them shortly."

Belisle whirled around at the voice as the soldier drew his pistol. It was not halfway out of its holster when a shrekka ripped through his chest. A geyser of blood followed it as it flew across the room, embedding itself in the far wall. Clutching at his savaged ribcage, the man crumpled to the floor.

"What do you want?" Belisle whined. "Money? I've got millions of credits in the vault in this office. I can give you anything you want! I–"

"Oh, shut up, Belisle," Thorella's calm voice called from the anteroom. "It only makes you look more like the coward you really are."

Reza eyed Thorella carefully. An enemy who acted calmly in the face of seemingly overwhelming force was one not to be underestimated.

"I suppose," Thorella went on, stepping further into the room, "that since the explosive in the basement did not go off when I pushed the button, all of your traitorous friends managed to escape?"

Reza did not favor him with an answer. Thorella was hiding something. His eyes narrowing in concentration, Reza swept the room with his senses, but could detect nothing that seemed overly threatening. Yet something was wrong...

"What does he want, Thorella?" Belisle hissed.

"He's come here to kill us, Mr. President," Thorella said nonchalantly.

"Yes," Reza said as he leveled his sword at Thorella, the blade steady as the stones of the ancient Kal'ai-Il in his hands. "The world has no need for such as you. Too much blood is on your hands, and there is no one – not even the Confederation's senior Counsel, whom you also murdered – to avenge the lives you have wrongly taken, the pain you have caused."

"Please don't kill me!" Belisle pleaded, his hands clasped like a repentant sinner.

Reza suddenly swung his sword in an arc that appeared as a golden ring in the office's mild light. Belisle's mouth continued to move for a moment as it tumbled from his neck, bright arterial blood spurting to the ceiling from the torso, creating its own gruesome fresco.

"Bravo!" Thorella applauded as Belisle's headless body at last collapsed, still twitching, to the carpet.

"Excellent swordsmanship, as always, Captain Gard. I'm sure the General Staff will enjoy watching it."

Reza looked up sharply, eyeing Thorella more closely. The colonel walked through a sofa as Reza might through a wall.

It was a hologram.

"Yes, that's right, you fool," Thorella's image said as recognition dawned on Reza's face. "You didn't think that I would let you get anywhere near me, did you? Even during the interrogation, I wasn't behind the glass. It was only a projection with an appropriate olfactory representation to fool you. And it seems to have worked quite well, eh?"

Reza's anger threatened to boil over like a volcano, but there was nowhere to direct it. Wherever Thorella was, he was safely out of Reza's reach. How could he have been so foolish?

Because, Reza thought savagely, cursing himself, you thought that even Thorella would have had enough courage to face you and not run away like a terrified rat. Or a cunning one.

"Well, my friend," Thorella went on, "I'm afraid I have to go now. Your blue-skinned friends are getting a bit too close for comfort." His smile faded. "One word of advice, Gard: die here, now, or turn your coat again and go back with the Kreelans. Because if your face is seen again in Confederation space, you'll be arrested and charged with murdering a sovereign planetary leader, not to mention a host of other lesser offenses." A contemplative look. "I might even be able to arrange it to have you charged with the murder of the General Counsel." He laughed. "People will hate you so much that they'll curse your name in their sleep. And your friends will suffer their share of society's rightful vengeance on your treasonous life."

"In Her name," Reza whispered, his blood a burning river of fire through his body, the power that flared within him stayed only by the knowledge that he did not know where to strike, "I shall somehow get you for this. If I die here, my spirit will reach you from beyond the Darkness, Thorella. My spirit and my vengeance shall haunt you until the day you die."

"How thrilling," Thorella said, amused. He looked at him as he might a steer that was being sent to the slaughter. "Good-bye, half-breed."

Somewhere beyond the city, Reza knew, Thorella was probably lifting off in an assault shuttle, trying to join up with the incoming human fleet.

His soul burning with impotent rage, Reza fled the Parliament building and Mallory City just as the first salvoes of the Kreelan bombardment began to fall.

TWENTY

Seven hundred men and women stood on the Plain of Aragon in the shadow of the crystal heart's mountain crater, watching their world burn. As Reza had foretold, the Kreelan battleships now orbiting close to the planet were devastating every human defensive position, turning the cities around them into rubble and flames.

They watched the sky glow bright orange and red as huge crimson, green, and blue bolts of energy crashed into Mallory City from the great Kreelan guns. The waiting Mallorys knew there could be no survivors.

"Surely, Sodom and Gomorra saw no greater wrath from the Lord," someone said quietly as fire rained down from the skies.

The bombardment went on for what seemed like a long time, the ground trembling with salvo after salvo as the Kreelans pulverized the settlements. The ridge where Reza's Marines had landed was no more than a smoldering scar in the earth; Walken's tanks, the artillery, and the First Guards troops that had taken over from Reza's company were gone, annihilated.

The smoke that poured from the smoking ruins of Mallory City and the Territorial Army garrisons blotted out the sun. A rain, a black rain, fell for a while and left behind an oily mist that swirled about the great plain like a funeral shroud. The Mallorys, cold and frightened, waited for whatever was to come.

"Where is he?" Markham asked. In his enormous right hand was the ax he often used to split logs as big around as a man's chest. He figured it would kill a Kreelan just as well.

"I don't know," Ian said, shivering in the wet chill. "He said he'd come. He'll be here."

"I suppose it doesn't matter," Markham said after a while. "One hand more or less isn't going to change things."

"I am here," Reza's voice flowed from behind them. From the glow of the flames that shimmered through the mist, Reza strode toward them like a wraith in human form. The people parted before him as he made his way to the place of leadership, to the front.

"I was beginning to worry about you," Ian said.

"Belisle is dead," Reza told him. "Thorella escaped my hand, but justice shall someday find him." He only half-believed the words. In the human world, people such as Thorella as often as not lived their lives through without the justice they deserved.

"I'm sorry," Ian told him sincerely. "I know how much your Marines and Counselor Savitch must have meant to you. To see the one responsible for their deaths escape is a hard thing."

Reza nodded in acceptance of Mallory's condolences before pushing the matter from his mind. There was much yet to do this day. "Are your people ready as I instructed you?"

Ian nodded. "Axes, knives, picks, anything we could lay our hands on that wasn't a gun or bomb. I don't know what good we'll be, but if nothing else we're fighting with things we've held in our hands all our lives."

Reza fixed him with a searching gaze. "Are they afraid to die, Ian Mallory?"

Ian looked around him. While he could not see every face among the crowd that had gathered around them, he knew all the names. And when his gaze touched them, they seemed to stand taller, their eyes brightening in the dim light. These people, some from Mallory City, some from a long distance away, many from in between, were his people, his friends. And he knew why they had come, why thousands more would have come if they could. "They didn't come here to be cowards," he said proudly, his heart swelling with love for the people he gladly called his own. "They came to protect what is theirs. There won't be any Mallorys running yellow from the Plain of Aragon today."

Reza nodded. "Then let it be done," he said. "Form them in a line, arm's length apart, facing as I do. Our wait shall not be long, for the enemy shall soon be with us."

He stared into the mist as Markham bellowed his instructions across the field, Ian Mallory standing thoughtfully beside him. The Mallorys, long used to teamwork in the mines where one man or woman's life depended on another, had already formed themselves into subunits that reacted quickly to Reza's commands.

It was amazing, Reza thought, that such fierce warrior spirits dwelt in people who so cherished peace.

In only a few minutes they were ready, the ends of the skirmish line just visible in the mist on either side of Reza. There was no need for a modern Napoleon or Wellington this day, for there would be no maneuvering and no need for tactical genius. When the battle was joined, it would be warrior against warrior, human against Kreelan, in a battle fought with courage and ferocity that only one side could win. A battle to the death.

"They come," Reza said, the softly spoken words carrying amazingly far. Beside him, men and women gripped their makeshift weapons tighter, adrenaline flowing through their bodies as they prepared to defend the right of their people to exist.

"Where?" Markham growled. "I don't see–"

"There," Ian said, nodding to their front. In the early morning mist, shadows danced in the glowing light of the rising sun, gradually taking form as the line of Kreelan warriors strode forward to meet them.

"Good Lord," Markham whispered. He had never seen a Kreelan before, and suddenly wished he were not seeing them now.

"Are you afraid, Markham?" Reza asked him.

"Naw," the big man said. "I'd much rather be in the pub, but I'm not afraid. If they get me, fine, but I'll take a few myself."

The Kreelan advance stopped. They waited.

"Markham," Reza said, "you will wait here with the others. Ian, you must come with me, as my First."

"What are you going to do?" Markham asked.

"We must greet them." He turned to the big man, who was obviously uneasy about letting Ian get so close to the enemy. "Do not fear; treachery is alien to the Kreela. The greeting is part of the ritual."

"Be careful then," Markham said, still not pleased.

"We'll be back, Nathaniel," Ian told him.

While Markham issued orders for the line to hold fast, Reza and Ian set out across the no-man's land separating the two forces, moving toward their opposite number.

As they got closer and more details of the two approaching figures, their opposites from the Kreelan line, became apparent, an uneasy feeling began to stir within Reza. There was something familiar about the leader. Something...

For just a moment, he faltered, his heart stopping with realization.

"What's wrong, Reza," Ian asked. "Reza?"

The two Kreelan figures continued to advance, slower now, and Ian saw that one of them had hair that was completely white, the snowy braids coiled around her upper arms like stately serpents around gleaming ebony trees. As they got closer, he could also see that her face was black below the eyes, as if she had cried in tears of ink.

Reza watched as she came to within arm's length, but his mind refused to believe what his eyes told him. His heart had begun to beat again, but with the surge of warm blood through his limbs also came the heat of tears to his eyes as he looked upon the woman he thought he would never see again.

"Esah-Zhurah," he whispered, unable to believe his eyes. "Is it possible?" he said in the Old Tongue, "Can it truly be you?"

For a moment, she only stood there, her deep green eyes searching his, her mind grappling with her own disbelief. "Your eyes do not deceive you, my love... my Reza."

They reached out to one another in the greeting of warriors, of peers, clasping their arms tightly. Each was afraid that the other was only an illusion, that a mere touch would shatter the dream. But they were real. They were together.

Reza reached a hand toward her face, the armored gauntlet seemingly invisible to the nerves in his trembling fingers as they made contact with her skin. Her own arms reached for him, cupping his face in her hands, his skin where she touched him burning with a wondrous fire.

"How I have thought of you each day of my life, my love," she said as they drew closer, the world around them fading to nothing, the Universe itself contracting into haunted, loving eyes, the touch of flesh upon flesh. "The pain of your banishment has never left me. The mourning marks have never gone away."

"My own heart has been empty without you, Esah-Zhurah," he whispered as her face came close to his, and his senses, denied the communion of blood that he had given up when he left, drowned themselves in her touch, her look, her scent. "I have lived each moment in hopes of someday again seeing you, touching you, one last time before Death came, but I never believed it would come to pass." With her face so close that he could feel the heat of her body like a roiling flame, he said, "I love you."

Their lips touched, just barely, and Reza felt the hard and terribly lonely years that had come between them melt away like soft steel in a white-hot furnace. A kiss more gentle, more passionate, there had never been.

They ran their hands along the braids of the other as their lips pressed together more firmly, their tongues greeting like the old lovers they were. Time kindly stood aside to let them enjoy this one moment that it could not, in good conscience, deny them.

As one, as if the union they had once made in spirit and blood had never been broken, Esah-Zhurah and Reza pulled themselves away from one another with no less reluctance than two planets overcoming their mutual attraction to spin away toward opposite ends of the galaxy. Shivering with the power of desires and needs that could never be satisfied, their hearts crying in anguish at the hand they knew Fate would this day deal to them, they stood face to face not as lovers, but as warriors.

As enemies.

"You would defend them, Reza?" Esah-Zhurah asked, fighting to control her trembling voice.

"Yes, Esah-Zhurah," he said unsteadily, his tongue leaden in his mouth. "Long have they lived in this place, and much have they suffered for it. According to the Legend of The One, in Her name I claim the right of Challenge."

Esah-Zhurah surveyed the human who had accompanied Reza, noting that he had already suffered physical harm before coming to this place. But she felt no fear from him, only determination, courage. Behind him, standing silently in the swirling mist, were the others who had come to serve the Challenge. Males and females, large and small, dressed in rags and without armor to protect their fragile bodies, she sensed that they had come here with no intent to flee. Their hearts beat quickly, but with anticipation, not with fear. "You choose your companions wisely, my love," she said. "The right is yours," she said quietly. "I accept your Challenge."

Reza bowed his head deeply. The sacrifice the Mallorys were about to make would not be in vain. Their people would be spared.

"In Her name," Esah-Zhurah said, her heart filled with bitter ashes at the knowledge that Reza had come here to save the kin of these people who offered themselves up to her, that he had come here to die, "let it be done."

With a final embrace, their hearts broken by the weight of duty and the injustice of Fate, the two separated, turning back to begin the short march to their respective lines.

"Who is she, Reza?" Ian asked uncertainly.

"She is... my wife," Reza replied with an effort to keep his voice even. It was the closest relationship he could imagine in human terms to describe his relationship with Esah-Zhurah.

Ian did not hide his shock well. "I can't ask a man to kill his own wife," he said. "This is our land, and we'll pay for it, Reza. There's no need–"

"It is as it must be," Reza told him woodenly. "Pray to your God that I may have the strength to do what must be done." Reza knew that the only sword on the field that could slay Esah-Zhurah was his own, and that to save any of the seven hundred Mallorys who had gathered here this day he would have to kill her.

"I don't know how to thank you for all that you've done, Reza," Ian said quietly, "but your name will never be forgotten on Erlang."

They took their place in the center of the line, a few paces in front of the rest.

Reza drew his sword, holding it easily in his right hand, the blade shimmering in the sun. "Let it begin," he whispered.

As one, with hearts beating cadence to their marching feet, the fourteen hundred warriors of the two battle lines started forward.

TWENTY-ONE

"Stand by for transpace sequence... Five... Four... Three... Two... One..." The ship's klaxon sounded twice to announce that Gneisenau had reentered normal space, and the swirling starfields of hyperspace resolved themselves once more into individual points of light.

In the massive port launch bay, Nicole sat in her fighter, impatiently waiting. "What is the matter?" she snapped into her comm link. "Why have I not been launched?"

"Standby, CAG," the chief of the bay advised. "We're showing some problems with your catapult."

Nicole could feel the thumps in the hull as the ship's other catapults began to hurl the fighters into space. They were not able to launch in hyperspace, of course, since the fighters had no hyperdrives themselves, and if they went outside the hyperspace field of the mother ship, they would find themselves left far behind in normal space.

Merde, she thought, suddenly furious with a passion that frightened her. She needed to get out there! "Pri-Fly," she said, "get my ship out of here. Now."

"CAG, the inductor circuit's fluctuating way outside the safety norms," the ops chief told her. "I can't launch you until–"

"Get this ship into space, damn you!" she shouted. "That is a direct order!" Her body felt like it was burning up with fever, and her only thoughts were those of the battle that awaited her beyond the obstacle of a mere piece of machinery.

"Wait one." The chief had known Nicole for only a month, and suddenly wished he had never met her. He turned to his exec, who shrugged.

"Looks like the thing's back on-line," the younger woman said. "Green across the board, now."

The chief frowned. He did not like it when machines decided to be finicky. It got people killed. His gut told him not to launch the CAG's fighter, but he was not left with much of a choice. "Stand by, CAG," he said. "You're up."

Nicole's heart rate picked up as she anticipated the launch. She eagerly watched for the visual signal from the control booth that hung down from the ceiling of the launch tunnel. Red. Yellow. Green.

Her ship suddenly accelerated away from the blast gates, the tunnel rushing past her in a blur as the stars outside seemed to grow larger, tantalizingly closer.

Something went wrong. Without warning, the magnetic field that accelerated the ship, and that was also responsible for ensuring the craft's safe passage down the center of the catapult tunnel, lost its integrity. Nicole's fighter slammed against the catapult tunnel wall, the Corsair's right stub wing disintegrating in a hail of sparks and electrical discharges. The ship yawed further to the right, the slender nose of its hull crumpling under the force, the metal screaming but the sound lost to vacuum. In the cockpit, Nicole reeled from the violence of the impact, the dampers in her ship unable to completely compensate for the horrendous forces that had taken hold of the fighter.

Long before humans could react, the launch safety computer intervened. Terminating the failed launch field, the computer activated emergency dampers that rapidly slowed Nicole's ship, bringing it to a stop twenty meters short of the tube's gaping mouth. Blast vents snapped open in the floor and ceiling of the tube; should the fighter explode, most of the force would be directed out the mouth and through the blast vents, lessening the force on the blast doors far behind that led to the vulnerable insides of the ship.

"CAG, can you hear me?" the launch chief asked tensely. He had seen this before. And worse. "Please respond."

"Oui," she said numbly. "I am... all right."

"Get her out of there," the chief said to the emergency crew that was already pouring through one of the tunnel's service entrances. "Move it."

Nicole Carré would not be doing any dogfighting this day.

* * *

"Sir," the intel chief said quickly, "it looks like we're facing two squadrons. One with a heavy division of two battleships and a heavy cruiser, and a second division with three cruisers."

Sinclaire nodded grimly. The odds were in their favor. For now. Turning to his ops officer, he said, "Order Mackenzie to take out the three cruisers. We'll handle the other lot."

"Aye, sir."

A few moments later, Sinclaire's orders reached Jodi as she led two Corsair squadrons from Gneisenau toward the enemy fleet.

"Roger," she acknowledged tightly. She was still unsettled by what had happened to Nicole. She had heard her over the common channel, screaming as her fighter was torn apart in the cat tube. Jodi had bitten her tongue so hard it had bled, as much to keep herself from tying up the channel with her own voice as from fear that Nicole might be hurt. But then the emergency crew had come. Nicole had been all right, just a little shaken up and with a mild concussion.

With difficulty, she pushed the thoughts of Nicole from her mind. Fifty-three other pilots from Gneisenau were depending on her now; as the second most senior pilot, she was in command. She was now the fighter force strike leader.

"Rolling out of your line of fire now," she told the controller on Gneisenau. She did not want her fighters anywhere near the massive gunfights that would soon erupt between the opposing capital ships.

Like a massive living thing, the two squadrons behind and to either side of Jodi's Corsair swept toward the three Kreelan cruisers that had the misfortune of being separated from the other ships of the Kreelan fleet.

As Sinclaire watched Jodi's fighters clear the field, he turned to Colonel Riata Dushanbe, the commander of Gneisenau's Marine regiment, the Fifty-Eighth African Rifles. "What is it, colonel?" he asked.

"Admiral," she said urgently, "we've finally gotten through to the colony, to some Marine forces there."

"What?" Sinclaire asked, incredulous. "When the hell did Marines arrive there? Why the hell didn't MARCENT inform us?"

Dushanbe shook her head. There was no way for her to know that Thorella's regiment had been dispatched outside of Marine channels in extreme secrecy, and Reza's contingent – a reinforced company – was so small that probably no one had bothered to report it as being on Erlang. No one had been expecting trouble like this. "I don't know, sir. Apparently, however many there were, there is only a company left, now. Alpha Company of the Red Legion's First Battalion, with a First Lieutenant Washington Hawthorne in charge. They've only got a single boat to lift their company and some injured civilians."

"What about the rest of the civilians?" Sinclaire asked. "There are supposed to be over a million people down there!"

"I asked him that, sir. He said he didn't know other than that the capital and probably the other settlements had been bombarded from orbit and completely destroyed." She paused. "He also felt sure that a lot more Kreelan ships would be headed this way, and quickly."

"How the bloody hell could he know that?" Sinclaire muttered to himself.

"Admiral," Captain Amadi said, "main batteries are within range, sir."

Sinclaire scowled. Too many irons in the fire, he thought. As always. He turned to his ops officer. "Have Mackenzie pull off a flight to provide escort to the Marines down there. Coordinate it with Dushanbe here." Then to Amadi, he said, "Captain, you may commence firing."

* * *

Jodi had just pulled out of her first attack run, her weapons crisscrossing the lead cruiser with splashes of light and a few minor explosions, when she received her new orders.

"There are still Marines down there?" she asked, mortified. Much closer to the planet than the rest of the fleet, she could see the damage the Kreelans had done to the surface: the blackened pockmarks where cities used to be, clouds of smoke streaking across the emerald surface like rivers of crude oil.

"Commander Mackenzie?" a voice suddenly interrupted on the link. "Is that you?"

"Eustus? Eustus Camden?" she asked, the muscles in her jaws tightening up. Where there was Eustus, there was... "What the hell are you doing here? And where's Reza?"

"It's a long story," the voice came back, scratchy in her earphones. Jodi could sense the strain in it. "Reza is... gone. Lieutenant Hawthorne's in charge down here, but he's in back trying to get some more wounded on board. There aren't many people that survived the attack on Mallory City. Jodi, we've got to get out of here, fast."

"Wait one, Camden," she said, hauling her fighter up and away from the three enemy cruisers. From here they looked like rakish beetles surrounded by enraged wasps. "Day-Glo, Snow White, Whip," she said, "form on me after you've made your runs." In perfect sequence, the three pilots acknowledged, and had formed on her wing in less than a minute. "Hangman," she called to the remaining senior pilot, "you're in charge. Finish those bastards off."

"Roger," Hangman, the second most senior pilot replied. "Good luck, Commander."

"All right, Camden," she said after switching back to the established air-to-ground link, "where's your beacon?"

As the four fighters screamed down through the atmosphere, the warships above them grappled like scorpions in a bottle, engaged in a fight to the death.

But Jodi could not push Eustus's words from her mind: Reza was gone.

TWENTY-TWO

In the clearing mists that hung over the Plain of Aragon, the battle raged for the fate of Erlang. Like a living thing in agony, the mass of clashing humans and Kreelans writhed and twisted, their even lines having dissolved in the fury of battle. Battle cries and the screams of the injured and dying filled the air, accompanied by the crash and echo of sword against ax, wooden club against steel armor. The bitter smoke from the ruins of Mallory City swept over the once beautiful plain, masking the coppery scent of human and Kreelan blood that now splashed under the feet of those who remained standing, fighting. The humans fought for their home and their loved ones, the Kreelans for the honor of the First Empress for whom they had come.

Ian Mallory stood in a tiny eddy of the stream that was the battle, his breathing coming in harsh gasps as his eyes sought out another of the enemy to join the one that he had just slain. He turned in time to see Nathaniel Markham searching for his own prey. The big man's gaze fell on Ian, and he offered his old friend a smile that was cut suddenly, tragically short by the blade that suddenly exploded from his chest like a great silver tree from bloody earth.

"Nathaniel!" Ian screamed as he watched his best friend's face contort in puzzlement as his eyes took in the length of the sword that had just taken his life.

But then those eyes, normally those of a peaceful man, filled with a killing rage. As the Kreelan warrior who had struck him the mortal blow fought to withdraw her weapon from his body, he whirled around, seizing her by the hair with one great hand. Then, like a dying Thor, brandishing an ax rather than a hammer, he took his opponent's head from her body with a turn of his great weapon. Holding the severed head high above him, he let out a roar of triumph that boomed over the raging battle.

Before Ian Mallory could take a step toward his friend, Nathaniel Markham's voice died away. Without another sound, he collapsed to the earth, the Kreelan's head still clutched in his hand.

Like an all-consuming fire, the battle swept onward. And at its center were Reza and Esah-Zhurah, locked in their own battle of a higher order, refined well beyond the uncontrolled chaos that whirled around them like a great tornado of slashing steel and bleeding flesh. But while they stood as titans beside their warriors, they were evenly matched against one another, each denying the other the quick victory that would have spared lives on either side by the honor that bound them to the Empress and to one another. And so it was that their own private hell raged on in time measured by the blood spilled upon the ground from those around them, each dreading the blow that would kill their beloved.

The two circled and crashed together like beasts fighting for the right to mate, oblivious to the small ship that leaped from the forest but a few kilometers away, carrying Reza's company and a few Erlangers to the comparative safety of the human fleet.

* * *

"You look like hell, captain," Sinclaire told Nicole as she walked onto the bridge. While his comment seemed brusque, his voice was filled with concern.

"Thank you, sir," she said flatly as the lights suddenly dimmed and a deep thrum shook the ship as the main batteries fired again. One glance at the tactical display told her that she might as well forget about asking for another fighter. There would not be much to shoot at for much longer. Two of the three cruisers that Jodi's fighters had attacked were already destroyed. The third was severely damaged and obviously out of control. The battleships that had devastated Erlang from orbit were far from finished, but their efforts now were more out of spite than anything else. The guns of Gneisenau, Hood, and the other heavy ships would soon finish them, as well.

"Nicole," Sinclaire said, "I'm just glad that you're alive. I know you're upset about not being able to lead your people today, but I'm not one to push luck too far."

"I know, sir," she said, looking down at her shaking hands. "I am sorry." To herself, she thought, He just does not understand. It was more than just wanting to lead her people; combat had become an addiction, a craving that she had to satisfy. It often terrified her, but she did not know what else to do. Worse, since she had awakened in sickbay from the minor concussion she had received, passing out as the emergency crew freed her from her wrecked Corsair, she had felt terribly odd, as if ants were crawling on her body. She saw visions, flashes of some kind of battle, two warriors fighting, and felt her muscles twitch in time with movements other than her own. As she was coming from sickbay, she felt a horrible pain in her upper left arm, as if it had been torn by animal claws. She had nearly cried out, it had been so intense and shockingly sudden, but her tongue had remained silent. The pain had gradually faded to a dull throb, but her breathing remained abnormally rapid, and she could swear that she smelled her own blood. Turning away from Sinclaire, she stared at the viewscreen and the battle that raged there between human and Kreelan ships. But her eyes were far away. A muscle twitched in her face.

Sinclaire regarded her quietly as the bridge continued to bustle with the hectic activity of the battle.

He had seen the signs before, too many times. She had lost her edge. While it was a great regret for him, he would have to post new orders for Fleet Captain Carré. Her days of combat were over.

* * *

The sands of the hourglass in Reza's mind had run out. His Marines were well away, and he knew in his heart that Esah-Zhurah would beg the Empress to spare the people of this planet on his behalf. There was no point in prolonging the battle further, for that would only leave more Erlangers dead and increase the risk of harm coming to Esah-Zhurah, the one thing that he could not allow. He also knew that she would not attack him with his guard down; he would have to trick her.

With the ferocity of their sparring, it did not require much. Warrior priest and priestess, each was able to sense which attacks would fail, and which might not. Thus far, their only injuries had been mere trophies, a gash here or there for the healers to mend to a scar that would be a remembrance of this combat.

It was time. Esah-Zhurah lunged forward with her sword in an attack she instinctively knew Reza would deflect. But he surprised her by holding his sword arm downward at the last instant, leaving his torso completely exposed.

Esah-Zhurah's weapon did as it was designed, piercing Reza's breastplate just below his heart. The armor, sturdy as it was to a slashing attack, gave way like warm butter to the sharp tip of the sword's living steel.

Reza's vulnerable bones and flesh offered no resistance to the hurtling blade, whose blood-streaked point emerged out Reza's back, the armor peeled back around it. With a morbid thump, the sword's pommel slammed to a stop against Reza's breastplate.

* * *

Colonel Dushanbe was just informing Admiral Sinclaire that the boat carrying Hawthorne's Marines and its four-ship escort had landed in the starboard landing bay, when Nicole Carré suddenly screamed in agony.

Clutching her hands to her chest, she crumpled to the deck and lay very still.

"Lord of All," Sinclaire boomed, rushing to his fallen officer and friend, "get someone from sickbay up here on the double!"

Carefully turning her over onto her back, he saw that all the blood had drained from her face. Her eyes were open, but Sinclaire hoped never to see whatever she was seeing: it was as if she was staring into Hell itself.

* * *

Esah-Zhurah's shocked eyes swept across the blade of her weapon as it protruded from her lover's back, covered in his blood. Her nose, far more sensitive than any human's, was flooded with its coppery tang. She heard, dimly, the sound of his sword dropping to the ground, and felt the weight of his sagging body as he wrapped his arms around her neck, his head falling to rest on her shoulder. All around her, like sails sagging under a dying wind, the Kreelan warriors suddenly lost their ferocity, their hearts torn by the force of Esah-Zhurah's emotional shock.

The humans, too, felt something change, and accepted the break Fate had given them. Confused and exhausted, they backed away from their Kreelan opponents by a pace or two, many of them dropping to the ground, chests heaving with pain and exertion.

"Pull it out, Esah-Zhurah," Reza whispered into the sudden stillness, speaking in the Old Tongue. His hands clutched at the armor protecting her back, his talons issuing a high keening sound as they sought purchase in the metal of her armor.

"No," she whispered. Her sword's blade had a serrated upper edge. It would tear out his heart if she tried to remove it. "No. Reza, I cannot... The healers will take care of you. They can remove it without–"

"You must," he breathed, a trickle of blood escaping his lips. "Please, Esah-Zhurah. You know I cannot return... home." He felt hot tears burning his face. "Let this be done... Let it be over... Now."

"Reza," she rasped. Her voice was an echo of the agony that seared her soul. She held him tightly with her free arm, thinking desperately for another way – anything – but there was none. She smelled the salt of his tears mingling with the scent of his blood, and suddenly wished she could cry with him. For him. The black of the mourning marks she had worn since he had gone so long ago just did not seem to be enough. "Forgive me, my love," she rasped as she closed her eyes. With one smooth motion, her sword hand drew back with all the strength she had, freeing itself with a ghastly grating sound against Reza's armor and the shattered bones of his ribcage.

Reza cried out before he slumped against her. She threw her sword to the ground and held him with both arms, her teeth grinding with anguish, her heart cold in her chest, dead with pain. Gently, with Syr-Kesh's steadying hands, she laid him on the ground, cradling his head to her breast.

"Reza," Esah-Zhurah whispered mournfully. There was so much to tell him, so much wonder that he would never know. "Why did you do this?"

His eyes, still gleaming with the life that faded rapidly within, fastened on her. He struggled to free his hand from the armored gauntlet, finally succeeding with Syr-Kesh's reverent help. Unsteadily, he reached for Esah-Zhurah's face. She took his hand and held it to her, kissing his fingers.

"You well know why, Esah-Zhurah," he said, softer than a whisper, barely a sigh. "You are the successor to the throne... on you the Way shall someday depend." He shuddered, suppressing the cough that would rend further his violated lungs, his damaged heart. Already it slowed, nothing more than a leaky valve as it sought in vain to pump more blood into the ruptured lungs where it rapidly pooled, and would soon drown him. "My life is nothing beside yours. I only ask that... in my memory, the Empress let live the people of this world."

"So much do you care for them," she said in a trembling voice as she watched her lover's life ebb away, "that you would utter your last words on their behalf?"

Reza smiled. "Not so much as that," he told her, his trembling fingers stroking her face. He could no longer feel anything below his waist. "My last words I save for Thee, Esah-Zhurah. While I love the Empress with all that I am, I love Thee all the more." He labored for another breath, knowing it would be his last. His chest was warm, too warm. "I shall... take my memories of you... to the Darkness that falls upon me. Your face and love shall keep me... for Eternity."

She watched helplessly as his eyes fluttered, closed. His hand, the hand that had held her, that had touched her as they made love, lost its strength, the fingers relaxing in her grip. His breathing stilled.

Shutting away the Universe from around her, she held him close as she had the child she had born to him, the son who had never felt his father's Bloodsong, the son whom Reza would never know.

On the Plain of Aragon, Esah-Zhurah wept without tears.

* * *

"Your orders, sir?" Captain Amadi asked quietly.

Sinclaire scowled at the tactical display. Thirty Kreelan warships, none of them smaller than a heavy cruiser, had just jumped in-system. There was nothing Sinclaire's task force could do to save the people down below. They did not have enough ships to hold them all, even if they had time to evacuate them. The first of the new Kreelan arrivals would be in orbit in less than thirty minutes. Sinclaire had recalled all the fighters, and the last of them were landing now. In one of the starboard landing bays, the last of Reza's Marines were carrying wounded civilians from their hijacked boat. They were lucky to be alive.

"Turn the fleet around, captain," he growled. "There's nothing more for us to do here."

Nodding sadly, Amadi quickly began to carry out his admiral's orders.

* * *

"What's wrong with her, doc?" Jodi had come to the sickbay the instant she had gotten free of the flight deck. She stood in the sickbay's anteroom with the doctor, her face still sweaty and marked with the outline of where her helmet had been pressed against her skin.

"I don't know," the surgeon said uneasily. "She's in deep shock, like she experienced some kind of massive physical trauma, but there's no evidence of any injury. Not a thing."

"Please," Jodi said, "I need to see her."

She was not ready for what she saw. For all she could tell, Nicole was dead, for nothing but a corpse could look so white. Her eyes were all that seemed to be alive. But they frightened Jodi: they were the eyes of the insane. She took Nicole's hand. It was freezing. "Nicole," she breathed, "can you hear me?"

Nicole's eyes pivoted slightly, then again, as if the muscles were no longer capable of the rapid and fluid movements they once had been. "Jo... di." The sound seemed alien coming from her blanched lips.

"I'm here, Nikki," Jodi said again, holding her friend's hand tightly, running her other hand across Nicole's chilled brow. "It'll be okay. Can you tell me what's wrong? What happened?"

"Reza," Nicole uttered, a little more clearly. "Help him."

Jodi fought back the tears that wanted to come to her eyes. She knew that others often saw them as a sign of weakness, but it was how she coped with things that otherwise would break her heart and crush her spirit. "Honey," she said gently, "Reza's..." She paused. It was so hard for her to say it. "He's gone, Nicole... dead. There's nothing–"

"No," Nicole said with such force that Jodi blinked. "No... help him... must not... let him die."

"Nicole, I know this is hard for you, but he's gone. Let him go. Besides, we've got to leave. There are more Kreelans coming and–"

Nicole's grip on Jodi's hand suddenly tightened, so hard and quick that Jodi let out a yelp of pain and surprise. "Nicole!"

"Help him," Nicole said through gritted teeth. The skin of her face was stretched tight, exposing the outlines of her skull through the bleached skin. Her eyes burned with ferocious intensity, like a wolf making its final leap before the kill. Jodi felt her knuckles grating together as Nicole's hand clamped down on them like a vice. "Save him." It was not a request, or even an order. It was a commandment.

Suddenly, the energy that had taken her over vanished, and she faded into unconsciousness, her heart beating erratically, her breathing shallow and unsure. Her hand, limp now, fell away from Jodi's. Her eyes rolled up to reveal the whites, then closed.

"Jesus," Jodi muttered, looking with widened eyes at the surgeon, who only shook his head; he was as shocked as she was. "If there's no real trauma," she said shakily, "she can't die, right?"

One glance at the vital signs monitors would have told her otherwise.

The surgeon shook his graying head. "I wish saying it made it so, but it doesn't. If I can't figure out what's causing her to be like this, I don't think she'll make it another two hours. Her body is just shutting down."

"Take care of her," she told him decisively before turning to the door. There was a certain Marine first sergeant she needed to see.

* * *

Eustus stared at the landing bay portal, as big around as a football field and filled with the stars and vacuum, safely on the other side of the force field.

"Eustus," Jodi said urgently, "it's Reza we're talking about."

"It's mutiny," Eustus snapped back. "More than that, it's suicide. You weren't there when the bombardment was coming down. You didn't see a whole planet get flattened. I did. And the fact that there's a whole shitload of Kreelan ships coming down our throats doesn't thrill me, either." He turned to Jodi, mindful of the blue eyes in her ebony face blazing at him. "Look, Jodi, I loved Reza as much as anybody ever did. I fought for him. I gladly would have died for him. But it's over. He's gone, along with the rest of them. He told me himself that he had no intention of coming back." He looked at Enya, who tended to some of the wounded, most of them Raniers. She was the real reason he did not want to go, he thought, ashamed in a way. Enya was worth more to him now than anything or anyone had ever been, and he was not going to just throw that future away. "I'm sorry, Jodi. But I'm not going. Maybe Hawthorne will—"

"Come on, Eustus!" Jodi nearly shouted, causing a few heads – Enya's among them – to turn in their direction. She lowered her voice. Slightly. "Hawthorne's no good for this and you know it. He's too straight to pull a stunt like this, and besides, he's too damn big. I couldn't get both him and Reza into the rear cockpit." She stared at him, willing him to come. "It's you or nothing, Eustus. I can't do it by myself."

"Can't do what?" Enya asked from behind them. "What are you up to, Eustus?"

"Nothing," he said, shaking his head.

"Commander?" Enya asked, a look of concern on her face. "What is it?"

"I think Reza's alive down there," she told her quietly. "And I need help to bring him back." She looked pointedly at Eustus.

Enya's brow furrowed. "How could he be alive? He was going to the Plain of Aragon to fight, I know, but… How do you know this?"

"Captain Carré – she's in sickbay right now – told me. She and Reza have some kind of special bond, they seem to know things about each other when there doesn't seem to be any possible way." She glared again at Eustus. "Nicole's dying, and the surgeon doesn't know why. I think it's because she's linked to Reza somehow, and is reflecting whatever's happening to him. I think he's important in some way that we don't understand. And if what Nicole said is true, and we don't do anything about it, we'll live to regret it. And Nicole will die."

"Could you make it through all those Kreelan ships?" Enya asked quietly. Eustus opened his mouth, but was smart enough not to say anything.

"We'll never know if we don't try." Jodi looked at Eustus again. "Time's up, jarhead. What's it going to be?"

"Eustus," Enya said quietly, "go with her."

"But–"

Enya raised a finger to his lips. "You must have faith, Eustus," she told him. "Our prayers brought your captain to our aid, and my prayers brought your heart to me. We don't know what has happened to our people. Maybe they are all dead. Maybe none of them have been harmed save those in the cities. But we do know that your Captain Gard is directly responsible for saving anyone who is still alive, and perhaps that kind of power is something worth the risk Commander Mackenzie is asking."

"Enya, it's suicide."

She nodded, biting her lip. This was the hardest thing she had ever done, sending the one man she had ever really loved off to die. "It well may be. But can we afford not to try?"

Eustus closed his eyes, hoping that it would all go away. Instead, he felt Enya's warmth press against him, her lips gently kissing his. "Go quickly," she said. "And may the Lord of All watch over you."

* * *

Master Chief Petty Officer Clarence Mahan was enjoying what was, ironically, the quietest period during a war cruise. As chief of the starboard catapults, he was responsible for getting Gneisenau's fighters and attack ships off the deck. Recovering them was someone else's job down in Pri-Fly. Now that the fleet was hauling itself around toward its jump point, it was only recovering fighters, not launching them. The standard four-ship alert had already been spotted on the outboard cats, leaving the rest of his watch free of major problems. Or so he had hoped.

"Chief," one of his assistants called, "we've got engine start on the number three alert bird."

"What?" Mahan said. The alert pilots were not normally kept in the cockpits, but in a ready room a few paces behind the blast shields. "Denkel, if you're pulling my leg, I'll–"

"No, chief, I'm not shitting you. Look." On the big board that made up the main display for the starboard catapult system, one of the alert ships was indeed powering up.

"Goddammit," Mahan snarled, "somebody'd better have a good explanation for this." He snapped the intercom circuit open. "This is cat control to Alert Three. Shut down immediately and get your ass out of that cockpit. Respond, over."

"Chief, this is Commander Mackenzie. I don't have time to explain, but I'd really appreciate a cat launch. I hate bolting down these tubes on manual."

"I'm sorry commander, but nobody said anything to me about any launches," Mahan said, wondering what the hell was going on. "I need to check with Pri-Fly on this one."

"Don't bother, chief," Jodi said as she brought the engines up to ninety-five percent power. The blast shields behind her automatically slid into place to prevent the fighter's engines from vaporizing the adjoining part of the hangar bay. "Pri-Fly won't know anything, either. See you later, Mahan."

"Commander–" He did not bother saying anything else. Her fighter was already gone: Mackenzie had guided it down the catapult tube manually. Goddamn bloody dangerous stunt, Mahan cursed silently. "Get me the bridge," he said to his assistant. "Somebody's going to be really pissed over this one."

* * *

"Jodi, this is insane," Eustus said. He was not qualified to fly as a back-seater on this ship, but he also was not an idiot. The holo display that was projected on the console and on the bubble canopy around him told him enough. There were Kreelan ships everywhere, although none had fired on them. Yet. "Even if we make it down there, how are we supposed to find him?"

"Do you know where this Plain of Aragon is that Enya mentioned?"

"Not exactly," he said, calling up a map display of Erlang on the computer. "It's supposed to border the ocean, on the far side of the coastal mountains where that glowing crater thing is. Hmmm... Due east of Mallory City – what's left of it – looks like that might be the place to start, anyway."

Jodi quickly evaluated the information that was echoed on her display. "Make you a deal," she said. "If he's not there, we'll split back to the fleet, and I'll think up some bullshit about bending you to my will." She grinned to herself. "I'll tell them I suddenly went straight and just had to have wild sex in the cockpit with you. No one else would do. What do you think?"

"No joy, commander," Eustus said, ignoring her attempt at humor as he clumsily called up the scanner data on what he hoped was the right place. "We've gone past the point of no return. We either come back with Reza or we don't come back at all."

Jodi nodded grimly. Around them, more warships of the Kreelan fleet sped toward Erlang.

* * *

Reza was in the temple, kneeling before the crystal that was the spirit of his order, the host of the cleansing fire that burned away the old to reveal the new. The crystal was light and warmth, wisdom and power. All else was darkness, without order. Chaos.

He was not alone. Sitting across from him was a warrior whose face he could not see but for her glowing silver-flecked eyes. Her hair was white as the snows of Kraken-Gol, her talons the color of his own blood.

"It is not yet your time, child," came the voice of Keel-Tath

Reza looked at his body, his eyes widening when he saw the armor of his breastplate, untouched, gleaming as when it was first made by Pan'ne-Sharakh.

"Pierced was my heart, Empress," he said, uncomprehending, knowing that he should be in Darkness, the place that was beyond all, where Time itself did not venture. He was dead.

"This I know, young priest," She replied. Her hands reached out to him above the crystal, and he took them, his flesh against Hers. "I have seen The One who shall inherit my spirit, who shall be the vessel of my Resurrection, the guardian of your heart. But She-Who-Shall-Ascend is only a part of the whole of which you are the other half. If you die, so shall she, in spirit and heart, if not in body, and the Great Bloodline shall come to an end. My Children shall perish from the world."

Reza felt his very soul chill at her words. "Can this be?" he whispered.

He saw the look of sorrow in Her eyes. "Indeed it can, My son," She said. "The cycles are few that remain to the Empire under the curse I set upon them so long ago. Soon it will be that no longer shall they bear any male children, and those who must mate will perish of the poison in their blood, and those who are barren shall witness the destruction of their race. Only in The One is there hope for the future, for My Children."

"What must I do?" Reza asked softly. Even in the dim light just beyond the crystal's glow, he could see the mourning marks that flowed down her face, so much like Esah-Zhurah. Even the immortal First Empress, he saw, could know remorse and compassion.

He felt the pain of the blade across his hand, the flesh of her palm pressing against his. The crystal glowed brighter, pulsing in time with Her heart. He felt the tingling of Her blood in his, felt the warmth, the fire. He heard only Her voice in the song that took his blood, but it needed no accompaniment; it was a universe unto itself.

"You must live," She said.

* * *

"I've got something at one o'clock," Jodi announced as she guided the Corsair through the debris-choked clouds, trusting her sensors to keep her from smashing into the mountains she knew lurked nearby. Below lay the burning pyre that had once been Mallory City.

"Just don't fly anywhere close to that blue glow, Jodi," Eustus warned, keeping his eyes fixed on the eerie light that penetrated even the smoke of the burning city.

"Trust me," she answered. She had no idea what it was, but nothing and no one could convince her to go closer to it than she already was.

Ahead loomed the last of the coastal mountains, and Jodi pulled the Corsair's nose up to clear them. Beyond lay the coastal plains and the ocean.

"Oh, shit," Jodi hissed as her ship squawked an alarm. "We're being tracked. There's a Kreelan ship down there, some kind of assault boat."

"Don't fire on it," Eustus told her. "Are your shields up?"

"Of course they are–"

"Drop them."

"Eustus–"

"Drop them!" he ordered. "Dammit, do as I tell you."

Cursing under her breath she dropped her shields, leaving her ship naked to attack by anyone hefting a fair-sized rock, let alone pulse weapons.

"Look!" Eustus said. "Down there!"

Jodi looked in the direction Eustus was pointing. "Holy shit," she whispered. On what must be the Plain of Aragon, she could see hundreds of human figures through a light mist. Most of them, she could tell, were not interested in her fighter, but in the perfect circle of Kreelan warriors, hundreds of them, who knelt on the plain itself. And in the open center of the Kreelan circle, she could see three figures.

One of them, she knew, had to be Reza.

"Why aren't they firing on us, Eustus?" she asked as she circled over the warriors, who seemed to pay her no attention.

"I don't know," he said, "but we'd better hurry up and get this over with before they change their minds."

"Roger that," she said quietly. She started the landing cycle, lowering the Corsair's landing gear and transitioning to hover mode. "If anybody ever told me when I was in flight school that I'd be pulling a damn fool stunt like this..."

Jodi set the fighter down smoothly just outside the circle of warriors, some of whom, she could see now, had taken a sudden interest in the new arrivals.

"All right," she said, her heart hammering, "let's do it." Leaving the engines idling, she cycled open the clearsteel canopy and disconnected the umbilicals linking her suit and helmet to her ship. She left her helmet on the shelf over the control panel. Eustus followed her out. "Let's take it slow and easy," she suggested.

"Good idea," Eustus said uneasily. His blaster weighed heavily on his hip, but he knew his life expectancy would be measured in tenths of a second if he reached for it. He followed Jodi out of the cockpit, clambering awkwardly down the diminutive crew ladder that had popped out of the hull.

By the time both were firmly on the ground, the warriors around them were on their feet, and there was no mistaking the hostility on their faces. "I'm beginning to have second thoughts," Eustus murmured.

"Stay here until I call you," Jodi told him. She was looking at the three warriors in the ring's center. One, with white hair that Jodi had never seen on a Kreelan before, was cradling Reza's body, oblivious to everything around her. A shiver ran down Jodi's spine. I know who you are, she thought to herself.

The other one, with the regulation black hair, stood by like some kind of bodyguard, her hands poised over her weapons, her eyes locked on Jodi and Eustus.

Moving slowly, her arms outstretched, palms open to show she was holding no weapons, Jodi made her way toward where Reza lay in the white-haired warrior's arms. The bodyguard moved through the surrounding ring of warriors to block her.

"I've come for Reza," Jodi said slowly and clearly. She had no idea if any of them understood Standard, but they should certainly understand his name. "Reza," she said again, pointing to his lifeless form.

The bodyguard looked confused, suspicious, perhaps, but did not move. Jodi decided to play her ace. It was all you could do when you only had one card left in your hand. Addressing the warrior with the white hair, she called, "Esah-Zhurah."

The bodyguard's eyes widened at that. The woman behind her, holding Reza, slowly lifted her head. She fixed Jodi with eyes that were as green as his, and so full of pain that it made Jodi's heart ache, no matter that this was her sworn enemy, an alien. She said something in a raspy voice to the bodyguard, who saluted with a fist over her right breast and stepped out of Jodi's path.

Jodi made her way past the warriors, who parted before her, and knelt down next to Reza. "I've come to take him home with us," she said gently, hoping Esah-Zhurah would understand.

"His home," Esah-Zhurah said slowly in Standard, the alien words coming to her only with difficulty after so many cycles of disuse, "is in my heart." Her eyes turned to his face, peaceful now, and pale, the thin line of blood from his mouth almost dried. "But you are right," she whispered after a moment. "It was for your kind that he denied himself before the Empress and parted with all he once loved; it was for your kind that he gave his life. His body, his ashes – even the collar of his honor – I grant you, for he died without Her forgiveness. He died not one with our Way."

Reaching out with a bared hand, Jodi gently touched Esah-Zhurah's face. "I'm so very sorry," she whispered. "I... I know how much he loved you. All these years, he never loved anyone but you."

"Did you love him?" Esah-Zhurah asked quietly, her magnetic eyes fixed on Jodi's face.

Jodi flushed with a sudden pang of guilt and embarrassment, but she did not look away. This was not the time for modesty. "I cared for him greatly," she said. "I... I held him once, at a time when I think he would have died from loneliness, without you. When he slept, he cried out for you. He told me about you, about your love. That's how I know your name."

Esah-Zhurah nodded. "Thank you for your kindness," she whispered. "Will you honor his memory?" she asked.

"Always," Jodi answered. "He will not be forgotten."

"Then he is yours," Esah-Zhurah said, her voice trembling. She carefully laid his body down, smoothing back the hair from the face she so loved. Gently, she kissed him on the mouth. "Fare Thee well, my love," she whispered in her own language.

Esah-Zhurah stood up and nodded toward Eustus, who walked quickly to where Jodi was kneeling. "You must go quickly," she told Jodi.

"Jesus," Eustus said upon seeing the gaping wound in Reza's chest. He saw the weapon that caused it lying in the grass nearby, its serrated edge festooned with gore. His last delusions about Reza still being alive quickly evaporated, regardless of what Nicole may have said.

"Come on, Eustus," Jodi said, trying not to look too closely at the wound, "we've got to hurry."

Esah-Zhurah turned away as Jodi and Eustus struggled with Reza's body. The smell and taste of Reza's blood were still strong, too strong, and she feared they would always be with her. She watched the blue glow of the First Empress's pulsating heart, still resting in the mountain crater, and prayed to Her for salvation, for forgiveness. For her own heart was dead, and never would live again.

Eustus was now acutely aware of why Jodi had needed someone's help. It took both of them to get Reza's body to the ship. Jodi danced up the ladder to the aft cockpit, standing on the edge of the hull to help Eustus as he climbed up behind her, Reza over his shoulder in a fireman's carry. After a few minutes of precarious balancing and brute force, Eustus was secured in the aft seat, holding Reza's body.

"Let's get the hell out of here," he said as Jodi dropped down into the pilot's seat and began the takeoff sequence, slapping on her helmet as the canopy whined into place.

Thirty seconds later, they were airborne.

* * *

"We're reading a ship ascending from the surface, sir," the intel officer reported. "Checks out as a Corsair."

"Mackenzie," Sinclaire growled.

"Looks like it, sir."

Sinclaire only grunted in response. On the tactical display, a tiny blue wedge detached itself from the planet and set course for the fleet, now hundreds of thousands of kilometers away. And everywhere, crowding the display, were red wedges accompanied by a few lines of elaborating data that identified the Kreelan ships that were appearing around Erlang like salmon about to spawn. "How many Kreelan ships, now?"

"Eighty-seven major combatants, sir, plus scores of smaller ships," the intel officer reported. "STARNET is reporting as many more still on the way."

"Bloody hell," Sinclaire whispered. It was the largest Kreelan battle fleet that had ever been assembled in Sinclaire's lifetime, and more ships were still arriving; humanity would never have been able to amass such a fleet in one location so quickly. "How long to the jump point?"

"Nine minutes and forty-seven seconds, sir," Captain Amadi replied.

"And how long for Mackenzie's ship to reach us?"

Intel shook her head. "Almost eleven minutes, admiral, at the Corsair's top speed."

A little over a minute too late, he thought glumly. "Has anyone been able to contact her yet?"

"No sir," Amadi said. "Nothing since she left the ship." They had no way of knowing that Jodi had disabled the command datalink in her fighter that might have allowed Sinclaire to recall it on autopilot, overriding Jodi's own commands. And along with the datalink went the voice and video communications.

"She's on her own, then," Sinclaire said. "I won't risk the fleet for a single person."

"Sir," a yeoman called from the FLEETCOM position, "it's Commander Ivanova. She's in trouble."

* * *

Commander Ludmilla lvanova, captain of C.S.S. Gremlin, a destroyer guarding the fleet's rear as it withdrew, was more than in trouble.

"Admiral, we're taking heavy fire from a cruiser that just dropped in-system," she said quickly as her ship rocked under the impact of another salvo.

"Captain!" the engineering officer reported, "We've lost the starboard aft-quarter shields!"

"Helm, roll us nine-zero degrees to starboard!" she ordered quickly. The destroyer responded immediately, rolling its exposed side away from the withering fire from the heavier Kreelan ship. "Make your course zero-five-zero mark eight-zero. All ahead flank!" While Gremlin was outgunned and out-armored, she was still faster and more maneuverable, and had her own set of fighting teeth.

Focusing again on Sinclaire's concerned image, she said, "We'll try to draw them off, sir." She smiled. "Wish us luck, admiral."

"Good luck, Ludmilla," he said. It was a paltry farewell to the captain and crew of a good ship. Both of them knew that Gremlin would not be returning to port. The Kreelan cruiser had the uncanny luck to have dropped in right behind the retreating human fleet, where none of the heavy ships could bring their main batteries to bear, and where they themselves were most vulnerable to enemy fire. It was Gremlin's job to hold off any Kreelan ships long enough for the fleet to jump out; if she could not, and Sinclaire was forced to turn any of his other ships to face the oncoming threat, he stood to lose a lot more than a single destroyer. "Godspeed, captain."

On Ivanova's display, his image faded, disappeared.

An explosion rocked the ship, throwing her forward against the combat restraints of her command chair. "Damage report!" she shouted into the chaos that was the bridge.

"Hull breach in engineering!" someone replied. "Main drives off-line!"

"Weapons," she ordered the crew manning the weapons stations, "ready torpedoes, full spread, home-on-target mode."

"Torpedoes ready, captain!"

In the main viewer, she could see the Kreelan cruiser gaining rapidly. Her skin tingled as she could almost sense the enemy ship's main batteries charging, almost ready to gut her wounded destroyer...

"Shoot!"

Just as the Kreelan cruiser's guns erupted with lethal energy, Gremlin's eight torpedo launch tubes jettisoned their own destructive cargo. Seven of them cleared the ship before the final Kreelan salvo tore into the thinly armored destroyer, boring into its reactor core. The Gremlin disappeared in a huge fireball that consumed Ivanova and her crew.

The eighth torpedo, not quite free of its tube, suffered minor, but significant, damage to its guidance system before it cleared the blast and debris that was all that remained of the Gremlin. As its siblings began their dance of death with the Kreelan cruiser, the eighth torpedo wandered off on its own. Its electronic brain damaged, no longer able to distinguish friend from foe, it circled through space, looking for a target.

Any target.

* * *

"Somebody just bought it," Jodi said as she watched the fireball fade to the residual glow that was all that was left of whatever ship it had been. Not far from it, she saw several smaller explosions silhouette a larger ship that passed through the first fireball, only to explode in its own turn. Torpedoes, she thought to herself. Somebody nailed that Kreelan fucker.

"How much farther?" Eustus asked. He had loved Reza as a friend and commander, but was losing patience with him as a corpse. His uniform was soaked with Reza's blood, and Reza's crushing weight in the already cramped cockpit was giving him a case of claustrophobia. The smell was none too pleasant, either.

Jodi checked her instruments. It was going to be a lot closer than she cared to admit. And the margin was not in their favor. "About six minutes," she said. She was not about to worry him with details, like they were going to be almost a minute short of the fleet's projected jump-out time. Unconsciously, her left hand pressed forward on the throttles, which were already pegged against their stops. The Corsair was giving her all it had.

All around them, the weapons of the dozens of Kreelan warships in the area were trained on them, but none had fired.

A warning buzzer suddenly went off in Jodi's ear. "Oh, shit," she hissed, craning her head, scanning the space around her.

"What is it?" Eustus asked, looking around frantically, although he did not even know what he was looking for.

"A torpedo's got a lock on us," Jodi said urgently. "There it is!" Highlighted on the holo display as the ship's targeting computer calculated the weapon's trajectory, the torpedo was coming at them from almost directly ahead. "Son of a bitch! It's one of ours! Hang on!"

She pulled up in a wrenching, twisting corkscrew, hoping to throw the torpedo off, to make it break its lock on her ship. She watched in the display as it passed beneath them, swung around, and began tracking them from astern.

Goddammit, she thought angrily. She could clearly see the human ships now, Gneisenau's enormous drives shining like a friendly star. But they were too far, much too far away.

"Jodi!" Eustus cried. He was propped up in his seat, looking aft at the torpedo. Forgetting for a moment that he was looking at his own death, he was mesmerized by the sight of the thing, the weapon's speed sufficient to induce fusion of the hydrogen in space on a molecular level, generating a bow wave of ghostly reddish radiation.

He did not see Reza's eyes flicker open.

Jodi did everything she knew to shake the weapon, but to no avail. She knew that their time was up.

"I'm sorry, Eustus," she said as the cockpit filled with the blood-red fusion glow from the approaching torpedo. "I'm so sorry."

Neither she nor Eustus noticed as metal claws took hold of them, just as the torpedo exploded above the cockpit.

* * *

Sinclaire turned away, sickened at the lives he had just seen wasted. And he probably would never know why Mackenzie had done what she did, or even what she was trying to accomplish. But it did not matter now. "That's it, then," he said angrily.

"The fleet reports ready for jump, admiral," Captain Amadi said quietly. Commander Mackenzie had not been with him for very long, but he had enjoyed her company greatly. Her loss, and the effective combat retirement of Captain Carré, was indeed tragic.

Sinclaire nodded. "Let's be off, then. If you need anything or there's any news, I'll be in my cabin." Two of his finest officers, a good destroyer and her crew, a full Marine regiment, and over a million civilians on Erlang, all written off. He wished he was planetside already, where he could find a nice dark pub and get thoroughly, utterly drunk. He kept his hands close to his sides, hoping that no one would notice that they were shaking.

"Aye, aye, sir." Amadi turned and began issuing the instructions that would take the fleet home.

* * *

In the landing bay, the Marines had been watching the holo display, howling their support of Jodi's run through the Kreelan lines as if they were at a Marine-Navy soccer game, evening up the score. But the bay was filled with shocked silence as the display showed the icon representing Jodi's fighter wink yellow and then disappear after her desperate attempts to get away from the brain-damaged torpedo. She and Eustus were gone.

A moment later, the display cleared entirely as the fleet jumped into hyperspace.

The Marines who now belonged to brevet Captain Hawthorne turned away, sadness and exhaustion etched on their features.

Enya found a corner to herself where she slumped down and rested her head in her hands, too tired even to cry. Her world was gone, her people gone, and now Eustus was gone, too. She had nothing left.

"Hey," she heard someone say, "do you feel that?"

"Feel what?" someone snapped angrily. "Your hand on my butt?"

And then she felt it, too. The air had suddenly grown heavy and still, as if they had dived under water. Her ears popped. As she looked up she was blinded by a searing blue-white flash.

"Explosion in starboard bay!" someone shouted in the maelstrom of lights that clouded her vision. She heard an alarm braying and running feet guided only by flash-blinded eyes. But there had been no sound, just the flash, and then the heavy feeling in the air disappeared as mysteriously as it had come.

As the others crowded their way out of the bay, fearful of a hull breach, Enya stayed in her corner, her eyes shut, waiting for her vision to clear. She did not know the bay like the Marines did, and could just as easily find herself running out the shielded landing door.

After a moment that seemed like forever, she opened her eyes. And there, in a heap of tangled arms and legs on the floor, looking wide-eyed at their surroundings as if they had never seen this place before, were Eustus and Jodi, with Reza's torn body between them.

"Eustus!" she cried as she leaped to her feet and ran toward them, throwing her arms around his neck and kissing him. The remaining Marines, shocked by what they saw, slowly gathered around the new arrivals, looking at them as if they were ghosts, the result of a mass hallucination.

"Lord of All," someone whispered.

"Get Captain Gard to sickbay, now," Jodi managed, still in shock. She was conscious only of two totally unrelated things: that Reza was somehow still alive, and that she had peed herself. The change of laundry, she decided, could wait; Reza came first. She struggled to her knees as helping hands pried Reza's talons from her numb shoulder and Eustus's thigh before they carried the stricken captain at a run to the sickbay. She did not try to dissuade the hands that picked her up, carrying her after him. Eustus, helped by Enya and a babbling Washington Hawthorne, trailed dazedly behind.

If You Enjoyed Confederation...

The story of Reza and Esah-Zhurah is continued with *In Her Name: Final Battle*, which brings their story to an explosive conclusion. You also have the option of getting the "omnibus edition," which contains the entire first trilogy (*Empire*, *Confederation*, and *Final Battle*).

To give you a taste of what's to come, here's the first chapter from *Final Battle* - enjoy!

* * *

The world was strangely white, so unlike the darkness of Death, so unlike the place where the First Empress's spirit had waited all these generations for Her awakening, and where only he, among all mortals, had ever been. He could not imagine the power, the wonder that must come to the Empire upon Her return, and his heart stopped beating for a moment as he thought of Keel-Tath's spirit encased in Esah-Zhurah's body. He would have given anything, everything he had ever had, to see her in the white robes and slender golden collar, high upon the throne, the most powerful Empress his people had ever known. His only regret would be that he could never again call her by her birth name.

In the whiteness that was now the Universe, he saw strange shadows hovering above him like odd birds fluttering above a snow-covered field. Their jerky movements were accompanied by noises that were sharp and purposeful, but not threatening. Were they other spirits, perhaps?

But he knew that this could not be; the place of the banished was forever dark and cold, and all those who dwelled there did so in eternal solitude. Or did they?

The world seemed to turn slowly, the white turning to gray, the strange noises drifting away into silence.

He slept.

* * *

If any time had passed, he was unaware. Dreams of life, and things that were beyond life as any other human had ever known, came to him, played their parts upon the stage that was his slumbering mind, and left to wherever such dreams go. While he would never be able to recall the exact moment, at some point he became aware that he did, in fact, possess a body. He gradually became sure of this because of what his mind perceived with gradually increasing clarity: pain. It was not the sharp, excruciating pain of a weapon cutting flesh, the kind of pain that he had been trained and toughened to withstand, to endure; it was the slow, throbbing pain of his body struggling to heal itself. This pain also was something he was well accustomed to. But this was deep, to his very core, and he realized in that instant that he was still alive.

The shock of that realization was sufficient to send enough adrenaline through his sluggish body to bring him to the threshold of consciousness. He opened his eyes. He was still in the white place, but saw no shadows.

"Reza," said a voice, so softly that he could barely hear it. "Can you hear me? Squeeze your right hand if you can. Do not try to talk."

Not questioning the instructions, Reza tried to carry them out. Sluggishly, he traced the nerves from his brain to his right hand, commanding it to close. Nothing. He concentrated harder, ordering his hand to obey. At last, he was rewarded with a slight twitching of the muscles in his forearm, causing his fingers to move fractionally.

"Can you feel this?" the voice asked with barely contained excitement. Reza felt a gentle pressure around his fingers, the squeeze of another's hand. He replied with another feeble movement of his fingers.

In his vision, he saw a shadow appear above him that gradually resolved into something that, after a moment, he recognized. It was a human face.

Nicole.

He tried to speak her name, but somewhere in the complex chain of physical operations that made speech possible was a breakdown. His lips, feeling swollen and numb, parted. The tip of his tongue curled toward the roof of his mouth, behind his teeth, to its accustomed position for making the "n" sound. But that was all he could do. His lungs were too weak to force enough air into his larynx to make the sound of her name. He tried again, hard.

"Ni...cole," he breathed faintly.

"Please, mon ami," she said softly, placing a finger gently against his lips, "do not waste your energy trying to talk. We will have plenty of time for that later."

She smiled, and Reza saw tears brimming in her eyes. It took him a moment, but it finally struck him that she looked exhausted, haggard. Her face was pale and drawn, her normally flawless ivory skin creased and sallow. Her eyes were bloodshot, with dark rings beneath them.

She mourns, he thought absently. But that was at odds with the light that shone in her eyes now. They were joyful, relieved.

"You will be all right, now," she said. It sounded to Reza as if the words were more to reassure herself. "We were very worried about you for a while. You were hurt very badly."

"How... long?" he asked, ignoring her pleas to conserve what little strength he had. His range of vision began to constrict, the periphery of his world turning to a dull, featureless gray until all he could see was Nicole's exhausted face.

She hesitated for a moment, and Reza sensed a general feeling of unwillingness to tell him the truth. His senses were terribly dulled, blunted like a rusty sword, but they told him that much.

"Six months," she said finally, her eyes questing, hoping the news would not send him into shock. When she saw that he was not fading on her like he had so many other times over the last months, she went on, "It has been six months since we left Erlang. After you got Eustus and Jodi to Gneisenau – however it was that you did it – the surgeons worked on you for many hours." Her smile faded with the remembrance of how agonizing that time had been. She herself had to be anesthetized, to shield her from the pain that Reza was feeling as the surgeons worked on him, trying to reconstruct his shattered body. "You never came out of the anesthesia, never fully regained consciousness," she went on. "Until now. You have been in a coma all this time." Her own recovery from the psychologically-induced trauma had taken two months, and the news that she was being forcibly retired from combat duty sent her into a bout of depression that she had still not entirely recovered from.

"You... all right?" he whispered.

"I am... better, now. I know I must look awful, but I have not been able to leave you." She looked down at her hand holding his. "I had a great deal of leave built up, so I decided to take some. To be here for you, when you woke up."

Reza's heart ached for her. He sensed the long, lonely hours she had spent at his bedside for months, wondering each moment if the next he would be dead, or would never wake up at all. "Thank you, my friend," he sighed.

"I could not leave you here alone," she whispered. Tony had understood, and had supported her after Gneisenau had returned to Earth on Fleet HQ's orders. He himself had spent many hours beside her, beside Reza. The two men had not seen each other in a long time, since the wedding that had made Tony and Nicole husband and wife, but there was a bond of trust between them that went far beyond the measure of their acquaintance.

"Erlang?" he asked as his strength began to wane, his range of vision narrowing again.

"The Mallorys, and what few Raniers are left, are well," Nicole said, still marveling at how that was possible. While the cities and major townships had been totally destroyed with grievous losses among the population, the vast majority of Erlangers – almost exclusively Mallorys – had survived. The Kreelans, after retrieving whatever it was that they had come for, had mysteriously departed without inflicting further harm. "Several convoys of ships have taken them the things they need to help rebuild. Ian Mallory sends his hopes for your recovery, and his thanks."

She did not add that he had also petitioned to be a witness in Reza's defense at the court-martial that had long since been planned for him. He was charged with multiple counts of murder, including those of President Belisle of Erlang and Chief Counselor Melissa Savitch, as well as high treason against the Confederation.

Reza sensed that there was something deeply wrong, something that she was not telling him, but his body demanded that he rest. "I am glad that Ian lived," he said quietly

The last thing he felt before his eyes closed was the gentle warmth of Nicole's lips pressed to his.

* * *

Tony Braddock was a troubled man. Someone to whom he owed his own life and that of his wife was in a dire situation, and there did not seem to be any way for him to help. While he had told Nicole that Reza had been charged with murdering President Belisle, Counselor Savitch, and an Erlang Territorial Army soldier, plus what he took as nothing more than a gratuitous and hate-inspired charge of high treason, he had not told her how extensive was the evidence against him. Not only did Colonel Markus Thorella claim to have been a witness (by remote, naturally), the man had also produced an especially damning piece of evidence in the form of a recording of the soldier's and Belisle's murders. The holo had been validated by the court in the last months, meaning that it had been declared devoid of tampering, was genuine, and would be admitted as evidence in Reza's court-martial. The alleged murder of Counselor Savitch was based entirely on Thorella's say-so, but considering the other evidence in hand, Tony Braddock knew that almost any military or civilian court would convict Reza out of hand. Politically, as the war went on and worsened, they could ill-afford not to. The public wanted a scapegoat for the pillaging of their civilization, and they would have one. And who better than Reza, who was caught between two worlds?

Worse – How could it be worse? Tony asked himself – since so much time had passed and no one was sure if Reza would ever come out of the coma, they had dispensed with the pre-trial preliminaries that might have given him some sort of due process, at least in terms of technicalities. Most of the witnesses for his defense had been released to fleet duty, their sworn testimony recorded for the proceedings. But it was not the same as in-person testimony, Braddock knew, especially when Reza's chief accuser, Colonel Thorella, had conveniently been ordered to a posting on Earth after he had somehow explained away the annihilation of his own regiment on Erlang.

While Tony had no proof, he had no doubt that there were some dark forces moving things along. He suspected Senator Borge and his increasingly large and vocal militant following of having a hand in it, but there was no way to prove it. And even if that were true, what could he do? Go to the president and accuse Borge of subverting the legal process in the military?

He smiled bitterly. Even with evidence as solid as Kilimanjaro, that would be foolhardy, at best. Borge had few remaining political enemies except the president and a few older and more powerful senators who still remembered what democracy was like, and who cherished the ideal above the rhetoric of their office.

And there were still a few young fools like Tony Braddock.

He rolled over, careful not to disturb Nicole, sleeping beside him. She seemed so much better now, after the months she had spent recovering from whatever had come over her, all the while distraught over whether Reza would survive. Tony had found it maddening sometimes, but he had done everything he humanly could to be there for her, to comfort her and try to lighten her burden. He knew she had been, and still was, deeply depressed at being assigned a non-combat position, but he was relieved that she had finally been taken out of harm's way. She had done more than her share, and it was time for them to have some time together as man and wife, and perhaps to ask themselves again if they were ready to become father and mother.

He heard her whisper Reza's name in whatever it was that she dreamed. His heart used to darken out of jealousy, wondering if perhaps she did not really love Reza more than she did himself. But over time, his fears had subsided. She loved Reza, yes, but as a sister might a brother or close friend. Perhaps there had been a time when she had wanted it to be something more. But he knew, from both Jodi and Nicole, that Reza would never have accepted anything more than platonic love from her or any other human woman; Reza's heart lay elsewhere, deep in the Empire.

Braddock had also listened to Jodi tell him of her suspected "psychic link" between Nicole and Reza, but he had never believed it until Admiral Sinclaire himself had told him of what had happened to Nicole on Gneisenau's bridge when Reza was wounded.

Braddock would have to learn more about that, and many other things, come morning, he thought, as well as bring an old friend some very bad news. He would go and visit Reza, not as a friend, but as his legal counsel in a trial that he knew could only result in Reza's execution.

* * *

"...and that's where you stand, Reza." Having finished outlining his friend's situation, Tony sat back in the chrome chair next to Reza's bed, feeling drained. A week had passed since he had first resolved to visit Reza, but the doctors had refused any visitors other than Nicole, who seemed to be a catalyst in Reza's recovery. But after seven days the patient's condition had improved enough that the doctors had finally allowed Reza one additional visitor. His defense counsel.

Reza showed no reaction, but continued to stare out the window as he had the entire time Tony had been talking.

Braddock frowned. "Reza, did you hear anything that I just said?"

"Yes," Reza said, at last turning to face him, his face an unreadable mask. "I heard and understand."

Braddock's temper flared. "Dammit, Reza, they're not just trying to throw the book at you, they're trying to dump the whole library on your head! Everyone who knows you knows that you would never have committed these crimes, but the court will–"

"I did, Tony," Reza said quietly, his eyes glinting in the light.

Braddock's mouth hung open for a moment. "What?" he said. "What did you say?"

"I killed Belisle and the Territorial Army soldier," Reza went on, his voice not showing the keening in his blood. "The killing of the soldier was unfortunate, an act of self-defense, but I killed Belisle with forethought." He paused, noting the blood draining from Braddock's face. "And if I had to do it again in front of the Confederation Council itself, I would. He was an animal, a murderer. Had I not killed him, or had the Kreela not come and destroyed the city, many of Erlang's people would even now lay dead at his hands. As for Melissa Savitch, her death was Markus Thorella's deed. And I shall yet find a way to avenge her."

"Can you prove that Thorella killed her?" Braddock asked, seeing his case to defend Reza foundering as surely as a scuttled ship. But perhaps there might be enough to hang Thorella for murdering Savitch. At least that bastard could swing beside Reza on the gallows.

"None but my word."

"That's not good enough, Reza."

Reza nodded gravely. In the world in which he had been raised, the world of the Kreela, one's word was a bond stronger than steel, a commitment backed by one's very life. Among those of this blood, among humans, however, it often meant little or nothing. Especially if one stood accused in a court of law. "I would have taken his head, as well, had he not outwitted me," Reza told him, describing Thorella's scheme and what exactly had happened in Belisle's office. "He shall not deceive me again."

No, Braddock thought, he won't: you will be a dead man and he will go free. "Reza," he said, leaning forward to emphasize what he was saying and shocked that Thorella's accusations were even partially true, "confession is only going to earn you a quick trip to the gallows. The only way I can help you is if there are some mitigating circumstances, maybe by having some Mallorys testify as to Belisle's misdeeds. We might be able to get that charge reduced to a crime of passion in the UCMJ, or even dropped altogether if we can get the Council to cede jurisdiction to Erlang."

Reza was warmed but amused by his friend's determination to keep him from the hangman's noose. He shook his head. "My friend Tony, you know far better than I that the Council will do no such thing. They cannot. I killed Belisle and the soldier, but not Melissa Savitch. To try and convince anyone otherwise would be to lie. And what of the charge of treason?"

Braddock shook his head, wishing that this were all a bad dream and that he would wake up in a warm bed next to Nicole. Even if he could get the murder charges dropped or reduced, the treason charge would not be let go. "How could you have done this Reza?" he asked more to himself than his doomed friend. All Tony could do now was to ensure that due process was given and the procedures themselves were legal. "You don't have a prayer with the judges. You may as well have just stayed there and died."

"I tried," Reza said quietly.

Braddock frowned. "The only other alternative I can think of is to ask the president to pardon you. I mean, since you are the only real authority on Kreelan affairs, maybe–"

"Impossible," Reza said quietly. "I am accused of capital crimes, Tony, two of which I am guilty by my own admission. How can it be that your society, which claims to hold justice so high, could simply allow me to go free? I do not well understand the politics of the Confederation, but I do not see how even the president could manage such a thing without devastating repercussions. He would not pardon me; he could not. And I do not wish it. I knew what I was doing when I took Belisle's head. I simply did not intend to survive to receive the punishment I must under Confederation law."

"You could escape," Tony said quietly. He was not suggesting it as a counsel, but as a friend. He knew that Reza would not have done what he did without good reason, but that would not hold up in a court, especially if Reza confessed. "It would be easy for you," he said. He knew as well as anyone that Reza could disappear like a ghost if he wished.

Reza shook his head. "And go where, Tony? To the hills of this planet? To the desert? Even if I could whisk myself to Eridan Five and dwell among the saurians there, I would not. What would be the point? Even without a trial, I am an outlaw among your kind, having forsaken the cloth of the Corps and the Regiment, and I cannot return to my own people without disavowing the oath I made that banished me. And that is something I can never do, even at the price of my own head."

Braddock did not say anything for a while. He felt like his guts had been ripped out and stomped on.

"What about Nicole?" If Reza had resigned himself to death, then so be it. There was nothing more he could do for him. Now he had to worry about Nicole. His wife. "How will she handle your death?" Tony asked, imagining the metal cable tightening around Reza's neck, Nicole writhing in agony as it happened, filling her with the same grisly sensations that Reza would feel. "What is this bond, or whatever it is, between you going to do to her?"

Reza had been devoting a great deal of thought to that, but he had no answer. He simply did not know. Even the memories of the Ancient Ones that only seemed to unlock themselves in his dreams had left him no clue. "I do not know," he said helplessly. "There is no way to undo what has been done."

"Does this link still exist?"

Reza shook his head. "I do not know. I have not sensed her since I awakened, but that means nothing. The Blood that flows through her is much diluted, for there is little enough in me. The bond has always been little more than a filament between us. Perhaps the shock of what happened broke it..." He shrugged helplessly at Braddock's uncertain expression, his own heart filled with fear on her behalf. "Tony, if there was any way at all to guarantee her safety, I would do it. But I just do not know."

"Sometimes, when she dreams, she speaks in a strange language. Would that be the language... your people speak?"

Reza nodded. "It would be the Old Tongue," he explained, "the language used in the time of the First Empress. She would only speak it if the bond was unbroken."

Braddock's heart sank. He was afraid that would be the case. "She spoke that way last night."

Reza closed his eyes, his heart beating heavily in his chest with grief. "Then I fear that whatever I feel, so shall she."

"She'll die, Reza."

Opening his eyes, Reza looked his old friend in the face, his own twisted in a mask of emotional agony. "I know," was all he could say...

A Small Favor

For any book you read, and particularly for those you enjoy, please do the author and other readers a very important service and leave a review. It doesn't matter how many (or how few) reviews a book may already have, your voice is important!

Many folks don't leave reviews because they think it has to be a well-crafted synopsis and analysis of the plot. While those are great, it's not necessary at all. Just put down in as many or few words as you like, just a blurb, that you enjoyed the book and recommend it to others. Your comments *do* matter!

And thank you again so much for reading this book!

DISCOVER OTHER BOOKS BY MICHAEL R. HICKS

The *In Her Name* Series

First Contact
Legend Of The Sword
Dead Soul
Empire
Confederation
Final Battle
From Chaos Born

"Boxed Set" Collections

In Her Name (Omnibus)
In Her Name: The Last War

Thrillers

Season Of The Harvest

Visit *AuthorMichaelHicks.com* for the latest updates!

ABOUT THE AUTHOR

Born in 1963, Michael Hicks grew up in the age of the Apollo program and spent his youth glued to the television watching the original Star Trek series and other science fiction movies, which continues to be a source of entertainment and inspiration. Having spent the majority of his life as a voracious reader, he has been heavily influenced by writers ranging from Robert Heinlein to Jerry Pournelle and Larry Niven, and David Weber to S.M. Stirling. Living in Maryland with his beautiful wife, two wonderful stepsons and two mischievous Siberian cats, he's now living his dream of writing novels full-time.

CPSIA information can be obtained at www.ICGtesting.com
Printed in the USA
BVOW02s1001120913

331017BV00001B/39/P